WASHOE COUNTY LIBRARY
D0758364
DATE

Saint Fire

THE SECRET BOOKS OF VENUS
BOOK II

TANITH LEE

(Il Libro della Sparda)

THE OVERLOOK PRESS
WOODSTOCK & NEW YORK

First published in the United States in 1999 by
The Overlook Press, Peter Mayer Publishers, Inc.
Lewis Hollow Road
Woodstock, New York 12498

Library of Congress Cataloging-in-Publication Data

Lee, Tanith.
Saint Fire / Tanith Lee.
p. cm. — (The secret books of Venus ; bk. 2)
is cataloged under:
Faces Under Water / Tanith Lee
(The secret books of Venus ; bk. 1)
I. Title. II. Series: Lee, Tanith.
Secret books of Venus ; bk. 1.
PR6062.E4163F3 1998 823'.914—dc21 98-4789

Manufactured in the United States of America

Book design and type formatting by Bernard Schleifer

ISBN 0-87951-735-2
FIRST EDITION
1 3 5 7 9 8 6 4 2

The law of the Dreamtime is yet the law.

FROM THE KOORI (Aboriginal)

Contents

AUTHOR'S NOTE

In this parallel Italy, some names are spelled phonetically. But an *e* at the end of a name is always sounded, (as *ay* to rhyme with *day*.)

The Latin phrases should be pronounced as Mediaeval Latin generally was-*V*, for example as in *very*, (not as a W), *ch* as *K*, *ae* to rhyme with *eye*. (It should be noted too, the Latin used in this book is also that of a *parallel* Italy.)

For the revelation of the connections between the *Hymn to Aten* of the Pharaoh Akhenaten, and Psalm 104, the author expresses many thanks to Robert Scott B.Ed.

PROLOGUE

> And priests in black gowns, were walking their rounds,
> And binding with briars, my joys and desires.
>
> William Blake
> *Songs of Experience*

A bell was ringing Luna Vigile from the marshes. The inn was not noisy at that moment, they heard it clearly enough. Some crossed themselves. Many grew quiet in a restive respectfulness, until the bell fell silent. Then they picked up their cups, drained them and called for more.

"Another, Ghaio?"

"It's late. I'll be getting home."

"A last draught to light your path, Ghaio."

Ghaio Wood-Seller glanced at the merchant Juvanni. Juvanni, who had established a name but not much luck in trade, had just negotiated a hefty loan from the wood-seller, a trader in much lowlier goods. But a city always needed kindling, especially now on the threshold of winter. Ghaio, who dressed scruffily and lived in a slum, was haughty, and said to be rich.

"If you like, Juvanni."

"Yes, yes, my friend," fawned Juvanni, and snapped his fingers for another pitcher of wine.

When the girl brought it, she leaned low to the table.

"Be wary," she whispered. "*Sweet smell.*"

Juvanni's red agitation paled. Even Ghaio looked put out.

"In *here*?"

"Coming here, the boy says."

"He'll go by."

"Maybe not. And not *he*, *two* of them."

She slipped away, to carry on her task of warning valued customers.

Juvanni looked into his brimming cup. Then took their previous, empty pitcher, and thrust it under the table.

"Someone else's," he said. "This is our first, eh, Ghaio, and we're abstemious."

"Damn them, I say," said Ghaio.

Juvanni shook his head. "Hush."

"Eyes and Ears of God," said Ghaio. "I have nothing to fear from them." He smiled long teeth at the merchant. "I've just gifted the Church a hundred silver duccas."

"So much? I would to God I could still—"

"Yes, yes, Juvanni. Well maybe you should give up your trade in sweetmeats and try something more serviceable. But then, I never had your schooling. I can't read much, and I add up on my fingers. I expect that would make the difference."

The door opened. Into the ruddy warmth of the inn came a breath of cold night. The torches faltered on the walls. A new silence began.

Really they had not required the girl's warning. The fragrance of incense that came from the two black-robed creatures in the doorway was potent. Sometimes, it was true, such men moved through the City in disguise, and without even the whiff of sanctity to betray them. But this was blatant.

Their faces were bare, the candle-wax masks of priests. One raised his hand over the rigid figures of the inn, blessing them.

The innkeeper had come running. He bowed low.

"May I assist you, holy brothers?"

"There is nothing your house contains of attraction to us," said one of the priests.

The other said, "Except for the souls of men."

With the cold air of the Silvian Marshes, the words of the priest ran like a shudder from wall to wall.

Although not far from the marsh church of Santa Lallo Lacrima, the inn had been seldom visited. But the Council of the Lamb stayed always vigilant. Recently the Eyes and Ears of the Council were seen more frequently in most spots. There was talk of war. At such times, the Church grew particularly sensitive to the sins of Ve Nera, City of Venus.

A third figure had appeared behind the priests. Against the vagueness of the outer dark, it was only tall and lean, wrapped in black. As it stepped forward, there came three gleams of pallor, from white-blond hair, from a pair of brilliant gray eyes, from a sword swinging in a sheathe of steel and ivory.

The priests turned, and shifted aside.

Juvanni sucked his breath.

The inn-keeper straightened, seeming relieved and alarmed together. "Good evening, Soldier of God."

The Soldier of God nodded.

One of the priests said to him, "You are familiar with this sty, brother?"

"Yes, brother."

"You come here to *drink*?"

Ghaio Wood-Seller noted the blond man's long mouth twitch with what might have been distaste.

Certainly not fear. "Yes, brother. The inn well has the purest water in the marshes."

The priests had settled all their attention on this man. He was, in station, their equal, yet subtly above them, a priest-warrior of Christ, one of the elite who prayed but also fought for the honor of the Church. On his shoulder shone, white and gold, the badge of the Lion, the Holy Child astride it. He was young, not more than twenty-five or six. Strong, and sheerly masculine as no swordless priest could be. All this Ghaio assimilated, for he liked sometimes to study men, if only to bring them down.

And this one was regal, was he not, due for a fall.

But the priests drew away, and one softly said, "Does your Magister know that you're here?"

And the Soldier of God turned to the priest a face of stone.

"You may ask him, brother. It is Fra Danielus."

If it had been a play in the street, the inn would have laughed. But even street plays never mocked the priesthood now.

They were retreating though, these two, going out. Fra Danielus was one of the three Magisters Major, who lived high in the Golden Rooms of the Primo. This soldier of God came from the Upper Echelon.

Now he walked through the inn, straight through, the innkeeper hurrying beside him. As a leather curtain closed them away, the inn perked up.

"He has his own business here, then," said Ghaio, curious.

"I have been told—" Juvanni hesitated, "he visits a woman here."

"A *woman*?"

"Oh, hush, Ghaio—"

"And they vaunt their celibacy. Well, it comes as no surprise." He downed his cupful of wine. "And now I'm off."

"You won't forget . . ."

"Your duccas? No. Send your servant tomorrow. They'll be ready. I'll trust you'll be diligent with my interest."

Outside, Ghaio's torch-boy, hired for the trip, emerged from a doorway, shivering.

They went up the alley, the torch lighting them luridly and fitfully.

The Silvian Quarter was bleak at this hour and this time of year. The slop of water in the canals had the turgid sound that promised ice in winter, as in the summer it promised stink. In a gap among the house sides, Ghaio saw, black and thin on water, a Styx Boat, and the two Eyes and Ears of God seated in it, being poled away.

From the marsh blew the smell of a frigid salt sea. Last winter, and every winter before that for five years, the ocean had partly flooded the marshes here. An old Roman temple on a hillock had provided a fine crab pool, for those with the mind to row out to it.

The sea was eating, or drinking, the City. They said in a hundred years or less, these marshes might become Ve Nera's third lagoon. But Ghaio would not be alive in a hundred years and had no time for the future.

"Cristiano," said the woman. She rose and went to him at once, the Soldier of God, and put her arms about his neck, in a cloud of hair not quite blonder than his own.

"Yes, Luchita. What is it this time?"

"So cold. Winter-cold. Do they freeze your hearts in the Basilica?" He waited for the familiar tirade to pass. Tired of it herself, the woman let it go. She only said,

"You're my brother. Who else should I turn to?"

"Your husband."

"That sotten pig. He drinks more than he sells here."

Cristiano waited again. Luchita remembered how he had always waited like this, even when a little boy only two years her senior. Infuriating, his cool, calm uninterest, the sense of his impatience always held in check because it was—like everything, or so it seemed to her—a sin.

She said, sullenly, "This new tax, Cristiano, on food, on drinking—the Tax of Pleasures—"

"The Council sets it."

"You serve the Council."

"I serve God."

"God—do you think God wants us to live in misery all our days—Christ knows, they'll tax screwing next."

He shrugged. Although she knew, with his high-flown and impossible ideals, she had probably offended him.

Outside, a song was starting up, the one that was popular this month, about the pagan goddess Venus, and the god of war, Mars.

Every year, new taxes—on drinking, and fine food, on property and on luxurious garments—no trouble to Luchita there, God knew. Soon a tax on songs? Well, it would not amaze her.

"I'm sorry, Luchita. I can't help you. Every inn will have to pay it, and pass the cost on to the patrons in the price of beer and wine."

"And then the patrons will go elsewhere, where they can find inns that cheat."

"I have no say in the Council. My work is other."

"Couldn't you—some exemption—he's often sick—"

"From drunkenness, according to your own words."

"And I may be with child. "

Startling her, he looked sudden and hard into her face with his sword-pale eyes. "His? Or another's?"

Luchita glanced aside. "God excuse me, I don't know."

Cristiano stared at some invisible distance.

Outside the words rang clear.

When your heart is mine,
You may do as you will to.
When my heart is yours,
Then wish the world good-bye.

It was a corruption, he thought, of all things, of a holy plaint to God and the Virgin. The giving of a whole heart set against the turning of the full eye of Heaven upon inadequate man, among whom even a saint was unworthy.

The next verse, from its sounds, owed *nothing* to a priestly plaint—

"Well. If you won't help us—"

"I never can, Luchita." He came back, and pushed aside his cloak. As always, as all his order were, he was garbed in a soldier's maculum of close-fitted mail. He set a bag which clinked on the table. "Take this."

"God bless you, Cristiano."

"He won't, for that."

"No, God wants only suffering from us. So you priests tell us. And guilt and shame for any joy we snatch. Isn't that so?"

"And anger is also a sin, Luchita. Especially when directed at Heaven."

She wanted to hurl the money in his face. Afterall, the

pig would have drunk it in a dozen days. But she held her hand down. Her brother had done his best, in his pure and remote manner. (Heartless.) And whatever he said, he was the most, the only powerful man she knew.

After he had gone, some tears ran from her eyes. She rubbed them away and went out into the inn to serve, singing.

His house stood on the Canal of Seven Keys, a mixed blessing. In deep winter, if it froze, you could cross it or walk along it, on foot. In summer, it matured, and dead dogs, even men, sailed up and down with the tides. The house itself, fixed firm between two others, was peculiar in that the walls were of a dark red. Ghaio's Red House, locals called it.

Over the door hung his sign, painted with a bundle of wood tied by a cord of gold: wood-seller. The gold had faded on the sign. But only there. Ghaio, as several suspected, was wealthy. He owned three houses, the two on either side his own, and one further along, and took rents from the occupants, although sometimes only in wrung-neck chickens, or other flesh, female and alive. He also owned the broad yard at the back of the Red House, which crowded out the back premises of the other buildings.

Once inside the house, Ghaio glared about him. The room was quite dark and the walls peeling a little from damp. It had no look of affluence.

But then, primed by his tread, his slave woman arrived to light the yellow fat candles.

"Late, you slut." He slapped her. "It doesn't please me to come into a house black as pitch."

"You said—"

"Never mind that." (He had told her never to light

the candles when he was out. He was a miser, but a contrary one. She was supposed to guess the time of his return—and sometimes did from mere desperation.) "Where's my supper?"

She pointed mutely.

Ghaio's views on food, and one or two other matters, were not miserly, when applied to himself. The table, now lit, showed a trencher of black bread, a white loaf, a dish of olives and cheese, a haunch of cold roast pork. And wine of course.

"All right." He sat and took up a grabful of the food. He chewed.

Candles cast shadows. In the corners there seemed very many tonight.

Confound those priests. Like shadows, they were everywhere. Soon they might come knocking on the private doors of such as himself. But he had his gambits ready, including the flail he used on his three slaves, this woman, the old man, and less often, the woman's ugly, snotty child. "See, saintly brother. I perform penitence on my own body."

And he had gifted the Church. Gone to the Basilica, the Primo Suvio, great temple of God's crusading knights, and *paid*. One hundred silver duccas. Even God should be delighted.

But Ghaio did not like to think of God. Though not sure that He existed, yet He stayed for Ghaio a tiny, nagging doubt, like the little pain in a tooth one felt years before it changed to agony and must be pulled.

"Tonight," he said to the slave woman, "you come upstairs." She said nothing. He said, "You hear me?"

"Yes, signore."

It wouldn't take long. Against the wall even. She was hardly good enough for his bed.

When she opened the door to go out to the kitchen

in the yard, Ghaio caught the briefest strangest glimpse of something, outside.

What in the name of the Lamb—

But no, no, it was nothing. It was the woman's child. The child he had called *Volpa*—Fox—for its filthy reddish hair.

It must have washed that hair. The brat had been waiting for its mother, and as it moved back from the door, the hair—uncovered by the usual rag—caught the candle light, like a flick of fire.

The door had shut now.

Ghaio thought, after all, a flick of fire was to be expected here. The Wood-Seller's house.

He sank his teeth in the pork. How old was the child now? He seldom saw her. He had bought them as a lot, ten years ago, got the price of the woman down, since the child, he said, was no use to him, only an infant.

The woman kept the child hidden from him mostly, he thought, not to annoy, and it—she—performed the most menial tasks, emptying night-soil, washing floors, walking after the wood-cart the old man slave pulled to market.

Hidden, he had not thought of the child much. But it—she—was older now. Twelve—or thirteen, even.

Perhaps he should look at the child.

A wind seemed to be rising outside, bringing the tide along the Canal of Seven Keys, the salt sea licking at the islands of Ve Nera, City of Venus the goddess of lust.

Soon it would be midnight, and the bell would sound again from Santa Lallo Lacrima. Two hours later it would toll the Prima Vigile for the priests to go on their knees once more. Those at least not prowling the byways, searching for drunks and whores to chastise. It was of no account to Ghaio in any case. Fed, and eased of sex, he would be long asleep by then.

BOOK ONE

Alter Mundi

PART ONE

Instead whereof thou gavest them a burning pillar of fire...

WISDOM OF SOLOMON
The Apocryhpha

I

FIRST, SHE SAW THE MOUNTAINS—not knowing what they were.

The sky, perhaps. Yes, probably she thought they were the sky; stones built of thin fine ether. The foothills of Heaven.

Two thirds of the year, there was white on them, snow . . . clouds. In high summer they darkened and there was no white.

The farm was in the earthly foothills, and here the slaves worked, among the brown grass and the yellow stalks of grain. Her memory was of sitting, of running, of carrying things.

She did not know what occurred, and after, her mother never explained. There was anger and fright. Mother weeping. So she wept too.

Then a market-place, down on the Veneran Plain, in a town of stumbling little hovels and mud. It rained.

She was four.

Presently, the journey to the great City, whose name meant *Meeting Darkness*, or *To Travel By Night*: Ve Nera. The carter had a nickname for the City. Venus. He made jokes about Venus—now a city, next a goddess. Not the Virgin, the only goddess the child had heard of until then.

Finally, the carter lay over her mother in the cart.

Outside the awning rain lashed miserably.

The carter grumbled, "Took you on—hope you're worth it. And that pest of a baby, that little curse. You women. Breed like conies. Don't dare bud from me. You hear, I'll beat it out of you."

The carter was Ghaio Wood-Seller. Master.

In memory, entering it, the City was indeed a darkness. They were put into a boat—never before felt, the motion of a canal. Arches of shadow, and blocks of night. Water rippling black.

Christian slaves did not matter, the Church had said so. Bodies might be in chains, souls stayed free.

A month later, Ghaio beat her mother. He made the child, already new-named "Fox," watch the proceeding, as a lesson.

Volpa's mother was never pregnant again. Perhaps the beatings saw to that, or simply the generally harsh life in the Red House. Yet, although life was bad, they clung to it, as if to some granite rock-face. The alternative was to fall into the abyss.

Or was it? Volpa's mother, in the early years, spoke sometimes of God, and sometimes of the Virgin. Later, she mentioned them less.

"We suffer on earth," said Volpa's mother, "so that we can be happy in another place."

But why must we suffer? Volpa might have asked. Possibly she had done so.

Certainly an outlandish answer seemed to have evolved to just such a question: The world is a school, a cruel and exacting one. Only here can we learn from terrors and mishaps, which, beyond life on either side, are never encountered.

Why then learn? Why is it needful?

"Because only then," said Volpa's mother's sweet tenor voice, "can we be one with God, who has already experienced, and surmounted them."

So God did not send sorrows against mankind to punish or chastise?

No, simply to cleanse, to refine. God, lonely in omnipotence, longed for the company of creatures purified as He had been. He wished that every single soul should achieve such greatness and such wisdom as were already His.

Ghaio, truly, was a diligent exponent in God's school.

Master. Apt title?

Volpa knew to fear and avoid him from the beginning. But it was normally easy, since she lived in another country, the kitchen and the yard.

The yard of the Red House was almost entirely filled with timber, logs, bundles of wood, and the shed where the cart was kept. There was also a cistern to catch rain, whose water was not of the best. (Nicer water was fetched by the woman from the nearest public well.) Over Ghaio's cistern, however, there grew a fig tree. In summer the leaves were like dusty metal. Green figs appeared irregularly in autumn. Bare in winter, the branches had a rheumatic look.

Whatever the season, on nights of the full moon, when Ghaio slept or was from home and the other houses dark, Volpa and her mother would dance about this tree in a strange, silent circling. The old male slave, coming across the yard to the privy one night, saw this, hid his eyes and went away, Volpa had no other indications that the dancing might be profane. Unlike the lesson of God, she never queried it. They had danced in this way, she thought, in the foothills long ago.

Ghaio slept with her mother—that is, had swift, rough intercourse with her mother—two or three times a month, in the early days. In the past four years, far less often.

Volpa saw and knew nothing of these couplings. Thus once, Volpa's mother said an odd thing. "He'll be too old before you're grown."

It was less a statement, of course, than a prayer. Ghaio had shown no inclination to violate the child, who, besides, was kept dirty and muffled and as much from his sight as was feasible.

But time, which leached off some of Ghaio's libido, and some of his strength, was working an opposite magic on the woman's daughter.

Volpa, who had never seen in a mirror—would not be able even to recognize her own face—was at first aware only of slight changes. The ill-treatment which had, perhaps, kept her mother barren, delayed the onset of womanhood. But finally it came. Soreness blossomed into breasts. A thunder of pain broke like a crystal and spotted the straw Volpa slept on with ruby drops.

Then she saw her mother with her hands to her lips. Afraid.

"What have I done? Mumma—I'm sorry—I didn't mean to." (Like the day she broke the pot—and was whipped.)

"No, it's not your fault. It can't be helped. It's what I told you of—do you remember?"

"That? This—is *that*—"

"Yes. Don't cry. It's good. As it must be."

"But *you're* crying, mumma—"

"Only from the sun in my eyes."

For Volpa's bleeding had begun in her birth month, late summer, the time of the sun lion, patron of the Primo, the great Basilica of Ve Nera.

Volpa—even her mother now called her that—was fourteen.

Soon, trudging up the alley after the old man, who hauled the cart, behind the creaking wood and picking up any which fell out, Volpa heard fresh abuse. Before she had been pushed about, slandered as a slave child. Now she was man-handled as a slave who was a woman.

In the market-place boys and men stole up on her and cupped the shallow rounds of her body, breast, thigh, buttock, in unloving hands. Squeezed her like the vegetables. "She's a hot piece." "No, not ripe yet." Sometimes she was glad when the black-robed priests moved nearby, although they spread fear like the aroma of their incense. Then men left her alone.

The adult Volpa did not confide much in her mother. Intuitively she knew her increasingly silent parent had enough to bear. Volpa bore her own dismay, unspoken. It was life. It was God's school.

But sometimes she thought of the story her mother had told her, at the farm in the hills, and maybe again, once or twice, in the first two or three years of the Red House.

The mother was the heroine of this story. It was a real story, true.

Already carrying her daughter in her womb, but not yet knowing it, Volpa's mother had been one night at dusk on a hill.

The day's work was over, and perhaps she was in those days then, allowed rest; she had never said. But pausing, she had looked up above the bare winter fields, into a pale sky that had seemed, she said, the color of the emeralds on the fingers of the mightiest priests. And stars were set out in this polished sky, fierce, and prickled as hedgehogs with their lights.

Suddenly the air, which was cold, grew warm. A warm wind blew up the plain, thick as the gusts of summer. And on the wind, high, high up in the orb of the emerald that was sky, Volpa's mother saw a flight of angels pass.

"At first I took them for birds, Blessed Maria pardon me. They were against the light, and yet they had a gleam on them. And the wings, moving slowly, as gulls' wings do when they catch the currents of the air above the City. But they didn't have any shape of birds, beyond their wings. They were long, like men with their legs stretched out, their arms crossed over the chest. And on the head of each, a flame—like a star come detached, and going with them."

This story of the angels never varied, or only here and there an iota. Now and then some slight extra detail was added—as of hearing a cock crow in the valley, as if at sunrise, and thinking the cock had seen them too—but never anything left out.

"Where did they go, mumma?"

"Away, upwards—into the dome of the sky. Until they grew so small they vanished."

"Did they look at you?"

"I don't know. Perhaps."

"Why did you see them?"

"Because they were there, and I was looking up," Volpa's mother had replied, with dignified simplicity.

She had told no other.

Now she never spoke of it, and Volpa never asked to hear. In imagination only, Volpa relayed the flight of angels. She had seen it so often with the inner eye of her mind, that now it too had become one with the earthly memories of her infancy in the hills. As if she had witnessed it at her mother's side.

That winter, after Volpa turned fourteen, was very bitter.

Ice—they said—formed on the great Laguna Aquila, and the smaller lagoon called Fulvia, and ice pleated the hem of the sea beyond the bars of sand and the sea walls.

The canals froze solid. Even the cart was able to be pulled along them to the market, not needing the alleys, slipping a little.

In Ghaio Wood-Seller's kitchen in the yard, Volpa's mother kept the hearth going as long as she was able from the meager allowance of wood the master gave them. They were supposed to use it only to cook his meals. However, the old man slave stole, a few twigs here, a log there, from the tempting mounds in the yard. Ghaio presumably never guessed. In any case, they were often cold.

During this winter, Volpa's mother began to cough. She tried never to do it when serving Ghaio, for then he struck her: "Shut your noise!"

One morning, the air seemed to break. Suddenly a softness came, like breath breathed on a rich man's glass goblet.

Volpa, waking on the straw at first light, went into the yard, and saw a single pale flower, some weed, that had pushed up against the house.

When she returned with the first unfrozen water from the cistern, she saw her mother still lay asleep.

"Mumma—wake up!" And she shook the woman's arm because no slave could lie abed.

But the man slave was there, gray as a cobweb gone hard.

"Don't shake her. Don't shake the sleeping or the dead," said this old man.

And reprimanded, a little aggrieved—what one took from master one could not bear from another slave—Volpa stopped. Then she saw the straw was dark under her mother's head. As had happened that time with herself, blood had poured out on the straw. Now, though, it seemed to be all the blood the mother had kept in her body. And the soft new light showed her white as the ice which had melted away.

Ghaio blasphemed and complained. She had not lasted eleven years, this useless, slave bitch. He had her body sewn in the customary sack, and thrown on a boat for the Isle of the Dead, where the bodies of slaves were only burned, there being no room for limitless burials.

Volpa stood stunned and weeping. The boat was rowed away in the gray morning. The old man slave said to Volpa, or to the air, "Cry for yourself but not her. Her pain's done. She is in God's world now."

Volpa wept. She said, "That's no better."

"Oh yes," said the slave. "Why else do you think He damns us for suicide? His world is the best of all, and we must earn it." Volpa only ever heard this man say two meaningful things, and this was the second. (The first had been about the shaking.) Then, as they returned through the alley to Ghaio's yard, the old man said also a prophetic thing, "How I long to get there. Would this could be done. I won't raise my own hand, Lord. But fetch me—by any means you like, by whatever awful way. The road's stones, but the gates are pearl. Fetch me, Lord. Amen."

The wood-seller had a collection of debtors, among whom was no longer Juvanni the sweet merchant.

His house Ghaio had taken in lieu of the loan that winter. Where Juvanni and his family had gone was anyone's guess.

Ghaio did not want the better house, though. He preferred his hovel. He sold the other, and put the deeds and the money into a chest in the upper room of the Red House, which was reached by a ladder, and full only of a bed, some candles, and many, many similar chests.

In the evening after the mother's corpse had been rowed away for the crematory, Ghaio had Volpa serve his meal.

He took no notice of her, but neither did he strike her. This surprised Volpa, who had tried not to displease him, but knew she had been clumsy.

At last, Ghaio sat back.

"You'll have to take your mother's place. I won't waste cash on another." Volpa waited. "How old are you?"

"Fourteen years, signore. So she said."

"Now I see you, you look less. Skin and bone. Skinny red fox. Let me see that hair." Volpa drew off her scarf with reluctance. "Ah, you're nothing," said Ghaio. "Worthless. I might sell you. What'd you bring me, though? A copper venus and a sneering laugh." Then he said, "Go up the ladder and open the chest nearest the door. It's not locked. Inside is a paper with a list of men's names, men that owe me money."

Volpa did what he said. Her whole life had been molded in obedience to him.

She knew he looked at her as she climbed.

In the upper room, she glanced about. She had been there often to wipe the floor and collect the night-pot, but always when the Master was from the house.

There was a tiny window, shuttered against the weather and the dark. The bed was low and spread with a moldy fur—normally her mother would tidy the bed, but today the man slave had done so. In the room was a bad smell, not merely from its enclosure and the accumulation of bodily stinks. It was a corrupt smell.

When Volpa came down the ladder, Ghaio again looked at her. She had to lift her skirt away from her legs to manage the ladder. She gave him the paper.

Then Ghaio reached out and took hold, through slave's tunic and shift, of Volpa's center, the mound of her sex. Her instinct—entire and vital—was to leap away. But she was property. She kept still, as she had mostly had to do in the streets and market. Presently, apparently dissatisfied, he let go.

But, "We'll see," muttered Ghaio, as if promising her something. He was.

That night, Volpa dreamed.

Generally it seemed to her she never did. Rather it seemed that she went—elsewhere. And coming back at sunrise to the Auroria bell over the marshes, she was dazed from a long journey, exhausted by her slumber. And this lethargy mostly only left her gradually in the hour after she rose.

The place or places she had gone to in sleep she recollected only in fragments—some glimmering piece, like a bit of a broken dish, made of some costly substance, yet worthless since broken off. Besides, it soon faded. As she revived, she lost all memory, all *sense* of the countries of the night.

Her dreams she considered differently, and they were rare—or rarely did she recall them intact. The last one which she could at that time remember had been dreamed at the farm or estate from which her mother and she were sold off. Volpa had been then less than four years old. She was, in the dream, in an orchard, where all the trees were bold with fruit—perhaps only like the orchards of the foot hills and the Veneran Plain. Yet on one tree, at the orchard's center, was an unfamiliar crop. The globes that hung from its boughs were of gold and silver—the image not of metal, but of sunlight and moonlight. (Told of gold and silver once by some traveler at the farm, she had only been able to picture them as such.)

The tree of gold and silver, of suns and moons, attracted Volpa in the dream. She went to it, and began the slow circling dance her mother had taught her for trees.

Then, high in the branches, something moved that also shone. She thought it was a cat at first, but then she saw it had no legs, or ears, and instead of a pelt it was smooth and sheened as any of the fruits of the tree.

As she had told her mother this dream, the mother had grown anxious. "What did you do? Did you pick any of the fruits?"

"Oh no," said the child, "they would have burned me, I thought."

"And the snake?"

"Was it a snake?"

The mother nodded.

The child said, "It slid down and stared in my face. It had such beautiful eyes."

"But did it speak—or offer anything?"

"No, mumma."

Her mother's face had eased.

"And then?"

"Then you woke me."

"God forgive me that."

The night after her mother's death, and going up

the ladder with Master looking up her legs, Volpa dreamed she was on the plain again, under the foothills.

Now, however, there were no villages or towns, and the land was covered by warm powder, or dust, very deep, so that as she walked, Volpa's feet sank far into it. Also there was before her only one mountain.

Realizing this, Volpa halted.

The mountain was astonishing. It was long, and had a curved, flattish top, and was colored a lucid flaming red—like a hearth or a sunset. A scarlet red, that had fluted shadows chiseled in it, and veins like living fire.

In wonderment Volpa stood, watching the mountain, which seemed to reflect the passage of clouds and suns. Then, she saw between herself and its incredible rock, figures dancing on the powdery plain. They were black, as if being by the fiery mountain had burned them. But something touched Volpa's foot, and looking down she saw a golden serpent rippling away through the sand.

When she woke, it was night, yet through the high window of the kitchen a full white moon was blazing. Somehow the contrast of its color scorched the dream of a red mountain into Volpa's brain.

She got up silently. The male slave lay sleeping in his corner. The houses were soundless, but for the lisp of the spring canal.

When she went out, the whole City of Ve Nera, Venus, seemed laid to sleep. Nothing stirred. No human voice nor cry of any creature, not one bell.

Volpa went to the fig tree and danced slowly around it, as she had done with her mother.

The boughs were silver with moonlight, but showed no hint of renewal.

On the Isle of the Dead her mother would be ashes

now, and tipped in some hole. But the people in the dream were so black, surely they had been in fire and come back out of it, whole, and far stronger, better.

Once she had danced, Volpa leaned on the tree, holding it, and crying noiselessly. Her pain rose and fell like waves, and it occurred to her that perhaps God noted this, and the height of her suffering, and that by her grief she helped to buy the life beyond life in God's perfect world.

Then something rustled, up in the bare tree. And for half a second, Volpa thought it was her mother, become now an angel, perhaps black, and leaning through the branches to say something kind.

But when she looked, Volpa saw it was a scrap of some refuse, blown up there in the winter, now coming apart and so making movement and sound to deceive her.

2

As spring took hold, Ghaio felt new optimism. This was almost always to do with money. The untamed scents of sea and fish and sap that now filled Ve Nera, put a bounce in his step, but only so he went up the ladder more quickly to count the money.

Having counted it, he selected a bag of silver duccas and one gold venus, and dressed himself in his tatty best.

(There had been some talk of an edict against usury, when practiced by Christians. Ghaio did not think this could come to anything, but it was wise to stay friendly with the Church.)

The hired boat ferried him out on to the wide Fulvia lagoon. Ghaio Wood-Seller looked about. How much of the City could he now buy? How soon could he buy more?

The gift to the Church was a sensible insurance.

It was almost midday, and Ghaio was going to attend Midday Mass, the Solus, in the Primo.

The lagoon was a sheet of green silk. The very sort of silk for which Ve Nera had become a rival in the cities of Candisi and the East. After the winter, the buildings crowded round the lagoon looked dank and draggled, matted beasts that had slunk to drink. Then the shoreline opened into the great square, swept, and tinted like Juvanni's prettiest sweets. From which rose the moon-dome of the Basilica.

Ghaio would not mind the mass. Although impervious to the holy ritual and the ethereal singing, the gold ceiling was of some interest to him, and the jewels and magenta of the priests.

When his boat reached the bank, the bell began to call.

Ghaio got out, paid the boatman (meanly) and strutted across and in at an enormous door.

Black robes moved at the square's edges. Eyes and Ears noted the pious hurrying in to God.

Ghaio stepped into an alcove, and awarded his gift to the relevant hands, leaving his name as donor for the notice of the Council of the Lamb. He then moved on into the body of the temple. Here the poorest sat on the floor. The better classes had chairs. Several stared up, as now Ghaio commenced to do.

Arch rose through arch, minor dome through dome, until at last the ultimate circle lifted, as if weightless, high above. Gold. It was more like fire. And in the fire, the painted angels flew, pausing to raise their hands in blessing.

There were great treasures hidden here. Relics, standards, icons, thick with bullion and gems. . . . The apartments above, they said, had riches like those of Heaven itself—

How many chests of money would it take . . .?

Angelic voices rang from the balconies, and Ghaio basked in his insurance. With God. If God did indeed exist, and the afterlife. But Ghaio turned his mind from his own demise. He would live long.

O God, the voices sang, *If I render to You all my heart, I am free. Yet, when You turn to me, You will demand of me everything. For Your love I must forget the world.*

A tavern song—surely?

Ghaio watched the priests, a cross stuck with rubies and chrysoprase.

Nearby a woman wept. They always did.

Not much longer and the show would be over. Then some dinner at an inn. Then two debtors to watch squirm.

By the time the Venus star stood over this City, Ghaio would be at home, and the Fox would come in her rags, bringing wine.

A twitch of feeling moved in Ghaio. After all the spring had found him, there in church. Sap and sea, milk and salt.

After the first dream of the scarlet mountain, for a time Volpa dreamed every night. Not entirely acquainted with dreams, she did not think to ponder that each one followed from the one before. They were like pages torn from an illuminated book, and falling down into her sleep, one after another, telling a story in bright pictures.

In the second dream, Volpa was aware of the summer heat of the wide plain. The sand was a terracotta shade and softly burned the soles of her feet, which in her sleep were bare.

On the land, between herself and the mountain, that in this second vision was darker, more of a maroon color, though glowing like a lamp, a haze of heat trembled. And out of this came walking a figure, slowly.

It was Volpa's mother.

Volpa felt at once very glad to see her. There was no memory that the mother had died. Only a joy which might have indicated some previous parting.

Then, as the woman moved nearer and nearer through the wavering pink air, Volpa saw she was almost naked, and though recognizably still the woman Volpa had known, younger—and darker of skin.

Volpa did nothing, only waited. When the woman reached her she touched Volpa's mouth with her palm. The mother smelled of hot things, stones and cinders. Volpa thought, vaguely, *Oh, it's that she was burned, on the Isle.* There was no terror in that. Here her mother stood, compact and alive.

When her mother spoke to Volpa, Volpa realized it was in another language. Even so, Volpa understood it, and was able, in turn, to utter it.

After this, they walked away over the land.

Waking, the girl never knew what they had said to each other, beyond a phrase of two. Her mother seemed to be teaching her things. In Volpa's infancy, the mother had done this as a matter of course, and necessity. It was simple to resume the manner of it. In the later years, Volpa had perhaps missed her mother's conversation, her advice, her stories. Now the dreams themselves were the stories, and the advice was inherent in them.

After the second dream, came others.

When Volpa woke in the cold spring dawns, to skim frost from the cistern, to cook as best she could Ghaio's porridges and rice, and bake his bread, the dreams did not fade. They sank back a little, as if replaced neatly into the revealed book from which they had fallen to her mind.

They were also, the dreams, very similar, for the most part.

Always the mountain was at the center of them, curved, striated, and a rich red. Sometimes the land had tufts of grass, boulders, even groups of blond trees with tasseled foliage on the boughs. The time of day was always late, near sunfall probably. Things cheeped from the low thickets. Birds of wild dyes flew over, or settled in the trees like topazes, jacinths.

In every dream, however, Volpa's mother darkened. Her hair grew black and her skin like brown ebony. She seemed comfortable with this, changing her skin. Her teeth were very white, and often she raised her arms, lifting by the gesture her heavy naked breasts. She laughed. Every thing which she taught to Volpa—which consistently, as with the conversations, Volpa did not recall on waking—seemed nevertheless good. That is, benign. It made the girl happy, and made the mother happy to dispense it, like nourishing food or the kiss of love.

One of the few phrases of speech Volpa retained was this: that she said to her mother, "Why do you teach me all this now you've gone away?" And the mother had replied, "How could I teach it to you, when I was with you?" In the dream that had seemed, quite reasonably, to explain everything.

Sometimes, other people crossed their path, literally appearing to move on other specific but—to Volpa—invisible roads. They were invariably a little way off or greatly distant. All were black. Sometimes they raised their hands in greeting.

Volpa and her mother wandered. Now and then, the mother would lean and snatch something from the grass or the sand, or out of a tree. These things were often live animals, but curious in form. Either Volpa or her mother then carried them on. The animals did not struggle. When Volpa grew hungry, she and her mother would sit down, and the mother would make a fire. She did this by rubbing her hand along a piece of stick. Volpa watched, fascinated, seeing first a thin smoke, and then a tongue of flame lick up.

When the fire was ready, the mother would shake it off on to the earth, and here it would burn. Then she would place in the fire the animals they had collected. There was nothing horrible or bizarre in this. The animal would vanish at once, and reappear *almost* at once, on the ground a few strides away. There it would run or preen a few moments, before darting off. After that, Volpa would have the sense of having eaten something delicious. She was no longer hungry, but satisfied, as she had rarely been when fed on the scraps of Ghaio's house.

In rather a similar, equally peculiar way, as they wandered, once or twice Volpa saw one of the animals prey on another. There would be a chase or a struggle, but when it was done, the prey animal would only get up and go off, or, on one occasion, it lay down companionably by the creature which had stalked it, and together they sunned themselves under the metallic sky.

The dreams came, if Volpa could have counted, for twenty-one nights. They were very alike in all but slight details. She and her mother, though circling the red mountain and sometimes even seeming to approach it, never reached the place.

Yet the last dream had one great alteration. In this dream, night had come. As Volpa stepped forward into it, the sand was gray under her feet, and ahead of her stood the mountain, as ever, but now it was the blackest of all things, the fount of the night itself.

"Come, make up the fire," said Volpa's mother. So they sat down, and Volpa took the stick, which always came at once, from nowhere, and she rubbed her hand along it as she had seen her mother do. Her hand felt warm, then cold.

Through the dark, the flame birthed clear and yellow. She set it on the sand. The mother said, "Now always you can make fire."

Then they looked up to the sky, which was quite light, far lighter than the earth or the mountain. And it was scaled with brilliant stars. Over the sky too went a shimmering ribboning path, which seemed to rise out of the smoke of their fire.

Winds blew across the plain, that sang almost in human voices. Somewhere things chorused like bubbles opening on the surface of water.

Did mother and daughter speak? What did the mother say to her child? Volpa thought her mother told her a story. That years ago Volpa had come to her as the woman walked, but this was before Volpa had been born. "Let me in," said Volpa. "Who are you?" said the mother. But Volpa had only flown into the body of the woman like a tiny white moth.

"What are the stars?" Volpa asked in the last dream.

"Yesterday," said the woman, now black as the night mountain. "Tomorrow."

When Volpa woke, she began to cry. Worse than at her mother's death, she felt bereft. The mortal City dawn was coming up through the yard. The dreaming was over.

It was sunset when Ghaio returned to his house. The bells of the Venusium, the service of the evening star, were ringing across the City. The bell of Santa La'Lacrima sounded hoarse from over the lagoon, as it sometimes did in the spring.

Ghaio was disgruntled. The two debtors had both paid up all their debt, triumphant rather than squirming. Coins appealed to him less than power, although he was not aware of this, and blamed his mood on other things—the bells, the tedious mass he had attended, the bad cooking of the stupid slave girl who now kept his home.

Red dimmed above the canal. Ghaio's walls darkened, and the alley further along seemed black and ominous, as if robbers might lurk there.

Ghaio scrambled from the hired boat, and in at his door. He locked it thoroughly and let down the great bar. Safe now.

"What's this muck?" he demanded as the bowl was set before him.

"Fish stew."

"That old fool. He can buy nothing any more. Can't see. Can't hear. useless. Call this fish? You'll have to do it. Market for the food. And improve your kitchen skills."

The candles beamed as Ghaio thrust a lump of bread into the stew and brought it to his snout. The bread was burned, as often now, and Ghaio, having champed and swallowed, turned and cuffed the girl.

The touch of her resilient flesh, springing at the blow, reminded him. He grunted, and drank some wine.

"Tonight, " said Ghaio. "Upstairs." Then, a strange caution overcame him. He added, "I want you to help me count my money."

And the naive girl said, "I can't add up, signore."

"I'll learn you, then." This made him chuckle. "Yes, I'll learn you, Foxy. Climb up the ladder as soon as you hear the Moon Bell from Santa La'La."

* * *

When her chores were done, Volpa drew water and warmed it, and washed her hair. She had no idea why she did this, for hygiene was irregular among the slaves. The nights were cold still, yet the hearth had some fire left there, and here she dried the mass of tresses, seeing the flames shine through as she rag-rubbed and combed them with her mother's broken comb.

Already the old man slave slept in his corner, but Volpa did not dare lie down. She was afraid she would sleep through the Luna Vigile—the Moon Bell, which called the priesthood again to pray, about two hours before midnight.

Her mother had frequently had to be up late to serve Ghaio. Her mother had never specified what these late duties entailed, beyond the carrying of food and drink.

Had she too helped Ghaio count his cash?

Volpa, despite her care, dozed. She wakened with a start to hear the bell, eerie and far away in the vastness of night.

Her hair was dry, the fire was out. In the yard, as she hurried across it, she smelled the aroma of the stacked wood. And, for the first time, she saw the fig tree showed no buds. She realized with a pang of sadness, almost fear, that the tree had died that winter, even as her mother had died. Ghaio would cut it down to increase his stock. And then only the dead would be there, in bundles in the barren yard.

3

Climbing the ladder, the girl was glad Master was not sitting below, watching her legs—for that had made her uncomfortable. This way, he saw her head first, the hair all crushed in again under its cloth. And she saw him as she never had in her life, sitting on his mattress, which was ancient and stuffed with straw, and contributed greatly to the room's foul odor. He wore a loose robe, rather short, so under it his bony, veined and hairy legs stuck out. If she had been a child, she might have wanted to laugh at this, but now it only faintly repulsed her.

Far, far away, the bell ebbed to silence.

She was afraid for a moment that he would reprimand her for being late.

No such thing. He seemed quite jolly. And his color was high.

"Here you are," he said.

She could hardly fail to be struck—not by his hand this time—but by his changed demeanor.

Volpa did not know Ghaio had decided he might take her even into his bed. She was a virgin after all, and could prove awkward at this first exercise. They were better on their backs for that.

Besides, she was young, and smooth. He did not in the end dislike the notion of her by him, in the night, perhaps convenient for a second game. And this too tickled him, the thought that he might utterly surprise her.

"Now, Volpa. If you're to help with the cash, you must take off your clothes."

She stared at him. Which amused him.

"You see, you might thieve a coin otherwise. I daren't risk it. If you're bare, you can't stow anything away."

Even at the word *bare*, (pleasing him) his tool rose under the robe. Oh, he was man enough.

"Come now, come on," he said, pretending impatience, "are you daft? Do as you're told."

She was a slave. Molded in obedience. With a shrinking that—for Volpa—had no real reason, she pulled off her slave's tunic, and then, in a kind of frenzy of shame, her shift.

Ghaio lay back, and dropping his hand in his lap, fondled himself.

Now this was not so bad. Despite her ineptitude with the food, he had an article of value here. It would not last, of course. A year or so, and she would be dross. Feed well then, while he might.

"And that scarf. Take it off. Not a stitch. Or I can't trust you."

In one wild movement she ripped the rag from her hair.

Five or six candles were burning in the chamber. Ghaio had wanted a proper look.

Now, for a second, he was startled.

His possession was, as he knew, very young, and very slender—but not after all skin and skeleton. Over the fragile bones, the creamy flesh had covered her, well made and perfectly fitted, like a lord's glove. Yet she was so pale, even the round little beads on her breasts barely the shade of watered wine—a match to her mouth. And her eyes, which never before had he noticed, were also pale, a sort of amber color; now he thought of it—just like the eyes of the fox he had seen once, in a picture. In her groin, however, these pallors deepened and flushed alive. She was *red*-amber, there. But that had not prepared him for her hair, nor its evocation.

Had he not once thought her hair like fire? Yes, for so it was. It blew out from her head, framing the whiteness of her body. In length, it fell below her knees. It could be worth cutting, this hair, and selling. But he might let her keep it . . . It gave him quite a thrill, the sight of it, that red mantle round her white.

Indeed, she was *like* a flame. The blanched center, the carmine rim.

"Come over here," he thickly said.

He could scent her, this vixen, this flame. Her rufus tang, the youth of her body. Sweet—

When Ghaio caught hold of her and spun her down on the stinking bed, Volpa thought she had again enraged him, and prepared at once for cuffs and slaps or worse.

Instead, perhaps only slightly less brutal, his hands clenched, one on her right breast and the other on her sex.

Ghaio laughed in her face.

"Now we come to it, eh, Volpa?"

Before, when he had grabbed hold of her, (on the evening of her mother's death) she had not questioned it, though it had filled her with panic. That sexual affront had seemed only one more lashing out. (Another more ferocious extension of the assaults in the market.) Now, a recollection surfaced. She saw again the cart in the rain, and her own mother under the awning and under Ghaio, her body wracked and shaken by his use of it.

This use Volpa had never understood. Nor did she now. Simply, she was afraid. Yet it was a dread beyond anything she had ever known.

"Give me a kiss, girl," said Ghaio. "That rosy mouth. And those white teeth—oh yes. Let me taste you."

And Ghaio kissed her.

At this she managed, her horror acting as a bow, to fire herself away from him.

Ghaio fell on his face and breathed, in place of fragrant youth and charming fear, the smelly bed.

"Come back, you slut. Where are you off to?"

She had stumbled away, but before she could get up from her knees, he caught her leg. Ah, so smooth, like marble, yet not so hard, nor so unfeeling.

"Stay still. I'm your master." He dragged her back

and now, turning, not even thinking what she did, she hit him in the mouth.

Ghaio yowled.

No other had smitten him, not in twenty years, and certainly not a female, nor a slave.

His face darkened. A new stench, the effluvia of rage, streamed from his pores.

"You'll lie down here with me, or you'll be made sorry."

She was across the room. She stood by her discarded clothes, not bending yet to snatch them. A weird pose—her arms not clamped protectively to her body, coyly shielding breasts or loins, as even Venus, in certain lewd pictures, sometimes did.

No, the arms of Volpa were outflung. Her head poked forward a little, like a snake's. And the scarlet wind of hair blew all about her, seeming sentient.

Its color—it had increased, become extraordinary—orange, like the golden citruses brought on trees from the East—some effect of the candles, no doubt—he scarcely noticed.

"Lie *down*, you trull. Lie down and take what I give. Or I'll flay your back and peaches for you. Do you want that, eh? Have your master or have the flail—want *that* eh? Or *me*?"

Through Volpa's brain things flashed. Not thoughts, let alone words. Lightnings, gusts of intolerable brilliancy.

She let out a barking scream.

It checked Ghaio.

What was she, this bitch, truly some beast?

A motion, of her body or of some other thing which was in the room with them, put out the candles, every one.

But they were not needed. For now Volpa herself gave light.

She was incandescent. The white of her flesh was blazing, blinding him. He could no longer make out her features, eyes or lips—not even the fleece at her loins.

Yet the outer hair—surely it did burn? Oranges and gold, lava that poured from some erupting mountain Ghaio Wood-Seller had never seen.

"Stop this, you scunny harlot." He got up off his couch. He rubbed his hands together, as he thought, to ready them for violence. But they were slick with sweat. That posture of hers. It was like that of some bird of prey, the wings out, the head thrust forward.

Ghaio stood on the mattress. He could not credit what he saw.

The hair of his slave—was *bursting*.

Who made that noise? It was Ghaio now, screaming. "Holy Virgin spare me—God save me—"

The hair of the slave had exploded outwards, and for a moment the girl was the core of an incendiary storm. It swirled upward, to either side, behind her. Her hair had filled the room.

Ghaio's eyes scorched. The shrill hair dazzled him.

Abruptly he was freezing cold. He clutched his arms about himself and shrieked as flames rushed up them. He was naked too, his robe burnt off, but clad in fire.

Ghaio danced. In the middle of the light, he was turning black. And the shell of the room broke like an egg.

When the roof flew off, he might have seen the night held in a net of glory. But, screeching, he only danced, and swallowed fire, and was made dumb.

Volpa had lost interest in him. She felt herself droop, and as she did so, her mind grew cool and dim. Two wings seemed to fold about her, and her eyes shut fast. She rolled into a silent emptiness, exactly like a sleep that had no dreams.

"What's that glow? Is it morning?"

"No, Lucha. A house is on fire on the Seven Keys Canal."

"Fire—!"

"Lie still. It's not so close. We doused the inn roof with water, to be sure."

Luchita looked out wearily, between the pains, at her husband. "Only one house?"

"Three, to be exact. But they're dipping up water from the canal. It's almost out."

Another pain came, and Luchita cried aloud.

Her husband hurried from the room.

She would lose this child. It was too early.

"Oh God—why do you make me suffer like this? I never even *enjoyed* it—"

She hated God. Pointless to dissemble. He would know.

In the window the red glare faltered, then waxed again.

The girl came in, with the old midwife from the marshes, old Maria with her ten black teeth.

"Best be quick," said this crone, "Venus is afire."

The girl looked scared and sprang from the room. Luchita said, "Three houses only, so he told me."

"Three so far. And the alleys full of wasps—" Luchita stared. The witch pointed straight at the window. Some insects were buzzing there drearily, dropping in and crawling on the floor. "A nest in his wood-stacks. It was the wood-seller's Red House. The heat of the fire hatched them too early. Only one body's brought out. The slave man from the yard, curled up and black. But they say there was a girl, and the miser himself, Ghaio."

Pain came. Luchita cried loudly.

Dying wasps hardly born drizzled in twos and threes into the room. Poor things, like the child, forced on too soon.

The witch trod on the wasps. She would be as blunt with the woman and the baby.

But the fire was dulling now.

The crone peered from the window. "There's a beggar at your door," she said. Everything was of interest to her save her trade, she had seen too much of that.

Below in the street, the beggar looked up at the window as Luchita howled.

Two men, shouldering from the inn to visit the fun on Seven Keys, strode by the beggar, knocking her aside.

Volpa sat down on the ground by the inn door. She had forgotten who she was, and where she was, if she had ever known either. Lusterless wan brown, her long hair flimsily veiled her. Her skin was like unleavened dough. She had been reclothed in something, perhaps her shift—but did not know it. She was cold, so cold. She rested her head on her knees and forgot the world.

Above her, meaningless as bells, the cries came and went for another two hours, until Luchita had brought forth her stillborn boy.

PART TWO

Then saw I a vixen seeming starved.

DANTE ALIGHIERI
The Divine Comedy

1

THE NIGHT TURNED SLOWLY as a wheel, spiked with stars. But he had forgotten that. The heat of new summer had brought scents and miasmas. These were shut out. The thick walls fortressed a lagoon of coolness, and the flavors, solely, of olibanum and myrrh.

Heaven was like this. Pure, chilled, perfumed, and silent, save with faint fair musics. A sky of burnished ghostly gold.

The window rose behind the altar. In darkness without tints, until a flutter of summer lightning briefly and inaccurately colored it, the white face of the Virgin, framed in a damson mantle. She maintained her vigil, as did he, the knight of God kneeling at her feet.

It was required of them. But some kept the Vigil (from the midnight bell until the dawn Auroria) only for the six watches obligatory during the course of one year. Cristiano was of that number who kept the Vigil once in every month, save during times of war. In winter, evidently, it was the most taxing. Kneeling straightbacked before the altar from midnight until sunrise—some seven or eight hours. (Some slept, slumping. Others regularly got up and marched about the chapel. Some fainted.)

After his very first watch—he had been seventeen years of age, and it was winter—Cristiano, who had not moved all night, had gone out into the courtyard, his legs had failed him, and he had vomited. Within a year though, he had grown accustomed, physically, to the ordeal.

There was no overt competition among the Bellatae Christi, the Soldiers of God. The proofs of faith, both in arms and in prayer, were a private matter. So Cristiano perfected his skills as a worshipping priest in the same spirit that he honed his fighting ability. By the age of twenty, few could outmatch him in the practice yard of the Militarium. None, in the church.

Of course, the Vigils had long ago ceased to be for him a test of endurance. While he himself had never seen the act in that way. He had understood and believed that the Vigil would bring him nearer, not only to God, but to the *Will* of God. So, even pain had not delayed him. Perhaps, in fact, had driven him the faster to his goal.

For there was always pain, in the first hour or two. Under the lashes of it, Cristiano would rise up into his mind, which soon became then a clear sparkling crystal, not unlike the substance of a star. Here he would wait, timelessly indifferent to the qualms of a body which only youth—and considerable reserves of trained strength—kept in the desired position.

As his soul stood above the body, pain was next burned away by a sheer white radiance.

When the radiance began, which was usually in the first or second hour, but sometimes in the third, Cristiano would tremble. For this coming of white light was the announcement, the *herald*, of the approach of God.

Although he would give way to nothing human, to this Cristiano surrendered.

And then, he would enter into a sphere of ecstasy so otherwise unimaginable, and afterwards so unretainable, that all things, world, time, reason, life itself, seemed stopped or left behind. It was the foretaste of the immortal state, this transcendence. It was beyond any physical pleasure, impossible in its wonder and effulgence, yet nearly always now achievable, by him.

Only the sounding of the dawn bell could bring him down from the height. Then he would sink back, drained yet renewed, into the leaden casque of flesh. Thin sun beams on the stony floor would scatter as his shadow finally crossed them.

That he relished such delight was unavoidable. Was it thus greed, to keep the Vigil so often? No. He had faith that nothing would be given him, should he be found unfit. And once or twice, when the supernal had failed him, that is, he had failed *it*, he had felt a horrible downfall. But despair was a sin. He threw depression from him swiftly, and working the harder at his office of priest, fasting, scourging his body, so pushing this body further off from him, he would find always that the next Vigil brought him again into the realm of the Divine. Into the exquisite duality of awareness and oblivion, which he knew to be God.

Cristiano was a virgin. Among the Bellatae chastity was the code, as with every priest. If any broke the rule and were discovered to have done so, the order thrust them out.

To Cristiano such a thing would have been insanity to contemplate, too stupid to consider. Besides, what joy of the flesh could compare to the crucial and excruciating ravishment gained by communion with God?

In war, there was another joy, it was true, which came also, since such wars were holy, from God. Then the crystal of the mind was not diamond white, but a deep red, like the bloody spinel. The vigor that coursed through the knight was like fire and wine, carnal enough, permissible only since God had willed it. (Such had ignited the Crusades in prior centuries.) When Cristiano rode in a sea of gore, swinging blades of steel in hands of brass, he was, even then, God's instrument, less a man than a battle chariot, and Christ astride him, the Charioteer.

To take life in the service of the Creator was neither sinful nor cruel. It was just.

Returning to the world was always strange. The City, the beings which peopled it, were alien and curious.

Cristiano had attended the Dawn Mass. Now he visited the knight's castra, broke his fast, with bread dipped in wine, and washed in the cold water from the Primo's clean wells. He was no longer tired, and would not look for sleep until this evening.

Less than an hour later, the boat took him through the Silvian Marsh. Today, before the full heat of morning arrived, the smell of salt was strong. Green reeds and brown grasses grew along the water channels, taller in places than a woman. Gulls and other birds soared and sailed, and here and there in the reeds nests were visible, stocked with young chicks. Elsewhere, some men waded with nets and slings.

Houses still stood in the marshland. Many were ruinous. Gardens had become lakes, from which rose dying cypresses. The old amphitheater was only a ghostly hump on the horizon towards the sea, but they passed close to the Roman temple. Ragged boys, who were fishing there, shouting, went stone-still, seeing the warrior-priest rowed by. Between the greened-over columns, they squinted out at him.

Even the boatman was wary. They always were. When the boat bumped home against the bank of the channel, the Silvian Quarter rising in its yellowing summer tones behind, he took his payment and dropped to one knee.

"Bless me, brother."

Cristiano gave him the blessing—it was a fault, but with indifference. The man did not seem yet quite real. Nor any of it.

Only Christ Himself, a deity who had once been human, could take in the fall of sparrows after the height of the sun.

Cristiano walked up the alleys to the inn. The morning was loud with living bustle, like the activity of the birds in the marsh. Washing hung out, and there came the clang of pots, a fug of cooking and dirt.

By the inn door two or three beggars sat on the ground, their backs to a wall. Cristiano paid them no heed. Men had their stations from God, or a calling to some task, as had happened with himself.

His bother-in-law, the drunk, slunk out. "Soldier of God—Cristiano—welcome, welcome. She's much better today. Will you have a cup?"

"You know I won't."

"Yes, Cristiano. She's in her garden."

In the room, the early drinkers glanced uneasily. But the Soldier of God barely noticed them.

He went on through the corridor and out by the little door where he had to stoop.

The garden was not large, but high-walled. Peaches and vines stretched on frames. In the beds were herbs, and salads and vegetables, with his sister moving slowly among them.

A servant girl, one of the inn slovens, carried the basket and a knife for weeding.

Luchita looked no better, he thought. Her body had lost its shape with the last birth. Until this one, that had not happened. Besides, she had borne healthily three sons and a daughter. The dead baby was a shock to her. She had caught Cristiano's hand on his first visit. "You'll say it's my punishment." Cristiano said, "If you feel it to be so, then perhaps it is." At which she had railed against him so violently, he was afraid for her, took her in his arms and said, "No, Luchita. Your sin wasn't such a powerful one. And you repented, you told me so. Be glad for the child, He spared it the agony of this world." But Cristiano did not believe anything he said. She had committed adultery, which only Christ could forgive. And the world was the Militarium of the soul, where it learned to fight and fine itself for Heaven. To be spared was to be cheated, and God cheated no one, only gave what was earned.

Now Cristiano's sister walked to him along the path, and even her walk had changed, less graceful. She kneeled down suddenly, as the boatman had.

"Give me your blessing."

So he stretched out his hand and blessed her, and she became real for him. And the garden, warming, and a bird singing in a small twisted fruit tree.

"How are you doing, Luchita?"

"Oh, well enough."

They sat on a bench by the house wall, and the servant moved alone about the plants, now cutting something, now tying something up.

"This is a thriving garden."

"Yes. I'm the Good Housewife. I do my best. It's never easy. But I like these things. The way they answer care. I sometimes think," she paused, then said, "kindness and love might improve humankind. Better than struggle and suffering."

"God tells us this very thing, Luchita."

He expected her to say sullenly, in her unlessoned woman's manner, "Then why does He never show it us?" But she only sighed.

The servant cut off a large head of salad stuff with a crisp snap. It was forward, he thought, but then the garden caught the sun at this time of the year. He was going to congratulate his sister again, and realized that she bored him, and this was another fault.

"Tell me what you've been doing, Lucha."

"What do I ever do?"

(He had taught her to read when they were children. But she had, here, no chance for or use for books.)

"My poor girl. Remember, care also for yourself. You've received a blow, a wound. It must have space to heal."

"That child? Oh. It means nothing now. If it had lived a few hours, if I'd held it—but there wasn't anything to hold. I blamed old Maria, it's true, the mid-wife. Said it was her fault. Foolish. I always lose my children." Perhaps she saw him frown. She said, "Then Maria said it was a girl under the window who was to blame, a witch, who set a spell on me so Maria's wonderful cleverness was to no avail—"

Cristiano's thought wandered. It was the image of a window . . . The Virgin in her mantle, the delicacy of her face, beyond beauty. And the light which filled him—He brought his mind back sharply.

Luchita was looking up at him. "You're so handsome, Cristiano. So splendid in your armor. And your golden hair, so thick it breaks a comb—oh, I remember. What a waste. What a *waste* to be a priest—"

Anger moved in him, the dark beast he must resist. "You know, Lucha, I don't like you to say these things. I belong to God."

"You belong to the *world*. Look at you! Any woman could love you. Or a man—"

"Luchita."

"Hold my tongue. Yes. But you might have had sons, Cristiano. Think of that. God knows I mourn the loss of them more than that dead thing Maria pulled out of me."

Cristiano got up. Alerted by his closed fury, which seethed invisibly yet white-hot about him, even the servant cowered, and the bird left off its song.

And at that moment a raucous shouting broke out over the wall.

Luchita jumped up too, wincing and flushed.

"It's mad Berbo, I know his voice. The girl must be there, and he's seen her. The numskull. There are Eyes and Ears all through the quarter today—"

And leaving Cristiano, as if abruptly he had lost his value, she ran heavily back into the inn. The servant girl ran after her, clutching the salad.

Cristiano followed them, irritated, and keeping himself in check.

The inn had erupted into the alley beyond. From upper windows and from doors too, people pressed to see and jeer.

A man in decent garments stood shouting, frothing somewhat at the lips. Pointing.

And from somewhere, probably off the canal, two other men came, in black robes, and took hold of him.

Cristiano disliked the Eyes and Ears of God. But, impartially, he accepted their necessity—in certain areas. Not here, surely? This fellow was crazed, as Luchita said.

But the madman was turning now, clinging to the two black priests.

"Praise God that sent you! Brothers—see—that witch—that Making of Satanus—"

Cristiano turned his head a little. Who was it that this shouting imbecile had singled out for his obsession? It must be the waif there, barely more than a child, skinny and filthy, with matted brownish hair tied up in a cloth. She looked harmless, and unimportant. And yet, thin as a pin, white as sullied snow, she drew his eyes back, and back again.

Her own were downcast. She seemed not to know the outcry concerned her. Containment—guilt—also madness?

"Quiet," said one of the Eyes and Ears to the madman. "What are you saying?"

"I say she's a minion of Hell."

"Be aware of your accusation. *Who* is?"

"That one, there."

"What has she done?"

To his disgust, Cristiano detected a spice of interest in the priest's nasal voice.

The Soldier of God moved forward, and became the center of the scene.

At once the deranged man attempted to kneel to him (the third one this morning) and hung from the priests' grip, They glared, not liking to be, conceivably, usurped.

And Luchita spoke up hurriedly.

"Holy brothers—she's only a beggar. She wanders about. I feed her crusts and the scrapings of the rice kettle, from charity. I gave her a cloth to cover her hair. She does no one hurt. She's addled. And Berbo, too."

Berbo was kneeling, despite the priests, who unwillingly let him go, only looming over him, like black shadows cast up from his turmoil.

"Bellatoro—warrior of God—*you'll* listen. Let me speak."

"Very well."

Cristiano pulled his eyes away from the girl. He was almost glad to, and did not know why.

The kneeling Berbo, no longer shouting, now apparently in control, offered his words with the skill of an actor.

The crowd which had gathered, attended breathlessly. But Cristiano, resistant to such fantasies, set himself on guard.

"It was the night—over a month back—when there was a fire on the Canal of the Keys. Oh, protect me, blessed brothers. A fiend comes and torments me when I speak of it. I shout and stammer and no one believes—"

None uttered a sentence.

Mad Berbo, if he was, glanced round, then, averting his gaze from the beggar girl, continued without a break.

He lived over by the next canal, but came through the alleys to watch the fire. Men were drawing up buckets of water, but he saw no need to assist; as he put it, he did not wish to impede their work. Instead he went through another alley to the back of the houses, only one of which was then alight. It was the Red House of Ghaio Wood-Seller, who was said to have a hoard of money.

The purpose of Berbo was plain to most of those who heard. He had hoped to be able to locate some outer stash of coins and make off with them.

Reaching the back yard, where the smoke was less, he found all neighbors had seemingly fled in fear of the fire's spreading. Some refuse by the yard wall enabled him to climb it, and look over.

In the yard, the timber, in stacks and bundles, shone with the red light of the fire, and sparks spun everywhere, but had not yet caught anything but a tree by the cistern.

Berbo thought time was short for investigation, and besides it would be chancy. As he hesitated, he beheld a very frightening thing. In the upper story of the house was one narrow window, and this was filled by the fire. Until all at once the fire came out of the window, not in flames or sparks or smoke, but in an upright leaping shape.

This, flying into the air, dropped straight down again to the yard, and landed there.

Berbo, who had let out a yelp, discerned next instant that this apparition was only the figure of some hapless person, caught alight in the burning room, and jumping frenziedly forth. He expected it to roll shrieking on the ground. It did not.

Rather, it stood up.

At this very moment, a gust of flame shot through the house top, and rained spangles in the yard. (Sounds of alarm rose from the front of the house.)

Just then too, Berbo was aware of a golden liquid ribbon which ran out from the window. Was this Ghaio's gold, melting?

Something made him forget the gold.

The figure which had sprung down in the yard, and which he had expected by now to be dead, was still standing. Indeed, it had *righted* itself.

There was no doubt that it was on fire. It *blazed*. A

woman, as he could just make out. Her hair was a vivid red, and redder from the fire in it. He saw her *through* and *in* the fire.

"She was young, and wearing only a white shift. And it all was burning—the shift, her hair, her body—she was furled in flames that never went out—that never ate her up."

One of the black priests said, "He's mad."

Cristiano, to his own surprise, answered, "Hear him out before you judge."

Berbo exclaimed, "She burned—but she didn't burn, Signore Bellatoro. She burned but never was *burned*."

"So you have said. What then?"

Irked at the brusqueness of this blond untonsured priest, standing there in maculum and sword, Berbo rasped, "Doesn't the Bible speak of wonders, eh? And terrible uncanny things that attend the Evil One, Lucefero?"

"I'm more concerned with what *you* are speaking of."

Berbo pulled a face. He said he had been transfixed by fear, and as he clung on the wall, the woman walked—*walked*, neither ran nor stumbled—about the yard, and everything—she touched it. And where she touched, that thing took fire.

"Hadn't sparks already set the wood alight?"

"*No*, signore. It smoldered here and there. But where she put her hands—I could see them in the fire—flames burst up. She was a walking *fire-brand*."

There had been a darkened kitchen in the yard, and until then it had seemed unoccupied, but now it's roof was smoking, and the uprights of the door. All at once the door opened and an old man came out.

"I thought he'd been asleep perhaps, and I was sorry for the poor soul—but then I saw he wasn't in a fix, only standing there looking about at it all on fire, and he was grinning, and praising God."

One of the black priests said, "Too many madmen in this tale."

"I can't help it, brother. It's the truth."

The burning girl was by this time at the tree, which had been all but consumed by then. Still she was circling round and round it, like a sort of dance. "That's when I knew for sure she was a witch. The country witches do it. They dance about the trees. So then I knew the fire was her spell, and that was why she didn't burn up in it."

But, said Berbo, the old man, a slave, probably, now hurried across, and he stretched out his hands to the fire witch.

"Excuse me, signore, but I wet my drawers when I saw that. I went cold in my belly. Do you know what he said to her? No, I'll tell you. I heard him say, '*You are the torch of God*.'"

The crowd which had laughed at Berbo's admission of incontinence, now produced a silence as dense as iron.

Some of them crossed themselves.

Cristiano spoke very clearly. "And could you have misheard?"

"No. *Never*. But then, don't witches call *him* 'God' sometimes—him, the *other* one."

"You're well versed in the manners of witches."

"Who isn't? You have to be cautious."

Berbo said that the fire-witch left the tree and went to the old man and touched him. And of course, he too went up like a piece of fat thrown on the hearth.

"He never cried out once. He seemed dancing, too. Round and round, till he fell down and curled up like an insect. And then the wasps came out."

"Wasps."

"From the burning wood. Must have been three or four nests there in the timber. Hatched 'em. I've seen a man die of wasp stings. I got my legs under me and I ran."

Berbo stood up from his kneeling. He dusted the knees of his leggings, the action of a prudent, fussy man, not a mad one.

"And what has this to do with the girl there?" asked one of the Eyes and Ears.

Berbo said, mumbling now, as if embarrassed suddenly, "It was her, her in the wood-seller's yard."

"The witch you saw was covered by fire, you said."

"I saw her *through* the fire. It's her."

Cristiano did not want to look at the girl again. She was a shred of human life, pathetic, of no consequence. And for Berbo's story, how many cups of ale had he taken, despite the new taxes, before he climbed the wall?

The warrior-priest turned his head once more.

At that second, the beggar girl raised her own.

At the movement, the rag slipped back from her hair a little. Not brown hair, but a dull and dirty red. The face a white triangle with pale yellow eyes. A *fox's* face. The fox which, in legend, was the devil's familiar dog, even his disguise.

"And you, girl. What do you say?" It was a black priest again who addressed her.

And Luchita, again, interposed. "Gentle brothers, she doesn't speak. I never heard her. No one has. Look at her—does she look burned? Does she look cunning or supernatural?"

Yes. The thought jumped starkly forward in Cristiano's brain. Cunning, supernatural, both. And—*holy*, holy in some incoherent, awful and total way, as a fallen angel might, perhaps, that once had been bright winged in Heaven before its fall.

Berbo shook himself. He said, "All right. None would listen before. I've told it now. I'm done with it."

Both of the Eyes and Ears watched Berbo as he marched abruptly away. They would learn his house. He might well receive a call from them, or from others. To accuse, as to be accused, was not always simple.

The girl had lowered her head and her eyes.

One of the priests said, to Luchita, "Will you sponsor her, then? Swear that she's innocent?"

Luchita opened her mouth. Cristiano was quicker.

"The inn-wife is my sister. I vouch for her as an honest woman. But she can't pass judgment on such a thing. She's fed the wretch to save her from starving, no more."

"What then to do, Bellator?" The priests stared resentfully and arrogantly at him. "Should we take her to the Primo and question her?"

The crowd muttered. Ve Nera knew that some taken to the Primo on such business did not come out, or came out damaged. The Council of the Lamb was determined in its service to God: it was better to kill a man than risk his soul.

A woman cried, "She's only a kit! What does Berbo know?

But a surly man remarked, "If she's a witch, she needs seeing to."

Cristiano too was well aware of the interrogations which sometimes were carried on in the under-rooms of the Basilica. They had been a cause of discussion in his own mind. It was a fact also, if he had not stood in the path, they might have been off with her already.

He took a chance, rashly, like a boy. Half offending himself.

"I vouch for my sister, and she vouches for the

girl. That's enough. I myself will see to it."

"But," began the fatter of the Eyes and Ears.

"You will leave it with me and save yourselves the trouble. You've enough work in the City as it is."

2

That winter, a high tide had flooded the square before the Primo Suvio. Now artisans were commemorating, in black and gold mosaic, the large octopus found washed up by the Lion Door.

Fra Danielus, who had not partaken of the—reportedly tasty—corpse, looked down at the work from a gallery above.

On this sunny day, with its promise of heat, the Magister Major was conscious of much pleasure in the world. In the beauty of the Primo. Its enormous dome which, from the Fulvia lagoon, looked like nothing so much as a gigantic pearl. The courtyards with their busy yet sedate procedures, the cappella and castra (barracks) of the knights, their roofs of silver and gold, the pure fountain which plunged into a basin of white marble, supported by four lions done in gilded bronze. From the gallery of the Angel Tower, where Danielus stood, all this, besides the artisans, was visible.

Moving on, around the Tower's huge side, it would be easy to see, too on such a cloudless day, the phantom forms of distant mountains. While the Laguna stretched like silvered glass to the sea wall and the lit curve of ocean, the faint drifts of insubstantial islands like aberrations of some fine mind, profligate only with loveliness.

Yet, to every rose, a thorn.

Fra Danielus considered also this. Like the thorn, it was perceptible, (in the paper he had left lying in his book-chamber.) Like the thorn, it would not be felt until one put one's hand thereon.

Danielus turned his eyes down to the City. Which thrived and moved. Not having felt, yet, the thorn.

Last summer, from this very tower, the priesthood had hung out seven "bird-cages," low enough that the citizens might observe how the six men and one woman swung in them and starved to death.

They were persons of wickedness, thieves and murderers, the woman also a whore. But worse than breaking the commandments of God, they had been caught out in sins against God Himself.

The Council of the Lamb was forthright in its punishments. Without example, half-blind, Man would stray.

Yet the prolonged death of the malefactors, their cries and contortions, finally their corruption, had been aesthetic blasphemy. The Angel Tower was for angels to alight upon, not to hang out dying men like washing.

Though he had thought it, he would never have said it. He said very little, generally.

Fra Danielus was not much more than forty years, and looked youthful for that age. His hair was more black than gray, and his eyes were black still. The thin long nose, the thin but well-formed lips, the long, thin fingers—even without his belted magenta habit, and jeweled crucifix, his body itself revealed him as a man of thought and learning, a calm selective man, self-pared to the service of Almighty God. He had no vices, even those which the Church permitted. He drank no wine, ate sparingly, avoiding all meat, wore beneath his finery the most ordinary undershirt.

All excess, it seemed, recoiled from him. Perhaps miraculously. Fair women became, they said, in his presence more plain. A dog which had once run snarling and foaming at him, dropped at his feet, dying without delay.

At the age of thirty, Danielus had attained his present position, third of the Magisters Major, one of the Primo's highest religious authorities, beside the Council of the Lamb. More, he was the Master of the Upper Echelon of the Bellatae Christi. Perhaps an equal, in all but inherited luxury, to the Ducem in his island palace.

The Soldiers of God were in themselves a power, an essential asset to the City and provinces of Ve Nera. Their Upper Echelon was as famous through the world as some emperor's crack guard. Of course. They were the mortal guard of heaven.

Danielus was not thinking of this. He walked down the stairs of the Tower, then down the ramp, beyond which the cages had hung out. He reached the ground, and crossed through the inner gate to the courtyards of the Primo.

A young man, one of the Bellatae, was in the first court. He had paused by the lion fountain, but now came straight towards the Magister.

Danielus extended his hand. The cool lips of Cristiano pressed the emerald in the Magister's ring.

"Magister, can you grant me a few minutes speech?"

"Yes, Knight. And in turn, I shall speak to you."

"Have I offended?"

The pride, almost insolence, with which Cristiano had responded, amused Danielus slightly. He masked his amusement. He always did. Amusement, rancor, any vivid emotion. Even natural beauty he could regard unsmiling.

"No, my son. This is something our order must soon hear of. You and your brothers first of all."

They walked through a second court, from which led the castra of the Bellatae, and their chapel, in which

Cristiano had kept his Vigil. A wide marble stair took them up into the Primo's flank. From here, an indoor stair of stone ascended to the Golden Rooms.

The majesty of these apartments was lost, in a way, on Cristiano. As he expected everything of God, (seemingly this was mutual) so the magnificence of the Primo Suvio was inevitable. Not a marvel, merely a law obeyed.

"Sit, if you will."

Cristiano took a chair in the book-chamber.

Indirect sunlight from a window, paned in glass, burned his hand.

Danielus sat down at his desk, and rested, as he often did, one hand on a polished human skull of abnormal size.

To either side of him, on the wall at his back, were two panels, painted a century before by an artist unnamed, for the glory of God. In one panel the Biblical Danielo faced the lions in the pit. In the second, a single lion, now become the Primo's symbol, was subdued once more by the Christ Child riding on its back.

"I will speak first, if you permit," said the courteous Danielus.

"Naturally, Magister."

"It will be a war."

Cristiano thought, and nodded. "You've had a letter from the Ducem?"

"That's so. Ve Nera's ambassadors have failed in the Eastern city of Jurneia. Failed so profoundly as to have had their heads put up on spikes in that place."

"The Jurneians are savages," said Cristiano.

"So we hear. And infidels, such as we fought in the Crusades. They haven't forgiven us that, the spoiling of their city and capture of their wealth, nor the saving of so many of their kind from damnation by conversion to the one true Faith. Three hundred years and more have passed; they don't forget."

Cristiano said, flatly, "I thought, Magister, it was a war about the price of silk."

Although he seldom smiled, Danielus had a way of conveying a sort of smile, by something in his eyes and brows. This happened now. "So it is. Mankind tends to that, don't you find, Cristiano—the use of new excuses for an ancient grudge?"

"Then it's both a war of trade and holy war."

"As you say. The armies of the Ducem will be called for the first. The Soldiers of God for the second. In tandem, obviously."

"And the fighting ground, Magister?"

"There's some debate. Jurneia is readying her fleet it seems, and building more ships besides. So Ve Nera is to equip hers. But it may take a year for the enemy to be ready."

"Then we go to meet them?"

"As yet, the Ducem makes no decision."

"But that will come?"

"The decision, of course. What it will be is with God."

Both men left off speaking a moment. It was well known the Ducem of Ve Nera, unlike his predecessor, was a weak and idle man, and his advisors supposedly corrupt. Where the Church could over-master the sins and failures of lesser men, the highest-born could, for the most part, only be regarded.

Danielus said, after a while, "There is the letter. Read it, if you so wish."

Cristiano took the letter. It was written clearly in Latin and black ink, on fine parchment.

It was very polite, exact and vague at once. But, without any doubt, it smelled of war.

"You see, Cristiano."

"Yes, Magister."

"There will be a lot to do. I think the Primo herself will need to buy in commodities to safeguard the people of this City, and ensure our interests in the markets of the outer world, to the same end."

Cristiano's eyes, fearsomely clear and steady. "Trade again, Magister?"

"You don't see it, I think. What the delay may mean, if Jurneia is as powerful as she may be, and the Ducem slow, or his decision on the matter—ill-advised." Cristiano blinked. "And now you do."

"Unthinkable—"

"If their ships reach us, those who refuse or are unable to fly, will be besieged here."

"By the Christ—"

"Of course, you don't swear. It's a prayer you uttered."

"Pardon me, Magister—yes, a prayer for Ve Nera under siege—"

"The Jurneian ships are narrow, and oared, reportedly by slaves, although all sources do not agree on this. The rigging is heavy for the vessels' shape. They have the new weapon, unperfected here, cannon. The men wrap their heads in cloth and worship their mistaken notion of God, facing towards the dawn. A strangely spiritual image . . . Other than siege, they may wipe this City from the face of the earth."

Cristiano rose. His hair burned white in the glow of the costly window. A halo.

Danielus said, mildly, "Please sit, Knight. And tell me your own news."

Cristiano stared at him.

"It's nothing to this. Some witch by the Silvian

Marshes. But she isn't. The products of ignorance and malice hitched to one cart."

Danielus stroked the smooth pate of the giant skull on his table. A pious man kept always before him a *Memento Mori*. There was no life save through God.

He had come across Cristiano when, at fifteen, the boy entered the novitiate of the Bellatae Christi. Even so young, Cristiano was striking, and despite his start among the slums, intelligent and strong. It would be easier to doubt one's faith perhaps, than Cristiano's sincerity, his absolute steely *belief*.

A Magister Major had no favorites. Of course.

"Do I assume, Cristiano, that you intervened."

"Yes, Magister."

"It had caught your eye. I don't mean the witch, evidently. The situation."

"This happened by my sister's inn. The story's a fantastic one. If they put such imagination to the service of God, they'd do better."

"Let me hear the story, then."

Sometimes, she thought that she was in Ghaio's house. But the big room was larger and had many tables. The kitchen was attached to the house, though entered by a separate door. There was a garden, she had seen it. It reminded her somewhat of the farm, or estate, from which she had come. She did not see many people. The blonde woman who was now, presumably, her owner, kept Volpa mainly in the kitchen. Here she did much as she had done in the house of Ghaio, cleaning pots, sweeping the floor, carrying nastier substances outside to tip into an open drain leading to a canal.

Sometimes people stared at Volpa.

No one spoke to her aside from her new owner.

But who had ever spoken to her, much? Even her mother fell silent. Only in the dreams following her mother's death had there been conversations. And all those words, now, she had forgotten.

She had forgotten a great deal.

Volpa did not know why or when Ghaio had sold her, and did not recall the process at all. She had one half formed memory, of fierce light, and of being very cold. And someone had helped her pick up her shift, and put it on, and then led her outside into the yard. Who had that been? She had seemed just woken from sleep at the time, and still not fully aware. Was this helper the blonde woman? The helper had been gentle, yet firm. The blonde woman was neither. She pushed Volpa aside or into place as though not liking to touch her. And she vacillated in her orders: Go and do that—no, do this instead. Leave this and go there—no, come back, stay put.

Once she slapped Volpa. "Didn't I say don't let them see you?" And then the woman snatched at her own hand. "Oh—I never meant to strike you, poor thing!" While Volpa, used to blows, waited, puzzled.

The woman was called Luchita. She was the wife of the innkeeper. This was an inn. The patrons did not like to see Volpa, so she must be kept from their sight. The persons in the kitchen did not like her either. There was a lean piebald cat kept for the mice and rats. Nor did he like Volpa, and sometimes, without reason, approached and bit her. Seeing this, some girl had cried out—"Now the cat's poisoned!"

Volpa remembered a red mountain in a dream—or had she and her mother really wandered there? (Had the mountains been scarlet above the Veneran Plain?) Once they had been on a hill, and looked up, and in the green sky angels passed. Volpa remembered that well. And a snake in a tree.

Luchita rose from her knees. She had been praying to the Virgin, but only in the upper room, while her husband, laved in wine, snored an accompaniment. She had heard the Prima Vigile sound from Santa La'La—two hours after midnight. Useless to pray here. God heard only those who went into a church.

There was never time to make the journey. She was so tired. Too tired to sleep beside the jolting snores.

She struck the tinder and lit the candle-stub. She went down the narrow stair and into the corridor.

It was summer, yet still not warm at such an hour. She suspected none of the three inn servants slept now in the kitchen. It was a cause of resentment, her letting the girl come in, letting her sleep there. But what else was there to do? Cristiano had insisted the girl have some care. He would speak with his superiors, he said, find a convent where she might be taken in. That was always his answer. Everything was only to be found in God. Long ago, he had told Luchita herself she might be happier out of the world—she, a *nun*! Damn him, his loins were made of ice and his heart of stone.

No, no. Not so, not so. She loved him, he was good. He gave her money after the sot drank it away. He was beautiful—oh, to be chaste when equipped with such an armament. For certain, he was a godly man.

Luchita cried tears. Wiped them off. Went out of the door and three steps over the yard and into the kitchen which was built against the house.

Yes, as she thought. No one was there, only the mad girl lying by the hearth. Which was out, black and cold as a grave.

Luchita felt angry. Her moods were easily upset after the still birth.

She shouted.

"Wake up, you slut! Don't you know to keep the fire going?"

As the form stirred—slender and fluid as a serpent—Luchita glared about to find the tinder. The kitchen was untidy, greasy, and smelled stale. The tinder was nowhere to be seen. She must use the candle then, make the fire, put on some herbs and water in a pan for comfort and perhaps sleep.

At, least the fool was setting sticks on the hearth now.

"That will do. Where did they stow the flint for the fire? You don't know. Curse you, you wretch. Your brain's turned like milk. No, I know you're dumb. You can't speak."

(Volpa gazed up, thinking, trying to remember if she could.)

But Luchita was crouching by the hearth, thrusting in the candle. As it met too hurriedly, the sticks, the wick was quenched. The flame went out.

Luchita laughed with fury. She sat back.

"There. That's how this world is."

The tears returned. She let them drop. Who was to see but this idiot.

Through the high window a faint light stole. The moon sailed above Venus, changing every canal, every channel of the marsh, both of the great lagoons to opal.

A soft, crackling was in the air. It had a sound of burning. Luchita looked, and saw the mad girl running her hand through and through her dirty, sticky hair.

Yet how brilliant the hair was, after all. Its redness shone out, merely from the moon.

She had pulled some of the hair loose. It fluttered in her fingers. She let it pour, liquidly, on to the twigs—

"*Jesus our Lord—*"

Volpa seemed diffident and barely awake. Her voice, unused for almost two months, was hoarse. "My mother showed me how."

Flames sprang briskly along the sticks, from the fire Volpa had made in her hair. The hearth burned with a cheerful domestic light.

3

Down all the winding corridors, the nun glided precisely three paces ahead of him. Either she, or he, maintained the distance, despite his Soldier's stride.

It was a bare place, blank stone, cut here and there with the harsh shape of a crucifix, or a window looking on an empty court.

Then a gallery, steps, a wooden door.

Cristiano entered the narrow room. The door shut.

His sister sat at the table, her hands on a small cross the nuns must have given her. Her face was scrubbed and her hair plaited and put in under a long white cap. She looked older, and younger, both at once. Her eyes were dark and flat.

"You see. Here I am. Where you told me to go."

"Luchita, I never said you must."

"No. Someone has."

"Who—has he thrown you out? I'll speak to him."

"My husband?" She looked momentarily incredulous. "*Him*, that sop? I left his house. I'm to serve here, and then I'm to be taken in among the lay sisters. After a year I can begin my novitiate."

"It's unusual. You're not a widow."

"I told them who my brother was."

"I see."

"You're not happy. I thought you'd rejoice."

"Luchita, you yourself admit you're not a woman for such a life—"

"Now, I am. The rest—was burned out of me."

Cristiano went to the window. He looked down at the empty court. There was nothing in it, no well, no shrub. Only the high walls at its sides.

"You lost a child, Luchita. This—may have been a fancy."

"No."

"She has yet to be questioned. Suppose you were mistaken."

"I never was. She created fire. I saw it."

"Then suppose, Luchita, Berbo was correct and her gift comes from the Devil?" He spoke almost mockingly. He had never, she thought, credited contemporary miracles, only the stupendous wonders of an earlier world.

"If it was from God or the Devil, what do I care? It proved to me, Cristiano, it *proved* to me—what I have *never* believed."

"Which is?"

"Life other than this one. Omnipotent power other than the power of men. God exists." In her face he saw, and did not recognize it, his own adamantine certainty. "You won't shift me. Recollect, you never could. God Himself has done so."

This, she knew, was *not* the house of Ghaio Wood-Seller.

She had been brought here in a black boat, over a vast sheet of water she thought to be the sea. It had been night, when she entered some equally vast building.

The room was small and dark, windowless and lit by

candles even now, at noon. Yet there was a sweet smell.

Volpa sat on the stool they had given her, which was uncomfortable, but she never noticed this, being used to discomfort.

Three priests sat at the table, on chairs. Two looked at her, and one wrote down apparently their questions, what she answered. She recalled such priests from the byways and market-place. Everyone feared them, but Volpa did not. It was not courage on her part—she had never been brave. Was there a word for what she had been? It was that she knew that she, a slave, and perhaps insane—as others said of her, she had heard it—was of no importance.

Secure in abasement, she felt no specific awe, and showed none.

The priests for their part had noted as much. Yet neither was the girl rude in her manners. Her eyes were kept down, save now and then. She sat modestly. A humble and demure creature, who answered with a seeming honesty.

Any wrong-doer, blasphemer, murderer, witch—would deny the practice, until the full questioning began. Then all was brought out. But they had not been permitted to speak of torture, not even to show her the instruments. Was she then only mad? She did not seem to be. She knew her name, her position. When asked if she knew of God, she had said that she did, and crossed herself. Only in the matter of her former master was she somewhat vague. Witnesses had been found to identify her as the slave of the wood-seller on the Canal of Seven Keys. She acknowledged this. But when the priests demanded to be told what had become of him, and his house, (and three other houses besides) she affected not to know.

"The house burned, did it not?"

"Did it burn?"

"I said that it did. And you, girl, burnt it."

Her eyes were raised then, strange eyes the color of the wine of pale grapes. "When I lived there, it didn't burn."

She had told them, in response to their interrogation—apparently not frightened by their voices and louring, used to such things, glad only not to be hit—that since about five years old, she had lived in Ghaio's house as a slave. But one morning, she woke up in an alley and did not know where she had got to. Then, wandering about, she had, she acquiesced, seen some houses that were burned. She did not recognize them. Also, sometimes women gave her a crust or some clean water to drink and she came across an inn, where they gave her food, usually in the evening.

Why had she woken in the street?

She thought Ghaio had sold her. In fact, she had thought he sold her to the inn-woman with blonde hair, because subsequently Volpa had been in the kitchen there, and performed duties. But later she remembered that before this, she had been homeless in the alleys.

Did she remember too making the fire come to the hearth at the kitchen of the inn?

Volpa here seemed to hesitate.

The priests' large white faces swelled. Even the clerk glared up at her.

Volpa said, "Mistress wanted the fire. So I made it."

"How was it made?"

"How mumma showed me."

"The mother was also a witch," snapped one of the priests. Volpa heard him say this, but, it made no sense. Her mother had been a slave. "*How* did she show you? *What* did she show you?"

"In a dream. After she died."

The priests recoiled. As snakes do sometimes, before they strike.

"A ghost? A *demon*? Where did she appear to you?"

"In a beautiful place. With a fiery mountain."

"*Hell*!" exclaimed one of the men.

"*Beautiful—*" said the other— "in what way?"

The girl raised her head and her eyes again. Her eyes were very clear, as if washed in light.

"It was easy and happy there," said the girl.

The priests sank back.

Hell could not be described as easy, nor happy, even by a malefactor. Nor beautiful. But the Devil was cunning.

One of the priests rose. He moved around the table and came to stand by Volpa. He put his hand on her shoulder.

"Now, my girl you're not helping yourself. This business at the inn. Don't you know what you've done?"

She was a slave, with whom obedience was paramount. She said, without guile or omission, frankly, "I lit the fire."

Perhaps she was in that room five days and nights. She was allowed, as most were not, intervals of rest, and to eat, and to void herself.

On the sixth evening, two women came, nuns, with only one man as guard. They took Volpa away up many flights of steps.

In a chamber which had several windows, but these high up, showing only a summer sky fading, Volpa was stripped and washed by a servant, in a bath that had a fountain running into it. Then her hair was also washed. As this went on, both nuns stood by (the guard was outside) and chanted, holding their crosses.

Volpa was dressed in a shift and a plain long gown, and her hair and neck covered by a scarf and cap. This dress, that of a woman neither well-to-do nor poor, most relevantly a *free* woman, surprised Volpa. She said nothing. The non-slavish questioning nature of youth had mostly ended with her mother's silence.

The two nuns then conducted Volpa up further flights of stairs, the guard walking behind.

Until now, the inner landscape of the building had not attracted Volpa's notice, or not very much. Presently however there was a passage, whose deep red walls were patterned by golden flowers. Then came a sort of circular space, in the middle of which rose a marble pillar, painted around in plummy colors, with pictures of robed men. Beyond was a door of iron. Here stood another guard. Unlike the guard who had come with them, and was clad only as a lay brother of the Church, this one wore leggings, and a tunic embroidered by the sigil of the Primo, the Lion ridden by the Child.

The nuns did not accompany Volpa beyond the gate, nor did the lay brother. Instead, a lean, stooping man in black, and hooded, stepped through the door.

"Is this the woman?"

"It is." The nuns seemed taken aback, anxious.

"Is she named Vixen?"

"Yes, brother."

And turning on her his thin eyes—thin both in width and tint—he beckoned Volpa.

The iron door was shut behind her.

The second corridor was patterned by golden beasts—all of them rare, and mostly uncanny. It opened into a hall less large than high.

Those brought here had been sometimes overcome. Like the vast Basilica that ran below and alongside these apartments, the Golden Rooms suggested the glories of Heaven.

The walls were blood red, so thickly painted and inlaid by gold and gems that they gave the impression of a metallic tapestry. The ceiling was sheathed in silver and gold. There were seven great arched windows, set with diamond glazes of saffron, red and water-green. All this shone into a floor of polished obsidian, and so gave a sense of ultimate light floating on a lagoon—or in a sea of glass.

They crossed the floor, Volpa hesitating, her balance interrupted.

A door, painted and gilded like the walls, let them through into a rose-walled annex. A second door gave on a golden room.

On a backdrop this time of rich yellow, golden angels ranged. Candles burned like stars against a roof that was a sunburst.

Two huge painted images at once confronted the eye, a glowing golden man among a pride of amber lions; the Primo Lion of gold and brass, with a haloed infant god astride it.

Between these paranormal scenes, two men were seated upright at the table. One was another clerk, she discounted him. The other wore the habit of a Magister Major, and on his hand an emerald watched, like another eye.

Volpa, the Vixen, saw him only as part of the whole. (She was not alone in doing that.) He had the face of a disciple from the pillars of the Basilica, and although she had never entered it until now, she knew. His face had moved beyond the human. As a priest should, he poised between Man and God.

4

"Have you been taught the story of Danielo?"

Volpa shook her head. "No, signore."

"He was a Hebrew, made slave to the great and cruel King Nabucco, in the wicked city of Babylon. There Danielo, through his wisdom, his visionary skills, and his faith in God, gained such power that men were jealous of him. They entrapped him and had him thrown into a pit of lions. The mouth of the pit was then closed with a stone, and sealed by Nabucco's own royal seal. There is the picture of this event."

Volpa regarded the picture of the golden man among the lions.

Danielus said, "In the morning, when they opened up the pit, do you suppose they found Danielo still alive?"

Volpa said, "Yes, alive."

"Why do you think that? There were many lions, all kept hungry. I see you have no answer. But certainly Danielo lived. Because God had closed up the mouths of the lions as decidedly as Danielo's enemies had closed the mouth of the pit. God is capable of any miracle."

The girl sat quietly in the chair. Mostly her eyes were lowered. She raised them in response to tones of the voice, a slave trying to divine an owner's wishes. (Had she stipulated that Danielo lived simply since she believed the questioner wished for this reply?) Yes, a slave. But even Danielo had been a slave.

"I've been hearing, Volpa," the Magister Major halted, reviewing her ugly name, then went on, "that you also can perform a miracle."

She glanced up, away.

He said, "Why don't you do it now? Show me your cleverness."

She sat there, eyes down.

"The woman who saw you do this until now, hers has been an erring soul. But at once she's come to God because of what you did. Through your act, this woman has found solace and regained the hope of eternal life."

Volpa sat silent.

The scraping of the clerk's pen beside Danielus was an irritant. It answered where the girl stayed dumb.

She did not look either deranged or witless. Nor did she look like other women of her type—girls, rather, she was no more than fourteen. In another year, or less, might come the sudden blossoming one saw among the females of this City and this land. For now, she had a boyish quality, despite the curve of her breasts.

"Again," said Danielus calmly, "beside a marvel which seems to have brought only good, we must place men of the Silvian Quarter, who claim to have seen you set fire to the house of your former master, Ghaio. More, to have seen you walking garbed in flames. Can you do such a thing?"

Volpa raised her head.

She was a slave, but when she met one's eyes, it was not a slave you saw. A warrior who stood firm, ready for the blow, and half indifferent to it. Eyes as clear as crystal—where had he seen this look before? It was rare enough among men . . .

"You must, reply, Volpa."

"I don't know. The black priests asked me about my dreams, and I told my dreams."

"I have read your account of the dreams, Volpa. Journeying with your mother, and the curious animals and plants, and the mountain that burned always with red fire."

"She showed me how to make the fire. It's simple." Volpa said, he could have sworn *patiently*, "Don't others do it?"

Danielus' eyes and brows indicated, for a split second, inner laughter. "No. I've never known any make a fire in the way the woman Luchita says that you did. Nor do any walk in fire unburned, save the three friends of Danielo, that Nabucco flung into a fiery furnace. But an angel kept them from harm and led them to safety."

Something fluttered through the girl's own eyes. This was not laughter, more like a passing light.

"An angel then," she said. "Oh, I see. It was that."

"What are you saying? Take care."

She did not. She gazed at him openly, frowning a little, and said, "I was in his bedroom, now I remember it. And he wanted to hurt me. He threw me down on the mattress and pressed his face to mine. I ran away across the room. Then I forget, but I had no clothes on me. And yet someone put my shift on to my body, and led me out, through the window, and then I forget again. But I see now, it was an angel who led me out from the fire. An angel who clothed me in my shift."

Beside Danielus, the clerk gasped and surged up. Danielus spoke quickly, like the edge of a knife. "*Sit down.*"

Volpa said, "I understand it now."

"What, Volpa, do you understand?"

"It was one of the angels I saw with my mother, when we were on the hill."

The clerk had sat, frozen, turning the color of whey.

Danielus said, softly, "You say you've seen angels?"

"When I was a child. Only once."

"Describe them."

The flood of reason, the solving of her puzzle, had loosened her tongue.

"On a green sky against the first stars. They flew over. We thought they were birds—but they were men. Their arms were crossed on their chests. They had great wings. Flames burned on their heads."

Danielus heard the teeth of the clerk chattering. The room seemed very cold. Danielus said, "Volpa, do you know your Lord's Prayer?"

"No, signore."

"I will say it. You must say it after me."

She nodded. Her face was bright, almost happy, as it must have been in the easy, happy, beautiful place she had detailed from her dreams.

"*Father of all, who abides In Heaven—*"

She spoke the words carefully after him. All and every one. With no tremor she pronounced the names of God, then of the Virgin, and the Christ.

When they were finished, he had her speak the prayer over alone. Unlettered, unable to read, and a chattel, she had been used to learning by rote. She was word perfect.

"You perceive," said Danielus to the trembling clerk, "she has no fear of God's name. Write that down."

The clerk wrote. The sound of the pen irritated less.

"Now Volpa," said Danielus without inflexion, "won't you call just a little flame, to start this candle for me."

She looked unsure. But then, her eyes strayed to the frightened clerk.

Danielus saw the peculiar transformation which went over her. He gauged its secret as no other had had space—or mind—to do.

Emotion was her impetus. Ghaio had meant to rape her—lust—and rage? Luchita had been urgent and weeping—sorrow, pain. Now the clerk's religious terror.

Volpa drew off her woman's veil and cap. The hair spilled out—still damp from washing, a dark lion's mane, glorious red as a sunset. And from it, stroking, coaxing, she pulled a tiny little sun, and put it down on the candle, just as Danielus had asked.

PART THREE

MATTHEW: Why doth fire fasten upon the candle-wick?
PRUDENCE: To show that, unless grace doth kindle upon the heart, there will be no true light of life in us.

JOHN BUNYAN
The Pilgrim's Progress

1

ON THE FLOOR, carnations were strewn, as always in late summer. The feet of men crushed them, staining the mosaic with pink and red. At the great ebony table, resting on its ivory lions' paws, these thirteen men who had crushed the carnations underfoot, sat now, all in black but for one.

And above them, hung the banner of white and gold, with its lettering like a spell: *Pax tibi Vene.*

Joffri, Ducem of the City of Ve Nera, (popularly called Venus) to which the banner wished peace, leaned his elegant chin on his slender hand.

His eyes were luminous with distaste.

Once every month, the Council of the Lamb attended on him, as their ostensible lord and patron. Sometimes he was able to make an excuse, as when he had had to have a tooth drawn, or, with more difficulty, when his favorite hound, lovely white Gemma, had died, gored by a boar in the woods of the plain.

But here he was today. And he had listened as they told him, as always, the sins of Ve Nera. How many citizens they had arrested, how many more were being watched over by their Eyes and Ears. Their disgusting black boats, nicknamed for the Styx, Death River, were an eyesore to Joffri. He loved the mass, the drugging incense and beautiful singing, drowsing through the exhortations, with a box of sweets at his side, and wine. He respected God, who had given him wealth and pleasure, and a comely healthy body with which to enjoy them. But Joffri, who as a child had artlessly informed his confessor that Jesus Christ had said there were but two commandments, to love God and to love oneself, had no liking for shadows.

These twelve shadows about him now were powerful, however. More powerful than a Ducem? Possibly.

The Magisters Major themselves must dip the metaphorical knee to this Council. Men in black who had no title save for their composite Brothers of the Lamb. Hoods or half-concealed, opaque faces. Repellent faces, like old parchment, cut for lips and smeared for eyes.

"It occurs to us, Lord Ducem," one of them said now, "that as war approaches, our authority must be increased."

Who had spoken? He mislaid their names. Besides, sometimes they changed, one resigning his post (or removed) another mysteriously assuming it. But wait, Fra Danielus, that astute and intelligent man, had sent a list this very morning. Danielus seemed privy sometimes to the Council's acts, and would, if asked, assist his Prince.

Where was the list in Joffri's brain? Ah, here. Yes, lean, stooping, little-eyed—Sarco, a strange, foreign name.

"Brother Sarco, I thought the Council's authority omnipotent."

"I thank God, Lord Ducem, it is not. We too are bound by Veneran law, and by the proviso that keeps ambition, even in the best causes, chained."

"Indeed. Well, whatever you need, naturally."

They rustled in their robes, like things of black paper.

"We hear," said Sarco, "that the fleet of the enemy, when launched, may number a thousand ships."

The Ducem let out a laugh. Checked himself.

"No, brothers. I pray not. The spies of Venus—pardon my lapse—Ve Nera—reported less than four hundred vessels, and another fifty perhaps to be made sea-worthy. Our own fleet we have held at one hundred and thirty ships."

"More ships must be built," said another of them, a bulkier one, Jesolo, the Ducem thought.

"*Yes*, brother. So they shall be. But we have a small problem there. To get them, we must add to the taxes. While already the merchants and tradesmen must pay *yours*. And they're unwilling—"

Sarco interrupted the Ducem fluidly, as if without discourtesy, "Our taxes, my lord, are necessary to stay men from sin. Since they lack the will to curb their gluttony, drunkenness and vanity, such levies as the council sets restrict them perforce, for the benefit of their souls."

"Of course," said Joffri. "I didn't imply, brother, any feeling against the esteemed council. Only against myself, the poor Ducem, should I require to *add* to the burden."

Far down the table, another man spoke. He was a new one, Joffri thought, swarthy and hoarse-voiced. The name refused to surface.

"Already the City's stirred up with fear of war. When they're afraid, men become more pious, or else they give way and run amok. They indulge appalling vices. Things are done at such times that invite the brimstone of Sodomus and Gomorrah. Do we recall the years of the Death Plague?"

Joffri grimaced. He had been born too late for that horror, and was extremely glad of it. He nodded any way, to keep the unnamed misery in temper.

Sarco finished, "Such scenes must be prevented."

"Oh, quite."

"We have here a letter in which we, the Council, set out that extra scope we consider proper to us, for the season."

One or two of them rose, and came to Joffri, with the thick scroll, bound by a spotless tassel, and stuck with vermilion wax. The wax was imprinted by the seal of the Lamb.

It was a nice little lamb, as it kneeled there. A gentle lamb.

God knew what they wanted now. All a-bed at the Venusium bell . . . a new tax on any traffic along any canal—worth a fortune, that one . . . or on the carnal act, perhaps, within marriage

They could order a rich merchant or even a lesser prince to ride publicly in sackcloth, in a Styx boat, to the Primo, beating himself the while, for some heinous (exaggerated?) crime of blasphemy or sloth. Now and then, in the last two years, they had done so.

"I am grateful, brothers, for your care for my City."

Joffri did not think himself a coward. Only wise.

When Sarco said, mildly, "Your City, Lord Ducem, but also God's," Joffri bowed.

He was so delighted to bid them farewell. But despite the carnations he had had scattered, their odor stayed with him all up the stairs. A sour stale smell of bodies and minds bound always tight in darkness. For a moment, he knew he feared the Council more than Jurneia and her thousand ships.

* * *

After reading a copy of the Council's letter to the Ducem, which Brother Sarco had given him, Fra Danielus went down to the castra, to the practice court, to watch Cristiano exercise.

In the summer heat, all the Bellatae were stripped to the waist. Wrestling, they flung each other over, laughed or complained, and ran back together. They were like battling stags. And seeing the Magister, they vaunted themselves, excelled—or made mistakes.

Cristiano did not do this. He seemed to take no notice. He had tanned from the sun, and standing at rest, was like a statue of the Greeks or Romans, made in planed golden wood. But the hair was silver.

Then he lightly raised up the heavy sword, swinging it in flashing, veering thrusts. He had disarmed his third opponent in the time that might elapse between two strokes of a bell.

Before he walked to the Magister, Cristiano slung on the practice tunic. His was gray and full of holes. No pride? One could not pledge that. But he was young, and God Himself had made him strong.

"Tell me," said Danielus, as they moved through into the castra cloister, which was empty, "have you any curiosity concerning the little slave?"

Cristiano looked at him. He said, "You mean the girl who can call fire."

"Yes, just that little slave."

"Should I be curious?"

"You found her."

"She was there to be found."

"Do you still doubt she can do what she does?"

"No, Magister. Not since you told me that she could."

"I see. Should I then commend you for your faith in me, or chide you for accepting such a story secondhand."

"Either," said Cristiano. He leaned on a pillar of the walk, as Danielus sat down in the shade. In the middle of the sunlit square of grass, a fountain played into a bronze cistern. Insects buzzed. There was the honeyed scent of flowers, but summer had passed its peak.

"And your sister," said Danielus, "how does she manage among the nuns?"

"I haven't seen her for some while. She seemed content."

"Not joyous, then."

"Not joyous. The life's hard for her."

"She will have guessed that."

"Yes. She anticipates nothing now, from this world.'

"I'm sorry to hear it, Knight. The world is to be valued, if only as the preface to a greater world."

"On her knees until they bleed, scrubbing floors, awake all night praying, fasting or fed on bread and water?"

"You're angry. Why? You also have done all that. You would do it now, and count it nothing."

"She's a woman," said Cristiano.

Danielus said, "Women are so weak, evidently. She has borne several children. That was probably far worse than scrubbing a floor. Don't you think perhaps God chose the female race for childbirth, because He thought them more valiant? The more able to endure?"

Cristiano said, "It was a punishment, I believed, for talk with a snake in a Tree."

"That too, of course," said Danielus. "But both were punished, both Adamus and Eva. If punishment is a corrective, and her punishment being the worse, did God suppose the woman capable of learning more from it?"

Cristiano laughed out loud.

"I can't debate with you, Magister."

Danielus gazed across the brown grass at the fountain. "I must go and visit my own devout sister on Eel Island. I've neglected her. I leave this evening and will be gone some days."

"Is Veronichi well?"

"Well, but melancholy, and demanding, as ever. I do my best to cheer her. While I'm gone, read this thing the Council of the Lamb has gifted the Ducem. Others know and are reading it. Also, I should like you to visit in turn the slave we spoke of."

"*Volpa*? Why that?"

"Anger again. Why anger now, Cristiano?"

Cristiano bowed his head, a false humility striving to be real.

"Pardon me, Magister. Whatever you wish."

"She's kept secretly, as you know. You know to keep silence. But you'll find her changed—changing. Her name has changed, too. It was a graceless epithet she had. And foxes are enlisted by the Devil, it seems. Now she's known as Beatifica. A name to exorcise all doubt."

"And what would you have me do there?"

"See that they treat her as I instructed. Talk to her, perhaps."

"Of what?" Cristiano shook his head. "Again, your pardon."

"Of God," said Danielus. "Talk to her of God, what else?"

Like the palace of the Ducemae, the house of Veronichi stood alone, on an island. Admittedly one that would have fitted fifty times over in Joffri's gardens.

The Isle of Eels was sufficiently small that, among Ve Nera's muster of seven islands, it did not count.

Nevertheless, the place was pretty in a drooping,

mossy way. The old water-steps had sunk below the surface only last year. One wall, which ran down into the Laguna Aquila, was also going, and in need of repair.

Fra Danielus had given the house to his half-sister a decade before, after he had brought her from obscurity in the slums beside the wall of the Jewish ghetto. Though she undoubtedly possessed their blood, she was a Christian.

Those that saw her, and this not often, (she was reclusive) had sometimes remarked that she might have caught a husband, if she had mended herself and looked for one. But Veronichi served solely one God. Her rumored charitable works and drab clothing were her only fame.

As the boat was rowed across the lagoon, the sun westered behind the buildings on the shore, seeming to set them all adrift.

A City built on water, if not sand. Parable enough in that, for Venus was mighty and rich, and had lasted. Even the threat of war proved her superior station. Why else fight with her for spice or silk?

In the apricot light the small island drew near. Over the walls of Veronichi's neglected orchard, savage pomegranate trees dropped tangled baskets of branches and budding red pods into the water. Eels still sometimes swam there in autumn, to gorge. When netted, they carried the taste of the seeds. Death's taste, surely, since the pomegranate was the fruit of the classical Underworld?

The sunfall was—voluptuous. Overdone. The words of the Greeks came to Danielus, who had read very much and widely. *Nothing to excess.* Yet God employed brushstrokes of glory. In the hands of greatness, was excess quite different?

He must read in the library he kept here. This was

part of his reason for the visit, but he might not tell Veronichi so. It would depend on her mood.

She met him, coming down to the landing-place in a dull gown, her hair scraped back under a linen cap. Her paintless face was the shape of a pip, narrowing at the forehead and at the chin. Her eyes were black as his own. She hid them under lowered lids, as she kissed his ring.

A game?

"I didn't think you would come," she said.

"But I told you I would."

As they climbed the steps, the boat was rowing away, melting into the extravagant sumptuousness of the light. The Council would like to tax such sunsets, no doubt.

2

Because the day was hot, she had come to sit in the yard.

There was shade here from one tall tree. The walls were so high she could not see the canal which ran beyond them, an oily dark green. But hearing it lap on the wall sides, and catching wafts of its summer smell, she remembered it. She had been brought along the canal, and then in at this yard.

The canal was named for the Virgin, Blessed Maria. The building where now she lived she had heard called only the cappella.

Life was not as it had been.

Volpa was not certain if this were a chastisement or a reward. Besides, she expected almost hourly that it would alter.

She rose, as she always had, at first light. A woman, a nun, would come into the cell where Volpa slept, bringing her a cup of water. At first there had been trouble, since Volpa did not sleep on the hard little plank meant for a bed. She preferred the stone floor, wrapped in the blanket. As a slave, she had never known a bed, although the blanket was a luxury prized, if mistrusted. Seeing the nun was displeased by Volpa's preference, Volpa had initially tried to wake earlier and locate herself upon the plank. Often she failed. Then, the nun ceased to be disturbed. Volpa did not ponder on this. She was simply thankful to be left alone. In fact, as with everything to do with Volpa, a report of it had gone to the Magister Major, Fra Danielus. He then advised the nuns of the Little Cappella, saying they should allow the girl to sleep on the floor. ("While we attempt to smite out of ourselves the body's whim for softness and pampering, she must only be envied, in this inclination for hardship.")

After Volpa had dressed in the plain, good clothes now supplied her, she was taken to the Auroria, the Dawn Mass. Here, as the group of nuns intoned and chanted, the prayers were whispered to Volpa, who, accordingly, learned them all. These prayers were in Latin. However, she got them, and the whole service, by heart, and could soon speak everything perfectly on the cues, and with a pure pronunciation worthy of the Primo. (The diction of the Little Cappella was highly rated.) She did not, of course, grasp one word. Or perhaps, just one, here and there.

She knew the word for God, for example. Although not in all its Latin forms.

After the mass, Volpa broke her fast. In the beginning she was offered many things to eat, at which she stared, and from some of which she turned, revolted.

The nuns' first annoyance was once again translated into reluctant approval.

Volpa's breakfast came to be a piece of dark bread,

dipped in watered wine. She took no midday meal, but in the evening might eat a dish of unsalted rice or porridge, or a vegetable gruel.

As a slave, she had lived through necessity as a devout priest of the Church was admonished to. Lack had trained her to accept only lack. To be comfortable only with a hard floor, a meager diet, a blanket and a cup of wine—luxuries valued, if barely tolerable.

To the splendors of the cappella Volpa was also nearly impervious, as she had been indeed to the marvel of the Golden Rooms. *They* had disorientated her, the cascade of gold and crimson, the reflecting floors. Until she put them aside, one more element that she did not understand and so must not waste time on.

Here, shown the carvings, the glass, she looked, and looked away. She was able to recognize the silver cross. Seeing it, she crossed *herself*, as her mother had taught her.

They did not conduct her to any further daily service until that of the sunset Venusium. Again, she quickly learned everything and faultlessly joined in.

Her mind did not wander at these moments. The exquisite inflexions that now came from her own mouth, fascinated the girl as much as they did the ears of those who heard her. Sometimes even she spoke the lessons over, when alone, walking the corridors of the cappella for exercise.

The nuns, finding that, promptly taught her other prayers and holy songs.

Speaking on and on, in company or alone, Volpa's voice fined itself and gained a silvery quality. Only in normal speech did she still sound, sometimes, rough and guttural.

She went to her bed early, after supper.

The nuns had noted she was not quite a child.

She had breasts, and every month she lost blood. (Unremarked, she had reached fifteen.)

She was bored, too. The stitching the nuns gave her she did poorly. Also, finding she was not chided, often she left it undone. She could not read. She sat singing to herself the chants of the cappella, or walked slowly about the tree in the yard. At night, sometimes, she stole out, thinking to circle the tree, but the nuns were always about, performing penitential chores, going to and from their devotions, or watching by the altar, from where the yard was visible. Volpa knew instinctively that her dance must not be seen. Less than the interrogatory priests, she recalled the old man slave, and how he had seemed afraid of it, and yet afraid without *fear*. What had become of him?

Had she burned Master's house?

It seemed to her it had only burned. Then the angel led her to safety.

She would like to see the angel again. She could not recollect how it had looked. But presumably it had been like the flying beings she had seen with her mother, on the hill, the great wings spread behind it, and the feather of brilliance on its head.

Seeing the image of the Apostles in the cappella window, receiving the power of God each in a flame that stood up on the brow, she noted a similarity.

She was called now by another name. She liked its sound. She did not really think of it as her own.

Crickets were cheeping in the warm stones of the wall.

A stink of fish rose up from the canal.

The Solus was over—she often watched from the doorway, learning the words of this mass as well. (As, at night, unable to dance to the tree, she learned the Luna and Prima Vigile.) She repeated the orisons clearly now, not knowing what any of them said.

"Gaze upon us, O God, and shed the light, more wonderful than any sun, so that we may see our way."

Cristiano stopped still.

The slave stood in the long shadow of the tree, through which a blade of sunlight pierced to touch her shoulders and the white cap that covered her hair. She was singing sweetly, and in perfect Latin, the words of the Midday Mass.

She had the voice—of nothing human. Not even the genderless beauty of the unbroken soprano of a boy. Cristiano, until now, had never even heard her speak.

Something moved against his skin. It was like a brushing hand made from the air.

He marked himself with the cross.

Then his mind cleared, and the sun shifted. She was a thin young girl with nothing exceptional about her, who turned and blinked at him, then lowered her eyes. And when he said her name—the inappropriate new name the Magister had given her—she mumbled, "Yes, signore," ignorantly and without any grace.

Cristiano wrote to the Magister, who was detained on Eel Island. (It seemed his sister was sick.)

The letter, also in Latin, was formal. Nevertheless honest:

> "The Little Church, as you would hope, as it is your property, and being its chief confessor, is healthy. No summer sickness has manifested. The sisters are hale.
>
> "For the slave, this girl, Beatifica, they care for her as you commanded them. They say she is modest, and

shows signs of devotion to the Christ. They do not fault her in anything, especially since you told them to let her go on in her original manner, sleeping on the ground, and so on.

"They say she steals to the door of the Sanctuary to listen to the mass, even sometimes to the Prima Vigile, two hours after midnight. They have noticed that, where the glamours of the carving and windows leave her untouched, she responds to a sight of the cross, and the window which shows the Apostles. She says prayers over to herself constantly, distinctly, and with apparent delight.

"I too have heard and seen this.

"Some of them think she will wish, after some time, to become one of their number. You have not told them of her single talent. And they have had, demonstrably, no sight of it."

Standing with her, under the tree, he felt an awkwardness. He had expected nothing else.

His lowly beginnings he had left far behind. He could read and write, he could do battle, he was a Soldier of God. She was a slave, illiterate and, at her depth, unmotivated, and amoral as any beast. She was a woman.

Long ago (it seemed to him) he had lashed and starved any fleshly craving for women from him.

And a woman, stripped of her potential to satisfy male hunger, or produce therefrom children, was nothing. God's afterthought, made from a rib. Perhaps stronger, as Danielus had mooted, merely in order to bear her lesser life. For what man could bear to live as a woman must? And what woman could tolerate her life, if she had possessed the capacity of a male brain?

Even so, what he had seen—felt—in those brief instants before the sun vanished in a cloud, before she left off her prayer—disconcerted Cristiano.

There had been holy women, transformed by the mysteries of God, and, above them all, the Virgin. Woman was, by the miracle of the Divine, sometimes able to ascend from her body and her lot, and from all things.

"Do they call you Beatifica?"

"Yes, signore."

"Don't call me that. I am one of the Bellatae Christi. God's Soldier."

She hung there in front of him, eyes down. Said nothing.

He said, "They tell me you're a good girl, here."

Nothing.

He said, impatient, "What do you say for yourself?"

She mumbled again.

"*What*? Try to speak out as you say your prayers."

"I mean not to offend," she said, "signore."

"Didn't I say, don't call me that. Say, Soldier of God."

She looked up and straight into his face.

Her eyes grew larger, when she stared at you, or so it seemed. *Yellow* eyes. He had never seen that color save in an animal, a dog or cat. (Woman, the beast.)

"Soldier of God," she said, and then, in clear Latin, "Bellator Christi."

She had been a slave, and the Magister's nuns here had told him, too, her back was scored with previous whippings, one of five and a half ragged scars, perhaps many years old. The stripes would never go.

Inside her white skin he seemed to glimpse now, clusters of bruises, preserved like fossils in marble.

"Sit down, Beatifica." She sat on the bench by the tree.

Sufficient men had been unkind to her. At a loss,

thinking dimly of Danielus' words, Cristiano said to her, "Say one of the prayers for me."

"Which one shall I say?"

Naively, although he did not guess himself naive, he said, "One which you like the best."

He had forgotten nobody might have bothered to explain the meaning of the prayers and that she must have learnt them (like the title Bellator) from phonetics alone.

And she any way obeyed, always obedient. She chose a prayer whose *sounds* she liked. And because it had one word she knew.

"I will raise my eyes to the mountains, where God is . . ."

Cristiano was to write: 'She selected the prayer of a king, Magister. She spoke it eloquently. And then there was a change in her, I must admit it to you. Her face became transparent with a kind of brightness. Perhaps only a trick of the sun.'

As he wrote these words in the letter, Cristiano felt suddenly oppressed by the heat of the summer evening.

Moving to the window of his cell in the castra, he saw sailed fisher-boats like dragonflies on the surface of the lagoon. But imposed upon them, the image of the Virgin in the Primo window, her damson mantle wrapped about her.

A slave was not to be compared with Maria. Tonight he kept the Vigil. Before then, he must empty his mind and spirit of this clutter. It came to him again to wonder, as he sealed the letter, why Danielus had sent him to the girl.

During the night, as Volpa-Beatifica slept on the floor, two nuns entered the cell.

"Get up, Beatifica. Put on your clothes."

When they took her through the Little Church and out into the yard, whose gate stood wide, Volpa-Beatifica was uneasy.

Torches burned, and on the canal, black with night, a covered boat rocked up and down.

Another woman would have protested, pleading to know where she was to be taken.

But Volpa was a slave. The small chances of free will she had had in the cappella were swiftly mislaid. And she had expected change.

She got into the boat without speaking, trembling, and sat where they showed her.

There were also some casks in the boat, smelling of wine.

She was rowed away into the night of Ve Nera, between the high black walls. In some, gratings and narrow slots evicted loud light. Stars littered the sky, forgotten candles.

Some of the nuns stood crying at the water's edge. They had been told Beatifica was to go to a religious house on the plain. They feared their care was not deemed adequate.

3

All the remaining year, past Christ-Birth Mass, Beatifica was at a farm on the Veneran Plain. How many properties, aside from the Island of Eels, and these one or two farms, belonged to Fra Danielus, was unknown. But a Magister, particularly a Magister Major of the Primo Suvio, must have revenues, and also places he might loan or give away or sell, as the Church's needs dictated. Even recently, there had been a sale of another house, in order to supply the coffers of the Church, which in turn leant gold to the City's ship-building.

Beatifica knew nothing of this, of course.

She was aware mostly that from the farm buildings she could see, far off, the mountains. Either she recalled them from memory, or from her mother's told memories. They did not, certainly, seem familiar any more. They were gaunt and gray, and soon helmed with snow. Neither in the brazen sunrise of fall, nor the red setting sun of winter, did they turn to scarlet.

At the farm, she saw slaves. This was a stumbling block, but having stumbled on it, she righted herself and beheld the difference. They demonstrated by their activities, their segregation—unlike her own—that she, now, was a slave no longer.

Like the prayers she still regularly said and sang, this too she had needed to, and did, learn, by rote. Yet, she remained a slave.

She slept in a bare, clean room. When she ignored the bed, which had frame, mattress, and curtains, they removed it. But they gave her for the winter chill three blankets, and a cushion for her head. These she took to. Also there was a brazier for wood. It was kept alight for her, as if she could not have lit it herself. She could not—not, as it were, *cold*. She must have impetus. She would need to be freezing to draw from herself the power—and, still slavish, might only have endured the freeze, as she had always done.

She had candles, too. And a cross the nuns had sent with her, which she liked to hold. It was made of tarnished silver, which with her caresses, grew brighter.

After only a day or so, the woman who came in the morning, (like the nun) a servant not a slave, brought Beatifica new garments.

The girl looked at them, and the woman said, "The Magister Major says you're to wear these, now. They'll be warmer, and handier for your work." A sentence prepared by others; the woman said it with an expressionless face.

Presently she took Beatifica, as usual, down to the farm chapel. It was a vacant stable, perhaps a theosophic pun of sorts. The altar had been sanctified, but stood among wisps of straw. Here were some men of the farm, couth and combed always for the Dawn Mass, and two women, both elderly.

None of them looked at Beatifica any more than they had ever done. Her clothes may have escaped them. Or not.

She ate alone by day. At night, she ate with a man and woman of the house. They corrected her actions at the table as diligent parents might have done. The manners taught her, however, were higher than their own. She did not question this. Could anything surprise her? Little. In her limited world, most had been a surprise, and mostly a surprise that hurt or harmed. Amazements without pain she did not resist. But then, she had not resisted pain either, until it seemed to threaten life itself. (Eventually she might have ceased to resist even that.)

She liked the honey and milk she was given, and the raisins and olives. These became an indulgence.

Beatifica learned the use of spoon and knife and linen napkin, the trencher of bread that was not to be eaten but might be thrown to a dog, should she wish.

Probably she did have a memory of farm dogs, for some reason friendly ones. Where the man and the woman had thought they would need to coax her not to be timid of the huge shaggy animals, they found her careless. Now and then she petted one. Never for long. She was not affectionate, or not in a physical way. And what was lost to her she did not search or lament for.

(She had learned so many tenets of the priesthood in her slavery.) Unless, nothing had ever been worth lament or search.

After the dogs, maybe her tutors wondered if she would be frightened, even so, of the horses

Ve Nera's means of travel, as a rule, was by her canals and other waters. It was true, the Ducem maintained some horses on his island, for riding in the gardens. And more on his estates on the plain, Forchenza principally, for purposes of hunting. Even the Primo kept horses on the plain, for its knights. And sometimes too it was possible in Ve Nera to behold horses, transported on some barge, or gathered, fabulously decked, for a ceremony in the Primo's great square beneath the Angel Tower. But Beatifica had never seen anything like that. To her, a horse was surprising. Therefore, not unusual at all.

Not until two men set her on a horse's back, did Beatifica become alarmed.

For a month before, she had been exercised, given things to do with her body in the new clothes—which were those of a boy, leggings, tunic, cloak. Her body, already firm and supple and spare, had loosened and knit further.

So she kept a grip on the horse. But her mind plunged off. Another would have screamed for help.

The horse was a steady creature of the farm, used to plough and plod. They led him round, and Beatifica sat on his top, her long hair tied off her face and falling down her back in a tail much like his own. Seeing her going like this about the fields, those who did not know—most—took her for a boy.

She kept in her seat; when they took her off her legs gave way, both from the unused posture and from terror.

The woman said to the man, "Is he insane, this Fra

Danielus? What does he want from her? To ride like a man—"

"Shut your lips, woman, till you have some sense. How do I know? He's our landlord. We do what he says. Besides, for God's sake, have you forgotten what he did for *us*? Would we be living still, if not for him? So, she's in our charge. If he gave you a priestly robe to sew, you'd use a fine stitch."

"It's a woman we're stitching."

"Shut your lips if you want to stay wife of mine."

Nothing made much sense to Beatifica. No warnings such as were habitual to her tutors' kind of servitude, a *servant's* slavishness, for gain; from thankfulness. Beatifica obeyed, as always she obeyed. What sustained life she did.

So, next day she was put up on the horse again, without cries or struggle. She did her best. By example, doing what she was shown, feeling out the country of the horse's back, Beatifica once more learned.

(She was fifteen. Her mind, unfilled by knowledge, gaping like a hungry mouth of sharp white teeth.)

The lessons she devoured. Unconsciously mostly. From fright she moved to acceptance to an almost—interest, and so to aptitude. She rode. *Bold* as a man now. And when they brought the other horse, sword-slim and brown as malt, *immodest* as a man, she mounted him. She trotted with the horse and her escort through the bare fields, through the woods lashed by the tusks of winter boars. The air was spiked with coming snow. She had never known such freedom. Freedom which had come through obedient enslavement. The goal of the priest.

Nine days before Christ' Mass, the Magister Major Fra Danielus went to inspect one of his farms. Three of the

Bellatae rode with him, Aretzo, Jian and Cristiano.

Snow was down in the foothills, and dusted on the plain. The high woods wove nets of snow-blossom. Wolves were seen, a black wind that passed across the distance. A boar appeared near the village of Mariamba, ten miles from the City, and menaced the cavalcade. The young knights killed this boar. It would make enjoyable eating, save for the Magister. But it was not a time for traveling.

Fra Danielus rode in the customary litter jolted between two geldings. The Bellatae rode their horses. Villagers pointed out the white-haired knight, on his silk-white horse.

Snow fell as they approached the estate.

The faces of the young men were flushed with triumphant exertion and cold. (Cristiano had needed this color.) Danielus regarded them from the swaying litter. He himself seemed fatigued. He had been called to his sister's island once more. It was patent she wore him out, this Veronichi, chronically unhealthy, an obscure woman with no proper existence.

The boar gurned on its pole, gutted and dropping thick clods of black blood.

When they reached the farm, everyone came out. The women were kissing the Fra's hand, his ring, the men bowing low. Slaves ran to and fro. Chickens scattered, and on a post the cock crowed, not knowing six of his wives were due for the pot.

"Is there news of the Infidel War, Magister?"

Jian said, interposing himself between Danielus and his retainer, "No, not yet."

Danielus spoke gently, "I'll send you word, as always. But you will need to butcher and salt down this winter."

"Yes, Magister."

"Don't look so vexed. The number of their ships is exaggerated."

"Over one thousand, so we heard—"

"Less than five hundred. And Ve Nera's fleet will match them, by the spring."

"Thank God, bless the Virgin."

Aretzo said, on the outer stair, "You didn't forewarn us, Magister, to lie."

"Yes, but do lie. A little. For now."

"It's no sin," said Jian, "not a lie of this sort. To save them distress."

Aretzo frowned.

Jian amended, "Truth has varied somewhat in the matter besides. Depending on which spy has sent which report from Candisi. And whether he lived beyond its dispatch."

"Hell waits for Jurneia," said Aretzo. His cheeks burned, as when he put a javelin into the boar.

Cristiano, silent. He had been so most of the journey.

The stair led to the Magister's apartment, when visiting. The farm folk had seen to the bed and hung thick curtains. A fire burned, and there was a dish of winter apples, wizened but sweet. The Magister's three knights would sleep in the lesser room, the four outriders and two Primo guard in the barn beside the kitchen.

As servants sorted the baggage, there came the shriek of chickens chased with knives across the slippy courtyard.

"What's the matter, Cristiano? Sorry for the fowl?"

Jian and Aretzo, worldly enough to like the jaunt, with its hunting and novelty. Cristiano smiled mirthlessly.

"The chapel here's a *stable*," said Aretzo.

Jian said, "So was the birthplace of our Lord. What

bag is that? Hey, fellow, where are you lugging it?"

The servant replied, "It's to go up for mistress."

"Oh, take it then."

The woman came in with compressed lips. She did not look at Beatifica-Volpa, but the girl, as so often she did, kept her own eyes down.

"The Magister Major has sent this. You're to wear it." An order. A slave obeyed orders, always. "He'll conduct the service of the Venusium at sunfall. I'll come for you then. Here's the slave to help you dress."

This (second) slave came into the room. A true slave, Beatifica's reminder by example that *she* was no longer of that kind.

Over the chair which stood by the window, the clothing had been laid. It caught the glimmer of the brazier.

Beatifica-Volpa stared one long moment at it.

Then, with the other slave's assistance, she took off her garments of a wealthy farmer's son, and put on the new ones Fra Danielus had sent.

As sometimes happened, in the minutes before it set, the sun appeared out of the clotted gray-white sky, a maroon ball, lightless enough to be gazed at. The sky was torn all around it, bleeding. Then the sun became a semicircle, and then a slice, and was gone. Color left the sky, and in the courtyard a boy was banging on a copper vessel, to summon the household to prayer.

Advancing to the left of the stable-chapel, the women had entered in a group. There were five or six of them, the farmer's wife, his elderly widowed mother and widowed aunt, to the front. At the other side, the right, the farmer and his sons were closest to the altar.

For the Magister Major, Eastern incense-gum had been brought from its chest, and lit. The air was fragrant.

Fra Danielus stood by the altar, and by the altar to the right, the three Soldiers of God. These four, facing the doorway, therefore saw her come in, as always, alone.

Of the Bellatae, only Cristiano, who had seen her before, did not take her at first for some unexpected young man of noble birth.

He noted the eyes of Jian slant inquiringly. Aretzo looked haughty, flaunting his own priestly rank.

In Cristiano a shock-wave broke. He did not know what he felt—horror? Disbelief?

But then Fra Danielus began to speak the words of the Sunset Mass.

Were the peasant family, the Magister's retainers, aware of what lived among them? This—*changeling*.

Cristiano forced his mind away from the girl, standing now at the back, neither on the womens' side nor the mens', but in the middle, before the door. Her eyes seemed fixed on Danielus, or on the altar, perhaps. When the responses were uttered, and in the chant, he detected her voice easily, silver-pure, the Latin exact.

And when they kneeled before the uplifted chalice, so did she. But on one knee only, as did the knights. Dressed as she now was, it gave her no difficulty.

Cristiano sought for God blindly, and through his great self-discipline, shut out reaction to the girl. But even so, could not quite grasp the majestic otherness of the Venusium, its true meaning and heart.

Religion was his food and drink, desire, rest, his life's

love. He rose, cheated. Just as, six times now, from the Vigil he had had to rise. For six times the essence of God had failed him—that is, been failed by *him*. Each month, through the summer and the autumn, the arrival of winter, kneeling before the Virgin window, lifted high above his pain and able to withstand it—but achieving nothing. The sheer white radiance, the overwhelmment of flawless bliss—they had not been his. And though in the past, occasionally, he had not achieved this state, always then it had been his the next time. Now no fast or punishment brought him back to it. Before the last Vigil, Cristiano had stretched out three hours on the floor, beseeching God, requesting to be told what fault of his had barred him from the pinnacle. Frustrated, unanswered.

Was his fault so grave that God refused to reveal it?

Frustrated . . . that now always. Reining himself like the horse he had ridden today, fighting over and over a restless bitter rage, like the boar they had slain.

He must not become a petulant child, fractious because his toy had been taken from him for his own good, seeing that he valued it too highly.

Was this the message God had sent him, then?

Even holy delight might become the sin of greed?

He had believed, while he stayed worthy—Ah, then, he must no longer be worthy.

In what way? What had he done? Reveal, Oh Lord, my *fault*—

Cristiano held himself finally in bands of steel. Self-governance was all that had been left to him.

It was by now dark outside, and a torch burned on a pole in the yard, which was perfumed, after the incense, with chickens and sheep.

But indoors the candles were lit, and they went into the farmer's parlor to eat.

The table was finely dressed tonight with a white cloth, and water for the hands. The woman of the house and her servants brought the dinner. Only the elderly women sat down with the farmer and his five sons. Danielus was placed at the table's head, and his three Bellatae on either side. One place still stood empty.

Then, in came the girl, the abomination of Woman dressed as a man.

Cristiano stared at her. Her lids were not lowered, but she looked only at Danielus.

The perverse garments were white. Whiter than the common white of ordinary things, the old tablecloth, the womens' aprons. Church white. Pristine as the new snow. And the cloak, where it was looped back, was thinly edged by gold. While on her hips the low male belt was hatched with gold. She wore a golden crucifix, not large, but set with one smoldering red gem, to represent the Blood of Christ.

In the candlelight, as she came nearer and nearer, her unbound flood of hair was like the torch from the yard, a water of fire. Cristiano saw her eyes were not after all yellow, but, like her cross, made of gold.

"Beatifica," said Fra Danielus. He spoke casually. No one at the table, or among the women, stirred. As if nothing much went on.

Yet Cristiano felt Jian beside him abruptly alter. And Aretzo across from them, (by whom, it seemed, the changeling would sit down) craned his neck. His eyes started like those of a fish.

"Speak the Grace for us, Beatifica," Danielus gently said.

She brought her hands together, folded one on the other. Her eyes now lifted above them all. Motionless, she moved beyond them. Cristiano saw it, as he had seen it that other time, in the court of the nunnery.

She spoke the Grace.

The table bowed its collective head, even the Bellatae. Cristiano *felt* his fellow Soldiers *listening*.

Her voice—was not like a woman's, not like a boy's—certainly nothing like a man's. It was like an *instrument*. The sounding-board of the sacred words.

(Beside Cristiano, Jian shuddered.)

At the proper juncture, they marked themselves with the cross.

The Grace was finished, and Beatifica took the stool left vacant for her.

It was Danielus who glanced about at them. Who said, "The Maiden Beatifica has learned her orisons, as you see. And here, she learns other accomplishments."

Aretzo said, "To sew, Magister? To make broth?"

Danielus said, lightly, "As you learned to plough, Aretzo, and to break hods."

Aretzo flushed. "I was called to serve God."

"And thus," said Danielus.

The women were placing the central dishes and a rich savory aroma went up. The kitchen had labored to present its best, a pottage of chicken in a great pan, flavored with pears and onions, ginger and pepper; slabs of the boar, roasted, stuck with cloves and powdered by cinnamon and grain-of-paradise. The Soldiers of God, today allowed their fill, reached out hungrily, angrily. Only Cristiano was abstemious, selecting solely from the chicken. The Magister, as usual, touched neither meat, contenting himself with pancakes made with eggs and white wine.

The girl—the *Maiden Beatifica*—was served a separate bowl, some vegetable thing, while from a little wooden dish she took a sliver of boiled white meat.

Cristiano's belly had turned in any case.

The family ate heartily. They seemed to have no troubles. The sons were even becoming sometimes rather loud over their ale, despite the Magister.

The woman though, the Housewife, stood with her servants, her lips drawn in tight. Only when Danielus complimented and thanked her did she wrench them in a smile.

The slave—the girl—the *Maiden*—she ate nicely, like a princeling. But very little. By her trencher the wine cup filled just once, waited mostly unused. She was frugal even with the cup of water.

Danielus spoke to the farmer about the land, crops, weather, the horses.

Later some cheese was brought and winter fruits, and a frumenty with rose-sugar.

They rinsed their hands and wiped them on napkins.

"The Maiden shall say the prayer to close our meal." Danielus looked at Aretzo, at Jian. Not at Cristiano. "The Warriors of God shall make choice of which."

Aretzo spoke at once. "Let her say one of the King's Psalms."

And Jian said, "The forty-second Psalm."

"That has a few verses," said Danielus. He turned to the girl. "Speak this, then, Beatifica—" and he said the first words of the Psalm in Latin.

Immediately she took it up from him, and spoke it all, in the beautiful argent voice.

"Deep thunders to deep, the waves go over me and I drown. Yet the Lord will send to me His kindness by day, and by night His love shall be my song . . ."

There was no noise at the table now, as that silvery instrument played.

Cristiano recalled the silence in the street when Berbo accused her. He thought of her in the convent, speaking alone in the sunlight.

A pressure had risen in him. A child might have identified it as the upsurge of tears. But the man sat transfixed, locked in steel, at war with himself.

The Psalm ended.

Jian sighed. Aretzo, always the redder, was pale.

And the woman among her servants held her hand to her lips as if to hide their relaxation.

Danielus rose to his feet.

The roomful of people gazed up at him, the faces lit from low candlelight.

He called the farmer by name. "Marco, you have been a faithful servant to me. And your wife, a paragon. Now you shall see something to wonder at. Jian, I ask that you will get up and shut the door. And you, Marco, put out all these lights except for that one there, on the chest."

Oddly, from beyond, in the kitchen, at that moment came a noise of the Primo guard, and their servants, some joke told, and laughter.

It was unseemly, and the two old widows clucked their teeth. Marco half turned, scowling.

"No matter," said Danielus. "Always remember, my friends, God gave us the earth also to be happy in. Doesn't the Psalm say this, *benevolentia et carmena*."

As Marco and his eldest son dowsed the candles on the table, a luminous shadow gathered them all in. There in the heart of it, only the white clothes and the hair of the girl went blazing on—and Cristiano's blondness, too, had he known it.

He spoke quickly, quietly, to Danielus.

"Magister—if you want her to make her conjuring here—"

"It isn't conjuring, Knight. But I value your caution. And—your agitation."

Cristiano's guts churned. There was a swirling in his head like drunkenness, but he had drunk only water. The pressure was rising through the core of him, pushing, scorching, agonized as an arrow working in a wound—insistent and dreadful as nausea.

But he was accustomed to conceal and to restrain his flesh. He had ridden partly unconscious through battles and cut men down like a machine. He had kept the Vigil, eight hours on his knees, even when God avoided him.

Yes, the sea had drowned him. Yes, he cried for the kindness and the song by night—

It was very dark.

Miles off through the stillness now, not the laughter of men, but a wolf's howling arced over the plain. Danielus nodded to his made creature, the Maiden.

"Look, Beatifica."

Cristiano in his locked—fast turmoil, sensed more than saw the crystals of her eyes. Chrysoprase from the breastplate of a High Priest—

It was as if she found him in the dark as he had found her in the obscure alley, alerted by some sound. Did she hear then, in stillness, the wolf howl of his emotion?

Away and away, the other wolf cried slenderly again over the snow. And then no more.

She saw his heart. She, this absurdity, this abomination—this joke cruder than any told in Marco's kitchen.

He felt her eyes upon his heart, cool, like pearls, sliding through his flesh.

And then—Oh God who is in Heaven—then—the light of the fire—

Aretzo cried out. Marco too and one of the sons.

The woman by the door, the paragon, let go a wild scream.

(Did the wolf, searching the plain, in turn hear these animal noises?)

One saw the Christ shown in this way, the halo, the sun, behind his head. And she too, Virgin Maria.

Beatifica—

Her hair had become a score of torches, and behind them shone the summer sun.

And with her thin white hands, she reached upward, and clasped this sun, and it came away in her hands, a nest of flame, sparkling and crackling, *alive*.

She held the fire high up in the dark, and gave them light to see. Then softly let it down, and all the candles caught at once, gushed up with a hiss, and spume of smoke. And on the table cloth, some little rivulets of fire ran off—and faded, harming nothing.

Marco's wife sank to her knees. Men and women knelt.

But Cristiano came to his feet, and as he did so the pressure reached and burst in his brain and all the whiteness of eternity, which for six bitter times he had not been able to attain, entered in. For one second such joy, such ecstasy was there, it shattered him. He died. But only in a second. Only *for* a second. And then he simply stood in the earthly room, and there was low candlelight and the smell of food. And a brown-haired girl in the clothing of a man, her eyes downcast.

4

His two fellow knights had gone out to the chapel. Even though it was a sanctified stable.

The rest of them—God knew. The girl to her chamber, certainly. Slight and dowdy. Her damnable eyes cast down.

Danielus was in his room.

Regardless of the chaos, someone had come in and seen to the fire.

Cristiano looked at the fire, and then at the Magister, sitting in a chair, turning an apple in his hand. At each turn, the emerald in the ring flashed green. But the face of the Magister gave nothing at all.

"You're still angry, Cristiano."

"Yes, Magister."

"Anger is—shall I say a fault, rather than a sin?"

"I'll beat myself later."

"Oh. Sophistry. That's not you, surely, Cristiano?"

Cristiano stood, white with rage.

"Tell me, Magister. Was it a *trick*?"

"I see now, despite your words, you never believed me when I told you what she did."

"*What did she do*?"

"You saw quite well."

"I saw—something. Am I to trust my eyes?"

"Have your eyes lied to you before?"

"No."

"Then, perhaps, trust them."

"*How* can she—for the love of God—"

Danielus got up. He walked across the room and back, and in passing put the apple into Cristiano's unwary hand.

"Look. Here is a wholesome fruit we eat. Meat may be forbidden at certain times, and wine. But apples—never, And yet, Cristiano, on the Tree in the Garden of Genesis, the apples were forbidden. And eaten but once, brought about the fall of Man, as later only the rebellion of Lucefero felled the angels of Hell. By God's will, things may change."

Cristiano gripped the apple. His eyes flamed cold. *So he looks in a battle*, Danielus thought, having never seen it. He pitied those adversaries who had.

"The Bible itself informs us of miracles," continued the Magister Major. "Nowhere, I think, does the Bible say that miracles have ended. Rather that they may attend World's End, or perhaps the dawn of another age."

Cristiano stared at him.

But the eyes of Fra Danielus, as others had found, gave no purchase.

At last Cristiano turned away.

"Magister, does the Bible say a woman should be dressed as a man, and have a man's freedom?"

"Some would tell you it does not," said Danielus.

"Then she—"

"She dresses for her work."

"She's *female*."

"Do you go into a skirmish, Knight, without your shield or sword?"

"*Yes*, Magister, you amaze me—you dressed her as a noble *boy*—where then is *her* sword?"

Danielus laughed. He tipped back his head and laughed—and this Cristiano had, before, never seen or heard.

Danielus said, "You ask why she wears no sword."

"Yes, then. *Yes*."

"She," said Danielus, no longer laughing, "*she* is the sword."

"What are you saying?"

Danielus now looked deep into the fire on his hearth.

He said, apparently at random, "Do you reckon they'll keep silent about this? I mean Marco and his brood."

"*No*. Whatever oath you made them swear. How can they?"

"How can they, indeed." Danielus now smiled. "They'll blab. And then go to their priest in the village, to confess the sin of blabbing. And he will send a message to the Church. And soon, between the gossip in the markets of the City, and the questioning of the priests, everyone will have heard of her, a red-haired virgin who can call down fire."

"It was deliberate then, to let them see."

"Of course."

"And I—and Jian, Aretzo—"

"She requires emotion, generally it seems that of others, since nothing stirs her very much. Oh, attempted rape did. That began it. But afterwards, the tears, fright, fury of those about her. Perhaps, their *need*. Her fire isn't always awarded as a punishment. It may be a gift."

"So you employed us, Magister. The Soldiers of God. Our doubt and—anger—"

"You alone were enough."

Cristiano did not move. In his hand the apple, (crushed) began to bleed wine-scented juice that dropped on to the floor.

"Was I."

"Your brother Soldiers gave themselves over quite soon. You resisted. Anger, or terror? Have you ever experienced fear, my Knight, to know it when it comes at you?"

Cristiano reacted suddenly. He flung the broken fruit into the fire. It hissed, as the candles had done, and a wonderful smell rose where the white flesh began to bake.

"How can I credit any of this?" he said.

"You saw it. How can you credit anything, otherwise."

Cristiano's face was bleak and the eyes wide.

"There you have it then. How can I?"

Danielus walked again across the room. Close to Cristiano, they were of a height. Nevertheless, as a father would, he took the younger man in his arms.

"You suffer, my son. Do you really believe God wants only penance and agony? He loves us, Cristiano. He wants us to be happy, too. Yield to Him, only that."

"I always have yielded, to God," Cristiano whispered.

"Do it only this once more."

"But she—"

"What did you feel then?"

"What I've felt only alone—before the altar."

Danielus held the young man; he stroked the blond hair of the bowed head pressed now to his shoulder.

"God is your father. You must trust Him as the child must trust the parent. His purpose may seem unconscionable. But He will know more."

"I've said I can't debate with you."

"Then God forbid you should try to debate with Heaven."

After a moment more, Fra Danielus moved Cristiano from him. The Magister left him to stand there, by the fire, and crossed the room.

Danielus opened the shutter of the small window, and looked out at the snow and the night. Beasts might faintly be heard trampling in their byres. No other sounds now but the emptiness of winter.

"Beatifica recounted her dreams to the priests who first questioned her. Sarco obtained details of all her speech with them. But I found these dreams especially interesting. They're beautiful, and innocent. And bright with power. But they might well have swayed those men further to the idea she was a witch. How lucky they were not beneath corruption."

Cristiano glanced at him. "You bribed them?"

"How else do you think she came to me, after all the fuss that had been made?"

"The Council of the Lamb—"

"Oh, the business hadn't reached high. They thought her nothing much."

Danielus was silent a moment. Then he said, almost tenderly, "There are wolf tracks in the snow, down there. They've circled the farm, poor starving things, and gone away."

"You pity wolves."

"I pity all the world, Cristiano. Myself not exempted. If it weren't blasphemy, I would pity God. So much pain and such a little spice and sweetness."

"That's how we learn. The harsher the school—"

"The greater the achievement? Later, in Heaven, we can be glad of it. Let me tell you what the girl said she dreamed. A country of sands and stones, with slim tall trees that had a foliage like fringes of gold. And a scarlet mountain, which seemed to burn like a terracotta lamp, from within."

"Where did she see such a thing to dream it?" Cristiano's voice was almost idle. Exhausted, he leaned on the wall, watching the apple in the flames.

"Where indeed. She said she saw the people there, and they were black as if burnt. The animals were curious. She describes one like a hare, but taller than a man. And a bear that sat in a tree and ate the leaves. Except, the leaves weren't consumed."

"Her mind—"

"Curdled? Well. Let me tell you something else. Now while you lean there, dying for sleep."

"Pardon me, Magister—"

"Rest yourself a while, Cristiano, from being always perfect. I'd rather have you tired, to hear this. Perhaps then your own dreams will make space for it."

Danielus closed the shutter. The room drew close about them.

"I keep a library in the island house. While I was there, I searched for and found a certain book. The writings of Gaius Suetonius Tranquillus. You will know, he was a Roman much given to anecdote and to history. Suetonius reports the tale of a Roman sea captain who, while questing for a large and unknown island in the Mare Arabicus, was overtaken by a mighty storm. The vessel outlasted the tempest, but lost her course. For some while she was blown southward. Then when the gale dropped, having not enough crew left alive to man the ship, they were driven east of south. The legendary island had failed them. Instead they reached several small islets, which sustained them with water and peculiar fruits. Months passed. Suetonius heartlessly describes their prayers to their pagan gods, begging salvation, and thinking they must die."

Cristiano watched the Magister Major. *Watched*. On guard against weariness, and any miracle.

But up in the watchtower, O sentry, remember night must come.

"At last the ship reached landfall. No island. It was a country large as any they had come from. And in their talk of it, when years after some of them returned, they named it, this place, God's Other World."

Cristiano said, "Since it was so unlike anything they knew."

"So unlike. A land of mountains and deserts and lush forests, filled by plants and creatures never seen, never imagined, not even in the remote East. They had fallen, they thought, from the edge of the earth. But being imperfect, this was not Heaven. Nor was it fearful enough for Hell. Another world then."

"If they returned and said this, were they reckoned liars?"

"Of course. Simply because they had returned, as Suetonius points out. The captain and his men claimed to have brought proofs, nevertheless. Unluckily, if unsurprisingly, none of the animals or plants had endured the journey back, which had been quite as harsh as the setting out. Only the woman survived, and was taken with them to Rome, to be shown to the Emperor Vespasian."

"A woman. Was she as different as the world they said they'd found?"

"She was black. But then, she might have been from Africanus. The Romans were acquainted with Nubians. However, her features weren't of this type, and the language she spoke had never been heard."

"What became of her?"

"I regret to say, she was a slave. The Roman men had made her that, treating her, the writer comments, quite well. They thought her an inferior, as they thought any foreigner, especially one whose skin was unmatched to their own. The white and freckled skins of Britains, for example, seem to have disgusted them. She was disputed over in Rome, whether she should be shown as an exhibit, or carried by the ship's captain to his farm. In the end, bored no doubt, the emperor generously permitted the captain to keep his spoils."

Cristiano thought the apple in the fire perished

very slowly. It had not yet burned away. He said, "Is that all the story?"

"She lived as a slave. And died as one. She reputedly bore several children. They said she was docile and biddable, but for all that, a sorceress."

"Why?"

"She could bring fire."

"Yes, I guessed that would be it."

"According to Suetonius, they called her *Cucua*, the nearest they could get to her name. She told them her knack of lighting the fire and lamps had been given her from a mountain, which she visited in her childhood. A red mountain, which was the home of spirits."

"Did her gift pass on?"

"Well, Cristiano. Perhaps it did."

"But it was long ago. And do they say where she died?"

"Gaius Suetonius names the place. I can't discover it. In Italy, for sure."

"She might by now have many descendants."

"Blood dilutes. As water does."

Danielus slowly drew off his cross and put it down. It seemed heavy to him, as he handled it. "Maybe all of it is only my fancy. Or a Roman fancy. Or an ancient lie. But the fire, Cristiano, that's quite real. Go and sleep now. Yes, go on. Throw yourself off into the abyss of slumber. Perhaps the answer is there for you, waiting."

Cristiano straightened.

Danielus looked at him, thinking of the boy of fifteen long ago—the girl's age now, probably. And, strangely, *her* eyes also, here clouded only by another color, by masculinity, and by intellect.

It was in this one he had seen her gaze. And this one

who held also her power of fire, but frozen cold as ice and trapped for ever inside.

Cristiano approached and dropped to his knee.

The Magister extended the emerald for him to kiss.

Presently, in the chamber outside, Cristiano's step was firm, then sluggish. The pallet groaned. Then silence.

But even after the candles had been dowsed, the inner room smelled on and on of burning apples.

Beatifica lay curled on her right side, one palm under her cheek.

She was dreaming, and did not know it.

Most likely she would not recall her dream on waking, only that she had been, as always, a great distance from the earth.

It was not Alter Mundi—God's Other World—which now she traveled. Instead, against soft dimness she neither heard nor saw, she beheld an angel.

He was tall and spare, and behind him the great wings had opened, like the wings of a swan she had seen carved in the altar rail of the Little Cappella. They were darkly white, and touched with a watery glow, shifting, elusive. In one hand he grasped a drawn sword. Again, perhaps, like an image she had been shown, this time among the Primo's Golden Rooms, Micaeli, the warrior angel of the Bellatae. And, like the Angel Micaeli, this angel too wore a maculum of glistening mail.

The girl was spellbound, not awed. She was entranced.

She observed him until he faded in the depths of her sleep. She had not seen his face. Perhaps he had not had one. But within his diadem of flame, the hair hung long, a pale gold almost white.

BOOK TWO

Mundus Imperfectus

PART ONE

> And there went out another horse that was red: and power was given to him that sat thereon to take peace from the earth, and that they should kill one another: and there was given unto him a great sword.
>
> REVELATION OF JOHN THE DIVINE
> *The Bible*

I

APPARENTLY HE COULD NOT VISIT. She had guessed he might not, despite an earlier letter. She would keep the Festival for the household, any way. It was the Feast of Sweets, after which came the forty days fasting and penance of the Quadraginta, to mark Christ's sojourn in the wilderness.

Veronichi combed her long black hair with the sandalwood comb. A vanity from the East. Crusades had first brought such trifles into Ve Nera. What irony: going out to enforce God among the infidel, they had returned meshed in and trailing infidel pleasures, unguents and perfumes, curious foods and scented baths. Also things it was not wise to talk of—aphrodisiacs, sodomy, the theology of another God passing as the true one.

But her hair was very black; she thought so, almost amused, hiding it now inside her linen cap. The hair of a Jewess

Danielus had rescued her from that. That is, from living as the Jews of Venus were supposed to do.

To her last day she would never forget the morning that life ended.

The house had stood against the ghetto wall—of course, on its *inside*. Plaster had crumbled from the house, exposing wounds of raw red. It was the same with all the houses of the ghetto. Besides, mostly the ghetto comprised huts. Filth was everywhere. She had thought nothing of it, then, nor the stench of poverty. (She could not bear dirtiness or bad smells now. When the lagoon brought her the summer stinks of Venus, Veronichi's household on Eel Island choked instead on roomfuls of fresh roses and smoking gums.)

She was the niece of a rabbi. He, living alone, had taken her in during her infancy. Her parents were gone, and she learned, then, nothing of them, and never much. Later she would wonder if her mother had been stoned for adultery. For Veronichi—then called Yaelit—was the child of a Christian, a prince of the outer City. And by the death-bed confession he had made, Yaelit gained her escape. For the prince confessed to one of his legitimate sons, Danielus, by then a priest high in the sacerdocracy of the Primo. The confession was not greatly original. On a drunken sortie through the Jewish quarter, the prince had seen the woman who was to be Yaelit's mother. He felt himself enamored, had her abducted, stored a few months in some place he used for such sport, and made love to her until love ended. Then he sent her back to her Jewish husband, and the ghetto. Yaelit was the result.

Following the demise of her actual father, the prince, Yaelit was in turn taken from the slum within the wall.

That scene, never to be forgotten. Her uncle, the rabbi, pulling her back into the room. Threatening he would cut her throat rather than allow her to be defiled, (the inevitable fate) or worse, made into an apostate—a

Christian. Already he had been planning to wed Yaelit to a scholar of the quarter, a man even older than himself. She was by then seventeen, and had been kept single so long only in order to tend her uncle's house—his unpaid servant. With marriage, she would have much the same position, but now maintaining two houses. She would cook and clean from the scraps of existence, revere her husband and bow to him in all things, as she did her uncle. But also she would have to lie down under the ancient scholar and conceive for him a son. Worse than all this, though, was the knowledge she must cut off her hair, and put on instead the traditional dry horsehair wig of a Hebrew wife. This proposed robbery frightened Yaelit. Had not the hero Samson lost his strength and spirit when shorn? Her uncle slapped her: what did that matter; she was no hero, but a woman.

The Christian men sent by Danielus came through the ghetto gates, however, armed with staves and knives, and in the end the rabbi, hideously cursing them and spitting foam, let Yaelit go.

How tall the ghetto walls had seemed, and looking back, she saw men and women in black, wailing and gnashing their teeth at her destiny—as if she had been cast out of paradise. Then, the Christian guards outside the gates, jeering and laughing. But then she was through, and she saw sunlight, which seemed now different, and the glitter of the canals, which were that day filled by rippling chains of jewels rather than water.

Her uncle had been right. She had become a Christian, naturally.

Veronichi, no longer Yaelit, pressed home the linen cap. But all her hair lay under it. Her hair remained for her. Whenever she wished, she might let it down. She smiled. She would presently write to the Magister Major.

'Dearest and most respected brother, pray do not leave your promised visit too long. You know I am always anxious at my management of your house, here. And I have not been well . . .'

On the Island of the Rivoalto, the palace and grounds of the Ducem vividly fluttered with pitch brands, candles, hanging Eastern lamps. Joffri had declared the Feast of Sweets must be a "Sunny Night."

As Joffri strolled through the gardens with two pretty women, and with three ivory hounds trotting behind them, he and his ladies tossing candies covered by goldleaf into fountains, dogs, and the jaws of small children, a messenger waited in the shadows of an adjacent court.

He could hear the laughter and the outbursts of fun, the music of harps, bells and trumpets. Distant small topaz explosions denoted runners with torches. But nobody came for him. He sat there, kicking his heels.

It was not particularly warm.

His mind uneasily announced to him that, from what he had been hearing, it had been warm enough elsewhere. Where did those stories start? He had met them at once, coming into the City. Some farms out on the plain, claiming they had seen a naked virgin, clothed modestly in fiery hair, riding a pale horse through the fields at dawn. And from the bare furrows, a flock of birds flew up, all on fire, but not burned, not *harmed*. And later, someone saw a flock of burning geese, rushing down like the sun falling out of the sky. Their wings were full of flames, which gradually went out as they settled to feed. There had been talk of a Plague Virgin half a century before. This was a Fire Virgin. An omen of war? Did it mean God would help Ve Nera—or destroy it?

The dispatches and letters the messenger carried came from Candisi. Later they would be shown at the Primo.

Although not informed of the contents of his satchel, the messenger had some ideas about it. Probably such news was unsuitable for the Feast of Sweets. For this reason, the advisors of the Ducem were making the dispatches wait.

One thousand and ten ships were now, it seemed, assembling at Jurneia. With the first fullness of spring they would set sail. Ve Nera might expect them by the Crab Month—or before, if God did not deter the winds.

The messenger reached into his tunic and touched the old lucky coin, bronze, with the figure of Neptune, the sea god, cut on it. He had already sent his family packing to the hills. A panicked exodus later might have impeded them.

It was said the City had, standing, or building at the shipyards of Torchara, four hundred ships. But more likely that was less.

An enemy could only come at her properly from the sea, and then her channels were too narrow to let them in. But the sand bars of the lagoons would be nothing to them. They would haul their ships over by means of slaves, on logs if necessary. Besides, the tides could flood quite high even in summer. And the sea walls were not very much. The lagoons would fill with ships as well as water . . . Jurneia had cannon. On every vessel?

Screams of merriment burst up from Joffri's gardens.

After this feast came Quadraginta. The wilderness.

An official was approaching.

The messenger rose.

Not an official, a priest. More, one of the Council of

the Lamb—all in black, stooping slightly, with fish-pale, worm-thin eyes.

The messenger knelt.

"Holy brother."

"Yes. That's well enough. Take yourself to the kitchens, and eat. You may leave your bag with me."

Again, uneasy, the messenger held the satchel, still.

"My lord the Ducem—"

"The Ducem shall have it."

The documents, in the hands of skillful scribes, would only take an hour or so to copy.

Reluctant yet distracted, the messenger gave Brother Sarco his dispatches. He went to the kitchens, where he fell asleep over his food.

"When your heart is mine

"You may do as you will to—"

That song had come back. It was a disgusting and lewd song. The goddess Venus, married to Vulcanus, engaged in lechery with the war god, Mars. Give me your heart, she said. You will be the freer without it. But, she warned, if you cause me to love *you*, I shall make you give up the world for me.

Careless of her admonition, Mars stretched her on her back, smoothed her nacre breasts, parted the sea waves of her hair and thighs, and drowned in her. But his spasms, while drowning, rendered her such delight, she loved him, and he was lost.

It had been a chant to God. The soul, loving God, was made free. But if God should choose to love that soul above other souls, by which it was meant, *select* that soul for some duty to Heaven, then the world must be renounced, and all things, but the service.

They knew this, the four priests, (Eyes and Ears) as

they stood by the door. Behind them on the night canal, the Styx boat waited like a crocodilius from some fearsome bestiary.

Fists slammed on the door.

Within, the noise rose riotous, subsided abruptly.

They had to knock again.

A little boy came, in an apron—a slave—he was pushed aside.

From the drunken inner room, the master of the house came out, hot-faced with fear.

"Brothers—what can you want here? It's a Christian household—we celebrate the fore-penitence feast—"

"You're Jacmo Leatherer?"

"Yes, brothers, yes, but—"

"Look at your own sins, flaunted there on your body."

In horror, the leather-maker gaped at his own corpulence, his tunic of good wool trimmed by embroidery—for the feast. The leather belt his own shop had made, studded with silver.

"I paid my tax on it, brothers—yes, even though I and my son worked it."

"You're too gaudy always, Jacmo. And too loud. Come. You must tell us more. We will listen."

Dragged in the boat, and rowed away, Jacmo weeping now. Once leaning over to puke from terror in the lagoon.

Other boats were stealing on. In each, beside the priests, a man or two, or three or four, with sagging faces of dismay. One boat with five whores in it. Bony from malnutrition, or fat with it, fat on stodges that gave no life. But, "You eat too much. Gluttony. Gluttony and lust." "I never like my work, brother. I *give*." "You give? For coin? You *sold* the flesh the Almighty leant you."

Rowed over water, these lamenting souls. Styx boats, yes. Towards the pearl-domed Primo, which now, by night, was like the gateway to the Underworld.

And in the under-rooms of it, a light like Hell from the braziers, in which weird tools were heating up.

"No—holy brothers spare my hands—I need my fingers for my work—"

"For delving in the dish? For tickling in concupiscence?"

"My trade—my trade—"

"Then repent, my son."

"For what? For *what*? I've done nothing. It's my money you want—for the ships—very well—yes—take it—"

"No, my son. It's your soul we wish to cleanse."

Cries. Such cries.

Prayers. Confessions which were invented to stay the pincers and the iron burning white.

Rumor said the underlings of the Council threw the corpses off a bridge some way over the Laguna Fulvia. Not too close to the Primo.

"Is he alive?"

"I think not . . . No. He's gone. Prayers must be said."

On the long stone stair, a man was standing, watching, as the latest corpse—the leatherer's—was shifted. In the hood, the watcher's face was swarthy. When he spoke, his voice was rough, as if from coughing.

"Remember too, you scour Ve Nera clean. The enemy sails towards us, the Children of Satanus. If we're found wanting, what destruction may not befall us?" They heeded, looking up, their eyes glinting in the brazier light—black rats. "These foul sins of theirs must be cauterized, and the body of the City healed. Or He will blast us all. Remember those other cities of the plain."

One of the Eyes and Ears replied.

"It's true, Brother of the Lamb. Who hasn't heard the story of the creature, formed like a girl, who burns down the houses of wrong-doers?"

The priest on the stair said nothing. Then he said, "This is only some make-believe."

(On the floor now, the dead man lay as if listening too. Make-believe had not saved *him*.)

"But many saw it. She *walked in fire*—and since then several have seen the thing. A being wrapped in hair which burns—"

"They thought her a witch," said another. "But she vanished. It was even thought we took a witch and questioned her, but that witch was only a simpleton. We lashed her and let her go—"

And another said, "Brother of the Lamb, God may already have sent down an avenging angel. It might take any form, to test us."

"A female—" rasped the man on the stair.

From across the black room, yet one more black rat cheeped up. His hands had blood on them. He said, piously, "The Immaculate Maria was at first only a girl. And the luminous Santa Caterina, who chastely wedded Christ."

The corpse was being quickly borne out now. There were others to see to. How many more would perish tonight, to fund and clean the City?

The swarthy priest glanced at dead Jacmo.

"Did he confess?"

"Yes, Brother of the Lamb. He said, beyond his vainglory and noisiness, he had copulated, twice, with his neighbor's dog. A bitch. It might have been worse. Here's the paper. He signed it. That is, we assisted him to sign . . . his hand—Seven hundred silver duccas, and his house, to come to the Council. The fine is just."

"Was he long in his dying?"

"No, gracious brother. And he died in the end in a state of grace, may Christ be blessed."

The corpse was gone now. The underlings would be in charge of it. Off to the bridge . . . deep water could hold so much.

Jacmo, who copulated with dogs. Renzo, who had eaten meat on a fish day, challenging and cursing the Trinity. A whore known as Happy, who had worshipped the devil and boasted she had that month served as many men as Jurneia sent ships.

Into the water.

And for these falsehoods, whispered, shrieked, to save what might be left of a whole skin, these admissions to crimes which, in fantasy or nightmare only they had committed, that place was coming to be named. The Bridge of Lies.

2

It was Quadraginta. The time of fasting and sorrow. The forty days of payment for past faults. But, spring was forward, and took no notice.

On a chair by the high window, Beatifica sat quietly. She was dressed as normally now, like a young man, a lesser prince. Her clothes were white, or gray, and she had learned how to save them from getting dirty, moving carefully about, eating and drinking in the fine way she had been taught. As she generally did when alone, she had spent some time saying over prayers and passages from the Bible, to enjoy their sounds. Now every day a priest came, who was teaching her both

Testaments, chapter by chapter, and in Latin.

This priest, young and gentle, blushed on and off and on with confused indecision when he was with her. Even so, he would tell her always the meaning of each passage he was to help her learn.

In this manner, although still not understanding the majority of the individual words, Beatifica was coming to grasp the narrative behind each section she recited. Also the names of Patriarchs, heroes, villains and celestial beings. As others had found before her, the richness of the Bible as a story book was virtually limitless, while the poetry and symmetry of the wonderful, unknown words, consistently pleased her. However, the appalling threats and unearthly inspirations jointly passed her by.

"She speaks so flawlessly, one would swear she knew every sentence, every letter she utters," this, from her flushed teacher. Then, urgently, "Truly, Magister Major, I think she *does*, by some supernal intervention, know them *all*."

Fra Danielus had nodded. It had been his hope that most would come to believe this of her. Her ignoramus's power of learning by rote was worth much more than mere understanding.

Beyond her window, which was high up in the Primo's side, Beatifica could see down between high roofs, into a small garden, where lay brothers were gathering herbs, the only form of seasoning, with a little salt, permitted for the Forty Days. Tiny flowers covered the lawn like gems and coins. On a peach tree, blossom massed like the white sea-foam from which the goddess Venus had been fashioned.

Beatifica had re-entered the Primo with Fra Danielus and some of his people, scribes and servants. She had been dressed then as one of the lay brothers, in a loose brown habit. No one noticed her. Outside, (unknown to the girl) her fame of fire had spread. But in most of the tales she stayed an uncanny phenomenon, manifesting without human agency, vanishing in thin air.

Into the garden suddenly walked a Soldier of God. He wore the shining maculum, and was girded by the sword belt. The shoulder badge of the Child astride the Lion, from this distance, was just a smudge of sunlight. His hair was dark.

The priests drew back. The Bellator talked to them, shortly. Beatifica heard the voices, but not what was said.

She knew the Bellator, however. He was the one they had called Jian, at the farm on the plain. He had ridden beside the uncomfortable jouncing litter which brought her back to the City. On the journey, three times every day, he had asked her if she required anything. She consistently said No. What could he give her? As always, she expected nothing, and to ask of her her wishes had remained, in her view, at best an irrelevance.

Now the priests left the garden, their baskets laid with green.

Jian, Bellator Christi, stood, foursquare below her. Far down, and made small.

The sun on his hair altered it to silver.

Something moved through Beatifica. This was like a low tide, passing from her heart to her brain, and away again. She did not recognize it. But she leaned out a little way.

And Jian, turning all at once, tipped back his head and looked directly up at her.

Her hair fell round her face and shoulders, over the window's edge, drifting. She wore it unbound and unconcealed now, as a boy or a man would. Sunlight caught her, too.

Jian crossed himself. Then he went down on one knee on the velvet lawn, crushing the little flowers.

Beatifica watched him, puzzled, unsettled as so often by the actions of others, and yet, as usually too, indifferent.

He was worshipping her.

She did not know it. Nor did he.

With a strange sensation of disappointment, (not knowing either what disappointment was) the girl withdrew inside her room.

She went over to the icon of Maria that stood on the chest. It was a small statue, of alabaster, only the veil colored rose, and painted with gold stars, which also appeared, one each, on the dainty feet.

Beatifica now crossed herself as Jian had done. She said a prayer to the Virgin, one of the prayers whose meaning no one had told her. She said it melodiously. She had been taught how to worship, its forms. And this too, for her, had become a valued pastime.

Outside, Jian was still kneeling. Still committing his own act of devotion.

Then the midday Solus sounded from the Angel Tower. Getting to his feet, Jian strode away.

The nun Purita knelt also in the Midday Mass. Here, this fell some minutes later, since the bell of Santa Lallo Lacrima, (lullaby of tears) invariably rang after that of the Primo.

Like all the women of her order, Sister Purita wore gray, her wimple only being white. Against it, her skin looked sallow. Under it, her blonde hair was cropped short—but she had seen, as it fell, some gray also in the strands. At the inn, she would soon have had to cover her hair completely, anyway, or to bleach it with the not-always-obtainable urine of a donkey or horse.

Luchita—Sister Purita—prayed.

Her back ached, but now she had the balm for that, and the herbal drink which helped her to sleep. There was the dispensation too, which allowed her, if unwell, to miss the Prima Vigile two hours after midnight. As a rule though, Purita had one of the novices wake her in time.

He had been so very kind to her. Possibly, it was for the first that anyone had. Even her father had beaten her, and her mother too, as they had all the children, excepting Cristiano. The local priest had taken an interest in the boy from infancy, instructed him in reading and Latin, and entered him for the priesthood. Their parents had been proud. Cristiano, she had always thought, (and sometimes enviously, belligerently) had *escaped*. Now, so had she.

Last summer, when she had knelt differently, weeping slightly from tiredness and soreness, on the stone floors of the nun-house, a man had come for her, a priest. She was taken through the marshes, to the big church of Santa La'La, whose late bell she had so often heard from the inn, and never heeded. She thought she had failed at the nunnery, all her remorse and punishing work gone for nothing. She would be castigated and thrown out. Then what?

When she was taken into the room, and saw the priest sitting there, she had trembled with shock. It was a Magister of the Basilica—more, a Magister Major. She knew him in another moment, from the description Cristiano had once given her.

He had the ascetic face of a saint, pale, and lean, like body and hands. His eyes were black, large and calm, and from his thick dark hair the tonsure seemed carved, like a disc in the fur of a dark cat. There was gray there, too. Like herself, he was no longer young.

He told her she should sit down.

When she had done so, he said, "You must find this road very hard, my sister."

"It is. But I don't mind." She did. She could see no other way.

"How long have they told you you must wait for the novitiate?"

"Until next spring. Then, if well judged, I can begin."

"Tell me, please," he said, "why you came to this? Was your husband harsh? Your children ungrateful?"

"Oh—my children are all far off. One way and another. The boys went for soldiers. Two died in the last war with Candis."

"That is sad."

"Yes." She corrected herself quickly, "You're very good to say so, Magister."

"What of the others?"

"Trade took them away."

"Even the girl."

She hesitated, then said, "My daughter became a whore, I'm sorry to say it. I never see her. My husband—he wouldn't have her in the house. I don't know what became of her."

"Maria Magdelena was also a harlot, Luchita. Nothing is irredeemable. But I perceive why the life of a nun may eventually have appealed to you. Your last child died, I think."

"You'll know from my brother," she said.

Danielus nodded. He had thought she might not be a fool, nor was she. In her scourged and emptied face, he could detect a trace of Cristiano. When young perhaps, she had been fair.

She said, "Magister, *he* must have told you I didn't seek this because of that. But because of the girl."

"Tell me of that, then."

She told him. Her words were halting, not from uncertainty, only through trying to find the proper ones, those which would summon back the event both for herself and another.

When she finished, Danielus said quietly, "And you have no doubt of what you saw?"

"None."

"Someone will have mooted the chance that Lucefero worked in this, not God."

"Many times. How can I know? But I never thought so."

"Why?"

She lifted her eyes and looked directly into his. "It hurt me when she did it. I felt a sort of splitting pain—it was—forgive me, Magister—like a birth pang. And most of my self fell from me. I was left only with my inner self. Not much, you'll agree, I'm sure. Yet no longer—bowed down, laden—*free*. It was as if I needn't cling anymore to the life I'd had. Nor to anything. I could begin again. Do you see? Surely Satanus doesn't give us anything like that? He'd weight us down the more, even if it was with luxuries and charms. It would be *heavy*—not lighter than the air."

Danielus got up. So did she.

"Do you know the symbol which is in this ring I wear?"

She stared at the emerald. "The emblem of your authority, Father."

"It is the stone blessed by the Christ, and from which his final drinking cup was made. Also, it was the stone of the goddess Venus, patron in ancient times of our City." He extended his hand. Unbelievingly, she realized he was allowing her to press her lips to the mystical jewel. She did so. (The emerald felt coolly warm, and smooth as water.)

Danielus said, "You've served your novitiate, Luchita. Now you need only learn your duties as a nun. Do you still wish it?"

Bemused, she nodded. "But I—"

"Nothing is random," he said, "that comes from God. He chose you, Luchita, never forget this. To be the witness and to throw off your earthly chains. Don't cry. You shall serve here in the sister-house of this church. You've paid your dues already in the world. I shall make it my business to see you're well-treated here. The Domina is old and charitable."

Luchita now, kneeling in Santa La'La, raised her eyes to the soft light of the glazed window. She prayed for the charitable Domina, and for the Magister, Fra Danielus. Let God bless him, as Christ blessed the green stone in his ring.

O God, sang the nuns, *I render you all my heart and am free. You demand of me everything, and I forget the world.*

3

The room was very large, and had required to be. It was crowded. The walls were covered by long tapestries, and painted panels that told stories, both colored like jewels, and gilded. Silver lamps hung down twice the height of a tall man, yet well clear of the throng below. The candles were uncountable, and all starred with light. Instantly slaves removed and replaced those which had burned out. Music played. The servants stalked to and fro, kitted in plum silk, the color of the Ducal house. At the long tables draped in white, and set with silver platters and spice-cellars of gold six mid-finger lengths high, (in the shape of towers) guests of the Ducem were eating and drinking. The Forty Days were over. Christ had died and risen from the dead. And here, the taxes and the dangerous opprobrium which hung over Ve Nera's apparel and food, went unconsidered.

Men in stiffened tunics, or long gowns, edged by bear fur and the tails of weasels, velvet hats stabbed by flowers of ruby and beryl. Women with bared lily shoulders pushed up from tightly buttoned over-gowns, which sprouted patterned waterfalls of sleeves, and headgear that was a heart, or padded hoop wound by gilt cord, netted in transparent veils from Inde, and spattered by pearls.

Even so, no joints or poultry were served on this meatless night. Crab flesh and eels had been brought instead, and wide-fish in honey, the scorpion crab in its coral shell, and stew of oysters in the Roman manner. Now, however, a trumpet blew. The salt-swans were coming in. Birds it was true, but, from their greenish tint and fishy taste, allowable.

Each rested on a bronze charger rimmed by gold. Each was re-clothed in its feathers, beaks covered by silver-leaf and with diamonds, no less, set in the eyes. Down the room they sailed, long necks curved, proud on their lakes of vegetables.

Twelve in all. The room applauded. Knives were sharpened. The slender dogs, in collars of gold, lifted their muzzles.

As the feasters tore the swans apart, neatly hacking a way in past the quaint feathery illusion of life, Cristiano watched, expressionless.

"You grasp now the Council's need for curbing the appetite of men?" said Jian softly.

"Yes. I have always grasped that."

Water green feathers littered the floor, among the strewn camomile and asphodel.

Further up the high table, from his place beside the Ducem, Fra Danielus courteously declined the swan. But inclined his head to the two seated Bellatae.

"He says we may."

"You eat it. It isn't to my liking."

"Cristiano, you needn't mask your virtue with a falsehood."

Cristiano grinned suddenly. It was as startling as the rare times the Magister Major smiled. Jian, englamoured despite himself, laughed.

"No, I hate swan-meat. Turbot with feathers."

As the salver came, the riven swan, leaning now, Jian carved off a modest portion. The servant craned near, offering other vegetables, sauce, pickled oranges.

Cristiano had lapsed back into his impenetrable and somber gaze.

He was thinking of the girl, due to be brought in soon, like the swans. Similarly to be hacked and cut up, as by the jeweled personal knives of these rich princes and their women?

On the other side of the Ducem sat two men from the Council of the Lamb. As a Bellator went abroad in his mail, so the Council Brothers did in their night-black, and hooded. One of them was that evil-looking creature, Sarco. And beside him, the man who was coarsely-spoken. He had some ailment of the throat, it seemed. The Magister had called him only 'brother'.

At first Joffri had seemed rather cramped between these two arms of the Church. But as the wine flowed, this lessened. His young wife, Arianna, arrived late. Now she sat along the board in her white gown, neck crystallized by olivines. It was just possible, from the profile of her body, to surmise she might be with child. Joffri looked at her now and then, absently, affectionately, without any passion. She had a sad little face under the extravagant headdress.

A male Jew, Cristiano had heard, thanked God every day for not making him a woman.

And outside, with her guard, for so they must be considered, of seven Bellatae Christi from the Upper Echelon, *she* waited.

A woman, but not solely a woman.

Beatifica.

Since Christ' Mass tide, he had kept the vigil, as he always did every month. But God did not grant Cristiano his vision of Heaven. The ecstasy. Perhaps never again would that rapture be his.

Only at that time she brought down the fire.

Only then.

What did it mean?

He had eaten sparingly. Had not wanted much. These feasts he found distasteful, pointless and dull. Nothing in the world could compare with God.

Where God was, there waited all purpose and exhilaration. Was God—with *her*?

Cristiano dipped his fingers in the water bowl, where petals floated, and wiped his hands on the napkin. He closed off his Cup—it was silver—to the servant with the pitcher.

Tonight, here at the City's temporal hub, was to be recreated that miniature night at the farm on the plain. Joffri had heard the rumors. Of course he had. Now and then, he cast a puzzled glance at the Magister. A puzzled glance lit with a sort of childish wish for surprises. The opposite of the looks he gave his wife and two mistresses.

What do I feel?

Cristiano did not want it to happen here. For it would. She would come in and there would be the sense of startlement, then scandal, and a score of women would giggle at her affrontery, and some of the jaded men, fancying this hermaphrodite thing, a boy-woman clad as a lord, would eye her lasciviously. Then she would call the fire. She could. She would.

He was armored now. He had put a maculum of steel upon his mind and soul.

But they, this ignorant petty crowd, attractive as all the similar scenes of banquets upon the walls, would respond with hysteria. Screams, prayers, women swooning, men falling to their knees.

The smell of smoke.

It was a show-piece, such as could provisionally be faked on any actor's cart, to please the rabble.

Yet it was real.

Had not Christ healed lepers and the blind before a crowd? Had he not, at a festival, changed water into wine? *Died* before a multitude.

Must even the sublime be cheapened to make good the truth?

But—she was only a girl.

The swans lay in ruins. (Twelve—one for every calendar month.) The odor of roast and grease and burning wax grew heavy, mixed with the squashed flowers, and the Eastern perfumes. Perfumes even from Jurneia, no doubt.

Jian had drunk too much, Cristiano noted. He would stay couth but then need to confess it and do penance. He was not thinking of that. His eyes were bright, thinking of Beatifica.

One saw it among all the Upper Echelon of the

Bellatae, for all were in the know. A raising of heads at the mention of the girl. Like the Ducem's dogs just now.

But the seven Soldiers of God who attended her tonight had never before seen what she could do.

The music had stopped. Joffri turned to Fra Danielus, his eyes brighter than Jian's.

Cristiano heard the Ducem say, "Will she come in?"

"Yes, my lord," said Danielus. "If you're ready."

"I long to see it, Father. Trust me."

On his other side, the hoarse priest from the Council said, gratingly, "If we are to believe she can."

Cristiano thought, *How can he doubt?* And then, *The simplicity of it is what is horrible to me. I believe. I know. I wish I could go out—no, I wish before God this was not to happen.*

But God must have decreed it. Miracles were in the provenance of God. God could not make an error. And yet, the Magister had told him she was descended from a witch—

Joffri stood up, and everyone became hushed. A little god upon earth, a man strutting in his crown. *Think of the skull behind the skin, Joffri*!

Cristiano's heart beat, a drum in his side. He tried to cool himself, half reached out for the wine. Took his hand back and sat motionless.

"Generally," Joffri said to the huge, worldly room, "I call jugglers now, and men who swallow birds and let them back out from their ears. Or a poet to sing his latest ode."

They looked at him. Men drunk, feeding their hounds on bits of swan. Women with the upper moons of their breasts shining.

Joffri said, "Christ's resurrection is scarcely past. And God has not forgotten us. Men say, let's eat and make merry and forget the grave gapes for us. But why fear the grave? Christ makes nothing of it. And He, knowing an enemy steals upon us even now, a dragon that slips across the ocean—" They stared. Faces had whitened. Here and there a woman clutched her male companion's arm, or held her own hand, as if to pray. "God sends signs to us, it seems. We needn't be afraid even of a mortal foe." Joffri flipped one nonchalant hand, and the trumpet sounded again. The wide doors at the room's far end were opened.

The Ducem sat. He shot one gleaming look at the Magister Major. The uncaring hand had said, Oh, let's do it then, let's see. The eyes said, You'll need God's help and to spare if you fail now, will you not?

It was exactly as Cristiano had thought.

Startlement first.

He had seen the red horse brought for her. But not reckoned on quite how she would look on it. Here in the City, it was at once a symbol of the rare, and too of war . . . It was a steady animal, despite its lean and graceful, hound-like lines. Ferried through the waterways on a barge, and here to the Rivoalto, it had needed to be. It placed its hoofs with the sure balance of a dancer. In color it was like burnished copper. The saddlecloth was white, sewn with golden stars and suns, and from the white bridle and halter, hung golden bells, which jinked faint but clear in the silence, as it brought her forward.

She was also in her white and gold. Her hair, unbound, was one pure shade brighter than the horse.

The seven Bellatae walked, three on either side, and one at her back. They had come armed into the presence of the Ducem, the only men who might, save for his own guards. And the swords were all drawn, the tips of them dipped earthward.

Down the room the red horse stepped.

Her face was blanker than unwritten paper. All but the wide eyes. Golden. Fixed, as Cristiano remembered, on the Magister. Until, suddenly, they moved, and fixed on *him*.

The drum in his side jolted. Missed, and began again.

But she looked at Jian now. (He heard Jian catch his breath.) And then straight at the Ducem. Straight, straight, straighter than any sword.

Joffri crossed himself. Then he said, very low, "You never told me, Fra Danielus, she was beautiful."

Cristiano heard Danielus answer instantly in his quiet voice, "Of course, my lord. Her beauty comes from God."

Joffri sounded shaken a little. He said, "Doesn't it always, holy Father?"

"By a conduit, it does. On her, it seems, the Almighty has directly breathed."

Cristiano heard another voice in his mind, which contemptuously said that No, she was not beautiful. She *had* no beauty, was more than beauty. Beauty was a tiny word of fools, used to describe what had no word, here on earth.

And a wave of fear followed the inner voice. The instinct to beware.

The horse had passed through the room, and come up to the highest table, where the Ducem sat with his family, and the priests.

They were aware now, most of the crowd, that the young man on the horse was not masculine. As he had predicted, Cristiano heard the quick rills of laughter, the smothered oaths. Until silence resumed.

But the rough-voiced priest spoke loudly.

"This is against the law of God."

The Ducem said, "Holy brother—"

And the priest said through him, not bothering with him, "A woman clad as a man is blasphemous and immoral. She must be wicked and an imbecile, and those in charge of her too."

Danielus now used his voice, pitched not raised, to find the far reaches of the chamber. "God makes the law and God can unmake it."

"You dare to say, Fra, that God—"

As easily as the priest had broken in on Joffri's sentence, Danielus overrode the priest's. "Who am I to speak for God, brother. And who are you to speak for Him. I say this: A sword travels in its sheath for battle. Not in a female gown."

The hoarse priest surged up and now Sarco, the other Council Brother, put out his hand and stayed him. "Let us only see."

The Magister would have told her what to do, and how and when. At some signal from him, now she dismounted from the horse. She did this without flurry or awkwardness, and with no display. She had the coordination of a knight, used to it.

"This," said Danielus, as he had on the farm on the plain, "is the Maiden Beatifica. Speak for us now, Beatifica, the Grace."

She did so.

As Cristiano had expected and predicted. In her perfect Latin.

Hands rose, a roomful of hands, faltering, belated. to mark the cross.

From a side door two of the Ducem's men were coming in. They carried between them a great black pot, and there was oil washing about in it.

They set this down between the girl and the high table, and went away.

One of the seven Bellatae guided the red horse aside. They all drew back, and left the central space clear for the girl and the cauldron.

She would do it now.

Cristiano braced his body and his mind. The Magister had said she drew her impetus from emotion. The room thrummed with it, like the strings of some instrument before a storm. But she should have none from him. Not one jot.

He felt but did not see her golden eyes go over him. He was one among so many.

The Magister spoke. "Bring the fire, Beatifica."

Cristiano, within a wall of milky adamant that could not be cracked, waited.

It would come.

It came.

He *heard* it, *felt* it—felt nothing.

Heard them screaming, and felt the heat of fire, absolutely present. The rasp of the oil igniting with the sound of tearing cloth. Chairs and benches scraped. Dogs volleying and baying in fright, voiding themselves—the silky bundled sound of a woman falling and caught by servants—sparks singeing his own cloak—*the smell of burning—*

Cristiano blinked to clear his vision, and looked and saw the pot full now of fire—and the Ducem, his eyes open wide and lips parted, and little Arianna, the Duccessa, shrinking away.

A column of smitch and smolder flaring into the roof where the banners hung.

A glass goblet, rare, brought to impress, smashing.

Purple light.

Her hair, deep colored now as blood, fading.

Her white face that seemed also burning from

within, paling down to a human paleness that was almost ghostly.

She was bowing her head. Her shoulders drooped.

It cost her something to do this. He had never realized that before. Now she was tired. Shivering perhaps, he was not certain. But she kept firm, standing there.

Oh, not as a warrior must. From obedience, duty. She had been a slave. It had been whipped into her.

He had remained on guard. She had not penetrated the wall. But inside it now, for a second, he too felt stunned and drained. Into himself however, he also had beaten the strength to withstand his own weakness.

She and he, some long paces apart, stayed upright and in command. And Danielus, and the Bellatae, and the obviously fire-accustomed horse. While the feast chamber of Joffri gave way.

Cristiano glanced aside at the unnamed Council Brother. He was ranting, slavering, clutching his crucifix, which was of plain and modest iron. Sarco prayed, his eyes closed fast.

The Duccessa was fainting now, and her Ladies gathering her. What had this sight done to the child in her womb?

Joffri swung abruptly back. He glared, then laughed shortly.

"Magister Major, you are to blame for this havoc. Come on, let's go into another room. Bring her, this Maiden. Bring your Soldiers of God. Yes, yes, Brother Isaacus, you and your fellow Council Brother must come with us, of course.

The Ducem's guards were opening a way for them. Others led the red horse off into the courtyard. As it passed by the dogs now, scented with fire, they shied and barked. A young woman with black, waving hair artfully emerging below her headdress, ran to touch the horse with her fingers. Having done so, she turned, crying for happiness. And on the tables sprawled the remnants of the cloven swans.

"She is proof of God's love."

"Of the wiles of the Devil!"

Sarco once more put his hand on Isaacus' sleeve. "Hush, brother. You'll hurt your sore voice worse." And then, "What the Magister says he most truly believes, of that we may be assured."

Joffri put down his wine cup.

He stared at the Maiden Beatifica, who sat now in one of the carved chairs, her eyes lowered, her hands folded together on her right knee. She did not look wanton, nor unsuitable in her clothes. He did not fancy her, either, which, if he thought of it, surprised him. God must protect her from the lewd inspiration. God, Joffri knew, was clever.

They were in the Scarlet Room, one of the three halls which led from the feast chamber. The ceiling rose to its rafters, which were gilded. The walls were sheeted with hammered bronze, and marble. There was nothing red in the room, (except for the Maiden's hair, which looked any way far less red than it had done in the feast chamber.) The Scarlet Room took its title from the pageantry which was sometimes enacted there. The recognition of sons, and betrothals, when scarlet and crimson garments were worn.

Fra Danielus stood by the Maiden. His Bellatae were ranked behind him. Nine of them now. They watched with professional faces, war-priests. But their eyes were dazed, or sparkling. All but that one, the one called Cristiano. His eyes were like silver discs found on the ice.

Danielus had lost none of his composure, and he was saying not much. He had told them God had sent them Beatifica. She was motivated by Heaven. In the conflict which the City must face, she would give courage in her turn. He did not say, it went by implication alone, the infidel would be afraid, if they heard stories of her.

Isaacus roared, spitting froth, "She must be questioned."

"So she has been," Sarco said.

Joffri said, urbanely, "Let *me* ask her something."

He thought Isaacus, (it had seemed essential to learn that one's name) would interrupt again. No. He only held up his cross, high in one hand.

Danielus said, "Beatifica, look up. There is the Ducem. Answer him."

Beatifica looked at Joffri.

What eyes she had. Were they gold?

"Tell, me, Beatifica, tell me if you're able, if you think God sent you this . . . gift?"

"What gift?" she asked. She did not say 'My lord'. However, her tone was gentle, inquiring, as if she wished to please—or comfort him.

"Your fire-bringing."

"My mother," said Beatifica, "showed me."

"Yes, the monster claims her mother taught her to do it, after the woman had died. A witch—a witch, what else.'

Joffri risked a small indiscretion. "Be quiet, Brother Isaacus, if you can. The Council of the Lamb has my reverence, but you are only one of its membership. I am Ducem, and you are very rude."

Did Danielus smile? Invisibly?

Joffri said, "If your mother taught you, Maiden, how did *she* learn? From a demon?"

"She told me nothing of demons. It was angels that she saw."

"Angels—"

"An account of that was sent you, Ducem," said Sarco.

"Yes but—never until this moment did I—" Joffri stopped. He said, "Other than angels, what have you seen?"

Beatifica did smile. She was pleased to speak of herself. In her previous life no one had been interested.

"I only saw the angels once. But also I saw the serpent in the orchard."

Now a great quiet filled the room.

Many had not learned of Beatifica's dreams.

"She saw the Serpent," grated out Isaacus. "Bear witness, Brother Sarco. You heard as well as I. The *Serpent*."

Beatifica said, "Magister," (him she gave a title) "do I tell them of it?"

Danielus said, "I believe you must."

"Then, I saw it in an apple tree. But the fruits of the tree were gold and silver, like the sun and the moon." From speaking the Latin, from talking so much, her voice had changed now utterly. It was a lovely voice, mild but of great clarity. It had scarcely any gender, not feminine—but not masculine in any way. "The snake came down the tree to me. I thought it was a cat—but it hadn't legs, or ears, so it was a snake. It stared in my face with eyes that were profound." (She had learned this word, found it apt, used it aptly.) "But I never picked the fruit. They would have burned my hands. I knew not to. Before the snake could speak to me, I was woken."

In the void, it was Jian who spoke, unable to prevent himself. "Eva, the first woman, heeded the Serpent, plucked the apple, and damned the world with her sin. This Maiden could not—*would not*. And God Himself woke her from her trance."

Isaacus, in his fury, cast down his iron cross on the floor. It rang.

"She is a *seducer* sent by *Hell*. This fire she brings comes from the Pit. Haven't I heard tales that she burns men alive?" He moved fast and ungainly, snatching a lit candle from its spike. "*This* is the natural fire of this world, and what she brings is filth from the guts of the Fiend, a sulfurous belch." Isaacus raised the candle and croaked, in his voice of pebbles, a blessing over it. "Now it is God's fire. Do we doubt *God's* fire is stronger than the flames of Hell?"

He went rolling towards the girl, like some boat cut loose on a lagoon. She gazed up at him, not moving. Changed as she had, still she was the slave.

Jian moved. With a vast thrust, the black priest shoved him away. Jian had not thought he would need much strength, but Isaacus was brimmed by his virtue.

Isaacus seized up the girl's right hand by the wrist.

"With *this* she calls her dirty genius. With *this* I *punish* her—"

Cristiano saw her start, flinch. Only a little. But she was used to ill-treatment and wounding.

Isaacus dropped her hand.

He waved the candle, victorious.

"She's flammable despite the Satanic influence. She *burns*."

Cristiano sprang around the chair. It was Jian, staggering still, who somehow caught him back. Danielus who reined him in.

"*Wait*."

Leaning to the girl, the Magister lifted her hand

and looked at it. Tenderly, perhaps. As a father might.

Then he said, "Get up, Beatifica."

When she did so—her face showing nothing, only her eyes, as if bruised—he raised her right hand in his own, and showed them all.

"You blessed your candle, Brother Isaacus, and called on God."

"You heard me, *Magister*."

"Then God has answered you. And everyone of us."

On her hand, at her palm's center, a red and awful, weeping mark.

"Where else," said Fra Danielus, "have we seen this sign?"

Joffri did not know whether to shout with laughter or hide his eyes. Not one of them was unfamiliar with the cross, the icon of Sacrifice upon it. Nor the holy pictures of its aftermath. How could they be in doubt? The insane Isaacus, seeking to reveal her as devilish, had scorched her hand. With the divine stigmata granted only to saints, the bleeding scar of the nail which had pierced the palm of Christ.

4

Sunset diminished on the sea. They had come far, and had further to go. As darkness bloomed, it gathered the ships, and formed them into one vast single thing, a cloud of wood and sails.

Those that could had answered the cry to pray.

God is great. There is no god save God. Hasten then to greet Him, hasten that His power make you rich in Him, richer than a thousand golden mantles. There is no god save only God.

Suley-Masroor, Master of the *Quarter-Moon*, came from the trance of prayer. He got up from the deck. The warmth of the day was softly going with the light. The sea was very calm. The oars were at rest.

On every vessel now, the lanterns were lighting high up in the fore-towers, yellow eyes blinking to each other. Sails furled in, described two masts or three. The *Quarter-Moon* had three, and the wind-catcher at his stern. He was male, the ship, like all the ships of Jurneia and Candisi, for it was the sea which was female, unpredictable, and lovely.

The Master walked forward to the tower. He climbed the ladder, and the watch stood aside for him.

"It's good to pray," said the watchman.

"Yes, always good. For those moments we become again as God would have us, and are without sorrow."

But after prayer, he thought, the world came back, and this sailing on to make a war.

As if he read the Master's brain, the watchman said, "They are deserving of wrath, our enemies. They cheat us for our silk and spice. They worship a parody of the Most High. A war of trade, but also holy."

"Have the three lost ships returned?"

"No, Master. There's no sign of them. The storm was bad."

"May those men be found, or ascend to Paradise," said Suley-Masroor.

They had lost five vessels in all since setting out. Four in the sudden spring gales, and one which had simply gone down, mysteriously, perhaps previously holed by spies. (They had caught a lot of spies, in Jurneia, prior to embarkation.) With the lost vessels, the fleet now totaled eight hundred and twenty-seven ships. It seemed the Lagoon City of Venarh had almost half that number again, over one thousand. And, as a last spy had confirmed, also ballistas and cannon.

Suley-Masroor remembered joking with his blind old father-in-law, telling the old man the Venarhans had only four hundred vessels. (He would gossip, when Suley was gone, and make his daughter, Suley's wife, afraid. Her three brothers were already with the fleet. It was sometimes best to dissemble.)

"I'll watch. Go down for your food."

Suley-Masroor stood in the fore-tower of the *Quarter-Moon*, staring out at the shining abyss of sea and night. Behind him, like a zircon, the evening star was rising up, Aspiroz, that the infidels of the west named Hesper, or Venus—another name they gave, so he understood, to their City.

He was reluctantly thinking about the dream he had had. Twice it had come to him. If it came again tonight, only then, would he permit himself to consult his sacred talisman. But it was strange, the dream.

In the dream, Suley-Masroor was hunting in the waste, alone but for his horse. The land was spare and dun, as he had often seen it, but then among some boulders a water-spout spangled. As he approached, he saw a yellowish fox, which sat still as the stones. Normally such a creature, of which there were several in the desert, would sprint away. But no, It did not shift itself. Even in the dream, he thought this odd, and hesitated, although the sight of the water filled him with thirst.

Then the fox got up, and trotting to the outlet, drank. But no sooner did the tongue of the fox touch it, than the waterfall changed. Suley-Masroor cried out in horror as spurts of steam and fire burst from the rocks in place of water.

Here, he woke. On both occasions at this instant.

The Chosen of God had, in the dawn of history, struck mountains to produce streams of water. This mocking mimicry of that act lodged like a burning shadow in the Master's mind. What did it mean? Was it only an inevitable anxiety—or some premonition sent to warn?

Cristiano dreamed of the Vigil.

He kneeled, not in the Soldiers' chapel, however, but in some open place of the Primo, which he did not recognize. It had a floor of glass, black glass. Pillars of gold, dull and ancient, rose to the dome, which was luminous and high, sounding with night winds, and with moonlit clouds that curiously passed through it, in and out.

He saw a window. The Virgin was depicted there.

As he kneeled below, slowly transcending his body's pain, as if dragging himself up a steep stair to the bell-tower of his own skull, he became aware that the hair of the Virgin was like copper. It was this, shaded by night, which had seemed to form her damson mantle.

Dreaming, Cristiano knew shame. But why?

More than the hurt of his body, he ached for God. But God did not arrive.

Instead, gradually, Cristiano grew conscious of other Bellatae, kneeling as he did before the window. Jian was to his left, and just at his back, Aretzo. Behind these he now saw, (leaving his body, drifting above them) the ranks of the Upper Echelon, and behind these, the lower militia of God. There were two Magisters Major present also, but not the third, not Danielus.

This concerned Cristiano, and he had a sense of searching for his own Magister, which kept him disembodied, moving on and on. The Basilica was filled, end to end; that in spite of being larger than it was. The priesthood was there, the lay brothers too, almost all the hierarchy of the Church. And beyond them, others knelt, men in mail like the Bellatae, faces locked in casques, their drawn swords held between hands in gloves of steel. Banners hung among them, leaning a little, or straight as the pillars. Emblems of the Lion and the Child, of the Lion and Star, of the Boar and the Bear and the Lynx—Ve Nera's Crusader banners from two centuries before. They were, these men, the first Knights of God. The warriors of the Suvio, the first cry to Battle, which had been uttered at the water's edge, when the Laguna Fulvia was choked with craft, and the sea, beyond the sand-bars, with high-sailed cogs bound for the Holy Land.

In the farthest reaches of the elongated Basilica, last of all, the people of the City stood humbly. They were very still, as if altered to carvings of wood. None of the children made a noise. The men were serious and the women devout. They wore the fashions of earlier times and of current time. He could not be sure of all their eras. But he noted a Roman matron, wrapped in her draperies, and beside her a broad-chested, bow-legged man in the armor of antiquity.

These were not phantoms. Nor quite immobile. Their eyes were living and bright.

At the Primo's end, in the dream, the doors were shut fast. It was here he turned, and looking back, viewed the colossal gathering, and himself, somehow, at their head, with Jian by him. And the Madonna Window, that too, which was like a slender rosy flame. Before it had been raised the secret icon of the Madonna Standard, kept close in the Sanctum, and shown only in extremity. He had never seen it. Now it was allowed him.

His sense of disquiet had left him.

Nothing was wrong, or inappropriate.

And in the upper air, where the clouds were, he saw the white light of God beginning, and was drawn up into it, and knew nothing else.

Beatifica dreamed a dream she would not remember.

She dreamed the angel had come back for her. He bore her up and flew with her across the sky.

She heard the vast beats of his wings, which were like the drumming of a heart.

Below, the world stretched out. Night was there, and lamps and other specks of light were being born, as stars were, in the higher sky. The sea and the lagoons seemed like salvers of silver, and the Silvian Marsh, and all the canals and channels, like a running of silver threads. Now and then, she saw their reflection on the waters, two flying beings upheld by the wide, beating wings.

In the East, on the sea, the moon was up.

They flew on, out towards the ocean.

She knew that soon the City would be left far behind and all the land. She did not mind it. She trusted her angel. For the very first, since she had been an infant with her mother, she was able to render the *obedience* of trust, which had nothing to do with fear, self-negation, or need. It was easy for her to let go, for there had never been anything to cling to. But now, in the clasp of the gray-eyed angel, she was free. In slavery, free. The earth forgotten, without any good-bye.

5

Caught in the tangle of pomegranate trees, new buds beamed a juicy red. The eels would dine well, this year. If the world went on.

The boatman optimistically sang about approaching summer. It was not a bawdy song. Besides, he had rowed Danielus before, and knew he would not be upbraided. Only when they reached the Isle of Eels did he say, "Bless me, Fra Magister. I can do with it. They say the Jurneians will be here inside three days."

"Not nearly so soon. You have time to get away."

"I? There's my wife and kits, my old dad, mumma, sisters, too, five of them, the youngest only twelve. Where are we to go?"

"Anywhere to safety, perhaps."

"You think it'll come to it."

"I think it may. Entreat God. Take this."

"Oh—Fra—that's generous. God grant you joy."

No one in the garden. (Veronichi had written she was too ill to venture out. Others saw the letter. None had been astounded he must come here, to reassure this querulous, nagging relative.)

Late afternoon. It was warm. Bees had found the waking fruit trees and the beds of flowers. From the highest point, by the house, he looked out over Aquila to the church of Maria Maka Selena. Today, its individual island stood to the waist in water. A riddle, this church. In some years the tides discarded it. Magically it appeared to rise up from the mud. Now it had sunk down. It was scales, like the balance of life.

The girl let him in at the door, and Danielus walked up a narrow stair to the parlor above.

"So you're here."

"As you see, Veronichi. How could I not come to you, after that piteous letter?"

"I had that in mind."

"I know it. Welcome me, then."

It was a small room, off which there led another

larger chamber, the door curtained by Eastern silk.

A table had been draped, and laid with platters of silver-gilt.

"Are yon hungry, my darling?" Veronichi asked, approaching him.

"Yes. But for what?"

"Whatever you wish. Several dishes have been prepared."

"I see you've put out the gold salt-cellars."

"And the glass cups, look. What else have you missed?"

"Little."

Her raven pelt of hair was down, silken as the curtain—like this, she looked quite wonderful. She had traced dark paint around her eyes, and a pomegranate salve on her lips. She was naked. Smooth from pumice, and almost hairless from a clever razor. Scented like a church and a garden, cream, with a core of black feathers and pomegranate bud.

She wound her arms about his neck.

"And here we are . . ."

As he kissed the delicious fruit of her mouth, she leaped lightly against him. A snake, she wound his body with her slim white legs.

"I am the first of the dishes?"

"Always. And the last."

"Perhaps not tonight."

There were no rushes on her floor. She had heaped carpets there, from Candisi. She lay back on them, and thrusting away the hindrance of the magenta robe, he possessed her.

There was hardly any play—a sliding of hands on skin, appetite of mouths. She flew swiftly through the gate, and he followed her. They were in a great rush. It had been too extended a wait.

After a few minutes, she left him, and returned with the precious goblets, filled to the brim.

"You seem tired, my love. Shouldn't I have called you here? I was lonely without you. But I can be patient as a spider—"

"Other things tire me, Venus, not you."

"If you call me that, am I the City or the goddess?"

"Let me decide. The goddess was wise in the sexual arts, I believe . . ."

More slow now. He watched her body unfolding like a lily, opening to infinitude, melting in exquisite death.

"Shall we do this when we're old?"

Of course. I shall need some machinery then, naturally, to support my aged limbs."

"I doubt that."

They walked into the larger room. A great tub of water had been lined with linen drapes. They got in together. The temperature was warm, the surface afloat with asphodel. Afterwards they put on each a loose white robe of Eastern style.

When they went back, the table had been filled up by food. She sent the server away, and saw to it herself. It was a meatless day, but they ate flesh, both of them, (all the house would.) Braised hare, and a roasted goose, pigs' livers with a janchia of garlic and ginger, also a dish of carp and one of spear-fish. She fed him sweetmeats, candied roses, quinces in honey.

"Do you want to sleep now? The bed is cool."

"Not yet."

"Soon you must. I have plans for your night."

"Indeed."

He took her hand, looking far away. She attended him, stilly. She had learned early on how to wait, and was adroit.

"Veronichi, sweetheart, I'd like best, tomorrow, if you would pack up your treasures and your household. Then a boat will come to take you away."

"If you insist on it, I will. I don't want to, Danielo."

"The Ducem is assembling the bulk of his fleet at the Island of Torchara. They'll be ready in five days. Meanwhile the ships of Jurneia are almost here. The likelihood is a meeting at Ciojha. But this may not be any solution. If they are unstopped and come on, we should see the Jurneians before the month is out. Picture it. They'll crowd the sea. Break the sea walls, and employ rollers and slaves to get across the bar into the deeper parts of the lagoons. They have cannon. You know all this. And that they think all Christians, especially Christian merchant cities, minions of the Devil. They will be raging from the fight, desperate from the journey, and merciless."

"Yes. They're like the Jews in that. Why else have Christians shut my people in ghettos, save as a man must imprison a tiger. They pull our teeth in case we rip them apart."

He stared, then roared with laughter, drawing her to him. "In God's name, dearest Venus, mankind's decisions are nearly always wrong. Why should they have *that* right?"

She kissed him. She said, "Danielo, may I speak to you?"

"You know quite well you may."

"Of matters where I'm ignorant—where I only *feel*."

"Veronichi, to me you can say anything. As to your ignorance, you read every day in books from the greatest minds the world has seen. It's your knowledge that knows to be circumspect, not your lack."

She murmured, "Nothing to excess."

"Nothing to excess, beloved, *but* excess."

"Then listen to me, Daniel. Can you give this up? I mean, what you've made your reason and your goal."

"You never said that to me before."

"Never. But now—"

"Now more than ever in the past, I say no. No, I must stay true to it. Remember what I told you, of my youth."

You were a boy—"

"And now a man. Nor an old man, yet."

She said, "Would you live to be one?"

He sighed. He put her back, and stroked her hair.

"Veronichi my Venus, when I was young . . . I saw two great truths. The truth of the teaching of the Christ, and the lie to which it had been corrupted, into mistranslation, stupidity, and evil. He told us we should live as the flowers live, glorying in delight, hurting no other, loving God and everything that is God's, which means also humanity, and the earth. Christ told us to have no fear of death and also no fear of life. If God had hated life so much, He would never have made it. Having learned these precepts, I saw the churches and their laws and lessons. That man must detest and obeise himself, crawling in the dirt as a worm, damned by a vast sin committed even before his birth. That he must loathe his natural inclinations, and go in dread and avoidance of every pleasing thing—good food, long sleep, the beauty of a woman, of a man, and the divine gift of lust, without which the human race must have ended long ago."

"Danielo—"

"So then, being forced to enter this bastion of lies, I came to think that, only by dwelling within the iron tower, I might secretly break open some windows in it."

"Yes."

"There's little enough I can do, Veronichi. But where I can, I do, I will, I must. Today," he said, "as I came from the Basilica, I saw the seventeen new bird-cages, as they sportively call them, which have been hung out there from the Angel Tower."

"Oh, God."

"Oh God indeed, my love. In those traps of torture, the Council of the Lamb, ever diligent to remind Ve Nera she must cower, has thrown thirteen men and four women. They are shrieking even now, and will do so until they can shriek no more. And below, the populace, trained like vicious dogs, throws sharp stones at them, and rotten eggs. It came to me long ago, and I think it now, that to tell men they are mired in transgression, and will only escape their filth by much suffering and denial, is to make monsters. There will be some strong enough—hard enough, like steel—who can beat and break out of themselves all natural weakness—and with it perhaps all love of life. But most will fail. They haven't the colossal strength the saints have had. And then, failing, what is there left but to become the beast the priests have shown them in the mirror? It's these subhuman things I saw, both in the torture cages—and jeering below. I see them everywhere. This is what the Church has made of men. And it is all—the misery, and even a lingering death—*to save their souls*. Today—today I heard the one called Isaacus, promise that if Ve Nera doesn't mend her sinful ways, we shall have burnings next. Yes, the burning alive of witches and other heretics, in the old Roman amphitheater in the Silvian Marshes. To demonstrate the virtue of this, he reminded us all in his letter, that it had been done there at the time of the Crusades. Am I being too canny if I say, I think he wants this because of the girl who can bring fire, to be even with me? It was plain enough he liked to scorch her. Though she's beyond him, he saw he would enjoy the sport. And these are the men of God, His lawgivers and examples—Veronichi, can't you see, my love, there must be also one or two like myself? Oh, simply for the sake of balance."

"There are tears in your eyes."

"I hide nothing from you. I must hide it from every other."

"And won't God condemn us, Daniel, for our own condition? That we lie together, brother and sister."

"You speak of the laws of men, made to control other men. God condemns those that do harm, Veronichi, not those that love."

She let her face rest against his face. She breathed his breath slowly.

"I won't argue, my lord. I'll do whatever you decree. Only—if you remain here, don't send me away."

"If not, you must still leave this house. They might well come to it, the Jurneians. These men we must call infidels—and who call us the same—in war, we'll *be* the same, no doubt. God has a million names and ten million guises. Man only a few. It's a shabby name, a dirty guise, Veronichi, when angry or afraid."

"Where must I go?"

"To the sister-house at Santa La'Lacrima, then. It's fortified like a castle, and has a storehouse I've seen is filled. I'm sorry. You won't be able to live as you do here, or might elsewhere."

"I'm content. The woman who witnessed your little saint is there, isn't she."

"Luchita. Yes."

"And you have great hopes of the little saint."

"Yes. The wall built by men between themselves and God—she has rent a tiny hole in it."

"She's your pawn, Danielo."

"The means to make another window. God help me to do it."

"And is Luchita also part of your plan? She will be. You waste very little. And besides, she is the sister of your Cristiano." Veronichi slipped from him, stood up, and held out both her hands. "Come and sleep now."

"Perhaps I will."

In the other room, the bath had been cleared. Behind its curtains, the bed was wide, with a mattress of down. He lay back on the pillows. As he did so, with a sudden glimpse of desolation, Veronichi thought she saw how he might look, near death. He was more than a decade her senior. It was likely she would have to behold him, one day, die. But not yet, sweet God. Not yet.

"Don't look sad, Veronichi. You've got your way."

"I'm not sad, my darling, but plotting. Tell me truly, do you love your white-haired knight more than me?"

"Cristiano? Perhaps almost as much. He'll never know. He would drop dead on the spot where I told him. How could I work that on him? But I gain great pleasure, both sensual and possibly pious, from watching him. Man in the image of the Most High. There it is."

The light was fading from the window.

She sat by the bed until he slept, then stole away, her robe whispering.

In another room, a young man got up at once. He had white-blond hair, and was of great physical beauty. He had a look of Cristiano certainly, and being only nineteen, a younger Cristiano, more flexible, less stern.

"You're ready?"

"Yes, lady. And—eager."

"He would refuse you if you weren't. Wait for an hour. Then admit yourself to the bed. He'll sleep a while. Let him find you when he wakes. Love one another well."

When the young man had gone, she sat down to comb her hair. There was no jealousy in her heart. Whatever would do her lover good, did good to her. And he would not send her away from the City. The Jurneians had been nothing to her terror of their parting.

Sister Purita waited quietly by the Domina, as church servants carried yet three more chests up the sister-house stair.

So many possessions for with this visiting lady. And yet, she was said to be frugal and devout.

Of course, there would be things of her brother's, the Fra's, kept in the island house, and now needing to be made safe. The library had already been brought; it had taken all morning to go up.

Veronichi was to have three of the guest cells. They must already be choked and impassable.

An ugly woman, though quite young. Of course she had never borne a child. Child-bearing aged women. It was a fact, she dressed modestly and unbecomingly.

The Domina sat in her chair, her hand on her walking stick. Now she motioned for the other nun, Permaria, to give her her medicinal tincture. (In the outer world, the fleet was gathering. How far off it seemed, here, how slight.)

"Purita," said the Domina, "it is you, there, Purita?"

"Yes, holy Mother." (This was the second time she had asked.)

"Purita, I should like you to read the lesson, as we dine."

"*I*?" Purita was appalled. The lessons read at meals

were transcribed from the Latin, to benefit the less able nuns. Even so—"My reading's poor, Mother, despite the help I've had—"

"Your Latin does indeed need work, but as you know that will not impede you in this. And you know the text, Purita. You've heard it often now. I'll go through the words with you. Remember, you may interpret, where you understand. God sometimes inspires us to do this."

Purita glanced at the other nun, who might have been a statue.

The old woman was saying Purita might *invent* the lesson, where she could not decipher it?

"I like you to read, you've read for me," said the old Domina. "You have a clear yet friendly voice, and the accent of the City."

"I'm common, Mother."

"That's not what I said, Purita. Besides, the rose is common in summer. Do we like it less for that?"

She could be crisp, when she wanted. Luchita-Purita wondered sometimes if the Domina acted out her occasional feebleness, her vaguenesses of mind, to trick them all. But definitely her physical strength was failing. They were both needed now, she and Permaria, to help the Mother to her cell.

But then she sat in her room, in the chair, like a cheerful, fat grasshopper, smiling. She loved her room, with its bare white walls lit by the sun, her wide window that looked on the well-stocked garden. You saw her filmy eyes roam over every object, the plain cross and the jeweled one, the hand-high Virgin with white flowers in a vase, the dark religious books, her velvet cushion for kneeling. She liked her walking stick too, which had carved on its top the head of a bird, much polished by use—and caresses. In repose she cuddled the stick like a toy, and now and then spoke to it, apologizing for her weight and her need, telling it, (oddly) that it reminded her of the boundless strength of Christ, who was the walking stick for every frail soul.

Permaria brought the Domina the huge Bible, placing it open at the lesson, where the transcription lay ready.

"Come here, and read it now, Purita."

Purita read the lesson stumbling, flushed with anxiety.

"There. You have it all."

"I stammer, Mother, when I'm nervous."

"That's pride, Purita. Did you know that?" Purita gaped. "In your case, it is. You know you can do well and expect so much of yourself, that you become afraid. Sister Gratzilia stutters, yet she reads. God won't object."

Unwillingly, Purita bent her head, trying to learn the lesson off by heart in the hour before the Solus and the afternoon dinner.

"Permaria, go if you will and fetch me some water. I'm very dry."

Purita, struggling with the words, heard the other nun go out.

Birds twittered in the garden. A ray of sudden sun found the hub of the jeweled cross. Crimson burst from it like fire.

It was harder now to remember the miracle which had brought her here. Had it happened? Surely it had.

"Sister Purita," said the Domina. Her voice was so soft, and like parchment. Startled, Purita looked up. "Listen, Purita. I shan't live many more days. God warned me in a dream. I'm not fearful. His life is lovelier than even this loveliness, which is only its shadow-image. And for all my lapses, I know I shall find mercy. In my heart I think that all men do, at last."

Purita stood, her hands on the Bible.

The Domina said, "I've told them, I want you by me. You must stay near. When the time comes, I have something to say to you."

"I—"

"You. You think they will be jealous? Perhaps. But only a few. And I've made provision. You have no knowledge, have you, Purita, of what you are."

"A sinner."

"Now, that *is* common, for so are we all. The Apostles that Christ chose were common men. They spoke with the accent of the land, some caught fish, they wandered about like beggars. They were his witnesses. And after Christ, his saints too are witnessed. You are the first pure witness to Beatifica, who brought fire from Heaven. The Magister Major has advised me."

Purita stood with her mouth open. She closed it. She said, "What are you telling me, Mother?"

"You're not a fool. You've seen the duties I have been giving you, and so have others. They see too that you're careful, and effacing of self. Above all, practical."

The door opened, and Permaria entered with a pitcher of water.

Purita's heart bounded inside her, blurring her sight, so the words of the lesson now became jumbled and illegible. *I'm willful, too*. They had forgotten or not known that, this Mother of nuns, this Father of priests, Danielus.

She stopped trying to read. She would *interpret* the passage instead. Let them see how they liked that. In such a mood she had several times committed adultery, once met her outcast daughter and given her money, fed the homeless at the inn door, *resented* her brother. The mood of rebellion. Or was it only liberty? As when, rebelling and at liberty, she became a nun?

6

> 'You will know, since I gave your order my permission—a matter of form, since the Ducem had already desired it—that I recognize your credentials, and your willingness to fight, for the City, and for God. This of you all, jointly and as individuals. But, Cristiano, as I have said to others of your brotherhood, be very certain you are essential there, and not needed here. The Ducem, as you see, is dispatching three hundred ships at last. His aquean army numbers at least six thousand men. Though Jurneia's fleet is larger—and here, we are aware, accounting varies—she packs less men on board each ship. She has perhaps a third again our numbers. Conversely, if the fight is lost at Ciojha, Ve Nera herself must be defended, from the land's edge.
>
> 'My gist, Cristiano, is that, while you wait on Torchara, you might think a second time. Many of the Upper Echelon I have persuaded in this. If you rebut my judgment I will, say no more. Christ be with you. Fight well.'

The returning letter from Torchara was, at core, brief.

> 'I have said, Magister, I cannot debate with you. I shall not attempt it. God be with us at Ciojha.'

It was a glorious summer noon. Torchara, an island of shipyards, showed her greenery high up on her inner hill. From her quays Ve Nera was visible in detail across

Fulvia, with the Laguna Aquila, and the Silvian Marshes held, as some poet had said, in her other arms. Out from Silvia on the Isle of the Dead, no smoke went up. They had left the fires unlit. Instead a hundred bells might be heard ringing clear as glass across the water.

Birds fluttered about Torchara, and the somber gulls circled and recircled the forest of masts.

They were white-sailed, Ve Nera's ships, almost every sheet crossed in Crusader red, and every greatest sail painted, in at least seventy different forms, with the old symbol of the City, the figure of a veiled woman crowned by a star. She had been Venus, once. Now they named her *Maria Stella Maris*—Maria, Star of the Sea. The vessels wore the Ducem's colors in their flags, and the colors of other lesser lords: plum and saffron, orange, black and gold.

Beautiful. The heart lifted at the sight.

What could stand against it, this perfect entity of wood, canvas and iron, flesh and bone and steel.

Two days to Ciojha. Propulsion from the slaves' rowing in the under-deck, a light wind to be discovered, perhaps, when on the open sea.

Only one Magister Major, not Danielus, had come to bless them, but nine members of the Council of the Lamb were there, black crows beside the magenta of the Primo's higher priests.

Boys were singing praise to God the Deliverer, their voices flung aloft and silencing even the predatory gulls.

Drawing out from land.

Three hundred shining ropes that slipped away. The water spreading, three thousand shining ropes that pulled them on.

Cristiano looked upward, his heart singing like the children on the quay, innocent, savage.

A solitary flotilla of clouds, peach-yellow from the sun, sailed above them, accompanying them.

"It might be some angelic fleet up there," Aretzo murmured, "some sign from Heaven. Like the Maiden's angels—"

Others had noticed. Gazed and pointed.

A war song rose sturdily from the decks, as the other voices faded on the shore.

The fleet of Heaven moved away, melting now into the east.

In the morning, after the easy rocking of night, a frisky wind blew up. The sails bellied out. The slaves were rested at the oars, and fed with meat and wine.

Ve Nera was merciful. She did not shackle her rowers in a fight. If a ship was stoven in, they could take their chance with the crew and soldiers.

Cristiano ate meat, like the slaves. Before a battle you did not fast. He drank the wine. Aretzo fretted. "We go like snails. It will be three days at this pace."

"So eager to sink your teeth in an infidel throat," another mocked him.

Jian was not there. He had heeded Fra Danielus and stayed behind. Among the ships there were some hundreds of the Bellatae Christi, distributed mostly in squadrons between five to twenty. On this ship they numbered ten, but all of the Upper Echelon. No one, apart from Cristiano, had received a letter from the Magister Major. No doubt, he had expected Cristiano to persuade others.

The sea was slightly choppy, dragon green in the shadow of the fleet, crushed glass under the sun.

There were a few cannon, purchased from other places. One straddled the fore-castle, an iron vegetable hooped in by iron rings. They were unpredictable furniture, liable to break loose. When fired, they could knock the cannoneer off his feet and slough his eyebrows. Or otherwise blow up and kill him. Cristiano had seen all this in previous actions, when Ve Nera's troops had fought with or by fellow cities.

Cristiano, glancing, noticed Aretzo had put on the new favor, pinned beside the Bellatae badge of the Lion and Child. This was only a piece of scarlet cloth. Many of them had taken to wearing it. He knew, though none of them spoke of it, the cloth represented the Maiden Beatifica's fire.

Some of the soldiers were now seasick.

Over the slap of waves, noises of vomiting and impatient nervousness, dinned the war-song. Or he heard the cannon rattling about in its ties, bound as the human slaves were not.

This ship was named *Virgo Maria*.

The white light of God had failed him. The red glare of war would not. (Hate always more vital than love?)

The red light did not fail. Nor was the voyage quite two days.

On the following morning, soon after sunrise, they saw Ciojha spread before them, perhaps two miles away, like a great whale sunning itself in the aftermath of dawn.

Before the whale, the fleet of Jurneia spread—and spread. And spread.

Like dishes laid for a feast, or the dusky waterlilies smothering some pool.

Sail upon sail, wooden shell on shell.

The sky was pale, losing the brilliance of sunrise.

Men cried out, and fell dumb.

Ve Nera stood on her decks, looking at the flowers of Jurneia.

The priests came quickly now through the Christian ships, shriving men. Warriors knelt, stuffing the Host even down sea-queasy throats. The Blood of Christ was gulped.

"How many ships, in God's name?" Aretzo, angry, priming himself.

"The Magister gave eight hundred as the last count."

"More. Over a thousand. *Look* at them."

"Perhaps."

"I hate a seafight," said one of the *Virgo Maria*'s other eight Bellatae. "I need to get close. Close as a lover to his leman, and sheath in my hot sword."

His coarseness was not rebuffed. Some of them chuckled.

Cristiano, his eyed fixed on the Jurneians, felt he rushed towards them through the air. His blood tingled. His face was to him like metal, his entire body, impermeable. Yet he was light. He crossed himself .stiffly, and the red blaze began to wake behind his eyes.

The ship groaned as her slaves rowed.

He felt the straining strokes, although his feet did not seem in contact with the deck. He himself, by his will, powered the ship onward. He and all these men, with whom, now, he was one.

The atmosphere bristled, glowed. From everywhere came the yells and growls of an army, readying itself, bracing itself.

When the first Jurneian cannon spoke to them, they were less than a quarter mile off.

A combusting scatter, like flashing gems—

The roar and hiss of approach.

It was often called *flying fire*.

It flew.

But the range was too great. The Christians saw the Jurneian infidel shot go down into the sea, with gargantuan splashes, sizzlings. Applauded and jibed.

On the *Virgo Maria*, the alien cannon poked its snout forwards. Men swarmed there. Along the line of Christian ships, one or two of the iron monsters had answered too quickly. The boom came of detonations, black fume, men shouting. And this shot too falling short.

But the fleets glided nearer to each other. Now Cristiano, partly out of his body, judged which vessel they would first come to grips with. They were slender craft, this one he had spotted with sails half looped in for the fray. She had Jurneia's picture writing on the side, curlicues and dabs—her name. No, *his* name. Their ships were male.

He noted fresh scurrying about their artillery. Around him, soldiers swore. Cristiano merely waited.

From the forward ship he watched, and from a hundred others, the cannon blast exploded now in a tempest. At almost the same moment, Ve Nera's armed ships replied.

The world reeled. Cristiano saw the great mast of the opposing vessel he had idly chosen, split cleanly. It cracked and tumbled in a billow of broken sheets, holing the deck as it went down. Splinters sprayed like rain; screaming came in another tongue.

But to either side of *Virgo Maria* the Christian ships had also been struck. Through one erupted a mighty water-spout like a dragon, venting. Others were at once on fire. All that beauty spoiled. Figures springing in the boiling sea.

The shots had missed *Virgo Maria*. Through a wall

of upsurge and flames, in sudden spark-lit darkness, she closed with a Jurneian vessel—not after all the one Cristiano had selected. That one was listing, going down.

Near enough now to see these enemies—

Through darkness, dark faces they had wrapped about with cloth, as women might. Bearded nuns—Eyes that glittered, white beast teeth—nothing familiar, nothing human.

The sword in his hand was like lightning. Cristiano raised it. It became alive. Eye to eye with them, their animal faces to his mechanical face of metal—nothing human *anywhere*.

The Soldier of God flexed. Marvelous, glorious, the wine red—

The red wine became himself. He stretched now to fill the world, and heard himself bellow far away. Head touching sky. Heart and lungs of sounding brass. The ecstasy sharp as any other sharpest joy, the battle-wrath.

The sides of the two ships bumped, then ground together.

Cannon barked. Another missile tore by above and this time clipped *Virgo Maria*'s topmost mast. A section of wood crashed behind Cristiano as he leaped, oblivious, over the bows.

God—I am Your slave—Nothing save You.

Sword was arm, arm sword. Body unbreachable shield.

He hacked and lunged. No one could come at him. A grinning man of metal, teeth bared—the machine of Heaven.

His voice thundering, *Ve Nera of God!*

God's holy war. They would win. They were unstoppable.

He smashed a man's jaw, treading over him, and cut two others free of life.

On all sides, the holy army, the slick of steel, blood bursting like a poppy.

Ve Nera of God—

(The third ship he had leapt to? The tenth?)

Miles below the stink of gall and offal, blood and excrement, the tinder smell of the ballistas and their iron cooking.

Jumping now across another rail. Ocean irrelevantly glimpsed and gone. Sword and arm, hack and lunge. Roil of brass and red.

A face—quite young—a handsome boy with honey skin and fawn's eyes black as jet, yet with a silver rim—sometimes these momentary images caught in the red net—then vanished—dead of Cristiano's war sword, and that other man-beast, knifed under the chin, both trampled underfoot.

This ship too was going down. (The fifth he had leapt from? The seventh?)

Aretzo punching at Cristiano, dragging him—"Come this way. Jump. She'll pull us under as she goes—"

"He, Aretzo." Lucid a moment, inappropriately lucid for Aretzo, who did not understand.

A scramble, up over the side—help forthcoming—which ship this one? Oh, a Christian vessel—blood-red darkness, heavy, and settling.

Cristiano shuddered.

"Drink this."

He drank the water mixed with wine. It tasted of soot.

This ship lacked any cannon. One mast was gone, chopped like a tree. The sails like wrung-washing on the deck. Men lying weeping, holding in their guts . . . He was coming up from the redness. Movement. Rowers working at the oars.

"What?" he said.

The ship's master, a third of his face a mask of blood: "We're standing off, Bellatoro."

"Yes," he said. Then, "We have won."

The master of the ship that was not the *Virgo Maria*, spat. "No, Bellatoro. Look, can't you see?"

"He's battle-crazed yet," said Aretzo. He sounded sulky. Cristiano saw abruptly that Aretzo had somehow mislaid his left arm. Which was bizarre—it could not have occurred.

Aretzo, losing consciousness, sank back against the washing-sails, coloring them.

Cristiano looked out from the ship.

A bank of cannon was belching once more, from somewhere. The missiles arced and dropped, flaming and smoking, into a wreckage of smoke and flame.

Like a ruined pile of brushwood, trodden on, the mess of ships. Those white sails, the painted crosses and Madonna-Venuses, brave flags, crests, burning, burning, on a water poison green and streaked with oil and fire. Loose spars and oars and planking rammed each other, and floating corpses. And men were swimming everywhere or going under. Heads that bobbed like strange fish, called in mortal voices.

Beyond, towards Ciojha across an interval of sea, the fleet of Jurneia, still clean and whole, grouped in a gracious cluster. Surely one thousand ships still. It was impossible. He—they—had killed Jurneia. But like the Hydra, she had grown these other heads.

The wounded ships of Ve Nera straggled away, picking up survivors, sometimes, where they could.

And now it seemed, Jurneia let them go.

"Ship's master, turn back. I order it."

The master, a head shorter than Cristiano, buckled into leather for the fight, his face divided, squared up to the Knight of God pugnaciously. "I will not. Scan about. Any vessel we have left is making off. If you're so razor-keen for death, signore, there's your way."

Aretzo, surfacing, let out a silly laugh.

"He would, but he doesn't swim."

From the ships of Jurneia a kind of ululation was going up. Mockery—triumph—who knew. They did not follow the retreat.

Not yet.

"Ve Nera requires we return and fight," said Cristiano.

The master spat again, at the feet of this steel-clad fiend. Then turned and left to go about the business of escape.

Cristiano lowered himself beside Aretzo. He bound the gouting stump that had been Aretzo's arm. They must cauterize soon.

Aretzo did not speak again.

The sky beyond the smoke, like the sea, was weirdly green. In it they saw the moon, as clearly as if by night.

7

When he came from the Chapel of Micaeli, by the Primo's South Door, Fra Danielus met Brother Isaacus among the pillars there.

They were like the trees of a wood, the pillars, gray carven trees, with gilded branches. You might expect to meet some creature lurking in a wood, after sunfall.

"Good evening, brother."

"Stay still. I'll speak to you."

"If you wish."

"You keep a woman in the Primo, Danielus. Not a holy sister, a nun. A *woman*. In this sacred place."

Danielus waited.

Isaacus snarled in his half-voice, foul breathed as any bear or wild dog, "You don't speak. Can't. You transgress, Fra."

"Then I must answer, must I not."

"You cannot."

"The woman kept here under my protection, is not a woman."

"Oh, a conundrum, Fra, is it? She is a *woman*. That bitch you paraded before the Ducem, like her whoresman."

Danielus said nothing.

Isaacus swelled like a toad. "If you were not what you are—I'd have our men come to you, our Eyes and Ears of God."

Danielus did speak. "They're welcome, brother. Meanwhile, there is other news than the Maiden Beatifica."

"What news? What?"

"Has no one come to you, Brother Isaacus? This grieves me."

"Ah—the ships. God favored the righteous. There was a victory. The acts of the Council were not in vain, and saved this contaminate City."

"No."

Isaacus drew back. His face in its hood quavered, then slammed itself shut.

"You say no."

"Most of the Veneran ships went to the bottom. A handful are limping home. They sent a messenger, one of the doves they carried for the purpose. Jurneia had the victory. We've only to wait for her."

Isaacus clamped tight his lips. Then rasped some incomprehensible sound.

"Your throat seems worse, brother."

Isaacus turned and went away, leaving only the ghosts of his odors, and the memory of his venom.

She had had her supper, a herbal gruel, and was in her room. Before lying down on the floor, with the blanket and cushion, Beatifica was praying to her pink-veiled Madonna.

Finishing three Latin prayers suitable for the Virgin, Beatifica crossed herself and rose.

Then she felt dissatisfied, kneeled down again, and began another prayer.

Her enjoyment of religion was very great, and had been noticed by very many. "She loves to be at prayer," they said. She attended every one of the services, including Prima Vigile, in a small chapel adjacent to the Golden Rooms. Here her tutor, the young priest, accompanied her for Prima Pegno and sometimes the Solus. Other higher priests came there on their own account, and sometimes Bellatae of the Upper Echelon.

Although clad always as a male, Beatifica's garments at these times were the soft gray of a nun's habit. She had no ornament and carried her little plain cross in her hand.

She should have covered her head, of course, as a woman. She did not.

Some of the priests evidently sought the chapel only to squint and frown at her. These she seemed not to see. (Even now, she expected nothing generous from people. While they did not lay harsh hands on her, she accepted and forgot them)

Jian too was frequently present, for the Venusium,

or Luna Vigile. Before the ships had sailed, some hundred or so others of the Upper Echelon crowded by relays into the tiny, elegant chapel, for one office or another.

It was suspected they were her guard of honor, although she scarcely glanced at them, nor did they look at her more than once or twice. They were gazing at her instead clandestinely, with the eyes of the soul.

"It is unwise for these young men, sworn to a celibate life, to hang about so round a female. Especially a female dressed so shamelessly."

Jian had responded, not realizing the Magister Major had somehow laid such concepts in his mind, "To us, holy-brother, she isn't a woman. She is the vessel of God."

"Take care. You're perilously close to the sin of blasphemy."

"Revered brother, I mean, in the same sense as a window may let in the light. She is so clear and open. One sees through her, to the Power beyond."

Besides Danielus, her patron, was himself a power. He had, in all his twenty-eight years with the Church, and by dint of his noble birth, made sure of that. Arguments were suspended.

And the Bellatae remained irreproachable. And the girl—she seemed properly aware, it was true, only of God.

Yes, she enjoyed all the matters of religion. She loved—although she did not fully know it—her hours of talk with the gray-haired priest Fra Danielus sent her as confessor. (She *relished* talking, and to be asked questions with such interest, to know so much—but what?—depended on her answers.) And the kind ancient confessor was swift to say to one and all, "I can tell you, there's no seal of secrecy to break with the Maiden. She is devoid of any crime or failing. I give her penances sometimes because, once informed of their purpose, she asks them of me. She loves to pray. She thinks only of Christ, the Virgin and God." And now and then he had been led to add, "Woman is a weak straw, prone to error. At certain times, God causes to be born a woman who may come to serve as an example, both to women and to men, that even for these faulty ones, grace is possible."

Danielus had always chosen well.

After the ships sailed, for four days, only Jian, with two other Bellatae, had come to every office in the chapel.

But two days before setting out, nearly four hundred of the Upper Echelon had come, in changing groups. And when Beatifica left the chapel, they had stared, for the first, intensely at her.

She felt their eyes, but she had felt eyes searing on her before. She did not look. They did not harm her. Even the few flickering touches of their fingers on her cloak's edge or sleeve, were not the prologue to abuse.

She had got used to them in a way. Perhaps, in a way, she was moved by them, just a little. (Their faces, fierce looks, the young male scent of them, the maculums of mail, their strength, the yearning that sang and trembled when they spoke their orisons.) One more interesting thing. Something else which was pleasant to do.

In the chapel, on the night before the fleet sailed, after the Auroria, one of the Soldiers of God—one only —cried out to her.

"Beatifica—Maiden—before this great battle, give us your blessing."

The disapproving priests froze, scandalized.

The girl turned, and said quietly, "No one has taught me how to bless. But the priests know how."

One or two of the scandalized were caught by this.

They nodded. She spoke the truth, and was modest.

Of course, she had only been speaking a fact.

But the Bellator left his place and went to her, and before she could become unnerved—he was tall and vigorous—he kneeled at her feet.

Beatifica thought. She had an inspiration.

"I'll ask the Virgin to bless you."

And she said one of the prayers to Maria, which began although Beatifica did not completely know it, *O most rare Mother, we entreat you, comfort your earthly sons, and beg from God, who will not refuse you, pardon and deliverance.*

"She dares to intercede—is she a priest then?" one of the still-scandalized exclaimed.

But another one said, "This is a prayer a mother would use. She makes herself their mother, and sister."

And Beatifica's tutor, who had come to the early mass, said quickly, though blushing, "This prayer is allowed to women, brothers. I myself taught it her."

Now, before the Virgin icon, Beatifica at last finished her general praying. She might lie down. Although she slept less well than she had in Ghaio's house, where exhaustion had always felled her.

She went to the window and looked into the night garden below. All blossom had left the peach, its leaves were dark. Thin light fell from another high narrow window, and colored a single red rose.

After all, in an hour she could get up again for the Luna Vigile.

Just then the door was knocked.

This always alarmed her. Not the summons, the recent courtesy.

"Yes, I'm here," said Beatifica.

A servant of the Golden Rooms was outside.

"Maiden, will you come, the Magister Major is waiting."

Beatifica smiled. She was happy: something to do. She followed the servant at once.

As she entered, Danielus regarded Beatifica closely. A nicer life, coinciding with the ripening of womanhood, had been kind to her. She had not gained any weight, but a soft bloom was added to her skin, and great luminosity to her eyes, and the remarkable hair. She must be almost sixteen.

"Are you well, Maiden?"

She accepted the name. She had always accepted the names given her, and the titles, whether benign or crude.

"I'm well."

No thanks, obviously. Her presumed superiors she would never think to thank, or to inquire after.

"Were you told of the sea-fight?"

"Yes. My tutor told me."

"You know it was lost."

"Yes, Magister."

"This City also lost a great many men. And of the Bellatae Christi, our Soldiers of God, five hundred went out, and less than one hundred and sixty return to us."

No response. No one was real to her. But wait—her eyes stole up, fixed on his, stared straight through him. What did she look for, in that unseen area—which others took for some divine, visionary place, or Hell, perhaps. Which he himself assumed was a kind of vacancy she studied when unsure, to see what might appear to her. Or was she really so uncomplex? Very likely. Light poured through the clearest vessel. Genius and intellect cloudily impaired the way. Most saints were simple. The Apostles had been, mostly, peasants.

She said, contradicting everything, "The Bellator Cristiano?"

Cruelly—was it being cruel ?—he delayed.

Her eyes had focused on him. Nothing to be read from her. Not self-control—more, surely, the inability to demonstrate her emotion.

"Cristiano," Danielus said, "survived the fight."

She looked away again. She said, "Yes. What else."

"What do you mean?"

"God wouldn't let him die."

"Why not?" He spoke slowly. "Beatifica, answer me. Why not?" And for a second, a breathlessness was in him, not unlike the pressure he had felt, waiting as the first ship back to the outer quays sent in its messages of survivors.

"God," said Beatifica, "loves Cristiano."

"He loves us all, Beatifica. Yet sometimes, through the evil and unwisdom of men, He must let us perish. Cristiano is subject to this law."

She astounded him. She moved, shaking her head. He noticed a wildness in her, as he had thought he had, long ago. "No, no." But her voice was not raised.

Danielus was torn between a strange delight, and a foreboding. That she might love Cristiano tickled him in a hundred ways, both spiritual and profane. Partly, surely, he had wanted it—these two extraordinary beings. Beyond that, she must *never* be caught out in it by another.

"Beatifica, you can have no favorites. Do you understand? That would be dangerous. I warn you now."

She said, flatly, "No, Magister. But he is my angel."

"In the name of God—what makes you say such a thing?"

"You say God shows me things."

"Yes, I have said so."

"The serpent and the angels and the red mountain. And my mother, who taught me to make the fire."

"Yes."

"God showed me my angel. I didn't remember at first. Then I did. It was as I was praying. The image of the Angel Micaeli in his armor, in the chapel here. It reminded me. But my angel was Cristiano."

If she was in love, she was cool. No alteration in her color. Her breathing slow and even. Only insistence had made her wriggle in her seat and shake her hair at him.

Danielus got up. He lifted her to her feet.

"Look at me, Beatifica. Listen to me. Never speak of this to anyone else. Do you grasp what I've said?"

"Yes, Magister."

She learnt quickly. He must trust in that. He was sorry, though, her eyes drooped away, losing for a moment their luster.

"You're our hope, Beatifica." Did that mean anything to her? He thought it did not. "Jealousy is everywhere. Treat all equally in deed and word."

"Yes."

And now, at this crisis point, he must take her to do the other thing, so vital and so risky. But all of it was risk. She had been put into his waiting hand, this slender fiery sword of God.

"Seven ships have returned from the sea-fight, Beatifica. And another five may come. Boats are rowing in the wounded and the dead, over the lagoon. Your white clothes have been brought. They're in the closet there, where you can put them on. Then come out with me. I want you to walk among the survivors and the dead. Beatifica, will you do that?"

She glanced. "Yes, Magister."

"Have you seen a dead person?"

"My mother."

"Forgive me, I forgot. Are you brave? You must be firm. There's no need to do much. Only pass among them. But if they call to you, what will you do?"

Wonderingly she looked. "Answer," she said.

Christ had told them, be as a child. Be simple. Knock upon the door and it shall open. Live as the flower lives and let God have care of you.

Doubt left Danielus.

"Go in then and change your clothes."

The dead, the dying, the crying, were coming in like cargo.

Torches sheered off the night in sulfurous rips.

Much too far away, the square about the Primo Suvio, to see the ruined ships lying crippled out by the bars.

This was enough. A scene from an artist's painting of damnation.

Cristiano stood on the square. He had watched Aretzo taken directly in to the hospice of the knights. (His bleeding had been staunched with heated iron. Now Aretzo was in the rambling stage, feverish, a stranger. Cristiano had seen it often; when sometimes wounded, had entered the state himself.) Elsewhere soldiers, and the crews of the ships, were being put on boats for the infirmaria by the wall of Aquilla. Others, luckier, (or not) had paid or promised payment to be ferried to a church, or to relatives.

Most were, for this while, piled up waiting at the Primo's walls, about the great doors, under the Angel

Tower. From which, all but three of the torture cages had been taken down.

His eyes went to those, nevertheless. A pair of criminals, too near death now to move or complain, hung out above the dying army of the City. And in the third cage, now he saw, the momento mori, a skeleton gulls had picked almost naked.

Cristiano felt his gorge rise in a thick wave. Against what he wanted to do, he must sit down by the torch pole, lean there, and catch his breath.

His body was cut all over, torso, limbs. The enemy steel had been superior. Blocked by his mail, the slicings were shallow, but had let out quite a lot of blood. He had felt none of it when he fought, of course. Not even the blow to the temple, which now ached and gnawed, a wolf trying to get in at his brain.

The world was dross. He had always known.

But tonight, Ve Nera was the city of Magni-Diabolon in the Pit.

There was a slight stir, over there by the Lion Door. More priests coming out to add the vapor of incense to the reek of butchery? Yes, here they came.

Cristiano clenched his teeth against a second wave, this one of fury, bitterness.

Here in Hell, what could they do, these black robes, those purple robes behind them? Swinging the censors, chanting over the groans and howls like a menagerie—

This horror was God's world, the making of God—

No—man's world. *Man*-made—

God's.

Cristiano bowed his head on his knees. He heard his own strangled whisper. "Let me lose everything, O Lord, even my life—but not my faith—Oh, God, not *You*—"

Never before had this come to him. Why now? He had been in twenty battles, more—

Dimly, through the rushing in his ears, the echoes of the awful whisper, he heard another noise.

He took it for some delusion. He ignored it. But it grew much louder, a single cry quickly taken up, concentrated by a score, a hundred, two hundred throats.

He turned his head on his knee, and looked.

After the priests, a young man was walking out among the crowd of vandalized men.

The Ducem. It must be Joffri. Odd, the story was Joffri had already fled.

"Maiden—" Close to Cristiano, a man on a blood soaked pallet, was holding out his arms.

Maiden. That was the cry.

Not a young man, a girl. Now Cristiano saw her hair as the torches burnished it. He had not seen her for some while, had not ever been among those who were about her in the chapel. Did he recall how she looked?

She wore her white clothes, and the gold cross on her breast that was only just perceptible as feminine; the gem winked scarlet.

The priests had halted, standing aside, lips closed.

The girl too had stopped, gazing about her.

She seemed serene, yet veiled, as if returning from a distance

Cristiano heard a man whimper, "See, she's been with God, but she sees *us* now."

And the crying became louder still.

"*Maiden! Maiden! Maiden!*"

It rose to a crescendo, breaking on her stillness like the sea. To silence.

And in the vacancy the shout had left, one man

again cried out to her. This time the name Danielus had given her.

"Beatifica, pray for me."

She turned towards the voice. Then, she stepped aside, through the crowd. It was a crowd for the most part lying on its back. Nevertheless, Cristiano stood up, holding to the torch pole, to watch her.

When she came to the man, she kneeled directly down beside him.

He had lost both his legs, and was nearly gone with them. It was a wonder anyone had heard him. But the silence had been vast, and even now it was, and the Primo Square was a sounding-stage.

She knelt in the blood and filth. At once her whiteness was sullied.

Then they heard her silver voice, rising up.

She was doing what he asked. She was praying for him.

It was a minor prayer, quite short. Perhaps, by now, she had even come to know what it meant.

The rumors of her had spread. Been helped to, no doubt, as the clever architecture of the square helped spread the utterances in it. They knew her. They listened.

When she stopped praying for him, the man murmured, "I'm afraid to die, Beatifica."

They heard this, too. They heard her reply.

Beatifica said, clear as a silver pin, "Don't cry. Your pain will be done. God's world is better. Why do you think he damns us for suicide? His world is the best of all, and we must earn it. Long to get there. He will fetch you, by whatever awful way. The road's stones, but the gates are pearl. Fetch him, Lord. Amen."

Something broke in Cristiano. Possibly it was his

heart, or some other enclosure less fragile. He seemed to stand in space, all the void about him, in which men lay bright as stars from the souls inside them, and across which Beatifica burned like a risen sun.

He could see the face of the dying man, lit now, radiant and careless. He let her go without any more entreaty.

And only the crying and calling began again, all the others, begging her. And she went to them, everyone. She went to everyone that called.

She went because she was a slave, and taught by vicious tyranny always to obey. He knew that. He knew.

He knew also the sentences she had spoken had been learned from someone else—maybe from Danielus, although they seemed unmannered, fluid—accessible. (He could not guess she had heard them from an old slave man by the wood-seller's Red House.)

But the words had come out of her at the moment of perfection. And she was like the words, made for this time, this arena of history and fate.

Not the pawn of the Magister. The pawn of God. As were they all.

Cristiano stood by the torch, watching her. Watching all she did. Kneeling, praying, answering in the simplest way their questions. So gentle. So soft. Even to the corpses that she passed, or was asked to touch or bless.

(The male slave's instructions had stayed. The second of the meaningful things he had offered her. *Don't shake the sleeping or the dead.*)

Had Cristiano been told this, he would have said, "That too. It was put into her hand for use. God also works most simply. You may see it in everything. Complication is a human failing."

She went by quite near him, once. She was trailed by two Bellatae, Cristiano now saw, one of whom was Jian. But he did not greet Jian, nor Jian him.

Beatifica did not see Cristiano, he thought. He would not have anticipated her to, at this moment. He could not know, of course, how Danielus had warned her.

But, seeing her near, Cristiano saw her for the very first. As other men did, who were on their feet, Cristiano knelt. Some hem of her cloak brushed over his head, and he felt it like a thread of running light.

She was mired in the blood and filth of hundreds, by now. And out of it she shone.

Not until every man who had called to her had individually received her presence, did she go in again.

By then the bell was ringing for the Prima Vigile, two hours after midnight.

They let her go without remonstrance. She had earned her reward, and they knew the Maiden loved best to pray.

8

Not baggage now, but bleeding men were being carried up the passages and stairs of Santa Lallo Lacrima's sister-house.

The nuns pressed back against stone walls. They were in awe. Less at the gravity of wounds, the largesse of damage, than at this general peacefulness. Even men writhing in agony, turning to say through pain-black lips, "Bless you, sister, for your charity." As if to reassure.

Word had come with them.

"It's true then. This girl who flaunts about as a man—"

"But look at her effect."

"Don't doubt, little sister," said a soldier carried by, "God sent her." He laughed, eyes shining.

There had been the usual dispensation of a war. Even the nuns might hear the last confessions.

"I thought I was damned, sister. She convinced me I'd paid, and never was."

Behind the officiating sister, another pursing her lips. "Only God can decide that, soldier."

Shaming her, as she needed to be shamed, the dying man said, "He promised, through her. But He prefers a tender voice, doesn't He, to a spiteful one."

As Veronichi hurried about the church, her arms full of salves, basins, bandages, fresh candles, her hair tied up under her cap so her face looked like a pip, and her gown streaked with ordure and blood, she too thought of Beatifica, this being she had never seen.

But in the rooms, in and out of which she went, she heard the difference Beatifica had made.

Waiting in rows, the soldiers drowsed fitfully, drugged with herbs and pellets of Inde. While a surgeon worked, splashed head to foot in the debris of his trade.

But this man under his knife was bearing it all, choking out between gasps and whines, that the pain of the world was but a lesson. Its suffering cleansed and brought one to the Kingdom beyond life, fit to companion God. It was good to bleed.

At which the surgeon's assistant blurted out, "So it isn't a punishment we're sent?"

"No—she says—she says it's only to learn from. Even God suffered."

At length he fainted.

The surgeon grimaced. "Heaven spare me chatterers."

But the teaching of Beatifica was everywhere now to be found. (Actually, her mother's teaching from the early years of Volpa's life.)

Veronichi labored tirelessly. She was strong and toughened by her first existence among the plagues and illnesses of the ghetto. Also, it seemed, passionless.

Sent on new errands, she passed Sister Purita on the stair behind the cloister.

They went by without speaking, yet each glancing once, curiously, furtively. Danielus linked them, but tenuously.

Veronichi thought, however, prudent and wily, *I must come to know her, I think.*

Purita thought nothing of Veronichi, except that she did not have the Fra's handsomeness, looked properly a Jewess, and had sent all her servants to safety on the Veneran Plain.

All in all, Purita felt prosaic. She had been told her brother had survived the battle—at which had come a gush of relief—and, peculiarly, irritation. Must his way be made always straight?

Then she came about the corner, and scratched at the door of the Domina's chamber.

The fat grasshopper was propped up high in her hard bed. Purita was glad to see she had been made more comfortable.

All about the bed, despite the turmoil of the war casualties below, fourteen of the nuns of the higher offices stood in a pale cordon. Were they reluctant to allow Purita by? Then one stepped aside, lowering her eyes.

Candles burned, but dawn was near. In the window a sort of nothingness had replaced the opaque immensity of night.

"I stayed to see, to behold one more sunrise," said the Domina. "I love it so, how could I leave before—and He has allowed me this."

So she was dying too. With what a guard of men she would go up. But she was worldly in her ascetic way. She would not mind.

Purita was sorry. The Domina was a fair woman. And what came next would undoubtedly be difficult.

Purita had given over trying to deny or evade. Luchita had previously let go her chains, her tribulations. Purita did not mean to take them up. Although, if allowed, the other burden she would accept.

Her own arrogance in that had amazed her, at first. But arrogance and amazement too she had let go.

The nuns in the room, some of whom must also know, struck her now as more friendly than expected. They were conceivably only uneasy. After all, what might Purita turn out to be? She must have already surprised them very much.

The Domina said, "I've been shriven, my own concerns are done. And now I have called you here to witness me."

Purita stood among the other nuns, head bowed, seemingly attentive.

As the old woman detailed her thoughts and wishes, sometimes pausing while they gave her sips of watered wine, Purita's mind strayed back and forth. These sisters had been in the order since girlhood. While Gratzilia there, had entered the religious life as a child.

Gratzilia stammered, but she was often impatient and often brutish. She sneered at the infirm, pinched the novices. In the garden she had, as Purita saw, killed helpful bees, and once shut a little frog under a bucket for no reason but malice. When Purita lifted the bucket, allowing the frog's escape, Gratzilia reviled her, stammering, and incomprehensible. Later Gratzilia scalded Purita's foot with water spilled from a pan.

Now Gratzilia was mute, and her habit had bloodstains as did almost all their clothes, from the assistance given below.

The window was changing further.

This was like any summer dawn. Bird song, color re-invented. There was a trace of golden cloud painted high on the thinning sky.

"Therefore," said the Domina, "it is my wish that Sister Purita take on my mantle. And to this end, I have written to the Primo. Here's my favorable answer, signed and sealed by Fra Danielus, Magister Major of the Upper Echelon of the Bellatae."

The nuns poised like petrified wood.

Purita thought distinctly, *Will they round on me and rend me in pieces?*

Then she heard their murmurings.

"Yes, Mother. God guided you."

"I have prayed for it, Mother."

To her own astonishment Purita felt her eyes let out two rushing streams of tears. They poured down her face. More fell.

She groped for the bed and crouched beside it.

"Domina. I'm not worthy. Oh, Domina, not me. How can I carry this authority?"

And again astonishing her, she felt the quick light touches of the nuns, smoothing her, softly, almost amusedly reprimanding her lack of faith. And the warm hand of the Domina holding hers.

"There, there, child. Remember how you told me you couldn't do justice when you read from the Bible? And then you read as if you had been accustomed since infancy. Rely on Christ. Then you need never be afraid. And here is my dear walking stick, for you to lean on if ever you have need to."

The window flamed suddenly rose-red. The old woman sighed and died, and her warm hand went abnormally cold. It was as if she had been dead some while, yet somehow stayed animate to see the dawn as she wanted.

Purita wept on, soothed among the flock of thirteen nuns. She did not think of the fourteenth now, the stuttering Gratzilia, gibbering in the corner, her mouth so full of maleficence she could not get it out.

9

The terror came after one more day.

Men fear the worst, and pray the worst will never be. They live only by forgetting that the worst must sometimes find them, as they fear. And sometimes, so it does.

The Jurneian fleet, lit foremost now by a sinking madder sun. Dipped in blood, like the wreckage of Veneran men washed in one day before them.

Up to the sand-bars and the walls that held off the sea. Up to the silver mirrors of the great lagoons.

Jurneia pressed her carmine tiger face against the looking-glass of Venus and was reflected there.

The pitiless enemy.

The ravenous infidel.

And sometimes, so it does.

Joffri had run away. He had been sobbing, as he did it, with humiliation. But he had done it. Taking his dogs, horses, friends, mistresses, and—an afterthought?—his wife. Now the City that had not so far emulated him, began to.

Barges loaded with baskets, furnishings, people in tears, or wailing, toiled through the waterways. There were collisions, drownings. Families fought and cursed each other and began feuds that would last for generations.

Some of the rich and noble had fled, like the Ducem. Others had shut themselves inside their palaces. Yet others opened their palaces and took in the less fortunate, out of the poorer houses and the hovels, before closing and barricading their gates.

Blocks of stone and hand-carts of rubbish were thrown into certain of the canals, in the hope of making them impassable to any of the enemy's smaller craft.

Under the direction of various officials who the Ducem had left with the charge of Ve Nera, soldiers manned the sea walls and the inner islands. Falling back from the former when the Jurneian cannon spoke, just after dawn the following day. This was when the Jurneians had finished their prayers, and the bells in the City were ringing the Auroria. Jurneia was ahead in everything, it seemed.

Belatedly boats had been put across the ocean end of the two lagoons Fulvia and Aquila. These too were all successfully splintered by cannon shot not long after noon.

In the Primo, priests had begun to pray on the previous morning, continuously, at the Great Altar under the Dome.

They prayed in batches. As men sank down exhausted or took sick, they were replaced.

The outer islands were almost deserted—Torchara, Isole. (More inward, also the Isle of the Dead, where the dead had been left to the mercy of God.)

Those who kept the outer (useless) defenses of Aquila and Fulvia, or on the Silvian Marshes—soldiers and hapless volunteers—soon saw the strategy of the Jurneians was to be as predicted.

Within half a day they had blasted flat the sea walls. (The infirmaria, marooned on its strip of land, took one blow almost incidentally. Laid indecently open, it displayed its two stories like shelves, stocked with corpses, and worse, the partly-dead and screaming.)

As the afternoon tide shifted, also as prophesied, the Jurneians used their sailors and their slaves to lay down wooden rollers on the sand-bars thus exposed. Their slaves then dragged over them the ships, by ropes. Where the sea had its narrow access to Fulvia, by the isle of Torchara, they pulled the ships through by means of little boats, taking no chances.

Into the lagoons, Jurneia came. Making soundings as they came, sensibly. The lagoons were not to be trusted, their floors uneven. Jurneia knew everything. Even not to move in too near. As yet.

Last isolate cannon fired from Isole, Torchara, and the marsh. And from five ships that sailed around the flank of the Isle of the Dead.

Jurneia returned fire, as if in courtesy not to belittle, and the Veneran artillery grew silent.

Like the smashed barrier boats, the five last ships of the fleet of Venus cracked and split, floated, turned over and went down, sails spread out once more like washing, belly full of water. Veneran men swam frantically away, and Jurneia let them.

Bells rang in Venus. Not for prayer. Everyone that could was praying, probably.

The bells, like the ballistas, presently fell silent, too.

Some seven hundred and fifty-eight Jurneian ships

had survived the fight at Ciojha. Now four hundred of them were mounted on the waters of the lagoons. They jostled a while. Then they were in order.

Now, Jurneia did no more. The ships stood there, hiding the water, tall and burgeoned with their rigging.

Seen from the City shores, they were like one more city.

They stood there.

Needing nothing else.

The Master Suley-Masroor, in the fore-tower of *Quarter-Moon*, was looking at Venarh, in afternoon light.

He saw no beauty in it. Like all cities, it had some glamours, the huge gleaming dome of its idolatrous fane, for example. But it seemed strange to him, *wrong*, the way this host of walls overhung, or went down into, the water. Besides, it was there only to be destroyed. Not by his will, but by the will of those he served. And through destiny, which came from God.

He was sorry for Venarh.

In the sea-fight he had not felt that. He slew the Christian devils and assisted in the wreck of their vessels.

This thing lay passive, and not well defended. It had its own unlovely but cogent life. Yet, men had souls, even if they threw them away in non-belief; there would be a chance for those Jurneia captured as slaves and converted to the true faith.

But a city's spirit died with its body. Crows would wheel above Venarh, and sea-birds make their nests in its ruin. The sea it flirted with would wash in and cover it.

Among the under-rooms of the Primo, the chamber of the Council of the lamb was lit by candles and by torches. It had no window. An iron room, filled full today.

The Council was in session. But along the great table of polished ebony, there also sat Fra Danielus, and his two fellow Magisters Major, with Ve Nera's Marshal of Arms, who had come here, swearing, from the quays. Captains of the Marshal sat by or stood at his back, and alongside them, nine of the Upper Echelon of the Bellatae Christi.

Of the Council too, eleven were seated. The twelfth was on his feet. And there was quiet, save for this one voice. A hoarse and crackled, hurried yelling, spitting out words like showers of darts.

"If we had cleansed this city—Sodomus, would we have come to this? If we'd done what was there to be done. We were lax—some of us. We let sin run like the water through Ve Nera. Now it will be blood."

The Marshal again swore. Softly as a leaf turning.

Brother Isaacus veered to the tiny sound.

"Ah—be careful of your tongue. These are the filthy things because of which God abandons us—"

The Marshal stared at Isaacus. A look of hatred, rage—and fear. He said, "Forgive me, holy brother. What I've seen has made me forgetful."

"*I* don't forget *you*, Marshal. I shall send to you, when this is done."

Danielus spoke. "If any of us live, perhaps you may, Brother Isaacus. To thank this man for all his labor on the City's behalf. Or should he have sped away with the rest, and left the City like a trencher for Jurneia's meat and knife?"

The Marshal said, reverting to his role, "We must send to them, and make terms."

"*Send*! send to them—" screeched Isaacus like some scraping, rusty nail—"they are the *Devil*! *Infidels*—"

"They won't make terms," said Danielus. "It was

attempted. The Ducem, while he remained, sent letters. And this was before they brought us low. Now they'll only settle for annihilation. Yes indeed, Brother Isaacus. It will be like the fate of Sodomus. Fire and brimstone. Leaving only a pillar of salt."

The Council shuddered as if a whirlwind raked through them. It was fright. They were the makers and causers of fear, yet themselves not immune to it. Or, only one of their number.

But as Isaacus began another tirade, Sarco got up, holding high both hands.

"Let's be calm. Yes, brother, calm. We are here to decide what can be done."

Isaacus said, almost gently now, "Nothing. It's too late. This City is tumbling in the Pit. Too *late*."

"You will tumble with it," said Danielus, dryly.

"I am of no account. And my soul's clear of dirt."

A silence fell here, as outside.

No sound might be heard, but the rustle of the torches.

Then Sarco said, "For myself, I prefer to let God judge me. And for now, I live. Fra Danielus, have you any advice?"

Standing at the Magister's back, Cristiano observed Sarco, Brother of the lamb, who seemed theirs, but who ultimately was in the service, perhaps the pay, of Danielus. Never before had such a thing occurred to Cristiano. It surprised, disgusted him, but remotely. Much had become remote to him.

As Danielus rose, the other Magisters turned to him. Even the Marshal did so.

Danielus addressed them in the mildest tone.

"We are at the brink. Our defenders are pared to a handful, our defenses ill-prepared and overthrown. Our shepherd, Joffri, has—been called away. The Jurneians don't practice clemency. They kill or enslave. They raze, so one stone fails to stand on another. We need therefore a miracle, sent by God."

Isaacus drew back his head and made some horrible noise of derision from his half-throat.

"Yes, brother," said Danielus. "I was about to say that we've been given one."

Sarco crossed himself. "It may be."

Isaacus cawed: "Satanus—"

It was broad Jesolo who rose from the Council, and he roared across the table, slamming down his fist upon it, "Hold your wind, brother! I've heard enough from you. Even in the Cities of the Plain, God searched for one good man. Are there no virtuous men in Ve Nera? Hold your foul breath and let the Magister speak." And turning he said, "Is it this Maiden they talk of?"

"Yes, Brother Jesolo."

"A virgin, a *saint*—"

"A virgin, yes. The nuns of the Little Capella have examined her. A saint . . . that's for others to decide. But you know her gift, I imagine."

The Marshal said, "I know she brought them comfort in the square. She was there three or four hours with the wounded and the dying. Praying with them."

Isaacus screeched and hopped in a frenzy of viciousness.

The bulk of the Brothers shrank away from him.

There came another voice. Above.

Cristiano recognized it, as did the other Bellatae, the Marshal and his captains, now plunging to their feet.

A long splitting rush. Then a concussion, at which the torches rocked and candles fell. The chamber shook.

"They're firing on the City!"

"The Primo's struck!"

"The roof will come down on us—"

Black dusts trickled down, and up, through the air.

Cristiano watched some of the Brothers crawling out from under the ebony table. There was the sharp smell of fresh urine.

"A miracle, then," said Sarco. "Magister, we're in your hands. All Ve Nera is in them."

Outside, when the bombardment had ceased, Venus sent up columns of dark dust, reminding Cristiano of the candle-soot below. How many candles here had been put out?

The Primo, clearly a target, they had aimed at. But the discrepancies in the depth of the lagoons had kept the enemy fleet bunched up and still some distance out. Range differed, and by a fluke—or divine design—no missile had hit the Basilica. One barrage had struck somehow behind it, however, and smashed the houses there, and the palace of a prince.

Towards the Silvian Marshes, the streamers of rising darkness were more pronounced. And from this square, Aquila seemed hidden by a drifting, horizontal pall, that almost certainly was, or had been, the silk market. Apt enough.

Cries filled the clouded air from all around. Bells came and went, starting and stopping.

The sun westered. Shapes grew flat and without color. As if the condemned City became unreal.

Cristiano stared up at the Angel Tower. In the torture cages, did the two lingerers notice any of this? Were they glad, or made worse?

He put his hand on the carved stone of the Lion

Door, to feel it. A war was also in his mind. Pain in conflict—with joy. Exhilaration. Tumult.

Beatifica.

Over the water, you could abruptly make out the huge maneuvering of the infidel ships. Testing, regrouping now, to come in closer and do more.

In the Primo courts a running man ran up to Cristiano, the Soldier of God, and told him Aretzo had died, just now. Cristiano signaled himself with the cross. He could feel nothing new. It was as if he had never known Aretzo, never prayed nor fought beside him. Cristiano was regretful. but it was a politeness.

"Heaven receive him."

"And all of us, Bellator."

10

Sunfall.

Watchman, in your high tower—what of the night?

The order had gone out along the waterfronts to make no light. Cannoneers might take sightings on every such beacon.

Ve Nera, meeting darkness, masked in the dark.

The Jurneians had not fired again, had not sent boats towards the quays. But like wolves they had come closer. And among the shore watchers, armed with pikes and clubs and hunting arrows, the word was that a horde more ships had been drawn in through Silvia, and through Torchara's needle's eye of sea. Five hundred now, in the lagoons.

Why did they wait?

Like the Christians, these Godless infidels prayed very often.

Ve Nera had heard their offices, in the afternoon,

and at sunset. A weird howling, it had seemed. Suitable, of course, to wolves.

Unlike the blackened City, their ships were bright with lanterns. They glowed, and the water sparkled under them as if to welcome.

They were wolves and tigers, the Jurneians. They liked best to attack by night.

Activity began to be seen on their decks. They were close enough now, it could easily be made out.

And then, after the stillness which the infidel had brimmed with animal noises, singing burst from the Primo.

Although there had been no bells, it was the office of Venusium, the Evening Mass.

And then the doors of the Basilica were thrown wide, and light, blinding sheets of silver and gold, flung heedlessly on the dark.

From her crannies and corners, Ve Nera peered to see.

The Basilica dome had bloomed like a white rosebud that sheltered a kernel of flame.

On every side of it, the torches were lighting up. Was this madness?

Among the Jurneian fleet, Jurneia too paid attention. Perhaps asking the same.

Now from the Lion Door, a massive procession issued. The priests in their black and white, their magenta and purple. Boys singing. Sound with light flared and flew into the other upper dome of night.

Incense blew so thick they smelled it on the ships. (Incense, which like the spice and silk, had come from the East.) There were a million candles, delicate butterfly points, yellow stars. And tall brands that burned ferociously.

On *Quarter-Moon*, Suley-Masroor looked, and thought, *They mean to sue for peace, but like kings*—affronted.

At Santa La'La over the marsh, seeing the sudden blaze of the Primo, certain nuns clustered crying that the Basilica had been set alight. They were not alone in this error.

But it was a pageant for those nearer, in the palaces and cannon-spoilt tennements about, as among the enemy fleet.

The priests filled the square, and moved aside. They made an avenue. Their singing ceased. Fearfulness crept back into their faces, which the chant had momentarily eased. The candles shook. This looked only charming: a million butterfly stars, flickering.

And through the avenue stalked the Bellatae Christi, the Upper Echelon, now numbering almost thirty knights. With, walking after them, three hundred more of the Militia of God. All that were left.

Their steel maculums, their mail, the white cloaks crossed with blood; helmed, each with the sword drawn in one hand. Some with a piece of red cloth like a rose above the badge of the Lion and Child. Within the cordon of the priests they too formed an avenue. Lastly, down this narrowed corridor, two Bellatae marched, bearing between them the Madonna Standard from the Primo's innermost Sanctum. Ten feet high, the banner swayed, heavy with bullion and pearls. The moon-pure face of Maria looked towards the ships, unmoved. Her pale hand raised to bless all that knew her.

Murmuring went over the walls of men, armored in mail or purple or black. From the roofs and windows all about. From stations of defense all but abandoned.

Would this special icon protect them? Or did it only signify the end?

Then, out of the Lion Door, behind the Standard, alone, as on a previous night, the figure came, but riding.

On the Jurneian vessels they exclaimed. These fools of Venarh. This must be their Ducem, sent to plead for them. But he was only a boy.

Nevertheless, they honored him somewhat, the men of Jurneia; they had heard he ran away, but no, he was here. A brave boy. Let them take him as a slave and break him, to reclaim his soul—How well he controlled the horse.

Cristiano stood among the Bellatae. As they did, he raised his head, and looked up, at the Maiden Beatifica.

In the Primo, in the floor, were mosaic pictures, parables and allegories. In one, a fox was shown, hoisted up on a pole by a dove, Virtue triumphing over Cunning.

She had been a fox, a vixen. And before her they had carried the image of the Virgin.

The brain, spinning with images, words, memory.

She rode the red horse, which in the torch and candlelight looked like carnelian, as did the waterfall of her hair.

In her white and gold he saw she was no longer a girl dressed as a man, or a female boy. No travesty. She was as she must be. Of neither sex. Of some other gender. Like an angel.

There was a humming note, low and tremendous in his ears. It was the murmuring intensity of all who stood here, priests and warrior-priests. A reverberation, part vocal, partly psychic.

And everywhere about, the City, upturned like a casket of beetles, running every way or petrified. *Attending*.

Emotion was her impetus. Danielus had said.

What had he said to *her*?

Her face was raised above Cristiano now, lifted over them all, as the slow horse brought her on. Could any human face be so white? Empty of any features but the eyes of gold.

Inside him, mounting, mounting, the glory and the terror of ultimate surrender, than which God would accept no less.

Her shadow, cast from the torches, swept over him. He felt his body drain of everything, of life, even. And how many others felt as he did.

He could have cried out, to her. He was dumb. Before this presence, he would not speak. But she had given him back his faith. That night when she prayed among the dying, saving them from Hell—she had saved him, too, from the Hell of a world without God.

Beatifica.

Beatifica.

Her shadow, golden as light, passed. He watched her travel on, his soul caught up, on air.

In some upper room, standing with Danielus, as he showed her the ships out on the lagoon, she would have waited passively, the way she did.

Had those ships meant anything until explained—their purpose and possibility?

Had the Magister said to her, gravely, "Only you, Beatifica, are able to save us"?

But she lit candles, she called flame like a garland and dropped it prettily into oil. She was domestic.

They said, when a slave she had burned her master, the wood-seller. But it was a vulnerable wood-yard. The madman Berbo, who was not mad, had said he saw her walk clothed in fire. But he was drunk.

"Call the fire, Beatifica."

Cristiano heard Danielus speak it, inside his brain.

Cristiano thought of the dream he had had, all Ve Nera gathered in the Primo, and the Madonna Standard.

Aretzo was dead.

Death did not matter. The road was stones but the gates were made of pearl.

Beatifica.

If they died now, she would raise them up. They would go with her on her wings. He would go with her, fearing nothing, into the unknown light of eternity.

When your heart is mine
You may do as you will to
When my heart is yours
Then wish the world good-bye

The red horse had come to the edge of the square, where the black water lapped below.

She gleamed, snow white and red as fire.

In the square, in the City, not a sound now. Nothing.

And on the ships also great stillness. They were intrigued, perhaps, by this last show.

Speak the Grace, Beatifica.

All across the short divide of water, aided by the square's design, they heard her voice, which was neither female nor male, speaking to God in the Latin tongue. She did not speak, the Grace. It was an ancient Psalm which invoked assistance, from the mountains. Had Danielus guided her too in this?

Undoubtedly the Jurneians did not follow it. But Cristiano, and how many more, felt his body part along its seams, painless, like a chrysalis.

The world itself is opening like some colossal door, to let another world come through.

The girl stands in her stirrups, well-trained to horsemanship on a farm of the plain. And the horse, well trained, stays steady as a rock. Through everything.

She raises her arms.

Oh Beatifica, the Word is God's, and now the Word is made Fire.

They saw, on the ships and on the land, an invisible great hand, which swept up all her burning pelt of hair, and as it rose, enfurled it into living flame.

Flame *towered*. It raced upward, higher than the walls of flesh and architecture, high or higher than the rose-white dome of the Primo Suvio. And in the flame, the heart of it, stood Beatifica, the Maiden, burning and unconsumed. (And under her the horse, a rock.)

For perhaps a minute this was seen.

For perhaps a little more.

And then the Maiden gestured with her fiery hands, and all the scarlet whorl of the fire curled over to them like some tidal comber of an ocean. She balanced this enormity in her grasp.

She held the monumental fire. All saw her hold the fire.

Then saw her set it free.

It sprang, the fire, redder than any sun, blinding hot, dry as a desert wind, balled and sizzling, with a shriek that tore the night across. It sprang straight for the Jurneian fleet.

Less than a minute they had. Some few seconds.

The time that was needed for one great breaking cry.

Suley-Masroor beheld, where dark had been, the burning wave, its heat scorching him, and casting up his eyes, saw *Quarter-Moon's* topmost sails alter, from dull white canvas clouds to a fire-cloud bright as day.

Thousand on thousand, all the white clouds were burning.

Flames leaped a hundred feet, tossing up and away huge limbs of masts that shattered as they seemed to hit the sky, falling in tails of gold. Flaming flowers, the rigging of five hundred and three vessels billowed and conjoined above the water, turning it to blood.

Through the roar and bellow, as the ships' wooden sides split wide, here and there interceded the screams of men, with a thin, disembodied sound.

Then thunder detonated, rang round the lagoons over and again as the powder of the cannons exploded. Black metal shapes hurled through the air. The water disbanded to receive them. Stripped skeletal, slender vessels tilted, diving like sharks with blazing backs.

The lagoons drank thirstily.

But now it is all the thunder, the lightning, and a rain of burning red, and sparks like shards of cinnabar, and ruby carbuncles and white gold, and streams of liquid gold that fissure the water of smashed mirrors, and the pillars of smoke that is black-red granite, pushing back the night to give—

this arson room—

this clamour space—

this apocalypse its legend.

PART TWO

By me this way is for the City Sorrowful,
By me this way is for eternal pain...
Your every hope desert, that enter in.

DANTE ALIGHIERI
The Divine Comedy
(Part of the inscription over the entrance to Hell)

1

FROM THE DUCAL ESTATE at Forchenza, the mountains were visible in some detail. Joffri sat long hours looking at them, brooding.

Those whose business it was to cheer him, tried. He wondered how long they would bother.

The dogs, as usual, were the best. Especially his second white Gemma, who sat patiently at his feet, not minding what he had done.

Joffri attempted to ignore what he had done. This was impossible, naturally.

He saw it very distinctly. Everything. Delay and indolence, not wanting to think of it. Allowing others to decide and make mistakes. Finally a dramatic unavoidable awareness. A bravura, (as at the feast, when the girl did her trick with the fire.) Even his letter to the Primo, in which he declared his sure belief in his own army, in his ships, in the Bellatae, in God. Then the panic. The packing. The running away.

If Venus survived, she would take him back. She would be, like him, too weak and lazy to demand another lord. But though she might forget with time what he had done, she would never *forgive*.

On the other hand, it must be faced, there was a probability he could not return to his enchanting island.

Jurneia might destroy it, and the City too. (He thought of the lovely colored birds in the trees of the Rivoalto, potted by heathen savages, and wept again.)

After a victorious interval, Jurneia would come inland, up the plain. They would harry the farms and burn down the old houses on the estates, this one included. And he would have to run again, up over those horned peaks he could so clearly see. Into coarse Frankish lands. Or else, he could retreat westwards through Italy, his house on his back, scorned, mocked, and a beggar in the courts of other princes.

The Ducem looked at the mountains.

When they brought him the messenger, Gemma the bitch hound stood up. Joffri meant to, but his legs were like leaden water.

He took the letters, and sent everybody out. Let them question the man themselves if they were so eager to learn of horrors.

Joffri sat with the letters in his hands.

He said to Gemma, quietly, "I'd do better at once to hang myself." At his voice, and inappropriately, his dog wagged her tail.

He smiled at the irony, and broke the first seal.

Joffri read the letters, one of which was signed by the Marshal of Arms, and undersigned by three captains, the second and third of which were signed by two Magisters Major of the Primo, (neither Danielus). The fourth was signed by five members of the Council of the Lamb, not including Isaacus. Having read the four letters, Joffri read them again. Then once more.

He had drunk a lot of wine that night she called the

fire. Even so he had, at the time, been partly overthrown by what she did. Joffri remembered now the bizarre tale of the man who discounted Jesus, saying the Christ had only risen once from death, who knew if He would be able to do it again.

Ah. If only he had had faith.

After this, Joffri sat on the chair.

Gemma came and put her head on his knee, because he was crying again.

> 'No sooner did the fire take hold, which was instantly, than a great many of their ships exploded, from the powder kept for the cannon, and stores of oil. The sky was red and the water boiled, and a rain fell on the shore of wood splinters and iron nails and other things, alight or melted.'
>
> 'Later we learned that the conflagration did further work. Seeing the distress of their fleet in the Laguna Fulvia, the Infidel sent in yet more ships from the sea mouths at Silvia and Torchara. And from Aquila, where the fire-blast did not go, also they tried to come in, by the wider canals. But no sooner did any draw near, than the fire spread contagiously to them, and so too through into Aquila.'
>
> 'The quays and waterfronts, even the roofs, and all the Primo Square, were littered with bits and parts of the Jurneian ships, which had been blown off. The citizens have since taken them for momentoes. One large wooden piece, thought to have been wrenched from a forecastle, was carried into the Primo and laid before the Great Altar. Strangely no fires were begun in the City from the rain of sparks, and the damage done by objects which fell is slight.'
>
> 'The sea and lagoons were full of swimming men, but many drowned, and countless others will have burned. Those we have are our prisoners. Their ships

cracked and went down. A few ships left afloat, though shambled, were consequently towed away. In all, the belief is they lost more than six hundred of their craft. As it was learned presently from the marshes and next the outer islands, the rest at length turned tail and fled. We had not the vessels to pursue them. But they have lost very much. Besides, they were shown, God was with us. They will not dare come back. And the word they sow in Candis and the East will muzzle all those cities there which will us harm.'

'For the girl they call the Maiden, whom truly God gave to us, she was carried away dead. Her fire, sent from Heaven, was too vast for her fragile vessel. There must always be a sacrifice.'

2

Before Cristiano was Jian, emerging suddenly from the shadows of the knights chapel, like a moving figure of steel. Defiantly, Jian said, "I am here, as you are, for her."

"Is that my reason?"

"What else, Cristiano. We must keep this Vigile together. We were her first witnesses among the Bellatae. Aretzo would be here, if he'd lived."

Cristiano said, "You know, I keep the Vigil alone. I'll come here tomorrow."

Jian's pale angry face, stony now as Cristiano's face. "You're petty, Bellator. You won't *share* with me? What are we, boys tussling for an onion? I'd use this night to pray for her."

"Yes."

Cristiano turned.

But Jian was after him at once. His hand fell hard on Cristiano's arm.

"*Stay*. Won't you do this for her? No? You're jealous then, I think. You want the Maiden to yourself, Cristiano. No one else must have her—and when they do, you avert your eyes."

"I assumed that was your own argument."

Jian stood back. He said, "You must always be the best, must you not? You treat God like some blind old father, who hears of your wonders and never sees the pride of you." Cristiano stood looking at him. Jian said, "You're swoll with pride, about to split from it."

The white glare of his rage and envy filled up the capella, but Cristiano reflected it back upon him like a polished shield. In his mind, Cristiano heard an inner voice telling him to be still. Perhaps Jian did also. Neither could heed it; And Jian's hand fell abruptly on the hilt of his sword.

"No," said Cristiano then. He stepped forward, and flung one arm about Jian, who resisted him a moment as (Cristiano surmised) a woman might. Then gave in.

"Pardon me, Cristiano."

"I do. I ask your pardon in exchange."

They fell back from each other and stared away in opposite directions.

"She lives," Cristiano presently said.

"So the Magister told us."

"You doubt him?"

"No."

Cristiano considered, as if they were events which another had undergone, the time—hours or moments—after the ships of Jurneia had been riven.

In the upheaval of the firestorm, the flickering light, the detonations, water and land, the City of Ve Nera, seemed equally to be quaking, collapsing.

To this he had come back. Perhaps for Jian too,

for many of them, it was like that. But not, Cristiano thought, (*And is this only my swollen, overweening pride?*) as it had been for him, what they returned from.

When she brought the fire—

He had not walled himself away, not protected himself. Rather, he gave himself.

The first time, at the Magister's farm, had been *nothing* to this.

Even to himself, he could neither describe it nor properly recollect.

This alone he knew. The white light of God he had found in the Vigil, the crimson light of war-fury, they were less.

There had been an upsweep, this he did recall. A whirling and soaring, as if in flight. And all the shore of Venus had gone up with him, caught on her fire-wings, to some realm that blazed.

The sweetness of it, and the joy—the *power*, which unlike any power of the earth, came from an assimilation, from a total *loss* of everything—

And no more remained of it, to him, when once it cast him back.

Then there were only the ships burning under their rose-red billow of sails and smoke. And Ve Nera, shaking.

The army of men shouted and screamed as in battle. Thunder. Leviathon the Dragon crashing in the deeps.

After this he saw that *she* had slumped down on the horse's back. It was fire-trained, and—unscathed as she was—had kept stock-still.

In a body that seemed made only from the hollow mail and armor of a knight, he hauled himself forward, to support and guard her, in case she should slip down.

He found Jian was on the other side of her, doing the same.

Somehow, through the great confusion and exaltation, they two led the horse.

Men had been leaping and running around them. The Bellatae were howling. Bells rang. A macrocosm of faces lit by fire. And through all this, which Cristiano barely saw, they led the horse away into the Primo's yards.

In the courtyard with the lion fountain, some grooms and servants dashed up.

They lifted her off the horse.

She looked asleep. Her mouth smiled a little, as the mouths of children sometimes did in slumber—or the dead.

But she was alive. The pulse thumped steadily in her throat.

Jian took her from them all and carried her inside the high walls.

She seemed a child, too, in his grasp. Or some creature of another race.

Her hair, hanging down along his arm, was faded and brownish, nearly gray, or flaxen, Cristiano thought, in the uncanny light.

Jian said now, "The Magister keeps her locked away. A secret. They're saying in the City she died."

"She never did."

"Aretzo died in the hospital, days after Ciojha. It could have been like that."

"No."

"The Fra spoke to you? Why to you and not to me?"

"He didn't speak to me. She's alive. Sleeping, I suppose."

"Perhaps it burnt out her mind or soul. Perhaps she's only a shell, the kind the crab-fish leaves."

Cristiano said shortly, "She's no fish."

"You know where she is."

"I don't."

"*Tell* me."

"Jian, take your hand from the sword. I won't stop you again. Do you think you can match me?"

"Can't I match you?"

"*Jian*. No more. In God's name."

"I'd die for her."

"I know it."

"But you—"

Ah, said Cristiano, *she has killed me already*. He did not speak aloud.

Jian turned away.

"Pray for her, Jian," Cristiano said. "There's no greater loving token."

"You talk to me as if—I were her *lover*."

But when Jian turned yet once more, to confront Cristiano, the capella was again empty, save for Jian himself.

In its black, lit room, the Council sat in silence.

Jesolo repeated. "It's very strange."

Sarco said, "Our dungeons are bursting, nevertheless."

"Perhaps they are."

"Remember, brother," said Sarco, "our task is to recruit for God all those men we may. These infidel may be converted, and their souls salvaged."

Jesolo answered bleakly, "Faced with the prospect, several have already taken their own lives."

"We've seen this before. Not all are so violent, or sinful."

Isaacus' crunching voice stirred in the dark.

"*They should be cinders*."

"The quick immersion saved them."

"Cinders—ash. Did you not see the fire, brothers? It burned."

Sarco spoke peaceably. "The fleet burned and is no longer a threat. Some of the Jurneians, evidently, drowned. Or died in other ways. And some are burned—"

"Scorches. Singes."

Another of the Council spoke ominously. "Brother Isaacus, what is the pith of these reflections?"

"This devil-witch called her fire. It burnt up the ships and made a show. But the men, these idolators, these infidel, these children of Satanus—these she *spared*. In such a conflagration, how could any survive? Yet many did. Beyond a few slight wounds, they have no mark of it."

Jesolo said, "It's so. It's strange."

"And yet," said another, "the City is rife with tales of men this Maiden is said to have burnt alive."

"*Christian* men," declared Isaacus.

"What are you saying?"

"What do you suppose I say? She incinerates true believers. The friends of Lucefero she spares."

Sarco said loudly, quickly, "Why then destroy their ships and save Ve Nera?"

"Are you a fool, brother?" Isaacus asked. "A fool, or in someone's hand?" Sarco said nothing. Isaacus said, "To gain power over us. Why do men ever turn to the Devil? They sell their immortal souls for help and comfort in this world. She has *helped* us. Saved us. Does she now receive our soul for her master in Hell?"

Danielus sat in his book-chamber, and watched the prisoner they had just brought him.

He was a tall man, dark skinned like most of the Jurneians, although the tones varied through amber and wood to a somber shade like bronze. Curiously, he had green eyes.

"Please sit."

"I will stand."

"Tell me at least where you learned the Italian tongue?"

"In trade. Where else. But you speak my tongue, so my countrymen told me. When they could not speak your own."

"I've studied some of the languages of the East."

Suley-Masroor, his turbaned head unbowed, said, "Oh, a pastime."

Outside, not very far away, came a soft rolling roar, then a sharp crack. The ship's Master started. Danielus said, "They're clearing the rubble of a house."

Suley said, fiercely, "Where we struck your city?"

"Just so. Be reassured. You've left us scars." He added winningly, "Please, do sit. It will make me more comfortable in your presence."

The Jurneian blinked. Then slowly he grinned. He sat down in the carved chair with its golden scrolls. "Are you a priest? You dress like a priest."

"Yes, I am a priest."

"That is astounding to me. You're couth, and quick. Unlike your religious brethren."

"I'm very sorry you were ill-treated. I have tried to alleviate the situation where I can. But we have another authority here, you'll have heard it mentioned. The Council. At this time, there's not a great deal I can do."

"How was it managed?" Suley asked. He no longer looked amused or collected. "The fire that filled the ships. It seemed—"

"What did it seem?"

"Like a magician's trick in the bazaar."

"But apparently it was real."

The Jurneian lowered his eyes. Danielus pushed towards him the crystal cup of water.

Reluctantly, Suley took the cup. He drained it angrily. Then, turning it in his fingers, remarked, "From Candisi?"

"Our own making."

"I thought so. Your glass-makers are inferior."

"Of course. But we will learn."

Suley said, "My fellows say you question them about the nature of the fire. How it took hold. Its swiftness. How we escaped burning."

"They tell me the same things, on every occasion."

"I have nothing to add."

"Did the fire touch you, Suley-Masroor?"

"Yes. Here on my chest, and down this arm. I saw my left leg burning as I went over into the sea-lagoon."

"How did the fire feel to you?"

"Very cold."

"So your fellow Jurneians described it to me."

Suley said, "That's usual, or may be so. At Khibris, when we fought your people years ago, my elder brother was burned across the back. He said it felt like ice and snow from the mountains. And afterwards he lay shivering."

"I'm sorry your brother was burned."

"No, don't lie, lord priest. He was an *infidel*, was he not?"

"But *we* are the infidel," said Danielus, "I believe."

"Yes. You follow the teachings of a great and holy man, but believing he is God. There is no God but only God."

Danielus poured more water into the (inferior) crystal cup. Suley-Masroor drank it. He said, grudgingly, "This water is good."

"The wells are pure, here. I see you have few wounds."

"The burns dried and sloughed from me inside a night. This sore here isn't fire, but from my irons in your prison. And this, from a generous Christian lashing."

"I shall see they are looked at. Forgive my harping on the fire—you suffered little, yet your ship was destroyed."

"How was it done?" the Jurneian asked again.

"Through God."

"Yours or mine?" demanded Suley, his eyes abruptly vivid and dangerous.

"As you pointed out, there is only one God. We merely award him different names, just as I might call Khibris, for example, Cyprus."

The green eyes flattened out, becoming almost opaque.

The Jurneian murmured, "I had a premonition of the fire. I dreamed of it three times. I have an amulet, from the City of the Dawn. When I addressed this talisman, it gave no answer."

Danielus said nothing. Then, almost idly, "Since you speak so excellently the language of this City, I shall keep you here, in the Primo. You'll be treated as a guest. Obviously, you'll be useful to me."

"To betray my brothers?"

"How can you betray them? What's left to betray?"

"What *use* then?"

"To salve my conscience. It will save you the prison and the ranting of men wishing to convert you. I've no interest in that. I will make it appear otherwise, of course. Are there any more from Jurneia you can recommend to me?"

"All. All."

"How I regret, Suley-Masroor, I haven't that much power. But ten or so, perhaps twenty. Write the names here. And I'll do what's possible to me."

"I write only in the script of Candisi."

"Of course. That will do. I can read it quite well."

When the Jurneian captain had gone, Danielus rose and walked about the chamber. He looked at it, at its ornaments, at the panels of Danielo and the lions. Some of the books he touched. Then drew out five of them, pondered, replaced one and drew out another. Had the Jurneian's choice of twenty men been as hard, or harder than this?

Carrying the books in his arms, he went from the chamber and walked through the glowing corridors of the Golden Rooms, where the servants of the Primo bowed, and the Primo's guards unlocked all doors.

Outside, the City was, day and night, loud with festival. Even the stern laws of the Council were being openly flouted. If Ve Nera were damned she would not have been saved. This notion gave them courage to outwit the Brothers of the Lamb.

On the Laguna Fulvia, countless little boats sculled about the glittering water, seeking, normally without luck, yet more relics of the miracle.

But it was noticeable, from the lagoon, that the Primo's nacreous dome had been besmirched by smoke. The smoke of a fire that burned selectively.

Festivals end. Trophies run out. Fear becomes remembered.

Entering Beatifica's room, Danielus set the books

down on a chest. The books were not for Beatifica.

She had been laid on the floor, as she preferred for sleep, only her head on the cushion.

Among the priesthood, most were certain the Maiden had been removed from the Primo. Even the Bellatae thought this, it seemed. There had, too, been certain decoys, and misleading maneuvers.

In Ve Nera however, the citizens were convinced their kind angel was precisely here. Where else? Ignorance fathomed where cunning over-reached.

The young woman who sat watching Beatifica, dressed as a nun, had been one, once. Later she was in Veronichi's household, on the Isle of Eels. Danielus had lain with this girl, who was merry in the carnal act, and achieved bliss uttering mouse-like squeaks, which had enchanted him. Later, he had supplied her dowry and seen her wed where she desired.

About Ve Nera there were many with cause to be grateful to him.

That might, finally, have been enough, to see done what he wished.

But then, the torch was put into his hand. Who could resist it, that bright and wondrous thing?

This was not God's cruel and unfair test. God did not perpetrate such deeds on men. They made their own pits, and duly fell in them.

Danielus considered briefly, if he had fallen. For had he, like the other cunning ones, over-reached?

"Has she woken, Milla?"

"No, Fra. Not since that last time."

Milla had told him, just after Solus, the Maiden stirred, and turning, opened her eyes. Looking at Milla, but seeming not to see her, Beatifica had laughed, almost a giggle, like a child's. Then lapsed back into her trance.

"I'll watch her until your sister comes."

"Thank you, Fra."

Knowing him, in several ways, Ermilla knew also this man would do the sleeping girl no disservice. Of how many priests could one say that? To her last day Ermilla would recall the monster, her strict and elderly confessor, who had fondled her when he should have given consolation for her sins, and later denounced her as a strumpet when she refused to go near him.

Danielus sat quietly in the chair.

Just outside some bees had risen up from the garden, smelling the sweet herbs in the room. Perhaps scenting the nectar of a saint.

Beatifica slept.

On her side now. The redness had come back to her hair. She looked thriving and at ease. Ordinary.

"Beatifica," he said softly. "How I've needed you to wake up. Now was the hour when I might have worked a miracle—almost as great as your own. But I asked too much of you. Or worse, expected it. Sleep, little girl. Only return unimpaired. When you will."

Beatifica dreamed a dream which—like the dreams of the serpent and the red mountain, and eventually, the angel—she would recall accurately.

In the dream she forgot the fire. (As had happened the first time, she would have little or no recollection of what she had done when awake.)

An old woman was leading her up a steep white stair. As she often had in the City, Beatifica marveled at the stair—through her early life there had been mostly ladders.

The old woman was black. Who was she? Beatifica thought she might be her mother, grown very old—

in the dream the memory had persisted of how mumma turned slowly black after her cremation—but then she had also grown young. Perhaps time passed differently here.

The woman was naked, and though old and thin, was firm, despite her embroidery of lines. Even her breasts, which had lost their flesh and hung down, had a gracefulness and symmetry nothing to do with sexual beauty.

At the stair-top was a terrace.

Below stretched a wide lagoon of silvery water.

Beatifica looked instinctively for the red mountain.

It was not to be seen.

Instead, along the terrace, near the water's edge, many of the priesthood of Ve Nera were walking about.

In that moment, Beatifica realized that she too was naked.

Something in the idea of being naked before men filled her with alarm and distress. Master had hurt her because of it, or had meant to, some new and awful hurt.

"They can't see," said the old black woman, in a smiling voice. She motioned with her hand that was like an artifact of carved ebony. "You so white and me so black. They think us a marble pillar and its shadow."

Beatifica believed the old woman at once. She relaxed her body, and watched the priests moving about.

Some were in the white or dark robes of the Primo, and others in the magentas of higher orders. Some wore black—the Council of the Lamb?

She did not recognize them, however. She could see no one she knew.

"Is Fra Danielus with them?"

"Oh no," said the old woman. "*Oh* no." She gave a laugh, like a stick rattling on a rock.

Something parted the water now. Beatifica thought it might be a drowned ship coming up, for somehow she knew ships had sunk in the lagoons of the City. But instead it was an enormous lizard, plated in a gray-green maculum. Its head was all snapping teeth. It pulled itself aboard the terrace, shiny, puddling. And only then did Beatifica see it too was clad in a purple robe.

When *they* saw it, all the priests began to make a great noise. This noise was not human.

There were squawks and trills, roars and grunts, and long foolish braying sounds.

Beatifica understood the lizard, now upright on its tail, was a crocodilius, for she had been shown one in a book. As for the others, two or three bent over, and then several more, and as they bent, she saw ears stand up on their heads. Cowls and tonsures vanished away. The priests jerked about, hopping heavy-bodied round the crocodilius—they were the huge hopping hares she had seen in previous dreams. And there went others on four little feet, and spines stuck up through their purple. Several had become birds, more gaudy than their garments, with crests, and pink wattles. They fought for perches where there were none. Another, like a pig with fur, rolled grumbling on the terrace, to get free of his priestly gown. A colossal toad sat burping.

Beatifica began to laugh. It pleased her, the silliness of it all. She was yet so young. An adolescent and a mage. She had never been a woman, even in her dreams.

But the black crone, again, was laughing too.

Then she said, "Go back now, girl. They call you."

Beatifica looked over her shoulder. There was a dim doorway behind the terrace, where the stair had been. She stopped laughing.

"Is Cristiano safe?"

"Yes, yes."

"I knew he would be. He can't come to harm. But then the Magister said he might—since, like Christ, he took on mortal shape. . ."

"Even the Magister lies."

Beatifica, troubled.

The beasts on the terrace had all begun to fight. They tore at each other and scratched and bit, snorting, defecating. No longer funny.

The old woman took Beatifica to the doorway.

"Where's mumma?"

"There," said the old woman. Her teeth were long and clean. She put her hand on Beatifica's forehead. Her skin was so richly black, would the fingers leave a mark? Like a flower, maybe, or a star.

"*There's* mumma. You, girl. Me and mumma, and all. *You*. Listen now, listen now."

But then she only shook her head.

The dim door enclosed Beatifica.

The last she saw before she woke, completely and at once, was the purple-robed crocodilius being tumbled back into the lagoon.

And after that, a woman's face, but quite young, and pale.

"God's mercy—you're wakened. Lie still, take care. I'll call to Milla. And the Fra only minutes gone—"

The girl lay down again. She felt dizzy and weak. She had none of the sense of strength and elation that had been with her in the dream.

There was a faint rumbling sound beyond the Primo. Thunder, perhaps.

Had she done what was asked?

What had it been?

Oh, as always. To call fire.

Because she must safeguard her angel.

The room was dark and closed by shadows. In her fluster, the running woman had put out the candle with the breeze of her skirt.

Beatifica took the candle up. She waited to feel the essence, so familiar now, rise in her. When she did not feel it, still she stroked her hair. Stroked as mumma had shown her. For the fire.

It did not come.

Her hand was empty, and warm with cold.

So the women found her, Ermilla and her sister, Ve Nera's saint, sitting forlorn on her blanket, the unlighted candle beside her, in darkness.

3

In a raucous voice, the boatman sang, rowing through into the Silvian Marshes. Sometimes he broke off and glanced at Danielus uneasily. "Be sure you don't mind it, holy Father?" Danielus said he did not. He did not add he wished the man could sing better. "It's relief, and proper thankfulness. Praise God."

"Yes," said Danielus. "Sing if you want."

Ve Nera had sung, and was singing. In the dusk, she was lit up extravagantly by an excess of candles and brands, and faces beaming in windows, at turnings between the walls. Here and there, where Jurneian missiles had struck, they were clearing rubble. The worst hits were about Fulvia. From those places rose businesslike noises, as if in a stone-yard.

On the narrow canals that led through from the marsh, they were out too, trying to gather the rubbish up they had dumped, to choke them off from small craft of the enemy fleet. In some areas the waterways were impassable. Probably they would not flow freely now till the winter tides, and the smell was viler than usual.

A woman pointed in the water, lamenting. "He flung in our bed—our bed we had from my uncle's house. We won't need a bed if the Jurneians come. That's what he said. Now he says, let's couple on the floor, but I say No, no, husband. Buy me another bed first." Seeing a priest rowed by, she made a motion of fake shame. "Forgive me, holy signore." He raised his hand gently.

He was glad for them, glad they were enjoying this respite from fear and worry. Indulging in petty events. It would not last. What could, in such a world?

They went by long outer ways, to avoid the closed canals.

Set in twilight, where the marsh broadened and liquefied to great lakes, Danielus glimpsed a ruin on its hill, the amphitheater of the ancient Romans. It was a smaller replica, a bastard babe perhaps, of their Colosso in Rome. Here, as there, they had watched men fight to the death, and criminals fed to beasts of prey. Through cunning drains and traps in the arena floor, they had sometimes flooded the theater from the sea, and staged mock battles in tiny ships, mock battles where gladiators and slaves died by scores.

Over it the gulls wheeled, crying mournfully. Nothing had improved for the gulls. Worsened, doubtless: ancient Rome and modern Jurneia would both have provided them with corpses to pick.

Santa La'La, also on its hill above the marsh, let him in.

He climbed up the stairs, preceded by two chattering nuns, a servant now carrying the books he had brought, seventeen in all.

Her rooms were not too unpleasant, but she had not been able to soften them much, which, where she could, she had skill in doing. Here, Veronichi stayed circumspect. However, when the servants and nuns were out and the door locked, she lit more candles, and pulled off the ugly cap to let her hair fall, newly washed, blue-black.

"Have you seen your Domina yet?"

"Not yet. After the Luna Vigile I will."

"She was anxious, I think. She's afraid she won't have satisfied you."

"She's only had the post a short while, and in time of war."

"I've seen nothing bad in her. She has a temper, but curbs it. She wept when the old woman was buried."

"Purita has a curious heart. Are you jealous?"

Veronichi smiled. "How well you know me. A little."

"Though never of my lovers."

"No. Never of those."

They ate the meal, which was sparse but well cooked.

"On the island," said Veronichi, "we would have chickens stuffed with pigeons and apples, and sit crowned by chaplets of lilies and peonies."

"And other, better things."

"Do you want—the door's fast—"

"No, dearest. Not here."

The wine, which he himself sent to the cellars of his churches, was very good. They ate and drank in silence. One by one, the candles burned down.

Danielus and his sister rinsed their hands, and sat side by side on a bench before the window of the second room. They leaned close, became disturbed by it, and in mutual consent, drew apart. Their bodies were used to love making, but must be denied. (Beyond, night hung low, its stars obscured.)

"Why have you brought so many books?"

"You also know me well."

"What else, my Daniel, when I've studied you all these years?"

"Your island's safe. Soon I hope you may go back to it. In which case, I'd like it best if you would store these books in the secret place."

"But—Pliny—"

"Perhaps all the Roman books, and the Greeks, must go in there. For a while."

"Carpocrates is there already."

"Wise Venus. Thank you."

You think that the Council will dare—"

"To question me. It's conceivable."

"And to *search* your rooms—"

"Also."

"Oh, Daniel—"

"Hush. Listen to me. Your race of all the earth knows the injustice and the pain of life."

She had put her hands to her face. She took them down. She said simply, "Tell me. I'm ready."

"I have many plans, and many who may assist. However, I'm vulnerable now. I have shown my hand clearly, and at the last moment, lost the valuable weapon—which obviously I considered mine by right. So the arrogant bring themselves to grief. The girl is still in her trance, this I wrote to you. I think she may wake quite soon. But—too late. In the days and nights directly after the firestorm, *then* she was needed. I've been a fool. How could such a power pass through her and not suck her dry? I only pray she'll come back of sound mind. Able to see and speak and walk."

"Pray God she will."

"Meanwhile the Brothers of the Lamb, and others discontented, are working like yeast in dough. The man Isaacus—I have learned his history. He was a felon, a thief and cut-throat, at eleven years sentenced to hanging. They duly hanged him. And he lived. Yes, after a day, when cut down, and as they carried him to the Isle of the Dead, he revived. Now we know the reason for his hoarseness. The rope impaired his voice, but could do nothing else. It seems he thought God had worked a miracle for him. He entered the priesthood. Such was his self-denial, his devotion—his fanaticism—that he rose high. To the spot where now we find him. No one is more zealous than a convert. One has only to consider San Paolo, after Damascus. This Isaacus is stronger than I thought—and still, it seems, immune to violent death. Since I've also learnt certain lords of the City recently tried to have him slain. But he survived the attack unscathed, and the assassins have disappeared."

Veronichi rose. She brought the wine and gave it to him. Danielus drank. He said, "Isaacus sees the world as the mirror of himself. It must be as corrupt and evil as he, in his beginning, and, like him, must go through the school of agony to redemption. Only through suffering can mankind be made whole. But this is the lesson our Church teaches men. The Church has made Isaacus." He sighed. "I was so careful all these years. I spoke publicly only what was permitted, merely seasoning it a little, tempering the whirlwind. And here and there, now and then, trying to let fall a little light. So the intelligent might see through the windows I tried to make. Some have. But the *slowness* of it, Veronichi—Then the girl with her fire. I thought I too had been given my miracle."

"I know, my love. You deserved a miracle."

"If she'd slept only an hour or so. A day. If I could have taken her out to them—I see it in my head a thousand times. The acclaim of her, the shouting and vivacity. They would have swarmed to her—a war won, without bloodshed, *gladly*. Yes, even the priesthood. How could they deny her gift or God's promise? It occurred before their eyes. And I could, by the light of Beatifica, have thrust the Council away, down to Hell where it belongs. Sarco would have helped me—he was primed and ready—not even for gain. From an anger like my own. That man, with his face that men see as ugly and evil—and his good, sensible heart. And Isaacus, who has no look of anything, who at ten years raped grandmothers and drowned cats for entertainment."

"Could you not—"

"No, sweet love. I have said, too late. She slept. She sleeps. The City already forgets. The old order is coming back. I saw a woman tonight who thought more of the loss of her bed than the incredible saving of her life. This is how we are. The many-colored Wonderful is no coat we can put on for everyday. And there's a new story besides. The Maiden, it seems, misled us all. She burned the ships—but failed to kill the heathen enemy, because she is the Devil's dupe. Ve Nera was spared destruction, in order to damn all the souls that are in her. As one spoils a child, giving it only sweets. We are the plaything of Satanus, now."

"I see."

"If the worst comes . . . It won't. It may. You too must deny me." Veronichi turned her head. "*Deny* me. If they examine you, speak of my harshness. That I beat you and kept you ignorant. If they examine you physically, then I forced you."

"Daniel—no—"

"Yes. I raped you, and have often raped you. You were kept in fear, and could never even confess it, for fear—of me."

"Very well."

"Deny you can read any script save Latin. They know you read Latin. I made you learn it to assist me. Of course in practices and strategies you never understood. I beat you worse if you asked."

"Very well."

"You are rejoiced that now you need no longer endanger your soul, but can speak to them freely. They are your rescuers."

"Very well."

He took her face in his own hands, now. He kissed her lips, abstemiously. "Remember, if I die—I shan't, but I may—I have faith in God. I believe this imbecilic world is not one half of what exists. Once dead, I shall know. And I am free."

"I shall die too. The Romans are fine teachers of method."

"Ask to become a nun. That will save you."

She leered now like a wolf. Her face was cruel. "What? And cut off my hair? Never. I'll die."

He nodded. "Only if it's your wish. I can wait."

Now, with no excitement, they held each other.

He said, "But this may never happen."

Outside, a hand struck on the door, and next moment tried the latch.

Veronichi got up at once, thrusting her tresses, with a practiced hand, inside the bald cap.

Into the room came a man from the Primo. He handed the Magister a paper.

Danielus read. He looked unhurried, almost indifferent.

"Yes, I'll come, then." He sent the man off with the conducting nun, for refreshment. "Veronichi, seek Domina Purita, will you, and beg her pardon for me. Beatifica's awake. Tell Purita, too. It hardly matters now."

"Is the girl—"

"In her right mind? They're unsure. She's weeping and won't stop. They can make no sense of what she says."

"Send me word when you can."

As she watched him go, Veronichi knew that she might never see him again. But she had always experienced this knowledge, every time he left her.

I was too proud. I must come down.

Cristiano contemplated the slope, a mental slope, a mortal one. So steep it was, he could not see the bottom. He had earned that trek by climbing up too high.

Around him, in the torch-lit dark, other men conferred, or rested briefly like himself. A woman sat sobbing, cradling a dead creature you took for a baby, until you saw it was a dog, its neck broken at once, (days before) by the plummeting roof.

Despise no thing. No hurt or sorrow.

She had loved the dog. Love was love.

Through these days, lending his strength to the soldiers in their Ducal livery, the desperate Venerans in rags, clearing the rubble of the buildings smashed by Jurneia's bolts and stones. Carrying out men and women, some living, although given up for lost. While most of Ve Nera celebrated, still this must go on.

He had dispensed with maculum and sword, and all the emblems of his calling. Warrior-priest, he had never been tonsured. No one knew him in his dark plain clothes now thick with blood and dust, (as hers had been that night when she prayed among the dying.) They thought him, so he had gathered, some well-off merchant, magnanimous enough to come out and assist. But his strength and endurance, which the Church had made, were valuable.

When it was finished, and they no longer needed him, he would go back to the Primo, and to Danielus.

"Magister," he would say, "I'm no longer fit for the Soldiery of God. Let me go over to the fellowship of the lay priesthood. I can serve better there. Man and Christ, both."

But would Danielus argue—debate—with him? Maybe. It would be more difficult then. Perhaps that had to be, so that he must fight for this, his fall, his *penalty*, as for the other things he had wanted.

So if he must, he would say, "I love her more than God. That's the greatest sin. I love her."

But Danielus would say, he thought now, "Through such a love, God teaches us the greater Love, which is only possible in Christ. *Love* her. Cease struggling. Let her show you the way back to sanctity."

And Cristiano would say, "I don't seek to cast out my love. I'll strive for her good. In every work of mine. In every prayer. But I must never look at her again, save from a great distance."

If he had to, he would beg. "Let me go. For my soul's sake. Let me go."

And then the circle shaved from his hair, the belt empty of a sword, the dull and mundane robe. He would wait upon men. Not in pride, as he had, but in humility. Their servant.

Let me descend the hill of my pride.

Cristiano rose, and moved to lift up another huge stone.

* * *

Ermilla stood to one side. Beatifica moved constantly about the chamber. Her body and limbs, now quite unconsciously accustomed to the liberty of male clothing, strode like those of a young man.

Her crying was of another order.

It went on and on.

At first Ermilla and her sister had tried to sooth and reassure. They had brought the clean water and the dish of ripe, nicely-colored fruits set ready. Beatifica had not spared anything a glance.

"What does she say?"

It was a gabble—the girl had gone back to her former slavish accents and mumbling.

"She said at first she'd failed. That the fire had never come. I told her it had—but she never listened. Then I saw the unlit candle. I think she's lost her holy, supernatural knack—is that why she's crying so?"

Ermilla wrote swiftly to Fra Danielus, and her sister, also clad as a nun, took the letter down.

But the messenger would have to cross all those part-choked canals, to the marsh. It might take some time.

It had. The Luna Vigile had sounded, and still he was not here. And the girl went on and on crying. Poor little thing, her face was swollen, and her gray boy's tunic all stained with wet. Somehow it was worse, the garb and the striding, with this womanly weeping.

Then suddenly Danielus walked in through the door, and Ermilla felt the awful tension shift away from her, like a veering sail.

"Thank you, Milla. Yes, I see how it is."

At the sound of his voice, Beatifica did not check. Ermilla had believed she would. Then after all she made a sort of slight motion with her hands, as if trying to catch hold of something.

Fra Danielus crossed to her. He stationed himself in her path, and as she turned about blindly and came towards him, he said, "Beatifica."

And at this, the girl stopped still.

Ermilla crossed herself.

Beatifica raised her face, bloated by tears, the face of an infant that has lost its mother but perhaps found someone who may help. Ermilla knew this from her own children. Beatifica said, in a small dead little voice, "Magister."

"Thank God," Ermilla breathed, "she knows you."

But Danielus said softly, "Forgive me, Milla. But go out now."

Ermilla obeyed. She was happy to be spared the rest.

Danielus placed his hands on the shoulders of Beatifica, lightly. He had a calming touch. Somehow all the legends of him were true. A lovely woman had made herself plain in order to stay with him. And once, a mad dog, running snarling up to him, had fallen dead coincidentally at his feet. But that had been because one of the Bellatae had killed it to preserve him.

"Now, Beatifica. Tell me why you're crying. Have you been to a terrible place in sleep?"

"No," she said. She hung her head. Between his hands he felt her fragile as a husk. Something was gone from her. It did not surprise, though it filled him with a kind of horror, when she said, in her former slavish voice, "The fire won't come. I do as mumma said, but it won't come. I couldn't light my candle."

"You mustn't be afraid," he said. He lied. She had reason. So did he. "What you've done has exhausted you."

"I couldn't—so I didn't do as you asked—the ships—oh he's dead—he's dead—"

The sword of her, worse than lust or anger, turned

in him. *Mea culpa. Oh God the fault is mine. Perhaps this is what I have always denounced—a punishment, and well deserved. Tears—water not fire.*

"No, Beatifica. You did all I asked and all the City asked. You saved Ve Nera, Beatifica."

"How could I? I never can do it now. He died. He died."

Danielus thought how he had stood with her before, explaining so simply, (just as he had about the farm, and the feast) that she must bring down fire to terrify the Jurneian fleet. He had not anticipated the magnitude of her response. He might have done. For when he had told her everything, he also told her the peril of Ve Nera without her intercession. He had said the Jurneians would slaughter them all. But, he had told her, that the Bellatae Christi would be tortured, for the Jurneians hated the knights of God. He had known, although she did not say this, that she asked him then, *And Cristiano, too*? Danielus had replied to her, "And Cristiano. He too they will kill, slowly and most wickedly."

The Bellatae had become the source of her inspiration, her *impulse*, through which she worked her magic. He did not leave this crucial act to that alone. No. He let her understand that Cristiano, whom she loved, her angel—being in mortal flesh—might be subjected to an agonizing death if she should not call down the fire of Heaven.

Her answer—she had burnt seven hundred ships.

Lovers are selfish. Though she had convinced others that Heaven lay beyond death, she could not bear to lose her love, even to God. Who could?

And now, remembering none of it, finding she could not light this bloody candle, she broke her heart, which was that of the purest and most naive of children, thinking Cristiano had died as Danielus had forewarned.

Yes, justly punished, I.

"Beatifica, Cristiano is unharmed. I swear to you upon the Wounds of the Christ. You know, do you not, I'd never offer such an oath for a falsehood. Look about you, where is the enemy? The City stands."

Out of the web of swollen lids and laval tears, her eyes were at once returning. Like lamps through heavy mist.

"Cristiano—"

"Is alive. And whole. You brought the fire, Beatifica. That's why it fails you now. Burnt out, my dear girl, my gentle girl. But he lives, through you."

Never in his life, he thought, had he seen such eyes on him.

And this also was his punishment. To be her savior, when he himself had first thrust her down to Hell.

Sickened, he let her go.

And Beatifica said to him, in the trained silver voice she had recently come to have, "Where is he?"

There was no other recourse. The game had turned into a snare. Meshed as he was, he owed her all the time he did not have. All the risks he must not take.

"I'll send for him at once. And while you wait, you must eat and drink."

"When I see him." Obdurate. As only women ever could be in such a pass. (Veronichi: *I will die.*)

"When you see him. But sit here. And sip the water."

"Send for him."

Danielus, her slave, hastened to the door. He called out into the corridor.

For an hour then, they waited. For another hour.

The secret of her concealment was out. Servants, then Bellatae, came to the door. None had found

Cristiano. Jian came, and kneeled to her, and Danielus beheld how she had learned to be truly gracious, for she touched his forehead, and thanked him, only her eyes again going far off. Danielus persuaded Jian to leave.

In the third hour, when Cristiano had not been found, her eyes went right away into the mist.

She began to weep again, in deep, convulsive, low cries.

Water, not fire.

Tears not joy.

The lesson of pain not the teaching of Heaven.

Mea culpa. Mea maxima culpa.

And in the fourth or fifth hour, when the Prima Vigile had long sounded and faded, other steps, other voices.

Danielus, going out, beheld the Eyes and Ears of the Council of the Lamb.

They had not come for him.

For her. This lost and weeping child. For her.

PART THREE

O, Burn her, burn her! Hanging is too good.

WILLIAM SHAKESPEARE
Henry VI Part One

1

ONE HOUR AFTER THE DAWN Auroria, the trial began of the Maiden Beatifica.

The day was, even so early, very hot. It was the Lion month. Soon, the prisoner would be sixteen years of age. And since she had never been sure of her dates, it was conceivable she might be sentenced to die on her birthday.

God's Chamber of Justice was a room kept distinct from the secular justice of the City. The latter was conducted elsewhere by Ve Nera's magistrates, or, in infrequent higher cases, the Ducem. All trials that had to do with the Church took place, as did the priestly inquiries and torturing, in one of the several under-rooms, reached by long corridors that ran below the Primo and the square. Many who had been questioned, (by voice or instruments) had come to learn the long winding walk (or drag) to the Chamber, and back to the cells and the black boxes of pain and terror, most without one window.

By religious law, as by common law, all were supposedly tried. But the trial was often brief, and the accused sent in minutes to be investigated more thoroughly. In some instances too, an investigation was conducted somewhat prior to the trial. For more general offenses—vanity, lewdness, the failure to declare eligibility for, or render payment of the Council's taxes—only the most cursory bow was given to the ethic of a trial. The wrong-doer never saw God's Chamber, having given up the ghost.

For the Maiden, a trial was decreed essential. And, though it had been thought unwise to conduct it publicly, (the rabble would crowd in and interrupt, mistaking it for a show) even so, representatives of the people must attend.

The Ducem himself might well have been called to do so; this was a rare case. But he was miles away, lying sick at Forchenza. He had sent instead two of his advisors, Prince Tizanio and Prince Ulisse.

God's Chamber of Justice, though underground, was powerfully lit, night or day, by flaring torches. It was a large room, and the torches needed for it numbered over a hundred. The rising heat of the City above would soon be nothing to the heat of this buried space.

On a raised platform, under the theological banners of the Lion with Child, and the winged Lion, and the white and gold banner which proclaimed in Latin *Peace to you, Ve Nera*, sat three judges.

Each was clad, not in black, but a heartening, cloudless white. They had been appointed by the Council of the Lamb, (which sat now, all twelve members, ranked to the right of the dais.) Collectively, these judges bore the name of Shepherds of God. Their duty was to drive off menacing sin from the soul of the accused. They would do this as sternly and brutally as any good shepherd faced by a ravening wolf.

Before the ranked Council sat the Interlocutor, in gray. Next, sat the Pro-Sequitor. *His* duty was to follow after any hint or scent of wrong, driving it towards the

Shepherds. This man wore red. He was not Brother Isaacus, and yet, in the strangest way he almost seemed to be. For Isaacus sat directly at his back, and was speaking to him often, very low, the hoarse words indecipherable.

To the left of the dais, on a bench, sat one Magister Major of the Primo. Normally no Magister would be summoned, but in such an unusual case, his presence was asked. And today his purpose was dual. He, and they, knew it. But Danielus sat composed, without any papers or books about him, such as the Council and the Pro-Sequitor had laid out. His hands were clasped lightly. And the emerald gleamed on his finger, steady, disturbed only by fluctuations of the lights.

Behind Fra Danielus stood a line of the Bellatae Christi, of the Upper Echelon. This was not, given the importance of the case, anomalous. However, the Council had looked askance at it. The Soldiers of God were counted. In all there were twenty-five of them. It was known besides that almost all the lower Bellatae Militia salvaged from Ciojha, were above, packed in around the square. There were also the bemused crowds, some of whom had come to the Primo, it was understood, because they thought the Council meant to honor the Maiden there. And how would it go when they learned otherwise?

Now the Pro-Sequitor rose. He bowed to the white judges, and then to the Magister Major.

The Pro-Sequitor spoke. "I ask you, Fra Danielus, to let off some of these Bellatae. They're needed more urgently to keep order upstairs."

Danielus raised his brows. "Surely not. The Primo guard will see to that. These, remember, brother, are the Soldiers of God."

The Pro-Sequitor, schooled, replied, "Then why are

so many Bellatae on the square and walks above?"

Danielus said, without rancor—or concealment, "To wait, brother, on what you will do in here."

The Pro-Sequitor turned to the Council. It was Jesolo who now rose. "Magister, *I* request you then, and the Council requests you, send out the Bellatae."

At his back, Danielus heard no movement among them. They too had been well schooled.

"Church law recommends a presence," said Danielus.

One of the Shepherds responded. "Seven only, Magister "

Danielus nodded. "Seven then. The rest may go."

As all this had been considered beforehand, eighteen of the Soldiers of God detached themselves at once, and left the Chamber, without fuss or formality.

Behind him now, as Danielus knew, waited the five he had selected with, at his right shoulder, the two he must not leave out: Jian, and Cristiano.

By the wall, the table of scribes was writing busily, with many hands, recording all this. Beyond these, down the room's length, the bank of priests and lay brothers sat agog.

The remainder of God's Justice Chamber was a wide space, which had yet to be filled.

Danielus watched, as, to the impatience of God's Court, the two princes now dawdled in, masking their unease with gestures and a great play with cushioned chairs. Once settled, their servants would go out.

The representatives of the people were let in next, men from the guilds and from positions of minor authority. Not more than ten persons.

(But how hot and stifled the vast room would shortly seem.)

Out by the wide doors, which presently would be closed, runners stood, to fetch and carry, to bring in and take away. At intervals also they must, by law, go up to instruct any crowd above how things progressed.

That would be a cause of concern to the court. Or not, if they had seen to things, as Danielus believed they had seen to rumor. Truth was adjustable.

Danielus knew, how well, their motive—also better than they did themselves. To make men carefree was not their aim. Men unafraid and charged with hope—were not governable. When once they grasped that joy was not a sin, as Christ told them, they would no longer be slaves.

And what chance then for the slave-masters?

None of this showed upon him. Nor the fact that he had ascertained by now, Sarco was not among the twelve members of the Council, had been replaced. But Danielus had warned Sarco. Had he eluded them? There was no means of knowing until Danielus might leave the court.

Behind him, the Bellatae were quiet and fixed as seven spears.

A runner now came trotting down the room, as tradition demanded, and standing before the dais, exclaimed, "Are you prepared to receive the prisoner?"

"We are prepared. Let her be brought. God watch over us all to bring this, her examination, to a perfect end."

They had not permitted the Magister Major to see her or speak with her through the days they had kept her here. Danielus had not, beyond the first, attempted it. To his avowal that the Maiden valued above all things her religion, and would need at least her confessor, they assured him they would provide one. They, the still-omnipotent Council of the Lamb. She could not read. He could not write to her. Besides, any letter would be scanned.

Cristiano had entered the primo on the morning after the Eyes and Ears, ministers of that supreme Council, had taken her. Cristiano knew nothing of it, as, then, the City did not.

Light was still gray. Cristiano was like a white flame burning through it. He had all the coolth and self assemblage of the very mad.

"Magister—I must leave off my pride—descend from it—"

"*Where have you been*?"

Never had Cristiano heard this voice from Danielus' lips.

"Helping them," he said. "The buildings that came down."

"More has come down than buildings, knight. Much more."

Danielus told him first how the girl had woken from her trance, and thought Cristiano to be dead.

"Why?—She brought the fire—"

"Now she can't. She believed therefore she failed, the enemy triumphed, and killed you." Danielus did not say that he was to blame for her belief. This was not subterfuge. He knew there was no time for the indulgence of his confession, now. He must shoulder it, if anything was to be done.

And Cristiano's face was like a boy's, all doubts, having missed the absolute way he meant to take—(*downwards* had it been? To Hell or to what? Oh, he had learned nothing. Or everything. Perhaps that was it.)

Cristiano said, "But—I'm alive. And the City—the proof's everywhere."

"She trusted nothing. None of us would do. It's you, Cristiano, who are her angel."

Exasperated at last, as Danielus had hoped himself never to be again—naturally, such a fallacy must fail him, as connivance had—Danielus sampled a moment's acute delight in Cristiano, confused, undone and falling from the sky. But it was not a cruel delight. A loving one. A thankful one. And he became, Danielus, instantly Magister of himself enough to say, not: *She loves you*, but, "She has seen the good in you. Your example shines. It gives her comfort, after the human swine she has had to encounter."

Then he gave Cristiano a glass of wine. Cristiano did not quibble that the glass was ill-made, knowing nothing better. Danielus described for him how the girl had wept like a child, and saw Cristiano go whiter still and then, very red. Red to the ears like a boy, indeed. And next master himself, as Danielus had mastered *himself*. And get out, "Before Christ—why didn't I know—why wasn't I here—"

"Never mind it. Now you are."

Then he told Cristiano, carefully, a little of the poison crumbs at a time, how the Council had sent for her, and he had had to let her go.

Danielus expected anything, despite his care. Cristiano might go raving mad, against the cool madness he had come in with. Faint even. One saw men who were capable of battling bare-handed with a lion, told that their mother was dead, or their son, and dropping headlong.

But Cristiano only stared.

And he whispered, "Is this my fault?"

"No. Dispense with that. How can it be."

"I love her."

"I know it. And she you."

"No, no—"

"And she you. No other must know but you and I and her. And we three *must*."

"Oh God. Oh God forgive me."

"Silence." Cristiano was silent. "Why do you think, Cristiano, God brought love into this world? For us to shut it up in a lead coffin and drop it in the sea?"

"It's sin—"

"Yes. To insult God, the worst sin. Accept His gift. Thank Him."

Cristiano said, after a moment, "The Council—what filth have they invented?"

Danielus informed him:

"She let Ve Nera off her necessary penance of rapine and slow death. She failed to kill all the men of Jurneia, who are infidel fiends. She be-glamored and damned us and is in league with Hell."

"*They* are in league with it."

"Bravo. Now listen. They must have a trial. She's famous here. And they will let me in to the trial, because one at least would like to catch me, too—"

"Isaacus. "

"He. And I may summon to the court seven Soldiers of God. Or more, if they're lax, though this I doubt. One should be you."

Cristiano had sworn to himself to end his knighthood. He said so.

"Not yet," Danielus said. "Think of her. She needs to see you as she knows you. Besides, only as a Bellatae can you be present. I wish I could prepare her, I have no means. Whatever else, when she stands before them in that Underworld of theirs, she'll behold you, living and whole. It's all that I can be sure of for her now."

Cristiano looked at him. "The Bellatae would rally to you, Magister. And to her."

"Again, bravo. You reassure me of your humanness

at last, speaking as you do. But the Bellatae are no longer enough. Ciojha saw to that."

"The Council's hated."

"And dreaded. Don't forget the power the Church has given them, direct from the highest, in Rome. Others remember."

"What will it come to?"

"At the worst, her death."

It had not been reasonable to prevaricate in this, as it had in the matters of love, and arrest.

And Cristiano said, making the heart of Danielus turn suddenly inside him, "If she dies—have I damned her?"

Danielus thought, *Your cold and frigid sense of only God. Ah, Cristiano. If God had wanted us tied by a rope to Him, would He have cast us from the Garden? The only means He could find to enlighten us was by infantile rebellion, by a forbidden fruit, and an angel with a flaming sword.*

Forget God, Cristiano. He made us in His image. Live in life for one small moment. Or you will never know His Face.

But aloud the Magister said, "If she dies she will go up to Paradise. But there's also the world."

2

"Beatifica, called the Maiden. This is your name?"

As custom ordained, the Interlocutor had risen, and addressed her as she entered. He had ringing tones, big even for the Chamber.

The girl looked at him. She shook her head.

There was some disarray.

Jesolo spoke for the Council. "She must not pretend to idiocy. We shall decide if she is sane or not. This, now, won't save her."

It was the Pro-Sequitor who got up, almost placatory.

He said, "A misunderstanding, I think. Woman, what is your name?"

Beatifica said, in her Primo-minted voice, "I forget my given name. Here I have another I'm known by."

"And that is Beatifica."

"Yes."

Jesolo said bluntly, "Were you never asperged for Christ?" Nothing. He said, "Sprinkled with holy water in his name?"

Beatifica said, "My mother told me I was."

"But in another name."

"I forget the other name."

"You were a slave," said Jesolo, "so we hear. How did your master call you?"

"Volpa," she said.

There was quiet then. She had been titled for the familiar animal of the devil. She could have said nothing worse. But she did not lie. Until now, her truthful answers had always been fortuitous.

Jian moved a little. Danielus did not check him, but Jian had quickly restrained himself.

Cristiano stood motionless.

As she came forward now, up the torchlit hall, he waited for her eyes to find him out. If she screamed then, aloud, he must not go to her. He knew this.

She seemed small and far away, as if behind a magus's distorting lens. They had not let her wear her white and gold, but allowed her male clothing, probably to better demonstrate her fault. She wore a padded black tunic, stitched breeches and leather shoes, and seemed inappropriately dapper, a young gentleman.

The princes Tizanio and Ulisse gawped at her. Cristiano thought they had not been at the Ducal feast when she brought the fire, had never clapped eyes on her before.

Behind her walked two of the Primo guards, and two of the Eyes and Ears, who had questioned her, although without instruments.

Her hair was beautiful, shining. It looked too strong for her, there was too much of it, as if it had leached away her vitality. Until she was nothing but the hair, and the gentlemanly clothes.

Now she reached the area where they wanted her to be, in front of the Shepherds on their dais. A stool was put for her and she was shown she might sit down. She sat down.

Cristiano, rigid, saw her head turn now, for the first. She looked at them, one by one, the judges, the Pro-Sequitor, the Interlocutor, the Council. Then, to the left, Danielus, and the seven Soldiers of God. Though no longer only a slave of lowered eyes, there was no curiosity and no interest in her face, and no alarm. There was hardly any face to display a mood. Yet, one by one, looking. And now

And now

And now at him. At him.

His heart twisted. Dropped down.

Her eyes were only a pale hazel.

He might run forward and take her up, and cut a way through several men with the sword. But they would not get more than a hundred steps, if so much. And if still she lived, then they might do anything to her. He must stay, as Danielus had told him, stationary.

Besides, he meant nothing to her. She had looked at him fully, and not seen. She had turned away.

Suddenly her whole body slipped bonelessly forward.

Despite himself, he moved. Wrenched himself back, rigid.

One of the Eyes and Ears had bent over her. Her sliding downward toward the floor was only like the action of someone exhausted, and for a second falling asleep. Was it only that? She had been lifted on to the stool again, seated.

One of the Shepherds said, "Does she swoon?" To Cristiano, the voice was juicy with enjoyment. Perhaps Cristiano mistook.

And she was sitting upright now, she looked straight before her. She looked up at her three judges.

She was changed.

Oh God, how changed. She was ablaze within. Her eyes like two bright flames. She looked at them, these men who might—who must—condemn her to death. She looked at them with radiant happiness and love.

She saw me. What now she is has come from me.

Better than any warrior, she did not say one word, but she was filled by light. The clothes, even her hair, returned to the place of mere apparel. She was alive.

And—she had disconcerted them.

"What is it?" one demanded. "Why do you laugh at us?"

"I don't laugh, signore."

"Call me Shepherd of God. I see you laughing."

"I'm glad," she said. "But I don't laugh."

"Why? You are here to answer dreadful charges."

Beatifica did not reply.

The Pro-Sequitor spoke to her, roughly at last.

"Don't add to your crimes by insolent sullenness. Whatever is asked of you, in this sanctified Chamber, you must give reply."

She glanced at him.

She said, "Then, I will tell you. I glimpsed my good angel."

A commotion. And under it, Cristiano heard Danielus take one abrupt involuntary breath, not exactly a gasp.

"An angel? In your inner eye do you say?"

"No, Shepherd of God. He is here."

"*Where* then?"

Beatifica considered a moment. Then she did smile at the Shepherd, individually for him. She had been warned, and also she had learned a little here and there. She said, without cunning, but only in order to obey them all—these men who demanded, Danielus who had said she must show herself to have no favorites, "He is at my right shoulder. Where I have heard the nuns say, one's own good angel always stands."

The Interlocutor exclaimed, "Take care. You blaspheme."

It was one of the Shepherds of God who rapped out, "She does not. It's some childish thing. She may be addled, or simple, we know that. The nuns do tell the children so. It's harmless. She isn't here to stand on trial for such a toy."

The Pro-Sequitor: "She says she sees him."

"Do you then, girl, see him?"

Looking directly at her judges, Beatifica, burning with her joy, (*Love casts out fear*) softly answered, "Not now."

"We must come back to this. She has always claimed to have seen messengers in Heaven, in childhood. Like her madness, it is a questionable assertion. But for this while, let's get on."

Turning, the Pro-Sequitor and the Interlocutor opened up their books on the bench; were brought, by lower priests, a sheet or two.

Cristiano, shaking and shaken, stood immaculate.

And the girl sat facing away from him, like a young bride on her wedding day. She needed only a crown of roses.

The Valley of the Shadow is entered by a million different gates. It has ten million million different names.

For Beatifica it had been this, the world, without Cristiano.

She had so little in her of autonomy. Though she had promised the glorious afterlife to so many, she did not wish to be alone and left behind. Yet, no concept of suicide even, could relieve her. She was, still, the fox. Animal, complex mostly in non-complexity.

To her also, that world of Heaven and this world of earth, were now so little divided that, ironically, she knew of no way to align them or get through. They were like a scene through a window—the angels, the serpent, the scarlet mountain, Paradise—but a window glazed by unbreakable glass. Immediate. Unreachable.

And also, in the midst of love, she did not know what love was. It had never been hers, or if it had, only for a moment. Unnamed, unrecognized, this stranger, powerful or more powerful than death.

What could he be, but her angel? And if through her he perished, what was left?

She had believed the Magister's reassurance instantly. But then, seen him to be wrong. If the lie were some game he played, or unkindness or punishment of her, it did not matter. All that she cared for was Cristiano and his life.

In this state, when the black-robed priests took her, she did not care. She barely noticed.

The Styx boat smelled of recent blood. That meant nothing.

They did not hurt her, physically. (Even the exploration of her virginity, carried out by holy sisters, was not ungentle. She had experienced such things—or her mother had, in early life.)

In every other way, her hurt was all-present. The walls of her cell groaned, the air writhed, the dull light ached.

She ceased to cry. She had gone beyond (lower) than tears. Despair was darkness. In darkness she moved absently about, and answered what was asked. They gave her crusts to eat, which would not have dismayed or offended her, but with which she did not bother. She drank the water, which was sometimes unpalatable. Her constitution was strong, and she survived those days.

Taken to God's Chamber of Justice, she felt no apprehension. Everything—meaningless.

Until, sitting on the stool, she felt somewhere in the walls or the air, or in the light—the groaning, writhing, aching—*end*.

Then, she looked, hesitant, not really knowing what she did—as perhaps she might have done in the cell, if a beautiful odor or color had begun inexplicably to drift about there.

When she saw him, she felt this: an absence of all things. There was no shock—or none apparent to her mind. It was, rather, as if all her horror and despair had been her *silliness*. Of course Cristiano lived. And here, of course, he was. Who has never lost that which is loved, and not felt this—the *certainty* that death is a mistake, a falsehood. Only turn the corner, fling wide the curtain and there the beloved will be. And for Beatifica, he was.

So, she looked away. And then the true shock met her, like a tidal wave. She plunged into a golden void, which swallowed her and then replaced her on the shore. Aspergation? Yes. Rebirth.

Had she ever been happy? Did she know the name of love? Now.

The Interlocutor had finished with most of his interrogation. The Maiden, (and so she was, examiners had made sure of it) had answered without delay, modestly and usually promptly.

The basis of *his* task was to elicit from her the story of her life. He did so.

She had been a slave from the foothills. Then she had served a wood-seller. Then she had been taken from his house—either by another owner, or a guiding, supernatural agency. The house had burned and so had her master, but she had slight memory of it. Presently she was at an inn, then removed to the Primo, and thereafter taught prayer and worship, which obviously she took to. After which she put on male attire, not by her own choice, but because it was given her. She could bring fire from air, having been shown how by her dead mother, in visions. She had prayed with the dying and wounded troops, who escaped the sea-fight at Ciojha. At last she had burnt the ships of Jurneia, although this too she did not exactly recall. She agreed she must have done it. When asked why, if she did not recall the event, she thought so, she said that the evidence was about her, here. With this none could argue. Jurneia victorious would not have left one stone on another.

Asked to say why she thought she had been brought to this Chamber to be judged, she said she did not know. But she seemed indifferent, casual. And, consistently, fearless and elated.

This had made her judges and many of the priesthood present, nervous. Not because it might denote innocence. But since it might mean she could summon up worse defensive powers.

The Interlocutor asked her to say if she understood the nature of the Devil.

She said she did not.

Did she serve him?

Beatifica stared, and answered no.

Who then, would she say, that she did serve?

"My new masters," she said.

"Name them."

She said, without pause, "Those in the Church."

"Who, for example?" relentlessly the Interlocutor insisted.

He had all the booming hectoring tone of any master.

Beatifica said, "Yourself."

"*How* do you serve me?" He was affronted, (despite the atmosphere, some of the younger clerks had laughed.)

"I am here before you, and obey you as best I can."

"*How*? In *what*?"

"In answering you."

The Shepherds frowned. One, the one who spoke the most, said, "If her wit is natural I doubt."

When the Interlocutor went back, Danielus rose for the first time. He seemed calm as deep water.

"We know, holy brothers, I think, that she has no terror of the name and words of God."

"Do we know this?"

Danielus said to Beatifica, "Speak for us, Beatifica, Christ's Prayer, and then the Psalm of God as the world's light."

And she, knowing them, uttered them. The beauty of the phrases, spoken by her clear as diamonds, stilled the court.

God covered with a robe of light,

Stretching the heavens like a curtain,
Whose beams are laid in the home of the waters,
Whose chariot is the clouds,
Who treads, winged by the winds,
Who for His ministers takes such spirits,
And chooses for his servants flames of fire.

(Let them dwell on those words, these resolute priests. They would have cried out sacrilege, too, if Danielus had told them this very Psalm began in Egypt, the hymn of a Pharaoh to the sun. God, by all his multitudinous names.)

When the girl had finished, Danielus said, "For now, I say no more."

Then the Pro-Sequitor stepped forward, in his fermented red. And an aid of the court, who had just brought it, set up a stand for his books and papers.

"Those that carefully questioned you, and without recourse to persuasion," (he meant torture)," say that, asked if your mother had taught you anything else, you revealed that your mother, while living, made you dance about trees. Is this so?

"Yes."

"Is this Christian? *How* is it?"

"I don't know."

"Of course not. It's a pagan rite, which treats the tree as a divinity. Yes?"

"She never told me that."

"But she said to dance?"

"No."

"Then who did?"

"No one."

The Pro-Sequitor scowled. He said, "You saw her do it, and followed by example?"

"Yes."

"And this pagan woman then taught you, after death, you say, to make fire."

"My mother taught me."

"How?"

"She rubbed her hand along a piece of stick."

"And fire came?"

"Yes."

"You thought this divinely inspired?"

Silence.

A Shepherd said, "Speak, girl. You have always to reply."

"I thought," said Beatifica, "many people did it. It would be useful."

"But you," said the Pro-Sequitor, "bring the fire from your hair."

"It seems so."

"What are you saying—*seems* so?"

"So it seems."

"Explain how it is done."

"I can't explain."

"Why not?"

"I only do it."

"What makes you do it?"

"Others ask me. And their need for it."

The Pro-Sequitor opened his arms to the court. "She has decided our wants. She rules us."

There was a rumble.

Fra Danielus, the Magister Major, rose.

"Holy brothers, that is like accusing the baker of ruling the man he sells a loaf."

The clerks laughing, and hushed.

From the Council benches, Isaacus spoke like scraping pots.

"Who bids the baker bake?"

The Pro-Sequitor turned and bowed to the Council, to Isaacus .

"Human need bids it," Danielus said. "Even Jesus fed a crowd with bread when they were hungry." He sat down. The clerks were almost applauding him. They were mostly young. The young tended to favor him. And the older ones, not.

The Pro-Sequitor—turned a page.

He said, "There are the burnings we must come to. Do you say you brought fire and burnt the Jurneian ships?"

Danielus rose. "Holy brothers. Many of us saw this very thing. It was a miracle, but it was well witnessed."

"I myself," said the Pro-Sequitor, "saw something of it. I saw the rigging and masts in flames, and the fleet sunk. But thousands of the Jurneian heathen escaped and are now in our prisons. How can this be? Meanwhile we have the tale she burned at least two Christian men in the City. To ashes."

Danielus said, "Her fire seems to find out those who will burn."

"What does this mean?"

"Some men are set for burning. They carry it in them like a spark."

"For their punishment?"

"It may be so."

"Then—why not these infidel? They were *spared*."

Danielus said, "In that instance, I think it may be called mercy."

"We can have no mercy on enemies—the enemies of this City—and of the Church." This, Jesolo.

The Pro-Sequitor raised his voice, unvibrant and thin but carrying. "Beatifica, why did you burn *Christian* men?"

She shook her head slowly.

"You must speak an answer."

"I don't remember it."

"Beatifica, if now an assassin, an infidel, ran into this room, raising his knife against the revered Shepherds, there, and we called on you to slay this man by your fire—*would you do it*?"

"No."

A great muddle of noise.

Again Danielus rose, but it was Jian, standing at his back, who cried, "Her fire's left her. She means only she *can't*."

Danielus turned. He put his hand on Jian's shoulder. Then turned back. Danielus said, across the racket, stilling it, "Answer, Beatifica. Does the knight tell us truly?"

"I can't bring the fire. Not since the night of the ships."

"In the service of this City," said Danielus, "she used up her gift, perhaps. Can it be God gave it to her only for that hour?"

"*Chastisement was the portion of Ve Nera! God willed it.* The City must be cut, and bled to heal. And we—the healers—are bereft."

Isaacus, standing now.

Danielus glanced at him, and looked towards the judges.

"Brothers, God is not put off, if He wishes to chastise us, by a single battle won. Even assuming a battle might be won, against His wish."

"*She is the devil.*"

"Brother Isaacus forgets. Women are the weaker vessels. Why choose a woman above a man, for such weighty work?"

"The easier corrupted."

"The easier found out."

"*So she is.*"

"No, brother. Nothing has been found. Nor is this court to be influenced—resist that error."

The Pro-Sequitor began, "I seek to find if any of these guides she vaunts so, these angels and so on, are demons, who have misled the wench. If that's so, and she will admit it, we may at least save her soul."

This was offered to them all, including Isaacus. But Isaacus gave an appalling crunching roar. He did not sound human, more like masonry knocked down in the aftermath of the cannon-stones.

"She—she—this *wench*—this *woman*—Satanus may take any shape. Who says she's innocent? What has she said of her visions—she rants of snakes and flying things. The Serpent *is* the Devil. Her angels may be *of* the Devil—did some not fall in the Pit with him? And her mountain is red, the very color of Hell fire."

"So," said Danielus sharply, "is the robe of the Pro-Sequitor." A true gasp went up like steam. He added, delicately, "But who among us would think to associate him with the Fiend?"

Isaacus moved about the bench. He came out into the open space. Like some incomprehensible beast from the shadow.

The foaming rabid lethal dog had died at Danielus' feet, killed by Cristiano, long ago.

Isaacus would not crumple. He had survived a day of rope. God was his. He *knew* God. The world must suffer as he had. All pleasure, since foul pleasures had nourished *him*, was foul.

"She speaks," said Isaacus, "of all her sights sent to her by God. But the Church is God's. His beloved and chaste wife. Where does she see the Church in this? Has she never been shown the Church in her visions, and told to heed us?"

"Perhaps," said Danielus.

But the Interlocutor had sprung up. He boomed out, like a bell, "Maiden, tell us then, has God never shown you, in your visions, his holy priesthood?"

She, a bride. Upon her wedding day. Her love. Her happiness. Aspergation in the golden void.

If she had had the sophistry to evade, even if she had, could she have side stepped at this instant? And they had insisted, she must always answer.

"Yes," said Beatifica.

More than silence, a sort of *deafness* which *heard*, this spread from her like ripples in the air.

The Shepherds leant forward. Eager or unnerved?

(Forgotten on their chairs, the sparkling princes goggled like sad fish.)

Danielus stayed on his feet.

She had not told him anything of this. What had she seen or dreamed? And yet, taken aback and unprepared, somehow it was quite expected to him. He knew it, as the spot of blood may be known. It foretold death.

But to gag her would damn her. The same, to let her have her say? She was naive. She spoke her mind. But might this not be only one more charming, spiritually disarming thing . . . Why did he *know* that it was not?

The Interlocutor again opened his mouth. Danielus interposed very quietly.

"One moment, holy brothers."

"What? What is it?" The Interlocutor, scoring on his target better than the Pro-Sequitor was loath to give over. "She must answer."

"That I understand. First, let me ascertain only this.

If she has had a vision of the priesthood, when was it?" They waited ominously. He turned to the girl. "When, Beatifica?"

"When I slept, after the night of the ships."

Danielus said, generally, "Her visions have been various. This may have come, waking or sleeping. But be aware of this, she lay unconscious five days and the nights between, after she burnt the ships. We thought her dead. You will be familiar, I think, with the notions of delirium, of a fever dream, and a nightmare. Her vision may not be of that order. Can we be sure? Or she?"

Isaacus let out another awful vocal noise. He was shouting, and none of them made sense of it. Jesolo and another of the Council rose and went to him, and Isaacus thrust them off. They allowed it. He had become, incomprehensibly, disgustingly, a power. Isaacus breathed, then spoke. "Look at him there, this Magister, with his army at his back. His *Soldiers of God—are* they God's? Or do they serve Danielus? His *mercenaries—*"

Danielus heard the shift and rustle of mail behind him, as the Bellatae, despite their discipline, moved. He raised his hand, and they were granite.

But Isaacus said, in his voice of broken bricks, "*See* it there. They hear no man but one. Send them out. Send them out, I say."

Danielus said, "Brothers, the law itself, quoted by you, allows for seven Bellatae in such a court. In fact recommends it."

The Shepherd who spoke the most, answered, stern and cold, "In such a court indeed. But who judges here? Who presides? Sit down, Magister. You're not here to debate. Sit down." Without protest, seeming unruffled and amenable, Danielus sat. "The accused here, before *such a court*, needs her chance to utter, without your interruptions. *In such a court,* she has God Himself to defend her, if she deserves it. You're redundant. Now, be still."

The Shepherd beside him added, "Nevertheless, the words of Brother Isaacus are very grave."

"So they are," said Isaacus.

The third of the Shepherds said, "Let us come back to this. Let us get on. Maiden, if God has shown you his priesthood, tell us now what he revealed."

Beatifica told them her last remembered dream.

They listened.

Of course, she had never considered tact. Others were almighty, impervious. That which is impervious to everything will be impervious to ridicule. Only when Prince Ulisse let out a snort of laughter, then turned his head, (yellow with fear at his lapse) did she half falter.

She spoke of the crocodilius in purple, wallowing up from the lagoon. the priests who changed to beasts. Their noises. How they fought and floundered. Toppled each other down.

Cristiano, hearing her, his heart changing to a piece of ice, thought, *If ever God gave her a true vision, here it is. Just so they are. The Church herself made into a monster, and toppled by their antics*.

She looked about. The lower priests were stunned by horror. The representatives of the people—picked carefully for their loyalty, their self-serving which the Council aided—were outraged. The judges had faces of white murder. The Pro-Sequitor—a grimace on him almost like terror—The Council blank as stone tablets unwritten on. Even Isaacus.

Beatifica did not speak for very long. The dream

had made her, while dreaming, laugh, but now seemed nothing to her. She had been careless with misery. She was only careless, now.

She was not a fool. Nor mad. But what had she ever met or learned to teach her another course? At first beaten almost for breathing, then protected in a shell of glass, and encouraged always to speak

If Danielus had known, he would have curbed her, and obedient, she would have kept this hidden.

In her despair—she had not thought to tell him. Caught too in her despair, he had not thought to ask.

After her voice, hubbub.

The judges, the Council, waited it out, until it ended in a bloated, rocking nothingness.

Then, the speaking Shepherd rotated himself in his chair. He fixed his eyes on Danielus.

Danielus spoke, not getting up. "Will you give me leave to tender some explanation?"

"No. *No*, Magister. What can you say?"

"She is unlessoned. To her—"

Jesolo said loudly, "Be quiet, as you were warned. The Devil pulls her under. Do you want to *go* with her?"

"The Fra is her patron," said Isaacus. "He is with her, never doubt."

Beatifica's light was gently dying in her face. She had been lost. Did she know?

All the Council of the Lamb was on its feet.

Jesolo spoke to them, and then one or two others spoke. A medley of low mutterings.

"End this session of the court, revered Shepherds," Jesolo said then. "Our scribes need time to put down all these terrible words. And you, Magister, take your Bellatae and go up.

"Yes," said the speaking Shepherd. "Leave this

court, Magister. Fra Matteo shall come in, instead. We have no need of you."

Danielus rose. "There are things I should say to you."

"Not yet," said the Shepherd. He said, almost bitterly, "But your hour will come. Be ready, Magister, for that hour."

3

Everywhere, as far as the eye could see, the crowds were roiling, moving together and apart and together, like waves. From the upper windows, they did not seem to matter so much, despite their spasmodic motions, and the whirring, rolling noise they made, now and then split by some higher, vaster cry. And they did not, in a way, matter much, truly. Just as they seemed to be, they had been swayed, and were altering. It was facile, to move them. Avowals and gossip, drinks bought or angers kindled. Not one single man at its back, this campaign, no not even Isaacus. Some almost unhuman force, streaming from the entity of the Church itself, driving the chariot. Powers behind powers behind powers. None quite aware, perhaps, what in turn moved *them*. Sensing only familiar mortal things, a wise rage, an essential piety, the need to survive, the wish not to crack the surface of a colossal code.

It would have been like this, Cristiano thought, in Gerusalemme, when the crosses jutted on the hill. In Rome, when San Pietro had been nailed up like a dead crow. And when a hundred saints were disposed of. Trouble comes in the guise of goodness—or great and perfect good in the guise of an enemy. Kill it then. Be rid of it.

No one had told Ve Nera that the City would have done better to suffer and bleed in order to be healed. Only that it had been spelled and misled by a witch, who performed one rescuing deed, in order to beguile and thrust Ve Nera down to Hell—

Legends surfaced like sea serpents from the ocean of the crowd. Had the woman not burned more than twenty fine Christian men? If they let her go on, what might she not do, with that talent of hers for burning things?

Yet, if she were possessed of fire—how could she be stayed?

There was now no need to fear her. The Church, alerted, had hold of her at last. It was possible to damage her, it had been done, it seemed. Before the Name of the Most High, she was brittle as a straw. God would drive the evil from her. God might, through his priests, do anything; all would be well.

"No, Jian," Danielus said.

"Magister—three hundred men, and more, will rush—"

"*No*. The Bellatae Militia won't turn their swords against their own City. No, not even against the Council. I have never taken a life, and will never do so, even to keep my own. Nor shall you, by my consent, do anything so injurious to yourselves."

"*Magister—*"

"Jian. I've things to do and little time."

"We must get you away. It can be done."

"There are other things to do. I've said."

"How can the Council bring you down?" Jian stammered. He was hushed with fury and disbelief.

"Simply, now."

"God's will?"

"Did I say that? No. The will of men."

Cristiano stayed silent. Danielus offered him nothing, let alone anything for the girl. They had already spoken, before the trial began. What need for more?

When the two Bellatae were out, Danielus went by another way across the Golden Rooms. He noticed, as he passed, their man-made beauty—frescoes, draperies, metal-work and jewels. Beatifica had been indifferent to these things. In a manner unlike her own, so was Danielus, now.

They had passed their days in the small rooms about the little courtyard. Sun came into the court, and by the sun they were able to judge the times of prayer. No one hindered them in this. Nor were they offered any forbidden or obnoxious foods.

Aside from the young male servants, Suley-Masroor and his twenty companions saw no one. But the high priest Daniel had previously described this solitude, assuring Suley he would not leave them to it for longer than he must.

Among Suley's twenty chosen men, were his three cousins, and the three brothers of his wife, four of his crew that Daniel's spies had been able to locate in the prisons of Venarh, and others Suley had named, knowing them to be virtuous and courageous.

These things too, perhaps, Daniel—though an infidel—might be. To Suley he was an enigma.

"Trust none of those benighted dogs," insisted the eldest brother of Suley's wife. And one of the oldest men from the wrecked ship *Quarter-Moon*, announced, "They are not even properly human."

"God has never told us that," Suley had answered. "This man took us from captivity. And their flies of conversion haven't bothered us since."

"Magicians, then. We saw it. They're in league with the Evil One."

Now, sitting under the shade tree in the sunny

court, Suley looked up and saw the high priest coming in through the gate in the wall.

All about him, Suley's men muttered. Only the three brothers and cousins, and Reem from the ship, came up and stood with Suley, to receive the priest who had been their saviour.

Daniel seemed older. The skin of his face, untouched by sun, looked thin. But the eyes were as Suley recalled. And he had told all these men to look at the eyes of Daniel, and then say again he was a dog, or a sorcerer.

Danielus greeted them all by name, politely, and with sound pronunciation, as if welcoming guests. Then begging their pardon, in the Jurneian tongue, he took Suley-Masroor to one side, and the men also moved off, glancing at them.

"We have been treated well, lord priest. You have kept all your promises. But one."

"To send you to your home? I will keep it, if I can. But for now you must go elsewhere."

Suley frowned. "Where?"

"To a farm I have, on the plain."

"That's some way to journey."

"You will be given permits, which I regret, as foreigners to Ve Nera, is necessary. My servants will then guide you. I request that you treat them well. From the farm, a method can be found to take you on, by some roundabout means. Others will assist you to the coast, or overland otherwise. As you say, a long journey. But it will eventually bring you where you wish to be. My plans, you see, weren't complete. Hence this unfortunate randomness."

"Then we will wait on you."

"I regret not. I think you must be gone."

Suley said, "There is some dissent over us, and what you've done."

"Not yet. Very few know. Those that do, agree with it, or else have been paid to find it very appealing."

"Then the bowman aims only at you."

"A nice expression. Yes, Suley-Masroor. You are acute."

Suley leaned back on the air, folding his arms.

"You should have left us to be fettered and scourged and made converts to your blasphemous religion, and so destroyed."

"Would you have converted?"

"To a strong cord, or a knife's edge. Am I to lose Paradise to make such dirty priestlings glad?"

"Suley, God is great. This you know. He gave you life to live. Did He ever say to you that to lie is worse than to deny?"

"A riddle."

"No. But there's no time for us to talk. Wait for my servant, and be ready, all of you. If any accost you, I fear you must after all pretend to our blasphemous religion."

"Some won't, lord priest."

"Then let them pretend to having been struck dumb." Over the face of Danielus there passed a swift dark cloud. Suley saw, oddly, how he had been when very young, hotter and more rash than now. But Danielus only said, "Arrogance is a sin, Suley. God knows everything. He knows a man's heart."

"So He does."

"How He must suffer then, Suley, at our idiocy and stubbornness. You will be given an unguent to lighten your skins and so perhaps save you from notice in the City. Think of your lies about conversion in the same vein. Both may be washed off."

"I will tell any who ask I worship your prophet, Yesu. And the others must keep quiet."

"Think of God, made happy by your freedom."

"He will also know to thank you, Daniel. And yes, my God too is capable of graciousness."

The priest smiled, solely with his eyebrows, but the Jurneian noted it. Danielus only said, "There'll also be money, and City clothing. I know you must cover your heads, but use the hoods to cover that covering. Your guide will be an educated man, who also speaks your tongue. He will appear to be nothing of the kind. His name is Sarco."

"Yes. Will we meet again?"

"I think—" Danielus halted. "No, Suley."

"What is this arrow that points at you?"

Danielus said, "That arrow which points at all men."

"Death."

"Death, Suley."

"From your priesthood here?"

"Enough now, Suley. Forgive me, but I have so much to do."

"Before the arrow strikes."

Danielus clasped Suley's hand, and the other men looked on. "Farewell. Go with God, Suley-Masroor."

"Can nothing save you?"

"A miracle."

Suley stood watching as the priest walked from the courtyard. Then, turning about, Suley crossed to these men that, in war, he had given orders. And his face too was the face he had for war, just the same.

The husband of Ermilla, the stone-mason, came from the Magister's book-chamber. Well and plainly dressed, head bowed respectfully, he received no challenge. He had been this way besides, often before. There were, now and then, things to do for the Magister.

But this would be fast work, even with the foundations laid.

How many men would he need for it?

A score, to be certain.

The stone-mason crossed the great courtyard with the lion fountain. From here, the noise of the crowds outside was hideously loud, though it would be worse on the Primo's other side, where the square stood over the Chamber of God's Justice.

A house the mason had built had fallen to Jurneian shot just beyond. He had obtained a right to take back some of the blocks. They might be useful as counterweights.

Of course, it was chancy, all this. But all life was chancy. And long ago, Fra Danielus had saved this man from penury. From near death. As he had also saved Ermilla.

The crowd boiled under the Angel Tower, from which one last dead rotting thing—that was once a woman—hung in its cage. Ignored.

They were howling now, a gust of howling under the cage and its unspeakable stink of decay. Demanding, jolly with viciousness, to burn a witch.

Changeable as the sea, and not as constant as the sea. She had been a saint not long ago. Though all kinds of provocation, untruth, slander and inducement had been used, to swing Ve Nera about, what scum they were, the race of Man.

Would I have shouted too? Saying that girl loved Lucefero, mocked God and lured us to the brink? Am I such a fool?

But the stone-mason recalled how he had been in youth, acts he had committed, thoughts he still had.

If you never see the light of day, how can you know there is a sun? And some were born blind.

4

She had liked to talk, and to answer questions. The sudden interest of others in herself, enjoyed. But now, so many questions. So much talk—hers, and theirs. And this fume of their emotion, like the slightly unwashed smell of scorching.

Additionally, many questions were repeated.

Sometimes prefaced by, Now can this be a fact? Or, Will you assure us that your meaning is such and such?

They had taken her out. She had been allowed water to drink, and was glad of it for the dark torchlit room was very hot.

When she was taken back, the room was hotter, or seemed so. The priests, even the Shepherds and Council, and the princes in their silks, were sweating. At last, one of the princes, Ulisse, begged the leniency—groveling—of the Council, and went staggering out on the arms of two servants of the court. He did not return.

Nor did the Magister return. Another man sat now where Danielus had. He was old and dry, with sad, accommodating eyes. Behind him, seven Primo guard. Not the Bellatae. Not Cristiano.

Her angel was alive. She knew this. But—where had he gone?

The powers of the court, though overtly threatening to Beatifica, were not fully understood by her. And she had missed many parts of her own trial. Waking dreams had obscured it. The image of Cristiano, thoughts of a cool place, of her accustomed habitual prayers which, now and then even here, she murmured.

(To this, once, the man with the loud crushed voice, had taken exception. He cried out that she recited a spell. But when the judges asked her what she had been saying, Beatifica repeated it at once. Her flawless Latin was received unfavorably. One of them said she masked her actual words. Or, she thought to impress them with her piety. *Deo volente*—God's will be done.)

She was exhausted, took no notice of that—for a slave, it could mean nothing.

But having been brought back to life, she was by now afraid.

She knew herself among extremely harsh masters, and no one to stand between herself and them. As in the beginning.

Beatifica was afraid. And yet, she had learned, inadvertently, to sit there as if collected and proud, to speak clearly when her own heart and breath choked her. But, if ever she had begun to *cease* to be a slave, that was gone. She *was* a slave. Without rights, without redress. No one to help her. But for God, perhaps, for whom she had no real name or true realization. (God, Invisible. Why else send down His heralds, saints and angels.)

"Why then did you dress as a man?"

"I was given the clothes to wear."

"By whom?"

"A servant."

"This woman plays with words—"

"Do you mean the servant of the Magister Major, Fra Danielus?"

Beatifica, unsure.

"Write down: it may be supposed so."

"Beatifica, was a reason given you for this immoral dress?"

"No."

The Interlocutor: "It seems, from other things she says, and that I have learned, that the Magister thought she would be discounted if she appeared as a woman, since women are naturally counted less. For a similar reason, he chose that she should be seen often, mounted and riding on a horse, as horses are not common in the City. The Soldiers, it has been said, took note of her in this way, for they themselves go mounted in war, outside Ve Nera."

The Pro-Sequitor: "That excuses nothing, makes it worse! He must know better than us all. An arch-manipulator,"

"Beatifica, when you danced about the trees, did anything appear to you? Any imp or creature?"

"Once I thought so."

"Describe it."

"I thought it was my mother. But then I thought it was a beast that lives in a fig tree and eats men. But it was only a scrap of rubbish."

"What thing is this you speak of? That lives in a tree—?"

She did not know. It seemed she had been told of it.

"Instructed in demons."

"Beatifica, what purpose do you have when you bring the fire?"

"No purpose."

"Come, come. *Why* do you do it?"

"Because I am asked."

"Why then have you killed some—and spared some?"

"I remember neither."

"You have said, you were shown God's priesthood changed to animals and birds?"

She *knew* this they were angry at. (Unreasonably.

Why should it concern them?) But she tried now to evade. "I was only dreaming."

"And in the dream, were shown it?"

"Yes."

She had never learnt tact, or to lie. If she had learned either, at the very first might she not tactfully have lied to Ghaio Wood-Seller, words, flesh, allowing him to rape her?

She knew not to ask for Cristiano, or the Magister.

Finally, they demanded, the white judges, if she would confess her fire came not from God, but from the Devil.

Stupidly, truthfully, she told them, "It comes from my hair. So others have said."

Then the one called Isaacus drew close, crouching, creeping, just—as she abruptly saw—like the sort of beast she had seen in her vision. He leaned over her and she smelled his physical uncleanness, the stench of his ruined throat, and of his ruined heart.

"You bring fire, but you too can burn. Do you remember how I burnt you with my candle blessed of God?"

And she perceived then, bending too close, a sort of second Ghaio, almost seeming to be about to glue his rancid mouth on hers. If she had been able, if the fire still waited in her, she would have brought it down. The whole chamber would have gone up, and every man in it. But her fire had left her. She was hot with cold. And with her fire, all else—all love, all possibility.

Instead, some part of her which had borne too much from the day she first began to live, broke in fragments.

She gave her fox's barking scream.

And they crossed themselves, jumping up. As if to scream was a sin. Perhaps it was. Isaacus screamed: "She fears it! She fears the flame of God! Burn the harlot—a rope's too good for her. Oh you strumpet of Hell! Burn to wax, burn to ashes, burn to glass—*burn—burn—burn—*"

Like a tattered flag that voice went with her. It put out all other voices. She had had nothing. She was Volpa, and all that there was—was this.

She was again taken through long corridors.

In a room—where?—cooler, a window—it was night—they bound her hands.

No priest came to her now.

She was an apostate. Could hope for nothing.

(Nothing but this, all there was.)

Beatifica—Volpa—grasped they were about to kill her. She had no concept for death. (Only for pain.) Cristiano's death she had seen in that way—his agony, and hers in loss. What else did death mean? Conversely, her mother had existed after death. The Afterlife, then, opened from the world like one room from another.

This she *knew*. But it made no difference.

When she was brought up on to the square, before the Primo, Beatifica found—but without finding—she was a single particle of a great procession.

Surrounded on all sides by soldiers—not Bellatae, but the Primo guard. Distantly, the priesthood, in black, and there a huge, gold, glinting cross held high. And beyond, everywhere, a wall of people, shouting and shrieking in a kind of merriment which, to Beatifica—to Volpa—was only like a hundred glimpses she had had before of human things.

Darkness, brightness. More torches flaring in this great black room of night. And above, the liquid black of terrifying sky, where no lights showed. And now black water, not liquid as the sky, but chopped and ragged with motion.

They led her, firmly, not gratuitously so, into a barge.

All about, the Styx boats jostling on the lagoon, torch-prowed, and the black priests, staring all one way, the dough-pale faces, and black holes of eyes.

This boat, sidling under her.

Guards either side. *Their* faces like wooden platters, not turned to her at all.

Alone in the world.

Volpa, the Vixen, alone, among these multitudes gathered only to see her.

The fleet of black boats set off, to cross Fulvia, and go in among the channels of the Silvian Marsh.

Bells tolling.

Everywhere the sound of praying and strange outcry.

Water lap-lapping. Oars.

It would be a long route, the choked canals—but had time stopped?

The torches red in ink water, reminded her of something she had seen. But, whatever it had been, she did not know, now.

She knew not one thing, now.

And as before, if any had spoken to her, she could not have used her voice.

She was all eyes. She felt that also. Two erroneous lenses in a flimsy frame. She looked, and saw the buildings of Ve Nera, called Venus, pass. The wooden posts, the overhanging chests of upper stories. From windows railed in iron, people craned and leaned. Pointed her out. "*The witch—the witch—*" "*May she roast.*"

A boy threw a stone at her. It hit instead one of the guards, who cursed, then renounced his curse.

Shades fell, and candlelight, over the prolonged traffic of the boats.

Mumma, she thought. Or a voice said it, in her spirit. What had the world ever been that she could make any sense of it? Harmed and abused, told always what to do, and the pretty prayers she could not translate. And joy and love, only the prelude to this.

Cristiano.

Cristiano—

I will lift up my eyes to the mountains.

Over Venus, Beatifica began to see the scarlet rock of her dreamworld, floating. Flaming red. A hearth or a sunset. On that black, starless sky. ("Mumma, what are the stars?" "Yesterday. Tomorrow." Neither, here.) And the fluted shadows chiseled in the mountain sides. Veins like living fire. All raised on a rosy blazing cloud.

Through the black of night, Beatifica-Volpa saw the tides of day rush in. Sand, not water, filled Venus to her heights. Sand shimmered in her canals. The lagoons a desert.

We suffer on earth, so that we can be happy in another place.

Why? Why? Why?

Let us only be happy. There, and here.

The procession of boats had at last entered Silvia.

The girl did not know, (who would have told her?) they had been building the pyre for her two days already, the platform and the shape of logs and dry tinder. For, without doubt, *they* had known she would be needing it.

In the marshes, the fitful torch light. The boats like a black serpent, some antique story of a monster which lived under the lagoons, surfaced now, glimmering, flashing gold and red.

There were other banks of boats, drawn off. People stood on them to watch.

The bell of Santa Lallo Lacrima, Lullaby of Tears, tolled like the rest. Did she isolate its individual note?

And there, another church going by, with a high and gesturing spire. On an islet in the marsh, desolate, and bell unrung. Gargoyles peered over, and behind, a hill rose free of the encroaching marsh, but a hill bare of anything much, some hovels clinging on there. (From which, people stared.)

Next, Roman pillars marching on either side of the boats, or standing like whitish nails hammered in, and on their tops, the nail-heads, weird beings of wings and draperies, wreathes, chariots—that once had been gods. But they were so high up, like the gargoyles, hardly to be seen.

A square, not unlike the Primo's, but empty, and this waterway carving through it, and on a pedestal a god with beard and weaponry fork—Neptune, the patron, long ago, of Venus, trident lifted, catching fiery crimson from the lights. (And would this god have saved her? He had been partial to maidens, Ovid said, liked them when they looked like young men.)

After that, a hump of darkness, just defined somewhat by other torches, that sprang out like flaming weeds. Ve Nera's little Colosso. The amphitheater where, in the time of the Crusades, the City had burned alive all those who were the foes of God.

Beyond that place, the marshes opened. Though half clotted, spilled with veils of grass and sand, they finally ran outwards to the silvered black of void. It was the sea. Perhaps. Or some other elemental thing that always rings the cities, bodies, *being* of mankind.

To the girl, nothing. Everything—was nothing.

A smell of pitch and salt and stagnancy. Of water. Of fire.

The priests far ahead and far behind, were dolorously chanting now.

Her mountain floated in the air.

Was it only an afterimage of flaming torches, left on the curve of her eyes?

In the day of the Romans, the sea had been farther off. Tunnels had led it in towards the stadium, for their shows of ship-battles and drownings.

Tonight the crowd itself brought a sea into that place.

They were scrambling in among the old crumbled tiers of seats, inconveniencing those already seated there.

In the mouths of entryways, up which victims had been herded or gladiators stalked, the crowd now jumbled. There was no longer an old smell of lions and bears to distress them. The moans of terror had died away.

The platform was at the center of the great arena. It had been built very large, as if for a giant. In former centuries, the pyres had stood in rows, twenty or forty at a time. But she was only one—so things must be exaggerated to display her importance.

There was a causeway. Out of the boat, and along this road of stones, they took Volpa, who had been Beatifica.

As she came into the amphitheater, an awful, incredible sound went up. Itself, the amphitheater knew it well enough. The walls had taken the impression of such noises, kept them better than the odors and whimperings.

One entity, a mob. Wordless. Yet there were words—*Feed me*.

The black and glittering procession, headed by its dayspring of a golden cross, (dragon-like) rippled over the arena floor.

It formed another pattern, with the center left open—for the girl, and the pyre.

Volpa looked up at the pyre. A huge, leaning, stacked pile of wood. It reminded her, the ultimate irony, of the yard of Ghaio Wood-Seller.

A man in black was before her.

He called, in a wild chant of voice, so all the crowd could hear:

"One last time, woman. Will you renounce your wickedness, and disown Satanus? Your body we can no longer, through your stubbornness, save. But we long to cure your soul. It is so easy. You need only throw off your crimes and beg God's mercy, even here at the foot of the stake. And though we, and He, must punish you for your sins, yet you will not altogether die. Oh turn from your vainglorious corruption. Turn from it, Beatifica. I entreat you!"

Volpa stared at him, as the crowd did. A spectator. He might have cried out in another language.

And now indeed, relinquishing her salvation, the priest belled in Latin, long gross sentences of excommunication she did not understand. But the crowd did, even the most untutored of them. They knew, and hung above and about, congealed in a wondrous revulsion at this fear which had missed them.

After that there was some delay. There had been a difficulty with the structure of the platform, or the pyre. The arena was old and ill-maintained. Engineers had had to come and make it sure. Or try to do so.

The eyes of Volpa wandered.

But everything was the same. The reeling tiers of seats, the circular-seeming space. Human figures, in similar attitudes. Craning, pointing, mouthing—or, like her guards, the dragoncoils of priests, motionless.

Her eyes any way were dazzled, and very tired.

She did not see two men, clad in black like countless others, standing to one side.

If any of the Bellatae Christi—Warriors of God, perhaps, Knights of the Maiden—had entered this place, which had been *forbidden* them, they did so unknown, and disguised. How many, Echelon and Militia, were there? Careless of the Council of the Lamb, or God, but not quite of summary imprisonment or death. Many.

They were known, too, found out, among the crowd. But the staring mob did not denounce them or go after them. They had prey already.

Cristiano and Jian had come up by one of the ghastly entrance ways of reeking, broken stone. Strong, young and male, no one quibbled that they pushed to the front.

The pyre was perhaps eighty feet from them. But it was much further. Beyond the moon. Under the sea.

Cristiano stood expressionless. He might have lashed and denied and forced himself on, for this one express moment. And he was sure, was he not, that no Hell awaited her. He was sure. And inside the case of steel, he burned already, molten and screaming.

Beside him, Jian, almost as armored. Not quite. Jian's mouth worked. It was as if he tried to remember speech.

Everything was lost. The world was lost.

Cristiano, burning in Hell fire, accepting.

Jian, writhing in the fire of earth, unable to accept.

Volpa saw neither.

And now, courteously, (at last) the priests and guard were propelling her to the steps, a wooden ladder, of the type she had often seen in the first hill farm, and in the house of Ghaio.

The executioner met them there. He bowed to the priests. A brown man with thick muscles and a brutal face. But the eyes were not brutal. They glared out in nervous agony at what the body and face consigned them to.

The priests drew off. Somehow, decorously.

The executioner spoke to Volpa.

"Too high, Maid. My boys can't get up again to you. We do, when we can. Break the neck. Make it quick. But not here, not with an audience like this. I'll say what to do. There'll be a deal of smoke. Breathe it up. It'll numb you, take you off a bit. You may die from that. But if the flame gets you, I promise, girl, I've seen it hundreds of times, it never takes so long. Trust me. It'll be over soon. Then you can rest."

Volpa turned and looked at the executioner. He was to say, after, he had never seen a woman or a man so serene. (This being how he interpreted her state.) And she said, "Am I really to die then?"

"Yes, girl. Yes. Don't fret. It's soon over. I swear it is."

And she said, "Cry for yourself not me. My pain is done. I am in God's world now."

The words of the male slave, by Ghaio's house, had again come to her. The executioner was not crying. His eyes always watered at strong light. His eyes wept, but he did not. He caught his breath, though. He did not know she had said these words because, in the shambles of her thoughts, the talk of burning had recalled her mother's cremation, as his watery eyes put her in mind of tears. Because all she had been told was that death was the end of pain. Not the beginning, as a zealot might have assured her.

Or did she say it because some vast intelligence, beyond her and all things, let fall the words on her tongue?

"God will be compassionate," mumbled the man. Then, "Do you need my help, climbing up?" (Sometimes their legs would not carry the condemned to the scaffold.)

"No," she said, listless, almost—he thought—bored. "I'm used to ladders."

5

After tying her securely to the post, the executioner's assistants leaped down.

They had paid her no attention, treating her like a side of meat, or bit of furniture, which needed only to be secured. In the same way, if so instructed, they would, under cover of the smoke, have gone back and snapped her neck, or punched her unconscious. Normally it would be several more decades, if they lived, before they realized what their job entailed.

The executioner came forward with a torch, and then his assistants with three more.

The priests were to bless these brands. How else could the fire work upon this witch who called fire?

Matteo, a Magister Major of the Primo, stood out before the Council. He too wore a black cowl and mantle.

He blessed the torches, calling on God.

The Council of the Lamb raised their hands.

A tableau.

It was spoiled.

Isaacus rushed out of the knot of priests. He jumped forward, and seizing one of the flaring brands, he held it high.

His face was livid, lurid. He waved the flaming staff at the tiers of seats, and at the sky where God must sit, watching.

And the crowd bayed.

How often, long, long ago, some Roman butcher of the ring, in such a stance. And such a crowd.

It was unseemly. The Council folded itself. Jesolo spoke stonily. "Stand back, brother."

"I never shall."

"This isn't your work."

"Yes. My work. God has touched this flame. It will swallow her up into Hell."

And turning, he strode straight forward, and the executioner and his men moved aside.

So it was Brother Isaacus who stuck the first torch in at the platform's base, to light the pyre. (Years after, the executioner himself would remember this. He would say, *The Church lit the fire. Not I, or mine.*)

But the flames at once took a grip on the dry wood, and on the straw packed in behind. Presently, where some of the logs had gone in dampened, there would be, as prophesied, smoke. But not yet.

The crowd, silent again, saw the fire catch. And made its noise once more.

Then the executioner and his men circled round the platform, thrusting in their torches.

And more noise rose. Then slackened off. To a complete silence, in which the rising crackle of fire and wood was plainly heard.

Cristiano looked up at her.

He did not know who she was. Inside his body his psyche seemed riven and pulling apart. He began to pray for her. But the words were meaningless, and even when he knew he was speaking softly but aloud, it did not seem to matter, being irrelevant.

He had been practical. He had willed it to be quick. Then she would be free. Now he saw it would not be quick. Hours would go by. She would see the flames fluttering, like golden birds, towards her. Feel the fangs of them. She would begin to scream.

Instead of Beatifica, better if he had died. He could have borne it. How could she?

Why had he not saved her? Why did he stand here now?

(And over all this, his voice quietly speaking for her. *I shall not be afraid for the sun by day, neither the moon in night . . .*)

Shall I climb up? Die with her?

Half moving. No. They had taken the ladder. He might manage to vault over any way—but the sides of the pyre were not able to support him, now. Or—would they? Why had he not gone up before?

She was not looking at the fire. She was staring away. She did not appear frightened—only—bleak. Like a child abandoned. Acclimatized to it. Indifferent.

Again, he half-moved forward.

As this happened, Jian went by him.

Jian was standing now, in the wide space between the crowds, the priests, and the pyre.

Jian, now, gazing up at her. His mouth working.

The priests over there were conferring. And a guard, summoned, turned towards Jian in his nondescript black.

And Isaacus, prowling like a mangy tiger at the pyre's foot, slavering, all his corded neck showing, as he stretched it to watch the girl. And on the neck a muddy scar, an old injury, that, to Cristiano now, looked like the lusterless loop of some ancient serpent—but which was the bruise of a hangman's rope—

Two guards reached Jian. One spoke. Jian reacted with an off-hand blow, and sent the guard sprawling. The other seized Jian.

Jian arched his whole body towards the top of the pyre, as if to shoot himself upwards and join her in the flames.

And his voice came breaking out of him. It was loud and very precise. His mouth had worked and worked to form this and have it right. Not one who did not hear. Like the Primo Square, this arena of death had been fashioned to relay, with trumpets and swords, a footfall or a whisper.

"Beatifica—you are God's own light! And this is the fire of wickedness—of the devil's putrefaction. Oh God, send her your divine spark—let her blast their bloody filth of fire with God's own flame—*Beatifica*—make the *fire* burn!"

The second guard had got up. He clubbed Jian across the head. Jian toppled.

Cristiano moved. Stopped.

A sound had burst out from the pyre. It was like something roaring there, then splitting open.

There was a flash like lightning. And a gush of flames and smoke poured suddenly upward.

The girl had been visible. Now she vanished. She was gone.

Plumes of thunder—smoke billowed, dwarfing the pyre. Flames scratched at the sky.

Was she screaming? Could he hear her screaming? He strained to hear.

No—women in the crowd—in a combination of horror and exaltation—they screamed, not she.

In fire, the throat was swiftly cauterized.

They were pulling at Jian. One of the guards kicked him, and then one of the men from the crowd did so. And a priest of the Council went to them pompously, and spoke, and they left off.

Only the crash of the fire now, was audible. Limbs of trees, laid there, cracked with the note of whips. Through all that pierced a soaring, whistling shriek, which was air escaping, freshening the fire.

Cristiano heard his voice then, saying over and over, "Quickly, let it be quickly. Quickly, oh God, be quick—"

You fool, he thought. *It may be only moments, and seem to her like a hundred years. And for me, it is forever now.*

He strove to see her in the flames. But there were only the flames, and smoke.

Be quick. Quickly. Is it over now? Let it be over for her.

Never for me.

He thought of Judeo at the foot of the cross, and then self-hanged on a tree.

As Cristiano thought this, stupidly his eyes roved back to Isaacus by the edge of the pyre. And Cristiano thought, *That man was hanged.* But some other might have been thinking it.

And then Cristiano saw Isaacus dancing. Presumably a dance of delight, of madness.

No. Isaacus clutched at his neck. His eyes bulged in the sockets. His face was turning to the color of a Magister's purple robe. He was strangling.

A couple of the priests hastened to him, trying to draw Isaacus back from the pyre. Many now were coughing from the smoke, and burnt and daubed with falling cinders. (As yet there was no smell of roasting flesh.)

But Isaacus was down on the ground. He was rolling and bumping there, clawing at his throat. Priests bent over him and jigged abruptly back.

His legs kicked out, again and again. He was like a man dangling from a noose.

All at once a gout of blood and matter erupted from

his mouth, and after it a stiff length of swollen and blotched tongue.

Isaacus flopped sluggishly on to his side. He relaxed. His starting eyes had now an uninterested look.

Cristiano watched all this. He did not know what it was, and soon forgot it.

But he did not look up again until a second explosion shook the pyre.

Huge bits of wood and charcoal showered down. A sawn tree trunk, the width of a full-grown man, was catapulted out, and landed with a smack on the arena floor.

The top of the pyre caved in. The smoke, scarlet now, creamed into the sky.

Nothing stood in the pyre. The stake they had bound her to had been devoured. She was devoured.

High in the air, the red smoke formed the shape of a mountain, long and low, fissured with veins of reflected fire.

Cristiano walked across to the guards and Jian, who was sitting half-unconscious on the ground. Cristiano's legs had no feeling in them. None of him had any feeling. His mouth had no muscle, but still said, slurred a little, "Let him go, boys. He's just bladdered on bad ale."

"What was he shouting? Saying the sacred fire was wicked—"

"*Her* fire he meant. Don't you know the stories? Come on, get up," he added to Jian, whom he could barely see, as he could barely see anything. "Get up and come home."

The guard, more interested in the fallen Isaacus, were not uninclined. Cristiano found he had pressed some coins on them, too. (To bribe. Where had he learned that?) They clapped his shoulder. There was a sense of disappointment in the shortness of the show. Other Bellatae, mostly Militia, clad as monks or laborers, were idling over. One got Jian on his feet.

With a sighing hiss, more of the pyre collapsed. And in the sky the red mountain had darkened.

Then wish the world good-bye.

EPILOGUE

> Does the Eagle know what is in the pit?
> Or wilt thou go ask the Mole?
> Can Wisdom be put in a silver rod?
> Or Love in a golden bowl?
>
> WILLIAM BLAKE
> *The Book of Thel*

THE SKY OF HEAVEN was always blue. So this was not Heaven.

Even so, today it was a Heaven sky, and Ermilla was singing in the fields, as she worked with the other women among the sheaves.

Her husband heard her, while he rode down between the long rows. She had a lovely voice, crystal in the sunny harvest air.

Then, through the sheaves, he saw her. Demetrio reined in his horse. It was a solid patient beast, always too ready to stand still. He sat there, looking at her. She was leading the other women in the song. Quite right. Though she worked among them, she was their mistress. But he was always glad, after her other life, to see her so untrammeled. She wore a light dress, saffron color, like the grain, and her hair was tied in under a white scarf.

Then she in turn saw him. She sang the last line of the song, and left everything, moving towards him between the golden land and the summer blue sky.

Reaching him, she said nothing, but put up her face, kissed by sun.

"We're to have a visitor." She only looked. "Yes, who else but Danielus."

Then her face did change. It became serious and thoughtful. At first he had always taken this gravity for unease. No longer. It was simply the face she kept for the Magister.

They walked back together, Demetrio leading the horse. His wife began to pick flowers from the verges of the hilly fields, and clumps of red poppies.

She was not a profound housekeeper. She preferred the work she did in the open, or her garden, where she was successful if haphazard. Peaches doubly ripened on the walls of the farm and great tussocks of herbs bubbled from their beds. She had known this sort of work, before cruelty and religion claimed her. Her cooking though was terrible, and others saw to the food. Demetrio did not mind any of this. Danielus had saved both of them—a thousand years ago it seemed—and now they lived, Demetrio sometimes thought, like the first couple in the first Garden. Except, this was the earth.

Even so, as they saw below the russet roofs of the farm, she said proudly, "I baked bread this morning."

And Demetrio visualized Danielus, chewing steadfastly through the black husks.

The sun had burned. But now the fire was out.

Gradually the mountains were mixed with the sky.

An apron of shadow spread across the plain.

Danielus thought he was tired, riding the slope up through the foothills. He had been in the saddle most of the day, many hours behind his messenger. Before that, he had been traveling three or four days, visiting all of his farms. This hill farm was the highest up. The summer air was sheer and sweet, and birds still rose and fell like notes of music through the twilight.

But he must be growing old, to feel so tired. Even last year, a ride like this would not have wearied him so much.

Then again, might it not be tiredness—more the enervation of a slight anxiety—or an anticipation—

He had not paid this visit to them before, his tenants here, Demetrio and Ermilla.

At his back, his servant, Lauro, had got off his horse, and was walking her. Kind Lauro.

"Not far now, Lauro, I think. Look, there's the path. You see that stand of poplars? Half an hour."

"That's good, Danielo." (Lauro called him always this, when they were alone; the guard had been left behind at the last farm.) "I was beginning to believe I'd fall asleep. It's this air."

Kind Lauro. He saw me flagging. Veronichi was clever, finding him. But, she always is.

He had gone first to her before setting out. She was back in her house on Eel Isle. There, since last summer, they had had five of those dinners, crowned with peonies, garlanded by the making of love. "You see," she would say, "I never had to cut off my hair." *Or die*, he thought.

On this occasion, he had had the new miracle to report.

Veronichi listened solemnly, and then said, very seriously, "Is it true, do you suppose?"

"True, yes. Not a miracle. How can it be?"

"But Danielo—you have always told me miracles may occur. And we know that, because of Beatifica."

"Not this." He had smiled. "I'm glad of it naturally. And it does good not harm. Or, only harm that once."

"He was an evil man."

"Yes. His tragedy."

"Almost ours. And *hers.*"

"In any case, Isaacus' death may not have been so Heaven-sent as it appeared. The rope ruined his throat in boyhood. And he overtaxed his voice. Then his extreme excitement, and the thick smoke—Of course, I wasn't there, but from what I heard described, he choked himself. Or some vital vessel burst."

"It thrills me to reflect on it."

"Ah. Veronichi."

"I can't pretend to your pureness of spirit. Remember, my God is still the Jews' God of vengeance."

"He is God, as is the God of everyone of us."

She had asked, however. for many details of the latest miracle. Possibly, it was that little jealousy of hers, too. For the miracles took place, most of them, at Santa La' Lacrima, where the Domina was Purita.

She had looked, Danielus thought, when he saw Purita again, a proper Mother of nuns. Though she had kept the accent of her inn, her Latin, when she read, had become more clear. Her general speech, too, was finer. So with all of her. She stood straight and quiet in her gray robes, and her face, which long ago was the pretty coarsened face of Luchita, had passed through a gaunt adolescence of middle-age and unhappiness, to this containment, remote—yet approachable. Her dark eyes had grown beautiful, large and luminous. The lined parchment lids enhanced them. Under her hand stood, (at her side) the walking stick with the carved head of a bird. Purita had told Danielus the previous Domina had given it to her, and therefore she cherished it. Also, of course, it had leant her some of the previous Domina's authority, a staff of office. She seemed not aware of that, and now had great authority of her own.

After pleasantries and a cup of wine Domina Purita asked two of her nuns to bring in the sister on whom the miracle had been worked.

Danielus then beheld a dried up little woman, with a spiteful mouth suddenly all softened, and wild eyes.

"Here is Sister Gratzilia, Father. I shall let her tell you herself."

And Sister Gratzilia began to speak. She spoke at great length, and no one checked her.

"I committed a great sin, Magister. I have asked for a penance for it. I went to the casket where the Heart is—the Heart of the Maiden which would not burn—and I said, You heal all these lame and diseased. You give the blind back their eyes. Then why not me? Why not me? Give me my speech like other women." Danielus nodded. Domina Purita had explained beforehand.

Sister Gratzilia did so as well. "You see, holy Magister, since I could talk, I stuttered. It was very bad. And the more I tried not to, the worse it was. In my family, in my family, I was mocked and laughed at. And they said, since I was ugly, too, I'd have to be a nun."

Sister Gratzilia lowered her eyes. Through her casing one saw the hurt and raving, inarticulate child. Then everything eased once more. "I've been a poor handmaid, Magister. I've been harsh and surly. I've taken out my pain on others. But I was miserable. I like this life—but have been useless. And when they let me read out from the Book of God—how patient they were, and only sometimes, the novices would—but I thought they all jeered at me, and made fun of me. I could hardly get out a word. And sometimes, trying to recite properly. I'd spit, not being able to help it—and make noises—like a chicken—or a pig, my brothers used to say. And I thought the sisters here said that, too."

They waited.

Sister Gratzilia resumed, "So I made my rude demand of the Heart of the Maiden in the golden casket, above the altar. And I turned away in anger, sputtering and cawing for breath. And then—"

Gratzilia stopped. Her face, from being only mild, suffused with a blush like a young girl's.

"Oh Mother," said Gratzilia. "Even now, now I can speak, I haven't any words—"

"You must try to tell the Magister," said Purita, calmly. "You underestimate your powers, sister. You always have. Say it as you did to me."

Gratzilia said then, "I felt myself—drop away *from* myself. Like a cloak thrown down. I'd never needed it. I was warm enough." She paused. Her eyes went far off and returned. "That was all. I opened my mouth and words came out, and I heard myself offering praise to God, like any other."

"This is a true miracle, Father," said Purita. "Like the rest. And like the rest, it has been written down. I've testified to it. And if you will add your authority and seal, the documents may be put away. Until the next time."

She was very efficient in everything. Of course, she had run an inn.

When Gratzilia was gone, Danielus asked Purita if she had awarded a penance, as Gratzilia had seemed to want, for her rough address to the Heart.

Purita said, "Doesn't Christ tell us only to knock upon the door, which will then open. I think He says nothing about the knock being urgent or too loud. If God rewarded her for it, who am I to punish? I've always felt, we learn better through joy."

"I am pleased with Purita," he told Veronichi.

"I know you are. Yes, I confess I like her too.

Sometimes I call on her, and we talk. Of you, rather more than somewhat. Does that please you, too?"

"Very much."

"She believes in every one of the miracles."

"The events do happen. No one can deny it. The lame do sometimes walk and the blind see. And the sick child carried in there, when the box was put by it, recovered. But Veronichi, Purita does not know what is in the casket. You know what is."

"A heart."

"The heart of a dead animal. A large dog found in the canal."

"That too is strange, Danielo. Why did the heart, even of a *dog*—not burn up on the pyre?"

"I imagine because the pyre abruptly collapsed inwards, as it was intended to."

"Most of the wood was consumed. And everything else but for a few bones."

"I wish I had been there when the executioner raked it out."

"You were . . . delayed."

"Indeed. I missed very much. The death of Isaacus at the pyre's foot, the fire-flash in the pyre itself, doubtless caused as the trap beneath gave way, but taken for another wonder. And then the Heart of the Maiden which refused to burn. It was lucky that the executioner had just had his conversion to Beatifica, and kept hold of the heart. He would not let the Council have it. He kept it secret, and finally brought it to me, as he said, a man now above the Council. If only that were so. And this was after, so he explained, did I tell you? the Heart had cured his watering eyes."

"Since the Heart isn't Beatifica's, nor even human, how do you suppose it works?"

"Belief. Faith. How most miracles are achieved. Through the power of God in each of us. It needs only a focus."

"Then all who pray in faith are answered? No, Daniel."

"The strongest faith may be interrupted."

"But—if even once—then these are true miracles."

"The true miracle, Venus, is you." He did not know she saw the weariness in his face. He thought, naively, he had placated her. "Come and bind me with your glory of uncut hair. I have to leave early tomorrow, for the hills."

Men walked out to welcome him, holding lanterns, and Demetrio went with them. Ermilla came out, too, like the Good House Wife. And the heart of Danielus sank. He chided himself, but to no avail. He had hoped, more than he cared to admit, to see—as they said in the streets of Ve Nera—her girdle lifted. But her belly was as flat as ever. She was not with child.

She seemed radiant, however. Not at all as he recollected. Certainly, a new woman.

They did not eat tonight in the great stone kitchen, but took Danielus into the parlor behind it. She sat down with the men like a lady, and they were served by the cheerful servants. She herself had only, luckily, baked three loaves.

And you, Danielus thought, *how are you, my dear Demetrio?*

He had noticed that Demetrio and Lauro had given each other a couple of almost puzzled looks. No doubt each thought he had seen the other somewhere before. Witnesses more impartial would be aware that there was a resemblance between them. More than that both were blond, handsome, well-made. Yet, where Lauro had grown more gentlemanly, Demetrio had not become a peasant out here in the hills. One had learned, he still practiced at his former trade, keeping as fine an edge in play as in earnest. He spoke the Grace, too, in the old way. The story was he had been a soldier, a captain at Ciojha, who gave up war for the land, and his wife.

Ermilla also spoke a prayer after the food. Nothing omitted there, either.

"And where is Suley?" Danielus asked, when the fruit and cheeses had come in. "I saw him last when he brought your letters down."

"With the horses," Demetrio said. "Of course he never will eat with us."

"Of course."

"When he's prayed, he'll be in. He loves to discuss God with you, as you know, Magister."

Danielus acquiesced. The comforts of old men, to sit debating late into the night, the chessboard between them, the candles burning red and low. Suley had reminded Danielus, in Ve Nera this spring, "The others went home to Jurneia by your generosity, Daniel. But I mean to stay rather longer. If I can, I will win you for the true God. I should hate it, my priest, to see you fall down among the lost." "But Suley, our Gods are one God." "No, Daniel, this you will never convince me of. I know your soul cries out for my God, who is God. One day you will let me feed you the sweetmeat of enlightenment." And Danielus had ceased to argue. Just as always, he allowed Suley-Masroor to speak to him of that one God who was God. And to quote from the sacred and exquisite Book which had proceeded from the depth of this God.

Who knows, one day I may even become a convert to the God of Suley. He will be the God I have always known. Is this not what Suley says to me? But we mean different things. Even so, we are fond of each other. We have each saved the other from likely death. This can make brothers of the basest men. And he is not base in any way. While I am not base in any way which would preclude or offend our friendship. Outside conversion.

Suley had affection, even, for Ermilla. She was shameless, he admitted, like most Christian women, but that was not her fault, she knew no better. She was a child, and a nice child.

He had never known her. Never thought to set together the two halves of Demetrio's wife, to make the whole woman. After all, he had only seen her once before, from quite some distance, and in an unnatural light.

Danielus did not burden Suley with the facts. Few were privy to them. That was usually best.

Beatifica was dead.

Ermilla sat blithely at the table, eating the red grapes which, in this candleshine, matched her hair. She had put on an azure gown, and on her breast gleamed the little cross her husband gave her on their wedding day, set with one stormy sapphire. He had got the cross in some battle. Why he had kept it he did not seem to know. Perhaps he had meant to present it to the Church, and then forgotten even he had it. He could never have thought of it as a bridal gift.

Demetrio and Danielus and Lauro talked about the harvest. That was reasonable enough. Later, Danielus would have some talk with Demetrio alone, and then they might refer to other things. Danielus thought that doubtless, as years went by, those other things—religion, war, the *past*—would be touched on less. Or with less care.

He was glad they were happy. You saw they were. Happy as most were not. Surely it could not be many more months before she had garnered his seed? Perhaps even now it had happened, not visible yet, and Demetrio, embarrassed even would tell him later.

Master of himself, perhaps always, Danielus did not drowse. He did not want to waste the precious time. How often could he visit here? Twice a year at most.

When Suley came in suddenly, winged by night, and with Reem beside him, Danielus caught that tiny flicker of something all about. A Magister did not *have* favorites. Yet the favorites were jealous. All the ones he loved, in whatever way he loved them, in some slight way of their own, subtly vied with each other. Before, Demetrio had had no rival. He had known it, without comprehending.

If he had been sent to the stake, could I have stayed aloof? Could I have planned as well as I did? I never loved the girl. I used her. I was sorry. And between us, I and God—or Fate—

Danielus went out for a turn around Ermilla's savage garden, with Suley.

"You're tired."

"Saddle-tired. It's nothing."

"There is a better horse here for you. Demetrio wants to give it to you. Don't refuse him, he has been perfecting the beast all summer."

Yes, they vied with each other, but also were protective. Siblings. "Then I will not refuse. You're wise to warn me. And you?"

"Look," said Suley. They looked up at the night. "I miss my wife. I make poems to her, which compare her to these stars of Venarh. And she is only a little plain round woman, with a skin like honey."

"Suley-Masroor, you must go home."

"Have no fear. None of Venarh's women tempt me. While I can stay chaste, I can remain."

"I should convert at once, and free you."

"I would know at once you lied."

"No. Your God is mine already."

"So you say. Listen, Daniel. One day you will die. On that day, you need only cry out to God, He who *is* God, and beg him to forgive and receive you. He will do it. If you do *not* lie."

"If I swear I will do that, will you go home to your wife?"

"A little longer. I shall stay a little longer. Besides, Reem's wife died in Jurneia. He feels more at liberty to enjoy a Christian girl. He has one. He's taught her how to pray. I think she may go with him, to the East. Never fear, for now, they hide it."

Surprised, Danielus gazed at Suley. Suley-Masroor raised his brows into his head-cloth. "Do you forget, Daniel, we also can deceive."

Danielus had been sitting that night in his book-chamber, when the Primo guard came for him. There were twenty of them and one priest. Perhaps not so amazing. The Council might have thought he would yet rally the Bellatae.

He got up at the summons and went with them. He left everything, even the glossily polished giant's skull that sat on his desk. In the end, one must leave all. Others would take interest in those things. Or they too would perish.

He desired that his enemies would not destroy any of his books, or smash the skull as an abomination. But even if they did, all things were always lost at last—and perhaps, nothing was lost. Men had souls, beasts too, he suspected. Why not a book, or an object. One saw, they would recur in other forms, yet the same. All lay in the limitless hand of God.

Noise had drained from Fulvia, away to the marshes, and the amphitheater. He too had considered going there. But he did not want the conceivably ultimate sight he had of the actual world—to be a girl burning alive. He was selfish in that. And immovable.

There were still things to do, anyway. He had made all the provision he could, until the last moment. His final agent indeed had gone down the corridors only a few minutes before he heard the tread of the guards.

If there were any chance, then Danielus had shored it up as firmly as he could. And now that too must be left. In prison he would never know. Dead—bodily dead—he would. Surely, he would.

It was possible, of course, that he was wrong. Although God surrounded everything, might Danielus himself not be strong enough to swim or leap the gulf beyond life?

He pondered this as they marched him across the courts below. It was the simple, the uncomplex who found it easy to enter Heaven. Thought was a wall, a tower. The needle's eye.

Then, leave also thought behind.

Danielus was conducted down into the the under-rooms of the Primo. Above, the silent-seeming City of Ve Nera. And here a silence that sounded in a roar.

He was promised no trial, though doubtless he must suffer one. Neither torture, nor death. Nor life.

Tonight, at the farm, would they again go over it, he, and Demetrio?

Who again would say, "Why did you never *tell* me?"

"I couldn't trust you. Oh, if it had been your life in a battle, then I would. But not with hers."

"I would have had some hope—"

"And if it failed?" Would Danielus then call Demetrio, not by mistake but through recapture of the past, by his former name? "Cristiano, your love for Beatifica was of an extraordinary sort. That's why you were prepared hopelessly to fight to the death for me—I am mortal. But in her you saw the light of her soul, you knew she could only go to God, and to God you gave her up. With *hope*, God alone knows what you might have done. Think. For all I knew, although my men had sighted and seen to the pyre and the platform, rigged up the trap below that led into the tunnel, still they must wait for the flames to take hold, to hide her. By the time it would be safe to bring her down, she might already be dead—or burned so terribly it would be a kindness to let her die."

Cristiano, last year, when this had been firstly discussed, standing there in his black, stripped of everything. No longer a Soldier of God, no longer anyone known. Cristiano, in honesty, might be said to have been expunged already. And Demetrio had yet to evolve and remake him.

And to this displaced being, Danielus outlined the plot and scenes of Beatifica's escape.

How certain men had made sure of the position of the pyre, and others assisted in its construction, supplying it too with the evidential corpse of a dog. The trap below had not been difficult to locate. Beneath lay a cistern and a tunnel. Through here, the Romans had pumped in the sea to fill the arena for their water-shows.

The trap was oiled, counter-weighted. The core of the platform was moveable and the core of the pyre loose, and fashioned to give way at once on the removal of certain props. Danielus' men must only wait and keep their nerve. Until able to precipitate the structure downwards as the trap gaped wide. Masked by fire and smoke, the girl would be plunged to a bed of mattresses and straw, and the trap heaved back above. *Then* water, to put out the flames.

If she lived—in any reasonable sense—they would take her, Ermilla's husband and his gang, through the tunnel, to the open sea. There was a boat in readiness. Along the coast, others were ready, for when the boat would come back to land.

Cristiano had listened. At first antagonistic, next excitable—then dulling down. Until he said, in a cold voice, "So. She lives?"

"She lives."

"But burned."

"There's no mark on her. Even her garments never took the fire. Or her hair."

"Then—"

"I don't know how, Cristiano. Perhaps judgment was unflawed and the men just swift enough. Alive and unscathed. Believe me. At the quay here is another boat to take you to her."

Danielus received no answer. And soon Cristiano, walking like a somnambulist, went away. Danielus sent a man with him, to be sure he reached the boat.

Some days after, on the coast northward of Ve Nera, Danielus married a woman and a man who were no longer Beatifica and Cristiano.

The chapel was a Roman one, but had been sanctified for God. It was a scanty wedding. In its manner also a Christening, for each had been renamed in Christ. Demetrio—the name of a saint chosen, perhaps, at random by the recipient. Since Beatifica did not seem to know her mother's name, nor properly any others for her sex, Danielus gave her that of the stone-mason's wife. Although this would be kept a secret always, the original Ermilla, he guessed, would take a rich satisfaction in it. Beatifica had been a saint.

Saint, and warrior . . . vanished. They were, for sure, two different people Danielus had joined. A bridegroom not stunned, yet very silent. A bride as silent, lucent, and in a gown. Much more than that. Much more. The service which created them one flesh—*superfluous*.

Without festivity, and at once, the couple went inland and turned back to the Veneran hills. The farm Danielus rendered them was far away, the mountains close. If ever they must, they could cross them, and be done with the City forever.

But that they might never need to do.

He had never dreamed of any of that, in the windowless cell beneath the Primo, which was always night, and which always soundlessly *roared*. There Danielus had stayed, (dreamless.) Waiting.

Eventually, as expected, guards came. Only ten of them. They marched him up to the surface. He had *not* expected that. Or, not yet.

Despite himself, he was rather disorientated. It was daylight, besides. Once he could see, he saw the blue sky. Which seemed unending, reducing all this below, to mere stupidity.

There were crowds on the Primo Square.

They were not spent and half-ashamed, as he had assumed they would be, having burned their victim—nor boisterous and seeking new carnage, which he had encountered too, in such mobs.

Most were still sooty from her fire. They spoke in mouthings. And seeing him, went mute.

Then Danielus saw the Council. Twelve men, as

ever, for the number of the Apostles. Sheathed in black, and more like avengers from the classical abyss. The Council of the Lamb, which he had wanted, and intended, to be rid of.

It was Jesolo who stepped forward. And then Danielus saw the Bellatae Christi, perhaps all of them that were left, hardly any of them in a maculum, but with swords, knives, burnished in their belts.

Had they risen, done what he forebade? They too did not have that look.

Jesolo reached Danielus. He looked deeply at the Magister from pouchy eyes. Jesolo said, "Isaacus died. At the foot of her pyre. The people are saying he was struck down by the Most High. For his sin."

One of the Bellatae moved forward too. It was Jian. He seemed unsteady, dizzy, or drunk. He said loudly, "She was the saint of God."

The crowd, murmuring, murmured more vibrantly.

Danielus tried not to search the Bellatae, the crowd, for Cristiano, whom he loved. Danielus, Magister Major, succeeded.

Jesolo said, "Some men are here. The men you had charge of. Once our adversaries."

Danielus looked, and saw the twenty Jurneians, and Suley-Masroor. He had not seen them because none of them wore their turbans. Their hair, wealths of it, and blacker than ravens, tumbled about them. They had shaved their faces. Both these things, for them, were fearful crimes.

In the name of God—what had these Christian clods done to them—Danielus felt a whirling fury. He could not quite control it, it was so long since he had needed to take control of such vast rage.

Then Suley-Masroor walked forward.

He called out, in his strongest voice, which seemed to quake the square, "Here is our savior, the Magister Danielus, who brought us to the light."

The sun beat down. God had made the sun. Or caused the sun to be. Or was the sun . . . And Danielus knew, from his reading of the Greeks, that the Psalm which spoke of this had been in the form of a song composed in Egypt, by a Pharaoh, praising the deity of the sun . . .

The guard was falling back from Danielus.

His eyes, stung by the sun's light, blurred.

He saw the Jurneians kneeling. Abominably, they were kissing a cross a priest was offering them, and the crowd murmured, murmured.

Danielus wanted to snatch the cross away and wipe their lips. For them—such sacrilege. As if they smeared themselves with dung—and worshipped that.

He had wept that day they had remade his sister, the Jewess Yaelit, as the Christian Veronichi. Even though he knew it did not matter. God was God. There was no God—but God.

But the skin of Danielus was ill-made glass, and all the light shone through and changed his blood to dust.

He heard Suley cry out, in a lion's voice: "It is he, this great priest there, who has brought us to the one true God. And only he could do it."

And then Jesolo stepped back, and Cristiano stood in front of him. He was white as a new skull. His eyes were black. He put his arm about Danielus, and, helpless, Danielus leaned on him.

"They say you made them Christians, Magister, by your preaching. After the fire—after that thing Isaacus died—the mob was turning. Then these men came up. Sarco brought them. See, he's there, in the Council, the twelfth man, to replace Isaacus. You converted twenty-one intransigent Jurneian infidel to the truth of Christ."

Jesolo, a little further off, said, "It's saved you, Fra Danielus. How can we doubt you? Thank God, and Amen."

Then Danielus was kneeling. He did not know why. His legs giving way, no doubt. Cristiano, who had lost his one great love, kneeled by him, holding him up. Cristiano, who was almost dead.

Everyone in the square was kneeling now, and praying. Including the twenty one Jurneians.

They think they damn themselves. And they do it for me.

Oh God, how can I bear this sacrifice?

Danielus thought, as he had done before, of Christ's rejection of the Cup of Agony, the cross, before he put away his human terror, and godlike, drank from it.

But had it been the agony He dreaded or the colossal power, the *godhead* itself, which suffering and death must bring?

No human thing could bear this. Even God-in-flesh could not. How can I?

Then Suley was there, leaning near.

He clutched the Jurneian's hand—"Suley—Suley—*No*—you must—"

Suley-Masroor's lips were at his ear.

"For a great one, great things must be done. But do you think our God cannot *see*—or forgive? Or that *we* cannot *lie*?"

And then Danielus wept. He wept because they had overthrown him quite. He had been returned to infancy, was a baby. And a baby cries.

All this the crowd saw and reported. Misread, it was considered appropriate.

Later, as Danielus, no longer a prisoner, and in

command of himself once more, told Cristiano of the plan for Beatifica, and of the message he had received of its success, the first three benign miracles took place. Although they were not broadcast for some days.

The carcass of the dog, put into the fixed part of the pyre as evidence of the Maiden's death, went mostly to black shards. Only the heart did not burn.

And, as the City learned later, a beggar, entreating for alms, when the Heart passed over him, though muffled in a bag, regained the use of both his legs. The executioner's son meanwhile, employing foul language and blasphemy in a wine-shop, took a fit of sneezing and had to desist. And beside the Canal of Seven Keys, where Beatifica, the story went, had once been a slave, a hen laid three score eggs in an hour, and lived.

Cristiano, it was Beatifica you loved, not me.

If ever I am proud, let me remember those twenty-one men who risked their souls for me, speaking the idolatrous prayers of infidels. And let me remember Cristiano, strong as steel to hold me up, until I could stand, and tell him she was not dead.

When I am a child, then I am invincible.

When I am most strong, weaker than any infant.

"Magister—your bed's ready."

"No, Demetrio, I wasn't asleep. We should talk—"

"Tomorrow, Magister."

Am I old, that he treats me so tenderly, like a father?

And he had been in error. Not Demetrio, but Lauro.

Danielus got up from the chair, and now it was Demetrio-Cristiano who went with him. And then the girl came, slipping from darkness.

"Ermilla—thank you. What lovely bread you baked. Yes, a candle. I must light it, mustn't I? Tomorrow then. Tomorrow."

There was a stair, but narrow, wooden. Beyond the parlor and the kitchen, only shadows.

But now he saw her lean forward. Her fox's smile. What a wicked face she had, he thought, this strange girl, like a Maenad almost, from the Grecian myths. Seen in a smooth glimmering—a lamp somewhere . . .

She put out her hand, and set there on the unlit candle stub Lauro had brought him, a tiny light. Not rosy. A hyacinth petal of flame. From her fingers' ends.

"Yes, Magister. It came back to her. She can still call the fire."

Was *this* a dream?

He looked at her clandestine face. Demure now. She was held fast in Cristiano's arm, as he had been, on the Primo Square.

Back there in the shadows, had Lauro seen the flame come? Danielus thought not. And Suley was gone. It was for him alone.

"Thank you," Danielus said, again.

The stair, as he climbed it, was like a mountain. So life was. Only in the afterlife could one reckon to fly.

Before going up to their bedroom, Demetrio went out to look at the horse. It was a fine one, malt-black. He had exercised and groomed it himself. Tomorrow he would show Danielus, ask his opinion on it—which could be nothing but favorable. Startle him with the gift.

He had seemed exhausted, the Magister, and fallen asleep after the meal. That would never have happened—*then*.

Demetrio did not admit to himself, was mostly unaware, that Danielus meant far less to him, now. Demetrio's feelings were of friendship, gratitude, and solicitous respect. Cristiano had seen in the Magister a figurehead, and a man standing in the sky. God, then the Magister. Not much else. And now—still God, but God reflected from the mirror of his wife. Who, in his inner mind, he still named Beatifica.

Before they ended their evening in the world, he should finish reading the letter that Danielus had brought, from Jian. Jian was with the Bellatae Christi at Rome. He served a higher power now. When he wrote to Cristiano, conscientiously, he never called him that. The letter spoke of mundane things, organized combats, monuments, and pageants of the Virgin. It was as if he tried to reassure Demetrio that the cosmos of earthly spirituality safely continued in the absence of a Cristiano. Or to make him envious.

Jian never spoke at all of Ermilla. Just as he did not know where Cristiano had hidden himself, he did not know the name of the woman Demetrio had married. Jian believed the Maiden to be dead.

Danielus had mentioned that Jian, in his other letter to the Magister, had inquired after the Heart and its miracles. *That* now, *was* the Maiden.

There was talk in Rome of another venture to the Holy Land, less a crusade than a processional. Jian would be part of this. He described his ambition to visit the Tomb in the Rock, the way-stations of Blessed Maria on her mule, heavy with the unborn Christ. The desert of fasts and visions.

Was I like Jian?

The horse was peaceful, its coat silk. Demetrio left it, and went to complete the letter under the lantern in the yard.

Jian's world, now, did not seem real. Nor this one.

Demetrio's pulse drummed. He put the letter away, still unfinished.

On many nights, he and she—farming folk worn out—would embrace, and lie down on their pallet on the floor, side by side, to sleep. Sleeping, they went away together, or alone, and in the morning, recounted their dreams. But they seldom did dream, either she or he. Tonight, they would not sleep.

He looked up at the higher window, soft-lit by a single candle. He looked at the window some while, his body tensed, attentive all through. Then he left the yard of the unreal farm, and climbed towards her light, through the unreal darkness.

When she saw the mountains again, she had remembered them. As the year passed, she watched their calendar of winter white, and later their lower mantles of green.

This farm was planted high, almost beyond the foothills.

The life was pleasant to her. At dusk, sometimes, she would gaze upwards, but no longer to watch for flocks of angels. It was her homage to the sky.

In the small room which was their bed-chamber, she sat combing her hair, hearing it crackle, and seeing the sparks fly out, bright blue.

Waiting for her beloved, she had no thoughts for anyone else, not even for herself. None for the past.

"Am I really to die then?"

The executioner had assured her she must.

She said some sentences to him in return. But she was going already to a great distance. She felt sleepy. She climbed the ladder, just as she had in the house of Ghaio.

She was on the pyre in the amphitheater at Silvia.

There were men around her. She flinched from

them, although she had become used to the nearness of men, unthreatening and dependent, at the Primo chapel and after Ciojha. These were not like that. And they stank.

They did not surround her long. Having tied her to the stake, they jumped away.

Some shouting was going on below. Crowd noises.

Then a sound like the wind, rising. It carried up to her the smell of smoke.

She had been told to breathe the smoke. But already she did not like the smell of it. She looked outwards.

So many people. But now a silence.

They were burning her. She had no actual fear. What had fire been, but her familiar. Yet, she might have recaptured the pain of the live candle against her palm, Isaacus' penalty after the Ducal feast. No, she did not. Human beings had always hurt her. If fire itself had hurt her, she did not reason it out. It was men, not fire, who hurt. The world.

Rushes of heat began to come. They slapped upwards, soaring against her body. And then the smoke she had smelled billowed between her and everything. It was not yet thick, but wavering and distorting—like water.

Volpa-Beatifica closed her eyes, because they smarted.

She began to leave herself behind.

It was then, on the boundary between flesh and spirit, that she heard a vast voice of brass that shook the outer places, but also the innerness to which she went.

Beatifica—

Beatifica—

Who—what—was it? She thought of the picture the

Magister had shown her, the man thrown among lions. She thought of the story of the burning fiery furnace, and how the angel had led the chosen ones from the fire. As she had been led from the blazing house of Ghaio.

Did the angel call to her now?

Beatifica, cried the angel like a trumpet, *God's light. Blast their bloody filth of fire—Beatifica—*

Beatifica—

Beatifica—

Make the ***FIRE*** *burn*

Who is that walking there? said the king, Nabucco. Into the furnace I cast three men. But there is a fourth man there with them.

In the smoke she saw, the girl, her angel. He wore the steel maculum and mail, the sword gleamed in his hand, his wings were spread, salt-white. His hair burned like white gold in the furnace. Cristiano. He said, now, softly, *Be quick. Let it be over.*

She flung up her head. She felt the torrent of her own pyrotechnic burst through her, as never had she *felt* it before. *She* the candle, *she* the altar. And to *her* fire, this other fire of the world—*nothing*.

A slave. She had obeyed.

And with her slave's obedience, the goal of the priest, directed by her angel, she took back her power and made the world's fire *burn*.

There was an explosive thud, and flash.

Smoke, an indigo column, rushing, thrusting.

She saw herself one moment, garbed in the flames of her own fire. They were cool. They tingled. And her skull filled like a cup with brilliancy.

This was the light of God. She had been told. She knew.

She gave herself to the light. And was received.

When the center of the pyre crashed in and she dropped to the cistern below, the Maiden was burning like a torch. When they threw water over her, shouting, the fire went out. And she lay unscathed, and fully clothed, on the weave of her hair which, for some moments, looked pale as ashes.

They picked her up, the men below, who had also risked their lives. But she slept.

"Is she gone? Is she dead?"

"No. Not a mark. Look, her heart beats in her throat, you can see."

They carried her away through the tunnel under the arena, where, knee high, water yet rippled like snakes. They put her in a boat.

She slept.

"She's cool. Not hot or fevered."

They rowed her from the land, across a web of blackest sea. They rowed her to the land again.

In a columned chapel, partly ruined, that the Romans had built on the stony shore, (to Neptunus) the Maiden lay asleep.

Night ended. Morning began. Day passed. Night returned.

Then the man arrived they had been told to expect.

He had been one of the Soldiers of God, and that was on him still. But he walked as if lugged by a chain, approaching wide-eyed, not knowing why or for what.

"Signore—Bellatoro—she's in there."

He went by them. At the back of the chapel, where a timbered cell had been attached, a red-haired girl lay asleep.

Cristiano stood looking at her.

He did not know that Jian had been, that once, and unrecognized, her angel also. He did not know that somehow she had heard Cristiano's own whispered prayer.

He did not know who she was, or what the world was in which she might have survived the pyre of sainthood and oblivion.

"He's lost. Doesn't grasp what he's doing."

"Come away. Leave him privacy. This is an age of miracles. We're favored and cursed to live in it."

Cristiano leaned above her, and then he reached out and smoothed the flame of hair back from her forehead. As a brother might. But, till then, he had never been even a brother.

It was the first time they had touched.

Her eyes flew open. She was there. Back from a long journey, she thought. Cristiano had been on the road with her. She gazed up at him. Danielus had believed she might not know this man without the mail of Christ. But she said, "You led me from the fire. You're my angel. Don't go away."

She never noticed Cristiano was no longer winged. Nor did he.

For she had burned. But now the fire was out . . .

Their sleeping room was bare, only the sparse mattress on the floor, a chest, a stool. One end, however, had been divided off, making the small chamber smaller.

Beyond the curtain they kept their private altar, where a cross of carved wood was set, a copper cup, and the flowers Ermilla regularly gathered, in a white jug.

They had not fasted. They did not, now. At all times they ate sparely.

They sipped the water from the cup.

It would not matter that the Magister was in the house. He would sleep soundly. Sunrise always brought them back, as it woke them on other summer days, blooming through the unglazed and unshuttered window. Better than a bell, the Auroria of mountain dawn.

They did not exchange a word, he or she. Alone, they did not ever speak at great length. Having no need.

Kneeling, they faced each other, by the altar.

In the warmth of the summer they were naked. As in the Garden, before nakedness became the mark of disobedient knowledge and the stigma of the Fall.

(Outside, soft noises. An owl across the fields. The stirring of animals. Stars turning in sky. The moon, singing, as it sailed its nacre boat.)

Cristiano reached out his hands, and Beatifica reached out her hands. Their hands joined.

The last image each beheld, as always, at this instant, the eyes of the other, silver, gold. And then the wave of eternal radiance, the light of God, swept down and spun them upward.

It came always the same. At the touch.

Together, one thing, they would enter the sphere of ecstasy so otherwise unimaginable, and otherwise so ungovernable. The foretaste of Heaven, and the immortal state. Beyond any physical pleasure, impossible in its wonder and effulgence. Yet always achievable. Always.

To this, mere sexual union—which they had never known, nor ever attempted, nor ever would attempt—like the fires of the world—was *nothing*.

In a glory above all delight, they hung together in the firmament. Would hang there like stars all night, until the dawn reclaimed them.

Across the wooden places of the house, Danielus, lying yet awake, might dream his waking dream. The Council had not been overthrown, inhuman lies still ruled the City, and the earth. He had lost the sword of flame. But oh, if they, the warrior-visionary, the priestess-saint, if they might produce, from their innocent lust, a child—what might that child not be? What true miracle might that child not work?

Alas, Magister, you must dream in vain.

They are virgins, these lovers, and will be till their death. And from their rare and soaring love, no child can ever be created—unless it is an angel.

For nine further years the mystical Heart of the Maiden Beatifica continued to work miracles in the City of Ve Nera. As belief in these wonders swelled, it became a common cause that the Maiden should be recognized as one of God's saints. At length the Council of the Lamb, eager to end this—as they perceived it—opposing cult, outlawed the idea of Beatifica, and threatened death by burning to her adherents. On this signal, the City revolted against them. And from Rome came the ultimate edict that the Brothers of the Lamb had exceeded their authority. The Council was overthrown, and most of its members, so the story went, secretly murdered by Ve Nera's princes.

In that year too, the name of Ve Nera was altered by her Ducem, Joffri, to *Venus*. This after the goddess of love, who also, like the City, had been born from the sea.

The Maiden Beatifica was never officially canonized.

One hundred years later, the golden casket, which contained her Heart, vanished without trace.

In heaven's luminous land, in splendour rising,
You, O living Aten, maker of life!
When once you have dawned in the east,
The country of the light,
You brim all places with your beauty.
You, the beautiful, mighty and aflame,
Upon the pinnacle of every land,
Your rays kiss the world
To the boundaries of creation.

From the hymn of the PHARAOH AKHENATEN
To his one true God, the Sun.